NORTH OF THE MOON

OTHER BOOKS BY ALLA CRONE

East Lies the Sun
Winds over Manchuria

NORTH
OF THE MOON

Alla Crone

Originally published by Dell

Copyright © 1984, 2004 by Alla Crone

ISBN: 978-1-5040-3030-4

Distributed in 2016 by Open Road Distribution
180 Maiden Lane
New York, NY 10038
www.openroadmedia.com

To Lois and Alfred Strode,
my cherished friends,
and
To my Guardian Angels of the Tuesday Workshop

ACKNOWLEDGMENTS

I wish to express my continued gratitude to Nicholas Slobodchikoff, Director of the Museum of Russian Culture in San Francisco, and to his wife, Valerie, for their invaluable assistance in my research for this work, and for making available to me rare volumes from their personal library.

I also want to thank Mah-Li Wang Shaw for her guidance and thoughtful suggestions for the Chinese part of my book.

AUTHOR'S NOTE

On December 14, 1825, there occurred an historic event in St. Petersburg, Russia, that was destined to be called the first Russian Revolution, and its participants—the Decembrists.

Members of the privileged class, the Decembrists were young noblemen, who, guided by high ideals and altruism, attempted to overthrow the tsar's autocratic rule. The moderates in the group favored a constitutional monarchy, and the radicals—a republic.

When the uprising failed, five leaders of the movement were executed and 116 were stripped of their possessions, rank, and privileges, and exiled to Eastern Siberia to serve various terms at hard labor and then be resettled for life.

Some of the wives chose to follow their husbands into exile and to share their fate.

There, surrounded by hospitable Buryats in the rural, beautiful environment of the Lake Baikal region, the Decembrists and their wives made a home for themselves.

Two hundred miles south of Lake Baikal, on the Siberian-Mongolian border, were two trading towns: Kyakhta and Maimachin. Those were virtually the only tea trading centers between Russia and China at that time, and some of the Decembrists made contacts with Chinese merchants and their trading caravans. The Decembrists learned to love this distant part of their vast country, and in turn, left their mark on the natives.

For decades to come, the Decembrists and their courageous wives were eulogized by poets and composers.

This work of fiction is dedicated to the devotion and heroism of those women, and although the main characters of this story are fictitious, historic events surrounding them are true; much of the detail is based on the existing diaries of Decembrists and their wives.

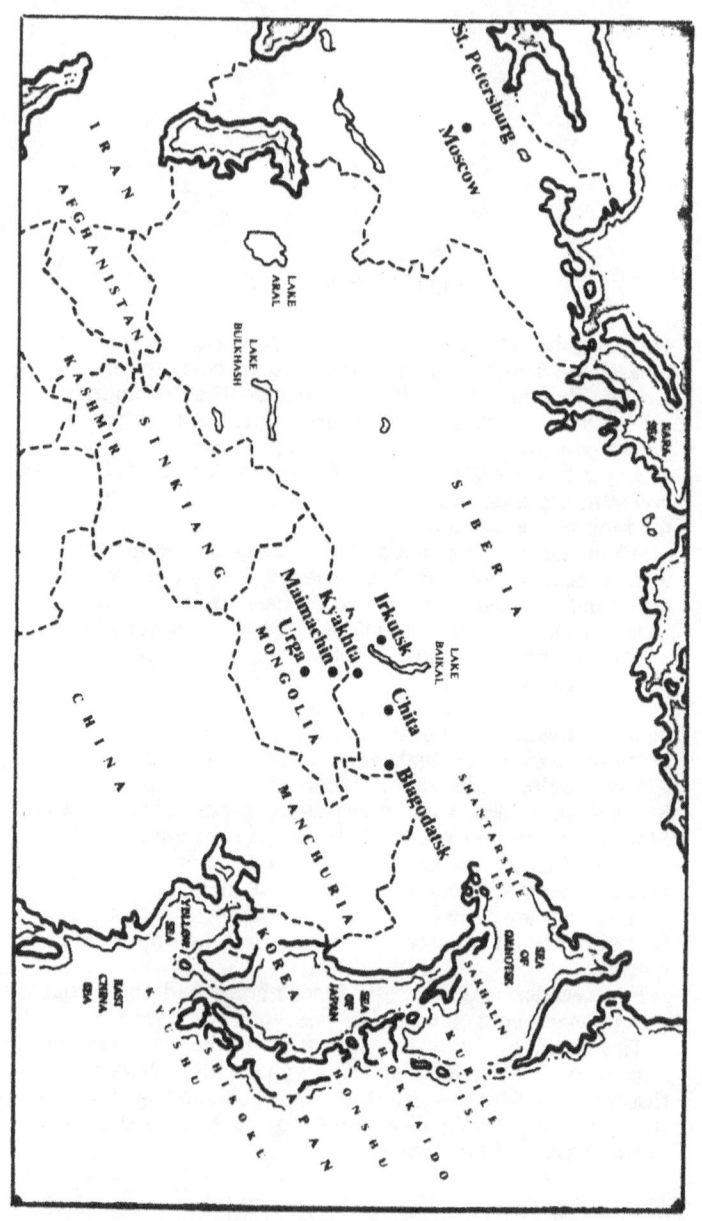

PART I

THE REBELLIOUS

Chapter One

Nowhere in the world were the summer nights as ethereal, as mystical, as in St. Petersburg, Russia, that June of 1825. The white nights of the north blended the city's pastels into a luminous hue of perpetual twilight, washing out the sharp contours and blurring the images of the capital.

Behind the lacy grillwork of the Summer Garden, amid the intoxicating fragrance of blooming lilacs, rumors abounded. They were whispered with relish, repeated in silk-paneled parlors, and carried back into the streets—rumors that the beloved Tsar Alexander called the Blessed for his conquest of Napoleon thirteen years earlier, had turned to mysticism and was withdrawing from the affairs of state.

Grandson of Catherine the Great, he was considered the most glamorous monarch in Europe and called Adonis of the North. In his own capital the aura of mystery pervaded the Winter Palace and spilled over onto the graceful boulevards of St. Petersburg, filling the air with speculation about his unfulfilled promises to abolish serfdom and his reconciliation with his beautiful but neglected tsarina Elizabeth.

On the night of June 16 the golden spire of the Admiralty Building shimmered silver in the pallid light, domineering the skyline and vying for attention with the somber towers of the Peter and Paul Fortess across the river. The Neva's lapping waters caressed the granite embankment in rhythmic cadence, and music and folk songs echoed from the elegant rowboats that were drifting downstream with the current. Clusters of pedestrians watched and listened as the noblemen, seated beneath the silk canopies of their boats, joined the musicians in song.

On the English Quay a pillared palace sparkled with lights. The French emigrant Count Lavale was giving a ball to celebrate the birthday of his married daughter, Princess Trubetskaya. Carriage after carriage of elegantly clothed guests pulled up at the brightly lit entrance. Diamonds twinkled in the opalescent light of the evening, spurs clicked, and peals of laughter trilled lightly in the air, fading out over the moonlit ripples of the gently flowing river.

Inside the palace, liveried footmen in gold-frogged red coats, white stockings, and buckled shoes opened the gilded double doors to usher guests into the main ballroom to be greeted by their host. Paneled in dark blue silk, the room was dressed with numerous baskets of roses and chrysanthemums grown in the hothouses of the count's estate outside the city. The red and white flowers against the blue walls were reflected in the tall pier mirrors, completing the tricolors of the imperial flag.

After the last guest had arrived, Count Lavale, a distinguished-looking man of medium height in black frock coat and white silk jabot, surveyed the ballroom, making sure that no one was neglected before the orchestra began to play the polonaise.

Well known and popular among the aristocrats of St. Petersburg, the count was pleased to have in attendance tonight the tsar's second brother, the grand duke Nicholas, whose wife, the grand duchess Alexandra, expected another *accouchement* and did not attend. *It's*

*a good thing that His Highness is so loyal to his
"Mouffy,"* Count Lavale thought as he looked at the
collection of glamorous women before him. It would be
scandalous for Nicholas to single out any woman in the
absence of his pregnant wife. The choice would surely
have tempted a less devoted man, for the flower of St.
Petersburg society was present tonight. The young
women favored white tulle and pastel silks, their jewels
glittering as they moved among the scarlet, blue, and
green uniforms of their husbands and escorts.

When the orchestra began to play, Count Lavale
watched the grand duke lead the polonaise and thought
that Nicholas was even more handsome than Tsar
Alexander. The tsar's appearance was almost angelic,
but this young man, though nineteen years younger
than his august brother, looked decidedly stern with his
high forehead, Grecian profile, and cold, clear eyes.
The count shuddered slightly. It was fortunate that
between this regal young man and the childless tsar,
there was another brother, Constantine, who would be
inheriting the Russian throne. Grand Duke Nicholas
would turn Russia into a rigid army camp with his
notorious military discipline, Count Lavale concluded,
and turned to see his daughter, Princess Catherine
Trubetskaya, or Katasha to her friends, a dainty girl with
saucy, upturned nose, approach him. But it was the girl
who walked beside her that attracted his attention.

Who was she? With so many guests coming in, he
had forgotten whose daughter she was, and he studied
her curiously. A stunning beauty, he thought.

The golden highlights of the girl's light brown hair
seemed to glitter from the double braided chignon on
top of her elaborately coiffed head to the carefully
arranged clusters of bouncing curls over her ears.
Large, gold-flecked green eyes rimmed with thick,
curly lashes looked intently from beneath a generous

sweep of brows. A half head taller than Katasha, she was dressed in a white tulle gown with a high-waisted satin band that accentuated her slim waist and small round bosom, and her low-cut lace-trimmed neckline framed a large ruby teardrop suspended from a single strand of pearls.

How fortunate that Katasha had a husband already, the count thought, for there was a presence about the young girl that completely overshadowed his daughter and, indeed, every other woman in the room. He smiled courteously at the lovely creature before him and then listened to his daughter's animated chatter.

"Papa," Katasha was saying, "this is Countess Irina Radina's first ball! I'm so glad that her parents brought her from Moscow specially for my birthday. We've just been pulling lists from our reticules to see how many dances we have already reserved!"

Without waiting for her father's reply, Katasha whispered something in Irina's ear and, laughing, whisked her away.

The music had ended, and moments later the dance floor cleared, with groups of guests clustering in various parts of the ballroom. Katasha disappeared in the crowd, and Irina Radina found herself standing near two elderly women who were talking to her mother. There was not the slightest doubt in her mind that the women were gossiping, for her mother's large neck showed several red splotches—a sure sign that she was angry.

Irina sighed. Her mother hated gossip. "Gossip is the most vicious of entertainments," she had said to her daughter once. "It's like an ink spot—no matter how much you try to wash it out, the suspicion of ink is always there."

How true, for tonight Irina was painfully aware that she would become the object of yet another choice bit of gossip. In the absence of her father, who hated these balls and never attended, she and her mother were escorted by General Temin, hero of the Napoleonic war, who drew attention to himself wherever he went.

At eighteen she had been of marriageable age for more than a year now, and her mother encouraged her to look with favor on the distinguished officer, who had recently moved to Moscow and had begun to frequent the Radin estate at Beryozovka.

Irina, however, had a mind of her own. "He's twenty-five years older than I am, Maman!" she cried. "Why do I have to marry such an old man?"

She didn't dare add that his drooping jowls revolted her and that his bony fingers sent shivers through her spine whenever he touched her. An old wound had left him with a slight limp, and he did not dance; but as the countess had pointed out while they were preparing to leave for the ball, General Temin would make a loyal and devoted husband, unlike their neighbor's flippant and unstable son, Prince Alexander Dolovin. Irina remembered the dashing young Alexander, whom she had met once, shortly before he left for St. Petersburg's prestigious School of Pages. She'd been only seven years old then, and he fourteen, and she had not seen him since; but the memory of a dark-haired youth with dimples and a flashing smile lingered.

Looking around the ballroom now, Irina studied the faces of the young officers around her, wondering if Prince Alexander was attending the ball tonight and, if so, which one he was. But it was silly of her to think that, for of course, if he were there, her mother would have reintroduced them this evening. Right now, though, Countess Radina was resolutely opening her lace and mother-of-pearl fan to cool herself, and as Irina moved closer to listen, one of the two women talking to her mother leaned forward.

"You know what I've heard?" she said, her voluminous bosom heaving in her red velvet gown. "It's about that woman, Baroness Krüdener, you know, the one who introduced His Majesty to mysticism in Heilbronn. They say that's what caused the estrangement between the tsar and the tsarina back in 1815, for the tsar has never been the same since he met that woman."

"Bah!" said the other woman, dressed in a bright green moiré gown trimmed with black lace. "That's not what I've heard." With curled lips and raised eyebrow, she went on. "After all, Baroness Krüdener was well over fifty when she met the tsar. No. There was a rumor that Her Majesty had an unwholesome friendship with one of her ladies-in-waiting at one time and—"

"I don't understand why this gossip is revived now," Irina's mother interrupted, the fan in her strong, fleshy hand doubling its speed. "True or not, it all took place a good ten years ago. Why tarnish the beautiful relationship that we see now between Their Majesties?"

The woman in red velvet shrugged and pursed her lips. "Whatever they have between them, let's hope they live happily for a long, long time, for I don't look forward to seeing Grand Duke Constantine on the throne. He's rumored to have his father's explosive temper, and I hope he stays in Poland with his morganatic wife. I see a lot of problems there." The woman paused, cast a furtive glance in the direction of Grand Duke Nicholas, who was talking to his aide, and then lowered her voice conspiratorially. "Even the next in line is someone to be feared. Grand Duke Nicholas is a strict disciplinarian; but after all, he's only twenty-nine, and maybe he will mellow with age."

Countess Radina snapped her fan shut decisively. "In my opinion, Grand Duke Constantine is loyal to the crown, and Grand Duke Nicholas is a good man and a devoted husband; but aren't we being too serious on a festive night like this? Let's enjoy the ball and celebrate Princess Trubetskaya's birthday!"

Irina smiled and was moving to join her mother when General Temin appeared by her side. She froze.

"I see that for a moment you're alone, Irina, and I have a chance to talk to you. In a few minutes the music will begin, and you'll be surrounded by young men begging for a dance. I'm sure your reticule is already filled with requests! As for me, I'm your humble admirer, who will bask in your beauty on the sidelines, as you dance."

Why does he always belittle himself? Irina thought uncomfortably. *Everyone honors him as a hero. Why does he still need reassurance?* Surreptitiously she looked around. People were noticing them together, the intent way he was looking at her, and soon tongues would wag. She wouldn't be envied, she would be pitied, and she couldn't tolerate the thought. She would have to make her mother understand. But once Countess Radina made up her mind, she was a formidable force in her household. Irina shifted her feet nervously, forcing herself to respond to Temin.

"You're very kind, General," she said smoothly, "but actually I was on my way to join my mother before the music begins."

General Temin twirled his handlebar mustache and bowed gallantly. "I'm sure Countess Radina will forgive me if I usurp a little of her daughter's time."

Irina lowered her glance and stood waiting silently for him to continue.

"I'm sure you're not aware how your eyes sparkle tonight and how your lovely ball gown enhances your beauty."

There was a brief pause, and then Temin added softly, "This is a lot more enjoyable than spending your time in the village teaching peasant children to read, don't you think?"

Irina squeezed her reticule hard, and the edge of the metal frame cut sharply into the palm of her hand. There was only one way he could have learned of her secret ambition. Her mother must have confided in him, must have told him how horrified she and Count Radin were at Irina's desire to teach the serfs to read and write.

"The more you educate them," her father had said then, "the more rebellious they'll become."

"It's below your station in life," her mother had wailed. "You should be presented at court instead!"

But Irina wasn't interested in court life. She had gone to the village on their estate, talked to their serfs, and found many of them intelligent and pathetically eager to learn. Determined to overcome her parents' objections, she continued to argue her cause. She felt betrayed now that her mother had divulged their private conflict to this man. She swallowed tears of embarrassment, forced a casual smile, and said, "I take it you, too, don't think much of educating the serfs, General."

"While I admire your good itentions, my dear, I'm sure you are not aware of what a waste of time it would be."

"That's a matter of opinion, of course, but tell me, General," she said, pointedly changing the subject, "what have you been reading lately? The last time we talked, you mentioned some interesting books."

She would not permit this man to involve her in a discussion of a subject so personal, so close to her heart. He would not be privileged to know her private thoughts! She was angry with her mother, so angry! It was small consolation that she had scored a victory with Temin.

Obviously taken aback, he blinked and coughed, then said, "Ah, yes, when we all return to Moscow, I intend to bring a few stories for you to read at Beryozovka."

Did she detect a slight possessiveness in his tone? With a polite nod Irina moved toward her mother, but at that moment the grand duke's aidede-camp appeared between them and bowed courteously to Irina.

"His Highness requests the pleasure of the next dance, mademoiselle," he said, and offered his arm to escort her to the grand duke.

Flustered, Irina glanced at her list. The next dance was already reserved by a young hussar, but her mother had overheard and shook her head.

"This is a command, Irina," she said quietly. "Go!"

Both flattered and apprehensive, Irina placed her gloved hand on the aide's arm and moved forward with small, gliding steps on the highly polished floor. Suddenly an irrelevant thought floated across her mind. Only the day before her mother had told her that the marble floor in the ballroom had once belonged to the emperor Nero of Rome. It wouldn't do—would it—to slip on such a floor, and before all those people! Would the grand duke still want to dance with her if she should fall? Irina thought, smiling inwardly to break her nervousness. For an infinitesimal moment she wished she were back in the safety of her home on her parents' estate outside Moscow. What wouldn't she give right now to be walking along the familiar lanes lined with age-old birch and maple, instead of approaching the awesome presence of the grand duke, standing erect and regal, waiting for her with an imposing smile.

The penetrating gaze of his large eyes chilled her as she curtsied low before him. Handsome he was, to be sure, with classic features and taller than average, but the legendary warmth that her mother described in Tsar

Alexander was lacking. Surely she couldn't be this intimidated by the tsar himself if ever they met!

The orchestra struck up the lilting rhythm of a mazurka, and Irina lowered her eyes as the grand duke led her onto the dance floor.

Her skirt was embroidered with steel plaquettes, and Irina, intent on not catching them on the grand duke's elkskin breeches, was startled when he asked, "Why haven't I seen you before, mademoiselle?" His voice was powerful, authoritative, accustomed to command.

Irina admitted shyly that this was her first ball. "I live in the country near Moscow, Your Highness," she said. "My parents brought me to St. Petersburg for Princess Trubetskaya's birthday."

"What is your favorite pastime at home?"

Irina replied, "Reading poetry."

"I enjoy Derzhavin and Zhukovsky, and who is your favorite poet?"

Without hesitation Irina said, "Pushkin!"

She realized her blunder the moment she said it. It was not a name favored at court, for Pushkin had been exiled to the south of Russia several years earlier for his inflammatory writings and only recently had been allowed to return to his family estate in Pskov.

If Grand Duke Nicholas was annoyed, he did not show it. After a moment's pause he said, "What in particular do you like about his poetry?"

Although Irina had read Pushkin's inflammatory *Ode to Liberty*, in which he criticized the government's autocratic rule, she was quick to refer to his lyrical works.

"Poetry is an escape from reality," the grand duke said, "and sometimes can lead the reader astray. Dangerous ideas voiced in poetic cadence can influence an unwary mind."

Although the rebuke was subtle, the chill in his voice

was not. But Irina, caught in her favorite subject, would not be intimidated.

"Pushkin once said that serenity is essential to artistic creation," she said, "and I would add that serenity and solitude are equally important to the reader, in order to understand and ponder that which the artist attempts to impart. How can this idea be dangerous?"

Perhaps she imagined it, but a glimmer of admiration shone in the grand duke's eyes for a moment and then was gone. She found herself relaxing and the grand duke Nicholas an attentive listener.

At the end of the mazurka he smiled frostily. "You are an excellent dancer, mademoiselle, and it is St. Petersburg's loss that we have not seen you here before. I realize that I have usurped this mazurka promised to another lucky gentleman." Releasing her hand, he bowed stiffly. "I owe you a favor, mademoiselle!"

Months later Irina would try desperately to recall the details of their conversation and the nuances of the grand duke's words, but now, standing at the edge of the ballroom, watching Nicholas's tall figure move away from her, she thought that although it was a dizzying experience to attend her first ball in St. Petersburg, the intimidating presence of the tsar's brother, and the gossip she had overheard about the royal family, made her yearn for the peace of her Moscow home.

Chapter Two

Two months after Count Lavale's ball Tsar Alexander gave a farewell reception at the Winter Palace prior to his departure for Taganrog, a quiet resort on the Sea of Azov, where he and Tsarina Elizabeth were to spend an extended vacation.

Long before the appointed hour of nine o'clock, when the ball was to begin, courtiers and guests arrived at the Jordan Entrance, with its huge columns and steps of Carrara marble, to enter the palace and climb the Grand Staircase, flanked on both sides by Cossack Life Guards in red tunics. They stood alongside troopers of the Chevaliers Guards, who were resplendent in silver breastplates and helmets crowned with double eagles. Farther on, the long halls leading to the ballroom were lined with lackeys in the imperial livery, standing immobile or swinging silver censers filled with incense to perfume the rooms. Every hall contained baskets of camellias and roses and, along with porcelain vases of scented flowers in the ballroom, created the illusion of an exotic garden. Crystal chandeliers with lighted candles and torchères with arms reaching up toward the carved and painted ceilings distracted the eye like thousands of twinkling stars.

Among the courtiers watching the tsar and the tsarina mingle with the guests was a young officer of the Imperial Guards. Dressed in a scarlet tunic with white breeches and gleaming high boots, he stood leaning against a polished column, one leg casually crossed over the other, his gloved hand absentmindedly twisting an aglet tip of the braided cord looped over his arm. His wavy chestnut hair was combed high above his forehead. Full, long sideburns outlined his pale face and accentuated his dark brown eyes, which now looked around the ballroom with apparent boredom.

But Prince Alexander Dolovin was more annoyed really than bored. Although the spectacle before him was so well rehearsed that he could detail each hour of the evening with military precision, his annoyance stemmed from an entirely different source. Concealed inside his dolman coat was a letter from his father, Prince Gregory Dolovin.

". . .I urge you to come home and spend your vacation with us," his father wrote from Moscow in his careless wide scrawl. "It has been entirely too long since you visited Dolovino, and while I know that St. Petersburg can be addictive, we, too, have some attractions for you. Besides, don't forget that your mother and I are not getting any younger, and we long to see you." He went on to remind his son how lovely the countryside was this time of year after the harvest and added, "The forests are full of mushrooms, and you know what that means—the young people are organizing to go after them, with picnics and song and dance a *khorovod*. So you see, you don't have to be housebound with us old people. As a matter of fact, our neighbor's daughter, Countess Irina Radina, comes over frequently. You probably don't remember her, for you met only once, when you both were children; but she has grown into a lovely young woman, and I can promise that you will not be disappointed." And then came the final statement: ". . . whatever ties may hold you in St. Petersburg, they will still be there when you return."

If his father had left that sentence out, then Alexander would have given in to the nostalgic pull of childhood memories and gone home. But Papa could never leave well enough alone. It never occurred to him that his family should be allowed to make their own decisions.

Ever since he was old enough to discern the world around him, Alexander was aware that his domineering father ruled the household with an iron rigidity that no one, not even his lonely wife, dared breach. Alexander learned early that his mother's gentle embrace was to soothe and comfort, never to protect or defend against his father's unwavering discipline, and he had tried to protect his younger brother, Nikita, five years his junior, a fair-haired, serious youth.

As he grew older and reached adolescence, Alexander's curious mind sought answers to the reasons for his father's severe treatment of his serfs. Once, when Prince Gregory ordered a servant whipped for failing to polish his boots to his liking, Alexander dared not question his father and turned to his mother instead, only to see her call for her smelling salts and wave Alexander out of her boudoir without explanation. Wispy and frail, she lived in comfort in their 10,000-acre estate, attended by servants for her every need and subservient to her husband's strong personality and seemingly content to leave all major decisions to him.

After many futile attempts to get her to listen to his adolescent anxieties over the years, Alexander gradually turned inward and distanced himself from his parents. In due time he learned from his old nanny that his parents' marriage had been arranged by their aristocratic families as a suitable match and his mother, timid and colorless, still a spinster at twenty-five, had been so in awe of her bethrothed that she had never crossed him in anything.

When the decision was made to send Alexander to the

School of Pages in St. Petersburg, he was relieved to escape from parental supervision and in subsequent years avoided visiting his family home as much as possible.

The not so subtle reference to Countess Irina could be turned aside as yet another effort at matchmaking on the part of his mother who, having married so late in life, was understandably eager to see him acquire a wife while he was still young. But then Papa had to let him know that he was well informed of his son's deepening involvement with Marianna Kosinskaya and was displeased.

At the thought of Marianna, Alexander tensed. There was no doubt that he had fallen under the spell of the fiery courtesan, but was he in love? Surely not. The idea was preposterous. He couldn't—he mustn't be! At twenty-five, he was his own man, and his father's interference in his private life was an annoyance.

Too bad that Marianna had not been born an aristocrat. She was the daughter of a widowed and ambitious modiste who owned a shop on the Nevsky Prospect and nurtured vain hopes that Marianna would marry one of her titled protectors. In her early teens Marianna was already on the stage and was soon recognized as a promising ingenue. Her first protector had set her up comfortably in a flat near the Neva Embankment, and by the time Alexander met her she was an established demimondaine.

Suddenly agitated, Alexander straightened, uncrossed his legs, and looked at the women around him. Marianna would shine like a rare gem among them, he thought; in their court dresses of embroidered silks and bejeweled headdresses, they all looked alike. His gaze roamed farther and settled on the tsar, who was moving slowly in his direction, stopping every few steps to chat with his guests. At forty-eight, the blond tsar had gained weight, and his brilliant blue eyes had lost some of their magnetic luster; but the contours of his rounded face were still smooth, and the soft lips smiled readily at his courtiers.

Suddenly the court pleasantries became oppressive, and Alexander wanted to avoid facing the tsar. After turning abruptly, he mingled in the crowd and made his way to the nearest door. Once in the quiet corridor, he walked briskly, his steps muffled by the carpeted floor.

A familiar voice from behind stopped him. "Alexander! I saw you leave the ballroom; where can we talk?"

Alexander turned around to face his friend Kondraty Ryleyev.

"Kondraty! I didn't see you in the ballroom! Let's go to the Malachite Room, it's right around the corner and should be empty tonight."

The two friends moved on in step and soon reached the vast room. Once inside, Alexander closed the heavily carved, gilded doors behind him, but not before looking up and down the hall to make sure they had not been followed. Then, after walking over to the fireplace, he leaned on the mantel and looked around the room, his gaze traveling over the malachite square columns built into the walls, over the inlaid tables, the artifacts, the vases, all made from the veined green stone in graceful symmetry. But all that was lost on him as he faced his friend.

"Well, what news, Kondraty?"

Ryleyev sat down at the round malachite-topped table in front of the fireplace and, leaning on one elbow, propped his chin in his hand. A well-known poet, he was an exquisitely handsome man with a dreamy look and soft features that belied his incisive intellect.

'We've split into Northern and Southern societies, Alex," Ryleyev said. "We can't agree on our theories.

Colonel Pestel is heading the southern branch now, and he is ruthless. He advocates radical measures in order to do away with autocratic monarchy." Kondraty moved uncomfortably in his chair. His wide-set eyes took on a clouded look. "What's more, we can't seem to reconcile our own differences in the north. Our moderate, Nikita Muravyev, favors a constitutional monarchy and calls me a radical because I insist on a republic. He should talk to Pestel!"

Alexander frowned. Things weren't going right with the society. Too much polemic, too many grandiose ideas, and little else. A vague uneasiness took hold of him. "If we don't come to some mutual agreement soon," he said quietly, "the whole idea of reforming our government system through revolt will become too big for us to handle and will have to be shelved." He smiled ruefully. "Future generations will judge us irresponsible, perhaps even naïve, because of lack of unity and organization. Don't you agree?"

Kondraty thought for a moment, then shrugged. "You must realize that something like this has to be carefully planned. Any rash act can land us all in Siberia."

"I don't mean that we must rush into it; all I'm saying is that we must soon come to some sort of agreement, at least in principle. We have to act while we are young and willing to undertake such a drastic change in our country. Moderate or radical, call it what you may, our principal goal is the same, and you know what that is."

"Yes, of course: to do away with the autocracy of the tsar."

Alexander started. "No so loud, Kondraty! This room is empty and large, but it might have ears; one of these doors could be ajar, and someone could be listening to us!" He moved a few steps toward the center of the room and looked at the grooved malachite pillars with Corinthean ormolu that supported the cornices by the doors. A perfect place to hide. Surely there was no one in the room, but one could not be too careful.

He turned to see his friend smiling. "What's the matter, Alex? Our conspiracy is getting to you?"

In spite of his discomfort, Alexander laughed a short, embarrassed laugh. "I don't know. I suppose it was not a good idea to talk here. Where's the next meeting going to be?"

"At my house, next Thursday. I'll see you then!" With that Ryleyev rose, shook Alexander's hand warmly, and walked out.

Alexander stayed in the Malachite Room a while longer. He knew well the dangers of having joined the secret society which they had named the Union of Welfare. It would surely be called something else by the police and by the tsar. High treason, that's what! And all in the society knew it. Yet he believed passionately in the Union of Welfare. It was made up of a group of altruistic, selfless men who wanted to do away with government suppression of free thought, better the lot of the underprivileged, and emancipate the serfs. There was something bestial in buying and selling human beings like so many head of cattle. Alexander had heard his father often enough, bartering over 100 or 200 *souls*. It was dreadful to think that this commonly used term had only one purpose: to distinguish the serfs from inanimate objects! The Union of Welfare firmly believed that the tsar's autocratic rule was ruining Russia. The country's bloody past hung over their heads like a bad nightmare. Ivan the Terrible had killed at whim, and Peter the Great's vengeance on his enemies had known no mercy. Tsar Alexander's own father, Paul, who was Catherine the Great's only son, had humiliated his citizens by having them whipped when they failed to obey his order to kneel or curtsy on the street whenever his carriage passed. When he had been assassinated by his courtiers after only five years of reign, it was said that his son and heir, Alexander, had known of the conspiracy to remove the tsar from the throne and had done nothing to prevent it.

Early in Tsar Alexander's reign, he had made sweeping promises to abolish serfdom and to dedicate himself to public service, but through the years he had become absorbed with personal salvation and turned inward, oblivious of the growing repression around him. Something had to be done about it, and Alexander's friends in the secret society all agreed with that. But what? How?

It was one thing to engage in endless discussions in the privacy of one another's homes, but quite another to take charge of a conspiracy and organize a revolt. Who among them had the necessary qualities of a leader? Alexander mopped his brow with a handkerchief. Strange, how hollow and dwarfing were these palace rooms when things didn't go the way they should. The palace rooms were kept too warm, and he suddenly needed fresh air.

Things were not going right for him today. Take his father's letter, for instance. Hidden inside his dolman, it rubbed his conscience, and suddenly the beckoning music from the nearby ballroom became irritating. He would not go back there. He was alone with his decisions and with his future. But he needed to talk to someone, to forget for a while about his problems.

Marianna. She was the only one who understood him, never criticized him, and seemed totally on his side. How fortunate to have a demimondaine who not only was intelligent but approved of his political views as well! Resolutely Alexander walked toward the exit.

* * *

Marianna's house was hidden behind the Summer Garden, on a quiet side street across the Swan Canal. Elegant, quiet, and discreet. He had bought it for her months ago and allowed her to decorate it to her own taste. Without portico or columns, it stood unobtrusively pale among other St. Petersburg's pastel fronts, but once inside, Marianna had let her flamboyant personality run unchecked. Alexander winced every time he saw the heavy red portieres trimmed in gold fringe, the gilded chairs upholstered in patterned red silk, and fancy porcelain bibelots everywhere. At first, he had tried to suggest a less garish decor, but as the months slipped by and his attachment to her deepened, he had abandoned the effort. After moments of intimacy when he had whispered feverish words of love and thought that never could he part from her, the red and gold decor stood as a sobering reminder of the chasm between them.

The short walk cooled him. It couldn't be otherwise on this mellow night, with gentle peals of laughter floating toward him from behind the iron grille of the Summer Garden. Dim shadows of strolling lovers, arms around each other, drifted slowly between the elms, while an elusive fragrance of delicate perfume teased his imagination.

At the house Marianna greeted him with bubbling pleasure, her silk and lace peignoir of vivid blue highlighting her bright turquoise eyes. Long curls the color of wheat fell loosely over her shoulders, making her small, rounded features look younger than her twenty-five years. Every time he saw her, he marveled at her ability to show herself to the best advantage, in spite of her rather ordinary face. But ah, her body and those long, slim legs! Aware that she was sensitive about being two months older than he, Alexander never failed to compliment her on her youthful appearance.

What a delight that he could be himself in her presence; how good that he did not have to listen to the inane banter at court, that he could remove his dolman and relax in her boudoir with a glass of Château Lafite!

He couldn't wait to tell her about his conversation with Kondraty Ryleyev. Marianna was an attentive listener, and what was more, she shared his views and knew about his involvement with the Secret Society. Good it was to have her loyalty, to be able to trust his random thoughts to her receptive ear.

"I'm worried about what will become of our society," Alexander said reflectively after he had told her about his meeting with Ryleyev. "Though it's exciting to be talking about our ideologies and dreams for a better system of government, what our country really needs is a *practical* leader who can organize an uprising and rally support of the army."

"Don't you have such a man in your group?"

"I think Colonel Pestel could be that leader, but he has now divided the society into two groups because he could not agree with our northern brethren. It worries me. Divided, we weaken our cause."

Marianna refilled Alexander's glass from a blue crystal decanter and reclined on the chaise longue, carefully arranging the folds of her peignoir. Then she looked at him with narrowed eyes. "What exactly does Colonel Pestel advocate?"

Alexander shrugged. "I heard about the disagreement only tonight. I may find out more next week, when I attend Ryleyev's meeting, but whatever Pestel's ideas are, he should certainly temper his wisdom with mercy; otherwise we'll get entwined in our theoretical ropes, and then who's going to cut our own kind of gordian knot?"

"Not only that, but the longer your society goes along without taking any action, the greater the risk of being betrayed by someone within your group. One of you might have second thoughts about the whole project and then, eager to exonerate himself, report your meetings to the police." Marianna leaned toward Alexander. "Oh, Alex, who knows what a man can do in his righteous fervor . . . I get so nervous thinking about it and what might happen to you!"

"You needn't be. Everyone in our society is a dedicated patriot, loyal to our country and not to the tsar. Believe me, no matter what our differences, we work for the common goal!"

"What a magnificent dream we all have!" she said, her voice full of wonder. "Imagine, Alex, the day may come when we can say what we want and where we want without fear of reprisals and censorship; ah, to be able to do good for those who now receive no justice!" She clasped her hands to her chest and then in one quick movement was beside Alexander, showering his neck with feathery kisses. "And all because of men like you—generous, altruistic, selfless! We shall be able to do so much then!"

Alexander smiled, slid his hand through her long locks, and, grasping a few curls, pulled her head close to his. "And you, my dear, when that day comes, will you still keep me sated and content and charged with energy?"

Marianna pulled away. "I'd want to do more than that."

"Like what?"

She lowered her gaze demurely.

Amused, Alexander thought: *What a superb actress, this one!* Restraining a smile, he asked again, "Like what?"

Marianna thought for a moment, shrugged, and then, laughing, tickled his ear with her tongue. "Like this!"

With a delicious shiver, he crushed her to him. Soft, pliable, eager to please, she teased and laughed and ever so slowly replaced his lofty plans for the future with private thoughts of pleasures at hand.

Minutes or hours later—what fool would count such passages of time?—Alexander heard her dreamy whisper. She was lying beside him, her head on his chest, the fluff of golden hair spread across his arms in disarray.

"I want you to know," she said, "that in moments like this, I feel I am more than your lover. We have so much in common, we understand each other so well . . . I feel . . . that we—we belong to each other. And should . . . forever and always!"

Alexander suppressed a smile. A well-rehearsed refrain, he thought. Was she aware how many variations on the same theme she had used in the past few months? How clever to make him believe she was deeply attached to him, as though he were her first and only love! She played her role convincingly, and yet . . . and yet was there something else he had failed to see? Ridiculous! With her flamboyant clothes, her flashy furnishings, and her delights, she was totally predictable.

He tickled her under her chin and kissed the tip of her nose. "Why such deep thoughts at a time like this? You surprise me!"

Whatever her reaction to his flippant remark, Marianna concealed it well. She turned away and reached for the decanter again, but Alexander caught her hand in midair and kissed it ceremoniously. "No more tonight, my dear. I've got to go over some papers at home."

Something had spoiled the intimate mood. He dressed quickly and was fastening his dolman when he felt the rustle of paper. His father's letter.

Perhaps it wasn't such a bad idea to go home for a visit. There would be no harm in spending his vacation on his parents' estate and meeting Countess Irina. It might afford him a pleasant few weeks of lighthearted escape from his entanglements in the capital. As he pondered the possibility, a vague idea floated across his mind. If Countess Irina pleased him, perhaps a marriage could be arranged, and he would then be safe from Marianna's scheme to ensnare him. Many of his married friends were keeping a courtesan in grand style . . . after all, it was an accepted, if unmentionable, custom in his milieu, and since he did not expect to fall in love with the countess, he could do the same. What harm?

Chapter Three

Long rows of stately birch trees lined the road from Moscow to Beryozovka. Although only ten versts from the city, it was secluded in the countryside, surrounded by oak groves, pristine pastures, and a few scattered estates. The Beryozovka mansion stood hidden in the park behind an iron grillwork fence and stone gates, flanked by pine trees and jasmine bushes.

Supported by Doric columns, its portico rose above the second story, and although its yellow limestone front was narrow, the illusion of smallness was deceptive, for the structure was twice as deep on each side. Numerous fountains and sculptures of Grecian and Roman gods dotted the park, tapping Irina's fantasy for hours at a time.

The only daughter of Count and Countess Radin, she had been reared in the genteel serenity of her family estate, where she spent a happy childhood, cared for by a doting nanny and indulged by loving parents. Educated at home, as was the custom of aristocratic families, by a succession of tutors, some French, some English, she had learned to speak their languages fluently and been praised as a bright and eager student. An avid reader, she had enjoyed Jane Austen's *Pride and Prejudice* and only recently had sat up most of the night reading Walter Scott's *Ivanhoe*.

But poetry was her favorite, and today, as she

strolled through the shady lanes of the park, she held a volume of Keats' poems in her hand. She had just finished reading his "Ode on a Grecian Urn," and although she found La Fontaine's French fables easier to read, she was nonetheless impressed by the English poet's depth of emotion. "Heard melodies are sweet, but those unheard/Are sweeter," he had said in his ode. Was the inner voice more powerful then, more lasting than the external one? She paused before the sculpture of Diana, bow and arrow in the goddess's hand, and studied the marble profile, gifting it with imaginary life. A resolute person she must have been, to hunt and kill and be a champion of women. Would she, Irina, ever have an opportunity to be this strong, this courageous? Her life seemed destined for quiet obscurity, a role of passive acquiescence. No. Not she! Determined never to marry General Temin, she had angered her mother with her cool reception of the general whenever he came to call, and to top it all, friction sparked at home each time she talked about the peasant children she yearned to teach. This morning had been no exception.

Countess Radina, her voluminous bosom heaving with excitement and threatening to burst out of her morning gown, was pacing her boudoir and impatiently waving away her maid, Dasha, who was trying unsuccessfully to remove curl papers from her graying blond hair.

"Leave us, Dasha, I want to talk to Countess Irina," she had finally said, and, settling into her gilded white chair, pointed to another chair in a silent order for her daughter to sit down. Irina remained standing. Her mother favored the dainty French furniture of the Louis XV period that Irina's father despised, and as a result, the rest of the house was furnished with sturdy Empire mahogany pieces.

"You pick a most inopportune time to talk to me

about your wild idea. I must say, dear child, it has become an *idée fixe* with you. Your father and I have told you repeatedly that it is not *comme il faut* for a young lady of your position to be teaching serf children." The countess fanned herself with her lace handkerchief—a sign of nervousness—Irina noted mentally, but she said nothing and waited patiently for further admonitions.

"I thought you had come to your senses. Of all the days to start talking about it again! After our visit to St. Petersburg, where you saw how young ladies of your rank occupy themselves, you should aspire to be chosen as a lady-in-waiting to one of the grand duchesses or to make a suitable marriage instead of thinking about the serfs. Your cousin and his wife are coming this afternoon for a picnic, and I already told you that Prince Alexander Dolovin is visiting his parents and has asked to call on us. Perhaps he is ready to settle down now, and since you're so high-handed with dear General Temin, I invited Prince Alexander to join us today. You should be thinking of what you are going to wear this afternoon instead of"—the countess threw down her handkerchief and having risen from her chair, went over to her dressing table, glanced at herself in the mirror, thought better of it, and turned to face her daughter—"instead of stuffing your pretty head with outrageous plans. What would Boris and Olga think if they knew this?"

Irina did not answer and, giving her mother a token curtsy, left the room. She hardly cared what her adventurous cousin Boris would think of her ideas. He was the son of Count Radin's older brother, and since Irina was an only child, she wondered if her mother had adopted Boris in her heart as her surrogate son. She suspected that Boris, who, since their childhood, was always ready to try new things, would be intrigued by her desire to teach. As for his mischievous wife, Olga—well, she lived in her own world of French fashion and neighborhood gossip.

At the moment, however, Irina was far more pleased by the omission of General Temin's name from the picnic's guest list than by the thought of meeting Prince Alexander, whose escapades in St. Petersburg were well known in Dolovino and repeated with relish among the servants in Beryozovka.

The weather was warm. It was one of those languid, shimmering days when the birds were hushed in the shade of the sprawling oak branches and the gold of the newly harvested fields reflected the brilliance of the noonday sun. Red poppies and blue forget-me-nots dotted the green meadow outside the Beryozovka park, where several young girls from the neighboring village, dressed for the occasion in their colorful *sarafans* and embroidered white blouses, were setting up tables for the picnic.

By early afternoon Irina had returned from her stroll through the park and with the help of her faithful maid, Tosya, put on a white muslin dress trimmed with green ribbon to match her eyes. Tosya, a robust, freckled peasant girl, placed a wide-brimmed flowered hat on a chair by the door and handed Irina her frilled parasol. Irina waved it away. "I won't need it if I wear the hat, Tosya," she said, laughing. "How can I look for mushrooms if I have to hold on to a parasol?"

In the main parlor of the house, the lined draperies were drawn to keep the sun out and the coolness in and to protect the mauve silk upholstery from fading. Count Ignaty Radin, a stocky graying man in a cool linen shirt that he always wore in the country, sat in his favorite leather armchair, talking to his nephew Boris Radin. As Irina stooped to plant a kiss on her father's high forehead, she caught the familiar scent of his shaving cologne. Papa was ready for his guests; he was being his usual affable, hospitable self, she thought, turning to greet her cousins Boris and Olga. A veritable dandy was Boris, with his pomaded brown hair and pouffed sideburns that rubbed against his silk cravat, which wrapped around his neck several times, as fashion dictated, in spite of the warm weather.

"How charming you look, *ma chère*," he said taking Irina's hand and giving her a brotherly peck on the cheek. She smiled and then turned to look at Olga, who sat fanning herself on a settee. Her black curls were caught off her neck with a ribbon, and her perpetually laughing eyes now looked at Irina with warmth.

Orphaned daughter of Count Rozov, who had been killed in the Battle of Borodino in 1812, when she was only seven, Olga had been married to Boris at seventeen, and although now, three years later, there were still no children of that union, she seemed content and lighthearted.

"I'm not sure your plan for a picnic is such a good idea on a hot day like this. I, for one, prefer to stay inside," she said.

Irina smiled and kissed her. "Nonsense, Olga. Boris can take off his fancy waistcoat, and by the time we all gather together and go outside it should be cooler. I heard Maman order the girls to set up tables in the shade of the trees. Besides," she added, nodding at Olga's airy batiste dress with a low square neckline, "you look very cool in that lovely outfit."

Voices drifted from the entry hall, and out of the corner of her eye Irina saw her mother rise to greet someone at the door. "Prince Alexander! What a pleasure to see you again! Do come in and meet our daughter and our guests."

Irina turned around to face the newcomer. His dark eyes sparkled with mischief as he bowed to her.

"The child I remember has blossomed into a beautiful young lady," he said, and his voice seemed to caress the words.

The conversation in the room turned to a murmur, the shadows lengthened, and she saw only the gold frogging of Prince Alexander's tunic, the white breeches contouring his muscular figure, and the sheathed saber that he was now unbuckling and handing to a waiting lackey. What was the matter with her? The heat in the room intensified, seeped through her skin, tickling her with beads of moisture. She fought the temptation to dab her handkerchief at her neck and, channeling her thoughts back to his words, smiled graciously.

"The years have been good to you, too, Prince Alexander," she said, forcing a steady look into his eyes, which now scrutinized her frankly. "I remember only a gawky youth whose main interest was pulling at my hair ribbons."

His glance traveled quickly to the green ribbon in her hair and then back to her eyes. "I am even more tempted to pull at your ribbons now, Irina Ignatyevna, and I regret that what was permissible to an adolescent cadet is forbidden an officer."

The tension was broken, and Irina laughed. How silly of her to react like this! After all, he was not entirely a stranger, for even though she hadn't seen him since childhood, she knew his parents well. His father, Prince Gregory, and his mother, Princess Maria, were frequent visitors at Beryozovka, and she had been invited several times to tea at Dolovino with her parents. Prince Gregory was an intense man with a booming voice that instantly intimidated those around him, including his slim, pale wife who always complained of delicate health and a weak heart. It must have been the contrast between the parents and their startlingly good-looking son that unsettled her so, Irina decided. How unexpected to see so dashing an off-spring of such old people! That was it!

After the introductions had been made, Irina's mother said, "Prince Alexander, I cannot bear the thought of your suffering the heat in your uniform. We are quite informal today at our picnic, and you young people will be outside. You will be far more comfortable if you put on one of Count Radin's country shirts. I insist that you borrow one!"

Alexander inclined his head graciously. "How very thoughtful of you, Countess. I accept gladly!"

Outside, it was hot, but the afternoon breeze rustled the leaves above the picnic tables and cooled the guests in the shade. The meadow sloped down to a meandering creek, its gentle waters sparkling in the distance. When Alexander joined them, Irina suppressed a look of surprise. Out of his uniform now, dressed in a loose-fitting white linen shirt with an embroidered side-buttoned collar, caught at the waist with a blue satin cord, Alexander looked younger, less formidable, and charmingly handsome.

After a picnic of buttered black bread with ham, roast chicken, dilled cucumbers in sour cream, and raspberries over meringue tarts, the young guests from neighboring estates went mushroom hunting, scattering in the pine grove behind the meadow. Irina found Alexander close on her heels.

Although she tried to suppress a smile, he must have noticed it. "I don't want you to forget what I look like in case we don't see each other for a while again!" he said, stooping to pick a mushroom under a tree.

Irina raised a brow. "How can I forget when every time I turn I find you at my side?"she said, accepting the mushroom from his hands. Their fingers touched, and she suddenly felt warm.

Alexander looked at her intently, an expression of

pleasant surprise on his face. "You've called my bluff! How candid!"

Irina smiled mischievously. "I hope I didn't embarrass you. I'm known to speak my mind and sometimes . . ." She spread her hands and looked at him apologetically, leaving the sentence unfinished.

Alexander laughed out loud. "Not at all! I'm charmed! And I shall try to get to know you better in the short time I'll be home."

"And how short is that?"

"About three weeks."

Irina saw another mushroom, stooped to pick it up, then straightened. "That will be long enough for us to decide whether we shall enjoy each other's company or be bored, isn't it?"

Alexander looked at her with unconcealed admiration. "Well, at least we'll be honest with each other! Now tell me, how do you pass your time? What are your interests?"

Irina hesitated for a moment, threw him a sidelong glance, and then said, "I pass my time arguing with my parents, trying to convince them that it is quite *comme il faut* for me to start teaching our serf children to read and write."

"Aha! I can hear your mother's admonition in those words. Instead of playing the clavichord or embroidering fine linens, you want to educate the serfs! Fascinating!"

Irina looked at him quickly to see if he was mocking her, but he seemed sincere enough. "Are you merely surprised, or are you shocked?" she asked.

"Surprised, yes; shocked, no. In fact, I admire your desire to teach the peasant children. It's not going to be easy. There is so much superstition among the peasantry that many of them look on education with considerable suspicion."

"Well then, I'll be a witch to some and a fairy to others."

Alexander smiled and bowed gallantly. "Let's hope the fairy will far outweigh the witch!"

Their baskets were full of mushrooms by now, and they walked out onto the meadow where all the young guests had already gathered around a group of peasant musicians with their balalaikas, ready to dance and sing.

Although Alexander's attentions were somewhat less than subtle and she had let him know that she was aware of his constant proximity, it was pleasant, nonetheless, to turn around and find him there, handling her basket of mushrooms or offering her another dish of raspberries at the table.

Now, as they sat on a white cloth spread for them on the grass, Alexander again found his way to her side. As the music started, at first slowly, then picking up the tempo, Irina felt Alexander's hand on hers, squeezing it in rhythm with the folk song. A thrilling day it was turning out to be; a perfect, cloudless day, the sky overhead so bright, it hurt her eyes when she looked up. Over the fragile branch of a white birch tree a bird hovered, singing an achingly sweet song, then disappeared into the brilliant blue. Yes, a perfect day!

Later that night, when the party was over and everyone had gone home, Irina lay in her bed for a long time, unable to sleep. Alexander's face floated before her, and she could not get him out of her mind. In his red uniform or peasant shirt, handing her the basket of mushrooms or holding her hand, he was before her. Was she falling in love with the handsome officer so quickly, she—the strong-willed girl determined to take her time in deciding her destiny? No. She had just been flattered by his attentions, enchanted by his good looks; that was it—a pleasant contrast with the staid and aging General Temin. Nothing more.

As the sun-filled days slipped by, Alexander visited Beryozovka almost daily. He and Irina walked hand in hand through the meadows and harvested fields, in the shady lanes of the family park, and talked for hours about literature, music, their childhood years, and gradually, cautiously, touched on their country's ills. To her unimaginable pleasure, Irina discovered that Alexander's physical appearance was not his only charm, that his concern for the serfs and the illiteracy of Russia was as great as hers, and that in this dashing man she had found a kindred soul with whom she could share her views and goals. That her heart stood still at the sound of his approaching horse, that his nearness endowed the afternoon with magic, that the lingering look in his eyes made the very air she breathed intoxicating—she wasn't quite ready to admit that it all added up to her falling in love. . . .

One particularly warm afternoon three weeks later General Temin paid her an unexpected visit. She and Alexander were returning from a long walk through the park when she saw the general walking toward them on a narrow path. Favoring his injured leg, he moved slowly, his lined face pale and inscrutable.

Caught unprepared, Irina groped for words.

"General Temin! How kind of you to call on us this afternoon." She was careful to use a plural "us" rather than single herself out. "May I present our friend and neighbor Prince Alexander Dolovin." She watched apprehensively as the two men shook hands—General Temin studying Alexander with reserve, and Alexander smiling with warmth and deference to the man's rank.

"I am honored to make your acquaintance, General," Alexander said politely. "After the campaign of 1812 your name has become a household word."

General Temin's face tightened. "You are very kind to give me that much credit, but I was entirely too young and immature during those years to earn that much recognition."

Irina was amused. Unwittingly Alexander had touched on the sensitive subject of the general's age, and the intended compliment had had the opposite effect.

"I brought you some works by Karamzin and Derhavin, Irina," the general said, "but I see you're not free now, so I'll leave them with you and pick them up in a few days."

How clever, Irina thought, *to find such a plausible excuse to pay me another visit so soon.*

After the general had left, Alexander looked at Irina curiously. "I had no idea that such a famous man was paying you court! He is quite a competitor despite his advanced age!"

Although Irina tried to remain serious, Alexander's last words made her laugh. "I'm flattered by his attentions, of course, but that's as far as it goes."

"What other writers do you favor? I'd like to bring some books to you, too, so we can discuss them. What a marvelous excuse to see you more often!"

Irina gave him a mischievous look. "We seem to see each other every day as it is, and there is no shortage of subjects to talk about." After a moment's pause she added impulsively, "But you don't need an excuse to come here; I'm always happy to see you, Alexander."

Alexander stopped and, holding her hands in his, looked into her eyes. "I've never met a girl so candid, so beautiful, and so full of irrepressible humor."

She gave him an exaggerated curtsy. "Ah, thank you, kind sir! Perhaps the mushrooms we pick in this area are responsible. Where would we be without our favorite pastime? I wouldn't be surprised to find that certain character traits are due to their magic!"

They turned into a side lane and sought the shade of a vine-covered gazebo, where they sat down on a cushioned bench close to each other. For a few moments they listened to the cooling sounds of water splashing in the fountains. Suddenly Alexander took her hand and pulled her closer to him.

"Are you sure General Temin's attentions are no more than flattering to you?" he asked quietly.

Slowly Irina turned to face him. "I have no reason to lie. Why do you ask?"

He took her other hand in his and held them both tight. "Because it is important for me to know. The last three weeks have been the happiest of my life. I'm afraid I have behaved like a schoolboy. Surely you must have noticed that!"

"They were the happiest in my life, too," she said simply.

He released one of her hands and slowly, reverently caressed the other, tracing her wrist and raising it slowly to his lips. Then he looked at her.

His face was so close to hers! Those eyes. Oh, those eyes! Changing color, darkening, they reached deep inside her soul. Beautiful. So beautiful that her own clouded with tears. He bent down and touched her lips with his. She held her breath without moving, afraid to lose the velvet of his touch, the dizzying pleasure of this new sensation. His mouth lingered on hers, and when he pressed harder, she responded with soft and trembling lips, parting them for a brief moment and then closing them again in hasty retreat, astonished at her own temerity.

He released her and looked into her face, pushing aside a curl that had fallen on her cheek. There was a barely audible "Ohhh!," or a moan of surprise, she could not tell, and then he pulled her to him once again in a gentle, tender embrace. His lips moved along her neck, tickling her skin with butterfly kisses. "Oh, my dear. My dear! How could all this happen in such a short time?"

She was being engulfed, smothered with a stunning emotion. Suddenly alarmed, she released herself from his embrace and pulled back.

He was looking at her, his eyes riveted to her mouth, sending a delicious shiver through her. Then slowly he raised his eyes to hers and shook his head in wonder.

"Irina, lovely, sweet Irina! We must not linger here anymore!"

She couldn't bear to look into his eyes any longer, dared not touch his hand. Taking a deep breath, she picked up her skirts and ran out of the gazebo.

"Maman must be waiting for us to have tea on the veranda!"

And so it was that the very next day Alexander came at the usual afternoon hour, but this time he asked to see her parents before seeing her. She wanted to join them; but the doors to the parlor were closed, and she fled to the park, running against the warm air until she reached her favorite gazebo, where Alexander had kissed her the day before. There she sat on the same cushioned bench and pressed her hands against her heart. It beat so! Her thoughts danced so! Alexander was talking to Maman and Papa behind closed doors . . . Surely it meant only one thing . . . What else could it be?

When at length she heard his hurried steps on the gravel path, she thought her heart would leap out of her chest and her face would betray her happiness before he spoke. He clasped her hands in his and smiled. "I've just asked your parents for your hand in marriage, and they graciously gave their consent." His mouth twitched treacherously. "How many more kisses must I steal before you say yes?"

Without waiting for her reply, he crushed her against him and kissed her, this time parting her lips with a demanding mouth, and Irina kissed him back with all the fervor of her young love.

In the ensuing days Irina's happiness bubbled over. She wanted to be married at the Beryozovka church, overriding her mother's desire for a fashionable wedding at one of the Kremlin's cathedrals. Thus the wedding day was scheduled to take place in three weeks to ensure that the country road to their estate would be free of early snow, so that guests could travel without difficulty.

In the dizzying flurry of activity during the next few weeks Irina's love for Alexander dominated all her thoughts. Tender vignettes of their few days together before he had had to return to St. Petersburg kept surfacing in her mind. The heart-stopping avowal of love and his proposal of marriage; that first timid kiss, followed by a bold, daring embrace; the laughter, the banter, the matching of wit, and the sharing of humor—these were the cherished moments she relived in the solitude of her nights.

Alexander had chosen her cousin Boris Radin to be one of his groomsmen, and Boris went to St. Petersburg with Alexander for the three weeks before their return to Beryozovka for the wedding. Olga was to be the matron of honor and helped with the preparations at home.

Two days before the wedding Irina was restless. Everything seemed to be in readiness for the big day, and it was strange to have nothing to do now. When Olga came by to keep her company for a few hours in the afternoon, Irina was grateful to her cousin's wife for her thoughtfulness, even though they had never been close.

In the early afternoon, when the older Radins retired for their rest and the servants were busy in the kitchen, Irina and Olga settled in the parlor for a cup of tea. Stirring a spoonful of raspberry jam into her cup, Olga shook her head and smiled at her cousin. "You certainly are well organized for a girl who is to be married in a couple of days. I marvel at you!"

Irina shrugged apologetically. "It helps wile the time away. If I had let everyone else do the work, I'd be a nervous wreck by now. This way I try not to think about Alexander and what he is doing every minute of the day. I miss him so much!"

Olga glanced at Irina and laughed. "It's best to divert your mind away from your husband as early in marriage as possible! One never knows what they're up to in the big cities!"

"Oh, but I'll want to know everything he does all the time he is away from me," Irina countered. She closed her eyes blissfully for a moment, then opened them wide and looked at her cousin. "Don't you?"

"Heaven forbid!" Olga retorted in mock horror. "With young and good-looking husbands like ours, the less we know what goes on when they're away, the better for us!"

"I don't understand what you mean!"

"Oh, haven't you heard of demimondaines and that *other* world that entertains the male? As far as I'm concerned, the less I know about it, the better! I just hope it makes our husbands appreciate all the more what they've got at home."

Irina stared at Olga. "I didn't know you were so broad-minded!"

"Well, we wives must be practical. Boris loves me, pampers me, and I love him. Whatever rumors I hear about him when he's away, I shrug off as something that may or may not be true."

Irina's face must have registered such surprise that Olga laughed again. "Don't look so stunned, darling. If Boris had fallen in love with *you*, for instance, that would have been quite a different matter."

Irina collected herself and cleared her throat. "I admire your tolerance, but in my case it would never work. One of the reasons I fell in love with Alexander is that there is total honesty and trust between us. I can't even imagine acccepting such a situation. Unthinkable!"

Olga gave her a sidelong glance, then busied herself with a mint cookie. "Let's say for the sake of argument, that after you are married, you find out that Alexander periodically visits a demimondaine. How would you feel then?"

"It would break my heart!" Irina cried instantly.

"Even if there were no change in his attitude toward you?"

"How can you say such a thing? It would be a betrayal of my trust in him! It would ruin my marriage, and my feelings for him would never be the same!"

Olga toyed with a spoon for a few moments, then looked at Irina with narrowed eyes. "And what would your reaction be if you found it out now, before your wedding?"

"Why, I'd call off the wedding, of course," Irina cried impulsively, "and I would—" Somewhere deep inside her an alarm sounded, and she halted in mid-sentence. Peering at Olga intently, she asked, "What are you trying to tell me, Olga? I can assure you, I want to know everything about Alexander now, before the wedding."

Olga rose, walked over to the window to look out into the park, then turned to face Irina. "I had no idea you were so uncompromising in your views on what constitutes a happy marriage," she said. "It's totally unrealistic."

She paused, carefully smoothed the folds of her skirt, then said, "I had no intention of telling you this, but I can see that you had better know the truth before your wedding. Alexander has been keeping—I mean, has been seeing—a courtesan in St. Petersburg for quite some time now."

Irina raised her chin and tensed her muscles to keep from trembling. "What Alexander has been doing as a bachelor before we met is certainly not my concern, and I'd rather not hear about it!"

"That's not the problem, darling," Olga said, pursing her lips. "You see, when Boris came home from St. Petersburg, I mentioned how starry-eyed Alexander looked when he left you and how reformed he must now be. But when I began to tease Boris and said that now Alexander would be setting an example to other husbands—" Olga hesitated, then bit her lip. "I'm sorry, Irina, but Boris only laughed and told me that Alexander had not ended his liaison."

Some invisible fist dealt Irina a blow in her solar plexus. Groping for the chair behind her, she lowered herself slowly into it. *Open, candid Alexander. How can it be?* She barely heard Olga's measured words.

"So you see, my dear, you have several choices now. Go through with the wedding, marry Alexander, and count your blessings for having a young, handsome, and loving—yes! *loving*—husband, then close your eyes to the situation, as many of us have done. Or you could postpone the wedding until he ended the liaison, but what assurances would you have that he won't stray in the future? Yet to be a nagging and distrustful wife is the quickest way to drive a man into another woman's arms!

"Your other choice is to call off the wedding entirely, and I shudder to think of the scandal *that* would bring! What excuse could you possibly give? Tongues will wag, concocting reasons far worse than the truth. You'll lose the man you love, and then what?"

Olga smiled smoothly. "Of course, there is always General Temin to come to your rescue. He might be faithful, although an aging man may need his pride built up by other love affairs, so there could be no guarantee there either."

Irina's vision blurred, and only a fierce pride before her cousins's wife prevented her from breaking down completely. Swallowing tears in rapid succession to keep them from spilling over, Irina turned away from Olga and stared out the window without seeing anything before her.

A scraping of a chair on the parquet floor, a rustling of skirts, and Olga's voice: "I'll be going now, Irina. You need time alone. I'm truly sorry I upset you so, but in the long run it's best you found out about it now. Ponder the alternatives, darling, and remember, they are far worse, believe me!"

Chapter Four

For a long time Irina stood without moving in front of the window. Fierce pride kept the tears in check long after Olga had left. Voices from the past few days crowded her: "What a beautiful couple . . . a perfect union, so young, so in love . . . their families are friends and neighbors!" The words pricked her like a thousand needles. She shivered and, after wrapping her arms around her shoulders, rubbed them up and down.

The view from her window stretched down two symmetrical pathways of the park, long rows of rose bushes between them meticulously trimmed. At the far end a fountain sprayed lacy prisms in clear afternoon light, dazzling the eye. Maple trees edging a pathway had begun to change color; soon their bronzed leaves would drop and be replaced by winter ermine. The inexorable turning of the seasons would then bring forth the delicate green of a new spring. It was ever thus each year. Ah, to be like those trees—untroubled, enduring!

Nothing had changed in the garden. But not so in this room. Now everything was different. Her thoughts jumped, collided, and exploded into a myriad fragments. Nothing made sense.

What was she going to do?

Memories drowned her: his strong arms around her in the gazebo; his skin fragrant with his cologne. A thrush, perched on the railing, had cocked its head and studied them curiously, then had turned and flown away. A strand of his thick hair had fallen on his forehead and shone chestnut in the sun; she touched its smoothness. The mischief in his eyes, his boisterous laugh, his tender kisses . . . With time she would forget them, or maybe she would keep the memories to remind her that such happiness could be only a dream, ephemeral, illusory.

Another memory followed. His firm hand with its long, tapering fingers holding hers as they had run, laughing, down the slope to the creek. They had taken off their shoes and waded in the cool water, splashing each other and giggling joyously. Pure, sparkling days of joy. Never, never again! Was it indeed a beautiful dream? Did the man she love not exist at all? She had been taken, used; an available, suitable bride for a marriage of convenience for him to carry on the family name.

She straightened, narrowing her eyes against the glare of the setting sun. Well, she wasn't going to be used. She hated him now, yes, hated!

"Think of the scandal," Olga had said.

How long would it last? It would be the talk of the town for a while, but then it would blow over and within a year would be forgotten. And for that, should she swallow her pride and submit meekly to a man she could no longer trust? She was young; she would meet other eligible men; Alexander was not the only one.

The door opened and her old *nyanya* walked in, carrying her lace-trimmed veil—dear Nyanya, crippled with rheumatism, complaining of gout, but still watching over her young charge. Irina stood rigidly by the window, fists clenched. "Take it away, Nyanya," she said tensely. "There won't be any wedding Sunday."

Nyanya stopped arranging the folds of the gown that

she had placed on the chair. "Say that again?" she said, peering at Irina with her nearsighted eyes.

Irina repeated it. Nyanya propped her sides with her fists. "You can't be serious! You tell me this two days before the wedding?" And when Irina nodded, Nyanya lowered herself heavily into the nearest chair and folded her gray skirt neatly about her heavy legs. "Sit down, child, and tell me what this is all about," she commanded. "What wild thing has gotten into your head?" she questioned, and through years of habit, Irina obeyed.

Nyanya listened until Irina finished; then she sighed and shook her head. From under the starched white cap a thin strand of gray hair fell over her brow. She blew it away, then looked at Irina.

"You're shaking like a leaf, *kasatka*," she began. "Why don't you cry? It will help, you know, and maybe it will clear your befuddled head, too. You can't change your mind so close to the wedding day. You'll bring shame on your parents. And think what an insult it will be to the Dolovins! How can you tell the truth, and what possible excuse can you give otherwise?

"So, the young falcon hasn't settled down yet; he will with time. Don't make a rash decision *pod goryachuyu ruku*—while your hand is hot. You may regret it for the rest of your life. Sleep on it. Tomorrow morning, if you still feel the same way, then postpone the wedding, but don't cancel it entirely. Feign illness, and I'll support you."

Nyanya leaned forward and shook her finger at Irina. "Now let's talk about alternatives. You'll meet other young men, you say. Possibly. But I can tell you that every time you meet one, you will compare him to Prince Alexander. There is more to him than good looks. You laugh well together. I've seen you! You're made for each other. He's no different now from what you thought he was then. He *is* in love with you. So he hasn't broken with his mistress yet. You don't know the details, his reasons for delay. But suppose he does stray once in a while. He is a man and a lusty one, I reckon. Is that reason enough not to marry the man you love?"

"I don't love him! I hate him!" Irina cried.

Nyanya looked at her for a few moments, then smiled. "So you say . . . but you needn't shout. I hear you. I hear you very well, and what you are really saying to me is that you still love him and because you are hurt, you want to hurt him, too. Remember, jealousy and love are sisters." Nyanya pursed her lips, and then her eyes began to twinkle. "There *is* another alternative," she said, a little too casually. "If you want to be sure that the man you marry is going to be faithful, then you had better consider the good General Temin."

Suddenly, Nyanya flipped her hands in the air. "Oh, this old head of mine! You shocked me so with your wild idea I completely forgot that the good general is waiting to pay his respects in the parlor! Go, child, and see him."

Her head high, her lips set in a stubborn line, Irina walked slowly toward the parlor. She was not going to go through the wedding ceremony no matter what her *nyanya* said. General Temin had been loyal and patient, truly sincere. Maybe—could she—was it possible to look at him in a differnt light now? She opened the door and walked into the parlor.

It was twilight outside, and in the graying shadows of the room General Temin looked old. His strained smile belied the sadness in his sunken eyes, and to her horror, Irina imagined those pale lips upon her mouth, perhaps the same insistent way that Alexander—oh, God, what was she thinking? General Temin! Never, never! A buzzing started in her ears, pushing his voice into a hollow distance. There were a few minutes of trite exchange, a thank-you for his wishes, and then he was bending over her hand and touching it with his cold, moist lips. She shuddered and stood rigidly until he said good-bye and left the room.

It wasn't until she was alone in bed that cold reality faced her. If she refused to marry Alexander, her parents and now her *nyanya*—her faithful, loving *nyanya*—would urge her to marry General Temin. After she had seen him this afternoon, the idea was even more intolerable. The comparison with Alexander sprang up, unbidden, and a yearning, so painful it was almost physical, overwhelmed her. Why not admit the truth? Yes, in spite of her anger, in spite of the terrible hurt, she still loved him.

Trapped!

Angry tears spilled over on her pillow. What could she do?

Olga was right. Irina couldn't be sure that the next suitor would remain faithful to her. Besides, falling in love with another man was an impossible thought. Nyanya was right, too. There was more to Alexander than his good looks. He had an enthusiasm for many of the things she enjoyed, and they shared a spontaneous humor. "You laugh well together," Nyanya had said, and that was important.

Yet could she marry him in two days without a word of protest and go to the bridal chamber, pretending her total unawareness of his duplicity? She had to do something, *something* to keep her self-respect. But what?

Somewhere in the hidden recesses of her mind a tentative idea surfaced and took shape. Irina sat up in bed, heart racing, tears no longer falling. With the palm of her hand she wiped her wet cheeks and, wrapping her arms around her legs, stared at the flickering flame of the vigil light before the icon in the corner.

She would tell Alexander after they were married that she knew of his duplicity, that she was not accepting the situation, and then—Irina did not finish her thought. She closed her eyes, and a slow, satisfied smile touched her lips. Ah, it would be a challenge, and her pride insisted on her course of action.

All the next day she avoided her faithful *nyanya's* probing looks, going about her preparations for the wedding with careful attention to detail, and toward the end of the day she caught a sigh of relief and a happy smile on the old woman's dear face. She couldn't bear the thought of having to answer Nyanya's questions— questions she had a perfect right to ask about how she had reconciled herself to go through with the wedding. No, it was her own private decision, and from now on it was between her and Alexander. Besides, Nyanya would be horrified if she learned of her plan, would call upon her sense of duty to her new husband, and voice all the other admonitions of a well- meaning old woman.

Another night came, the last in her parental home before she was to become Princess Dolovina. It was a restless night, confused, tumultuous. Fiery words, aimed to stun her unsuspecting groom, spun through her head.

When the stars began to fade, and dawn had washed the inky darkness out of the sky, Irina fell into a fitful slumber. Her maid, Tosya, awakened her in midmorning, and the excitement of the wedding day took over. She hadn't seen Alexander after Olga's visit two days before, and she dreaded facing him for the first time under the scrutiny of friends and spectators in the church. But maybe it was best that she would not be alone with him until long after the wedding ceremony was over. She had to believe that.

Her wedding dress of silk and lace was exquisitely

embroidered with seed pearls by Moscow seamstresses who had come to the house and worked long hours to finish it on time. It flowed freely from the Empire waist, and the pearl-studded *kokoshnik* headdress held a long veil that wrapped her in clouds of tulle. She had knelt before her parents, who had blessed her with the family icon, and now she waited for Nikita, Alexander's brother, to arrive at the house and tell her, as the custom demanded, that the groom was waiting for her at the church.

Hushed murmurs of admiration greeted her when she entered the church and joined Alexander, who was standing at the door, resplendent in his dress uniform. When the choir burst forth with the joyous "Come forth, oh, dove," she closed her eyes momentarily to hold forever the first image of the handsome groom before her. Whatever pain awaited her, whatever Alexander's reaction to her words, she knew she had made the right decision to go through with the wedding. How could she ever have considered giving him up? As she stood beside him now, her skin burned at his touch. Her heart fluttered like a trapped bird, struggling to get out. Unaware of her inner turmoil, Alexander smiled and squeezed her hand and stroked it gently.

With mounting apprehension of what she planned to do, Irina went through the wedding reception in a complete daze, smiling, nodding, answering platitudes to warm wishes from all the family members and guests, and through it all, her mind registered minor, seemingly insignificant vignettes: her mother in pink silk, unobtrusively dabbing at happy tears; her portly father, twirling his mustache and smiling benignly at Princess Dolovina, whose thin, veined hands fluttered in the air to emphasize something she was saying, while her faded, almost bleached brows moved continuously with a nervous twitch; and finally her new father-in-

law, tall and angular and formidable with a coarse
brush of mustache that seemed to run into his thick
sideburns, which he smoothed unconsciously as he
surveyed the guests with an impenetrable look.

The voices, the laughter, the toasts to the newlyweds—all floated above her in a merging, distant
hum.

And then the day was over, Alexander's parents and
guests had left, and she and Alexander were the last to
leave Beryozovka to ride in the family brougham to
Dolovino. During the ten-minute ride Irina talked
nervously about the food and the guests and the clothes
everyone wore, afraid to stop her chatter, pretending
not to notice Alexander's silence in the dark as he took
her hand and raised it to his lips in a slow, tender kiss
that made her tremble.

At her new home the older Dolovins were waiting to
welcome them with the traditional bread and salt and
their own family icon. As Princess Dolovina raised the
icon to bless them, Irina bowed to the ground, and the
smile that spread on her mother-in-law's face was an
eloquent sign of how pleased she was with Irina's
traditional obeisance.

In the elegant bridal suite, dinner was served to the
newlyweds, but Irina barely touched the rich smoked
goose stuffed with apples, or her favorite mushrooms in
sour cream, or the raisin-studded sweet bread, fragrant
with almonds and saffron. Later she let the two maids
undress her. Her faithful Tosya had come along for a
few days to help the new girl, Agasha, a healthy,
apple-cheeked serf assigned to her by Alexander's
mother as her personal maid. While Alexander prepared himself in the adjoining room, Tosya and Agasha
helped Irina out of her wedding gown and into a
flowing white silk and satin peignoir, decorated with
handmade lace. As the two girls brushed her long hair

of golden brown, Irina was so nervous that she was
barely conscious of the beautiful bedroom with its walls
paneled in turquoise silk embroidered with flowers and
birds, the gilded Louis XV furniture, or the pastel
scrolls of the Savonnerie rug at her feet.

Irina could hardly wait for the maids to leave. She
was ill at ease, aware that she was being prepared for
the mysteries of her wedding night, about which her
nyanya had given her explicit instructions only a week
ago. Maybe it was because of Nyanya's simple approach or perhaps the casual tone of her voice, as
though she were relating a minor event of the day, not
the physical intimacies between man and wife, that had
enabled Irina to listen more with curiosity than embarrassment, even to file away in her mind the practical
hints of her dear *nyanya*. If the old *nyanya*, so prim and
proper, found nothing shocking in all this, then, Irina
decided, she would not let herself be appalled at what
she had learned.

After finishing Irina's toilette, the two serf girls
curtsied and left the bedroom, but not before Agasha
knocked on the adjoining door to let Alexander know
that Irina was ready.

Now, standing in the middle of the room, waiting for
Alexander to enter, she pressed her hands against her
heart in a futile effort to control its violent beating.
How was she going to say what she had to say when all
the words she had so carefully prepared had vanished?
How was Alexander going to react? Feeling dizzy, she
closed her eyes. When she opened them again, Alexander was standing in front of her, smiling, his arms
outstretched, his eyes full of love.

*Oh, God, why does he have to look like that, so
handsome and so loving?* Irina thought in anguish,
staring at him in his satin-sashed lounging jacket of
turquoise blue, so fitting in the pastel bedroom. She felt

faint. Quickly she moved toward a chair and grasped the back of it, clutching its velvet-upholstered richness with trembling hands.

"Alexander, there is something I have to tell you," she began, but Alexander put his hands up in a helpless gesture and shook his head in bewilderment. "Darling, you look so frightened! I'm going to love you, not hurt you!" he said with such tenderness that Irina choked back a sob.

Be strong, Irina, do not succumb! a voice whispered in her ear. Taking a deep breath, she looked at him, blinked back gathering tears, and blurted out, "Alexander, I am not afraid! But I want to tell you something! Our marriage is going to be in name only!"

Alexander stared at her for a moment. "What—what are you saying?" he finally said, the smile gone from his face.

Irina swallowed hard, then went on, desperately trying to keep her voice from shaking. "I know of your liaison in St. Petersburg, Alexander. I found out about it only a couple of days ago, and I also know that you haven't ended it. I can't live with that!" Her voice rose, out of control. "I can't! Do you hear me?"

Alexander winced. "Oh, my Irina, I'd have given anything for you not to have found out about that!"

"I see! What a marvelous beginning to a marriage! I thought we were a special couple because we were so honest, so candid with each other!"

"Please, please hear me out!"

But Irina shook her head. "Whatever you say, I stand firm on one thing: I won't . . . I can't, not until that—that relationship is ended!"

"Irina, I have a right to defend myself against whatever gossip you may have heard. Please give me that right!"

She looked at him, forcing disdain into her glance,

but there was such anguish and disappointment in his eyes she could not hold it and averted her gaze.

"Irina, not only am I *in* love with you, but I love you with a deep, abiding love that comes only once in a lifetime and for some, never. In those heavenly three weeks we spent getting to know each other—surely you must realize—there was far more to our relationship than physical attraction! Whatever happened in my life before I met you can in no way be equated or even compared to my love for you."

"Equated . . . compared . . . I hope not!" Irina cried. "I'm not accusing you of that! You're avoiding the issue! Why haven't you ended your liaison? Am I to live with your duplicity?"

"Oh, darling! How I hate to have the shadow of another woman between us tonight!"

"Of course you do!" Irina couldn't keep sarcasm out of her voice. "You hate to have your—your plans for tonight spoiled!" Her lower lip began to tremble dangerously, and she bit into it. "Why haven't you put an end to—to—"

"Irina, listen to me! There is no way I can prove I am telling the truth, but you have to believe me! When I went back to St. Petersburg, I fully intended to make the break, but I hate arguments and emotional scenes, and—and . . . oh, darling, don't make me tell you the sordid details, please! I swear to you it will all be over when we return to—"

"We!" Irina interrupted. "What do you mean, 'we'? I am not going to St. Petersburg with you until it is all over, and I don't intend to share your bed until then!"

"I know how proud you are and how painful it is to you. I regret deeply that all this had to come about. But I appeal to your compassion—your understanding of my reluctance to hurt someone so abruptly, someone who has been loyal to me. I wanted to do it in the least cruel way."

Irina raised her hand. "Please spare me the details! You are so thoughtful, so reluctant to hurt the other woman! What about me? Have you given a thought to how deeply hurt *I* would be?"

"I never intended that you find out," Alexander said tersely. "If we're to start our life together honestly, you *must* trust me from the beginning, and your idea of marriage in name only will never work."

He reached her in a few quick steps and tried to take her in his arms. "Irina, I love you. Only you! Let me prove it to you now, my darling!" He buried his face in the silk of her loosened hair, but she struggled free and, backing away, hugged herself fiercely.

"Don't touch me! Don't you dare touch me!"

Suddenly the hurt was too much, and Irina sank onto the nearby chaise longue, covered her face with her hands, and began to cry. A few moments later she felt Alexander's arm around her shoulders, and she jumped, throwing his arm off.

Alexander rose. "Very well, have it your way. I won't touch you." His voice sounded bitter. "I promise, I won't touch you in *that* way. I have my pride, too, Irina, and I love you too much to force myself upon you." He hesitated, then reached out one hand and said, "But it hurts me to see you so heartbroken! Let me hold you in my arms at least and comfort you!"

He took a step toward her and waited.

Distraught, confused by her conflicting emotions, Irina suddenly felt an overwhelming desire to be comforted and to weep in his embrace. With a deep sigh, she went into his arms and let the tears flow again.

He held her gently, stroking her hair, as if she were a fragile doll that would break if he tightened his embrace. She pressed her face against his chest and circled his neck, the way she had done as a little girl seeking comfort in her father's arms.

Calmed at last, she became aware that this was *not* her father, but her new husband, who loved and wanted her yet had accepted her ultimatum. He wasn't going to force himself upon her. In her relief, incredibly, there mingled a grain of disappointment. What was the matter with her? She had won her point, and wasn't that what she wanted?

Suddenly she pulled back and looked up at him. He tilted her chin and smiled. "Some beginning, huh?" he said quietly.

Shyly Irina smiled back and stayed in his arms, reluctant to move from their strength.

At length Alexander cleared his throat and said, "There's a little problem facing us, darling."

At once alert, Irina moved away and looked at him in alarm. "What is it?"

He laughed. "Don't be such a frightened gazelle, my love. It's a practical thing, a matter of pride with me." He nodded toward the wide canopied bed with its down comforter turned back, lace-trimmed pillows piled high on top of the feather-filled mattress. "The servants will talk if I sleep in my own room tonight, and whispers will soon reach our parents. There is nothing else in this room except the chaise longue, and it's too small for either of us."

Irina felt a hot wave of embarrassment flood over her. To cover it, she tried to make her voice sound as casual as possible. "I have no doubt that you will remain a gentleman, Alexander. The bed is wide enough for us to be comfortably separated."

Alexander kissed her hand ceremoniously. "Thanks for at least *that* much trust!"

The ice was broken, and Irina shrugged. "At least

this night is one we'll remember long after we're grandparents!"

The moment she said it, she blushed, realizing too late what her words implied. Alexander tilted her chin and kissed the tip of her nose. "Darling, I promise to make up for this unusual—to say the least—beginning!"

Irina looked around the room. "I wouldn't want you to sleep on the floor!"

Alexander patted her hand. "I would get a backache if I slept on the floor, and"— he looked at her with a twinkle in his eye—"people have vivid imaginations and might misinterpret the cause of my pain!"

They were treading on dangerous ground, and Irina rose. "It's been a long day, Alexander. Time to retire!"

But she could not go to sleep. Lying stiffly on her side of the bed, she stared, wide-eyed, into the moonlit room. Maybe if there were no moon this night—if total darkness had somehow removed Alexander's presence beside her—if the silvery glow on the bedcovers had not shone so ethereally, she could then go to sleep. But now, alone with her thoughts, why deceive herself? Her body yearned for his embrace. In the silence she listened for the sleeping rhythm of his breathing; but there was none, and she knew he was not asleep either.

Suddenly Alexander threw off his covers and got up. Irina sat up in her bed. "What's wrong, Alexander?"

After a momentary silence he said, "Nothing. Go to sleep, Irina. I'm just restless."

She lay there watching him pace the floor, then look out the moon-washed window, and finally return to bed. As he slipped under the coverlet, she did not think; she did not know how or why she turned and reached out, touching his arm. His hand slid up her forearm, the touch so feathery, so slow, it sent shivers down her spine; her hand clutched his shoulder, tense and muscular; her own strength ebbed as though weightless, she were afloat in a nameless sea.

Did she move toward him, or did he wrap his arms around her? There was no warning, no warning at all; but the barriers had fallen, and she was clinging to him, her mind drowning in a flood of boundless love. All the yesterdays of courtship and the thousand tomorrows would never match this moment. The doubts, the hurt, had vanished in the night, and only pleasure filled the room.

"My precious one, I love you . . . My world is you . . ." he whispered once, and then there were no words to break the magic. So taut were her nerves, so sensitive her skin that each caressing touch of his unhurried hands evoked an echo of her tangled love, though fear still lurked somewhere in the hidden valleys of her being.

His arms were around her now, a tightening of muscle, a circle molding her to him with mounting, unguarded pressure. Her thoughts hovered on the edge of consciousness; she forgot her fear and let herself be carried on the rushing tide of endless pleasure. The room, the house, the world had vanished in a mist, and in this strange, unknown dimension, a mystery, a silent poem were unfolding in his silky, flowing movements, and with a sigh of final revelation, she gave herself to him with gladness.

In a flash of blinding brilliance there came a pain— yet not a pain at all—but deliverance from tension beyond imagining, beyond endurance.

No longer separate from him, she had no wish to be apart or think or act alone.

But time goes on, and seconds run into unchanging minutes, moving hours toward dawn. His hands caressed her hair, her face, her shoulders; his lips, a thousand brushings on her lips; his voice at last, a gentle breeze against her ear: "My love, my darling, such happiness I never could imagine."

She stayed awake a long time, watching shifting patterns of moonlight in the room: gossamer, silvery-blue, delicate. Outside the window a breeze made the birch leaves quiver, throwing dappled shadows on the chaise longue.

Through the beauty of the night the secret love of man and wife was no longer a mystery to her. Her body tingled with fulfillment; surely her *nyanya* had never known this! Dear, kind Nyanya with her starched cap and fat legs, who had moved to Dolovino with her. Irina giggled as she thought of it, then sobered, as a disembodied presence wormed itself into her mind. Did Alexander love her enough not to compare her to—to that other woman? Did he kiss her with the same ardor, whisper the same impassioned words? The nasty thoughts! The jealous, nasty thoughts! She wouldn't let them spoil her beautiful night, this, of all nights!

There was plenty of time to think and act tomorrow.

Chapter Five

They had two weeks of honeymoon. Alexander stayed by Irina's side constantly, guessing her wishes, showing her around Dolovino estate. Wrapped in woolens, they sat in a far corner of their immense park and read Pushkin together; around them, birches, alders, and elms stood tall and princely, their gold and auburn leaves a mottled carpet under their feet. Concealed from the outside world by the thick foliage of untrimmed privet and lilac bushes, so different from the pristine lanes of Beryozovka, Irina called this thicket an enchanted forest.

"Papa likes the natural look of our park," Alexander explained, "and since Maman rarely ventures beyond the veranda, it is allowed to grow wild." He squeezed Irina's hand. "A perfect spot for lovers, don't you think?"

Irina shot him a mischievous glance. "Your mind these days seems to run along the same track."

"But a singularly beautiful track!"

Hand in hand they walked across the broad meadow near the mansion, inhaling the crisp autumn air tinged with the pungent smoke of burning wood. The light poured diamonds into the morning dew, the sun pale in the autumn coolness. With her head against his shoulder, she walked slowly, the dome of turquoise high above. So quiet in the mornings!

In the spring, Alexander had said, he would take her to their Crimean estate on the Black Sea, where tropical foliage, sand, and waves enchanted the mind and all thoughts dissolved into delicious languor.

"But I love the autumn," Irina said. "The colors are fiery, as though nature were burning out its last passion before the winter calm."

Alexander smiled. "Sounds as if you've read too many of Pushkin's poems."

In the afternoons, while the parents rested after midday dinner, the newlyweds retired to their suite and loved each other. In the aftermath of sated passion, when the private hours flowed into dusk, they often missed the late tea and rejoined the family for supper at eight.

It took Irina awhile to learn the names of all the poor relatives and retainers who lived on the estate and ate with the Dolovins. There were rarely fewer than twenty people at the table, and frequently the village priest, Father Arseny, a tall and cadaverous man, joined them as well.

In no time at all Irina felt a mixture of affection and pity for her mother-in-law, who worried constantly about the welfare of various members of their household and whose sole purpose in life seemed to center on remaining in the shadow of her domineering husband. Irina could not warm up to her father-in-law. Prince Gregory rarely spoke to her directly but addressed his words somewhere to a point above her head, asking questions of no one in particular and going on to the next topic without waiting for answers.

Almost immediately after the wedding Princess Dolovina began to fret over Irina's comfort. "Does Agasha please you?" she asked, her nearsighted pale eyes peering at Irina. "She's only sixteen and fresh from the village, but she is quick-witted and learns fast."

Irina assured her that she was well pleased with Agasha, and indeed, she was. The young serf girl had endeared herself to her mistress at once with her sunny disposition, singing softly to herself as she went about her chores. She soon confided in Irina that she was betrothed to a young peasant in the village, Ossip Agafonov, and they were to be married next summer. Aware that marriages between serfs were frequently arranged by their masters, Irina asked, "Do you like him?" and smiled as the girl blushed. "I'm glad for you, Agasha. He must be a fine fellow."

Agasha covered her face with the crook of her arm and giggled. "He's a healthy muzhik, Barynia, and clever. He tells me that someday he will learn to read and write!"

Irina studied Agasha for a few moments. "Next time Prince Alexander and I go for a walk, you tell me where to find your Ossip. I may teach him."

Agasha gasped and, grasping Irina's hand impulsively, kissed it. "He lives in the third izba on your right as you enter the village."

A few days before Alexander was to leave for St. Petersburg, Irina told him of her intent and asked him to accompany her to the village. Alexander nodded. "I think it's a wonderful idea. And you needn't worry about my parents. I'll tell Papa that Ossip might work as a clerk in the estate manager's office; besides, Papa is too preoccupied with his own affairs to bother, and of course, in Maman's eyes, you can do no wrong!"

They found the izba without difficulty. Inside, a middle-aged woman said that her son Ossip would be in shortly. From the way she bowed to the floor and skittered around, gasping with short, frightened sighs, it was obvious that she was overwhelmed by such an unexpected honor. The interior of the izba was dark but clean. A bench ran along the walls, and several cross-stitched pillows were piled high in one corner. A wooden table stood in the center of the room, and on it, a steaming samovar beckoned invitingly.

Alexander and Irina declined the woman's flustered invitation to join her for a cup of tea and waited until Ossip entered, shuffling his feet in cumbersome bast shoes. He stood hesitantly on the threshold, his tall, powerful build filling the frame of the door, wheat-colored hair, neatly parted in the center, covering his ears. *What a giant of a man*, Irina thought, watching him nervously smooth the gathered folds of his belted shirt. His light blue eyes in a freckled, square-jawed face studied them with shaded curiosity.

"Ossip," Alexander said, "would you like to learn how to read and write?"

Ossip's face lit up, and he bowed several times in rapid succession. "Oh, Your Grace, what prosperity and happiness it would be for me!"

Irina smiled. Such eagerness! He should prove a good student.

"How old are you?" Alexander asked.

"Twenty-four, Your Grace."

"Well, you're still young enough to learn. The princess is willing to teach you."

The clear, trusting eyes came around and settled on Irina. *It will be a pleasure to work with him!* she thought, and as Alexander started toward the door, she nodded at the tall blond peasant. "I'll send word when I am ready to start."

Outside, the single dirt road that ran through the village was mired from recent rain, but Irina did not mind getting her shoes muddy. She picked up the hem of her skirt with one hand and, holding on to Alexander with the other, started toward the house.

"Happy, darling?" Alexander said, smiling, and she

nodded. "Oh, Alex, can you understand how it feels to have my greatest wish realized?"

"Your *greatest* wish?"

Irina glanced quickly at her husband and saw such mock horror in his eyes that she laughed.

"You're a terrible tease, aren't you? You know very well what I mean!"

Alexander turned her around to face him. "I won't let you take another step until you tell me what your greatest wish has really been! And you'd better hurry, before the downpour begins again." He pointed to the sky where ominous clouds buffeted one another and distant lightning flashed.

Irina thought quickly. How could she tell him her innermost wish was to hear that his liaison in St. Petersburg had ended? Perhaps honesty was not always the best policy.

"Well?" Alexander said, his eyebrows shooting up in surprise. "What takes so long?"

Irina lowered her gaze. "You know very well what it was. To marry you, of course, silly!"

Alexander released her arm. "That's better! Now let's see if we can race the clouds to the veranda!"

Another two days went by, and on the day of his departure for St. Petersburg, Alexander held Irina close and promised to return soon. He said nothing more, and Irina did not question him, nor did she ask her to go with him to St. Petersburg. It wouldn't be long before he came home, she told herself, and in the meantime, she would keep her mind on her new duties at home and would start teaching Ossip. She would not permit her thoughts to dwell on St. Petersburg.

The brougham rolled from Dolovino toward Moscow along the birch-lined track, and Alexander looked at the pastoral scenery from the carriage window, nodding absentmindedly to the bowing peasants along the road. It seemed to him that the serfs looked older, wearier than he remembered, or was it his imagination supporting the purpose of his stopover in Moscow today? The message he had received from Paul Pestel giving him the day and the hour of the meeting of the Southern Society could not be ignored, even though he hated to part from Irina. He thought that the ultimate happiness would have been to spend these last few hours with her, blotting out the apprehension of what was waiting for him in St. Petersburg.

He had meant it when he told her on their wedding night that he disliked emotional scenes. How dreadful it was to discover that she had learned about Marianna! He dared not ask who had told her, but he suspected. It shamed him to admit even to himself that he not only had deceived Irina, but had not yet ended the relationship. Instead of telling Marianna that he was getting married, he had once again succumbed to her exciting, expert lovemaking.

There was something else, too. Marianna approved of his dedication to the Union of Welfare, and he had needed to share his innermost thoughts with someone close who understood and did not condemn his actions. But that was before his marriage, before he had tasted the sweetness of his new wife. How could he have known that he was going to fall so madly in love with this innocent yet spirited green-eyed beauty, whose humor, ideals, and background matched his own?

Irina! The loveliness of her! He did not think, he could not imagine in his wildest dreams that he was capable of such a love. Everything about her enchanted him: the thicket of her golden lashes tickling his cheek as he kissed the tiny hollow near her eye; the delicate pulse in the curve of her neck as it throbbed under his lips; the way she turned her head to one side and looked at him teasingly from under a raised brow; her soft laughter. Everything! He thought: *Time is man's invention and can be stopped at will.* When he was with her, the outside world was hushed. The narrowed sphere of his existence became sharp, brilliantly outlined with the changing hues of autumn sunsets and pastel mornings, a symphony of color etching her face in memory forever. He closed his eyes remembering: her lavender scarf fluttering in the breeze, the silk of her light brown hair, the subtle fragrance of her skin. *Oh, my dear, my lovely wife!*

He knew she loved him, yet he worried about her reaction if he told her of his membership in the Union of Welfare. Her desire to teach the serfs by lifting the hem of illiteracy was one thing, but being involved in an underground movement against the government was quite another. He dared not test the safety of his marriage yet by telling her of this dangerous and seditious venture. What if she condemned him as a traitor and turned away?

He flushed with anxiety at the mere thought of such a possibility. Yet, in spite of the risk he was taking, he was loyal to the Union of Welfare, and it was important to find out how Pestel's radical ideas differed from those of Ryleyev in St. Petersburg. He hoped it would be made clear today. Members of the radical Southern Society from Tulchin and the moderates from the north were to attend today's meeting, and he felt a stirring of excitement. Boris Radin, who was a member of the Southern Society, told Alexander he would attend today's meeting also. Perhaps he should double-check the address even though he had memorized it: 34 Povarskaya Street. It would not be difficult to find, for it ran into the Arbat Square very near the center of town. Alexander reached inside his tunic to retrieve the paper. It was not there.

He frowned, felt his pockets again. Nothing. Then he remembered. He had put the address and the paper with a few of Pestel's ideas to be discussed at the meeting inside his morning coat before he took it off. Good thing he had remembered the address. How foolish to be so careless, but then the only person who would handle the coat was his manservant, Prokhor, and he was illiterate.

The large dark room was filled with smoke, swirling slowly in the light of a single green-shaded lamp. Alexander leaned against the wall and counted the members of the Union of Welfare present: twenty-one, including himself and Boris Radin. He knew very few of the others.

Colonel Paul Pestel, the leader of the Southern Society, fascinated him. In a dark green uniform with upright red collar, he looked short among his comrades, yet with his high forehead, sparse hair combed forward in the style of the day, and his dark, burning eyes, he had an air of authority. Right now, as he waited to start the meeting, he surveyed the group with a somewhat sardonic look. Alexander studied him curiously. That Pestel had been a war hero was obvious, for the decorations he wore had been awarded him after the 1812 Battle of Borodino, where he had been wounded. Reputed to be a man of iron will, pragmatic, and analytical, Pestel firmly believed in the principles of the Union of Welfare, and it was said that he would never allow unrealistic ideals to cloud his mind. *Not at all like Kondraty Ryleyev, our emotional leader of the north,* thought Alexander.

Among others he recognized was Peter Kakhovsky, whose narrow, pointed chin fitted neatly into the opening of his white shirt collar, giving him a birdlike look. An intellectual whose passionate belief in a republic had gained him Pestel's respect, he sat at the table, smoothing his black cravat, his eyes on Pestel.

The lean-faced Prince Sergei Trubetskoy and the older Prince Sergei Volkonsky, both scions of ancient, respected families, were also present. Alexander wondered if their vigorous involvement in the movement was known to *their* wives—the warm, friendly Katasha Trubetskaya and the very beautiful dark-haired Marie Volkonskaya. He regretted that Ryleyev, who worked in St. Petersburg for a Russian-American company, was unable to attend, for it would have been interesting to hear the two leaders debate.

"Gentlemen," Pestel began, "I've called you together to discuss our divergent views and to try to come to a common understanding. It is vitally important that we are united in our goals."

"Then please state exactly what your views are," Prince Trubetskoy said quietly.

"Surely," Pestel responded. "I believe in a republic, not a constitutional monarchy, as some of you do in the north, and that is why I've drafted a new constitution, which I have entitled 'Russian Justice.' It will abolish serfdom and distinction of classes and will give equality to all."

"And how do you propose to achieve all this?" Prince Volkonsky asked.

"It will be necessary to make a clean sweep at the top."

"And the tsar?" Prince Volkonsky persisted.

"The tsar must be assassinated."

For a few moments there was a stunned silence in the room, and then it was disrupted by a scraping of a chair as Kakhovsky pushed it back and surveyed the frozen faces around him. "Why are you all so shocked? Have you forgotten that our present tsar allowed himself to be implicated in patricide? Haven't we all judged the assassination of Tsar Paul an act of moral courage rather than a crime? Why, then, should this be so different?"

Shocked, Alexander moved forward from the wall and leaned over the table. "Although I am for a constitutional monarchy, there are some of us in the north, like Kondraty Ryleyev, who favor a less radical republic patterned somewhat after the American constitution."

Pestel waved his hand impatiently. "It will never work in our country. Let me remind you that we have a tsar who has fallen under the influence of a mystic, and a woman at that, and who, after signing a Holy Alliance with the European powers, trusted them to formulate policies according to the principles of Christianity. And you well know what has happened. In the ensuing ten years this Holy Alliance has become the laughingstock of Europe. I say no! A constitutional monarchy will never work, and I doubt that a democratic American constitution would succeed in achieving the necessary reforms either."

Kakhovsky pounded his fist on the table. "I agree! What we need is a republic with a dictator who will lead the masses into new order."

My God, thought Alexander, *these two are Russian Jacobins!* Aloud he said, "And what do you propose to do with the tsar's brothers?"

Pestel shrugged. "Ideally they should be killed, too, but as a concession to your northern and, I might add, unrealistic ideals, the whole imperial family could be exiled."

"What you are suggesting then," Prince Trubetskoy said angrily, "is to smear our consciences with blood."

"You need not be involved in it personally. The work would be done by members of our Southern Society," Kakhovsky replied.

"I, for one, cannot agree to regicide," Alexander said emotionally. "It would start an anarchy, bathe the new republic in blood. Look what it has done in France. Do you want to be called a Russian Robespierre?"

"I can think of worse comparisons than that," Pestel retorted with a disdainful smile.

"Radical changes require radical measures, Alex," Boris Radin interjected, exhaling a coil of smoke from his pipe. "We must have a government for the people, but not *by* the people. Do you realize that in Moscow, a city of two hundred and fifty thousand inhabitants, there are ninety thousand serfs? What do you think those serfs will do if they get a taste of freedom to govern themselves?"

The argument became heated, and it seemed to Alexander that everyone began to talk at once.

"I favor constitutional monarchy!"

"No! A liberal republic like the one in America!"

"Never! A republic with a dictator!"

Voices rose, then shouted at one another. Alexander moved slowly toward the door, appalled by what he was witnessing, disturbed by what the radical members were plotting, and dismayed by the discord within the society. He needed time to sort out his own feelings.

His coachman was waiting in front of the house, and with a curt order Alexander climbed inside the brougham and leaned back against the cushioned seat. On the long ride to St. Petersburg, he would have plenty of time to think and decide on his future actions.

Chapter Six

"This is the letter *K*, this is *O;* repeat after me," Irina said slowly.

Staring at the paper intently, Ossip repeated them, then looked up to see Irina's reaction.

He was learning remarkably fast, as though this were the most important thing in his life. As he mouthed the letters laboriously, Irina watched him with satisfaction. She had arranged to have his bast shoes replaced with leather boots and seen to it that Alexander's manservant, Prokhor, supplied new shirts for Ossip to wear to the house for his lessons. On her frequent walks through the Dolovino estate, Irina was appalled by how Prince Gregory neglected the serfs. In weather that was turning cold, small children ran around with mud-caked bare feet, and their frayed and scanty clothes made her want to take them in her arms and warm them.

Time and again she saw the village elder waiting outside her father-in-law's study, only to be turned over to the manager under some flimsy pretext. Prince Gregory seemed more preoccupied with his hunting expeditions, his horses, his games of billiards and cards with his retinue than with the care of the serfs he owned. It rankled Irina to hear him talk about how many souls he had bought or sold. Now, with Ossip, clean and neat, sitting in her study, frowning over a new letter of the alphabet, she was gratified.

It was three weeks since Alexander had left for St. Petersburg, and his letters arrived full of love and longing. Irina had resolutely locked away all her thoughts of the courtesan, trying not to imagine what was going on in the capital. Surely it was all over, to judge from the tone of his letters, so adoring, so full of eagerness to see her again.

There was something else that disturbed Irina greatly, but she had no one to confide in and tell of her alarming discovery. That day—the lonely first day after he had left—Irina roamed the rooms, touching his books, his fencing sword. His room was empty and still untidy, for his faithful Prokhor had gone to give Alexander's instructions to the stableboy who was tending his master's horse. Irina sat down on a chair, and as she lovingly stroked his carelessly tossed morning coat, she became aware of a rustling sound in its pocket.

Was it something he had forgotten to take with him? She pulled out a piece of paper, unfolded it, and read its contents. A Colonel Pestel was inviting Alexander to attend a meeting in Moscow that very day. Mildly curious as to why Alexander hadn't mentioned it to her, she read on.

At first it made no sense, and she read it several times until comprehension came slowly. Disbelief fought with fear, and her stomach tightened. Alexander a member of a secret society plotting against the tsar? She smoothed the crumpled paper, read it once again. The room had suddenly become terribly silent, her quickened breathing very loud.

Her lighthearted, her loving and romantic husband had kept yet another secret from her. This one, however, gave a new dimension to his character, one that required courage, moral conviction, and—her heart stopped for a moment—a great amount of risk. She shuddered.

He hadn't wanted to burden her with the responsibility of knowledge. Dear, thoughtful Alexander!

In the ensuing days she tried to sort out her feelings. She could not condemn him. How could she? She remembered well their impassioned discussions of their country's problems, and she was no hypocrite now to deprive him of her moral support, despite her apprehension. She dared not question him about it in her letters and waited impatiently for his return. As she watched Ossip's progress in his studies, she realized how worthy was the cause for which Alexander was going to fight, and she loved him the more for it.

She had trouble concentrating this morning and wondered if her thoughts had caused the queasy feeling in her stomach or if the extra amount of yoghurt that her mother-in-law forced on her at breakfast had upset her. *"Prostokvasha* is good for you!" Princess Dolovina had kept repeating.

Irina found it difficult to continue the lesson and rose quickly from her chair. Ossip jumped up, tipping his chair behind him, and it fell to the floor with a crash. Red in the face, he replaced it by the desk and bowed to Irina, mumbling his apology.

Unaccountably Irina became irritated. "You need not bow and apologize so much, Ossip," she said, picking up the alphabet book. "Take this home with you and study today's lesson. I shall see you back here tomorrow morning."

Gently Ossip picked up the book, then bowed again. "Thank you, Your Grace. I'll work hard, and God bless you for your kindness!"

As she watched him back out of the room, Irina shook her head. A fine man, so eager to learn and to please; how wonderful that he and Agasha—her two favorite serfs—were to be married! She must talk to her mother-in-law about a good dowry for Agasha.

Irina sat down to rest in an elaborately carved bergère. She spent a lot of time in this room, which she filled with mementos she had brought from Beryozovka. Her gaze roamed over the wall above her desk. It was covered with miniatures of her parents and herself as a child, all of which were framed in wood of various shapes and styles, crowding one another in studied disarray. She smiled. Homey!

In a few minutes her stomach settled, and Irina became aware of voices, tense and sharp, outside her room. She listened; but the double doors to her study were thick, and she could not hear what was being said. She would not tolerate arguments between the maids in her part of the house! Quickly she threw open the doors and stepped into the corridor.

An angry Prince Gregory stood facing Agasha, who cowered against the wall. Startled, he looked up at Irina with intense annoyance, then turned on his heel and, slapping his riding crop against his high boots, stalked away in the opposite direction.

Agasha covered her tearstained face with both hands and tried to dash past her mistress. Irina caught her by the strings of her apron.

"Follow me into my study, Agasha, this minute!" she ordered.

Weeping bitterly, Agasha obeyed.

"Now tell me what this is all about. What have you done to anger Prince Gregory?"

Agasha continued to sob. Irina waited for a few moments, then said impatiently, "That's enough, Agasha! I'm trying to help you, not scold you. Whatever you've done, I'm sure we can straighten it out. Now, out with it!"

Suddenly Agasha dropped to her knees and wrapped her arms around Irina's legs. Between sobs and gasps she poured out a wretched story, her words strangling against Irina's woolen skirt. Tears of pity and revulsion rose to Irina's eyes.

Agasha, her innocent, wholesome Agasha, and—her father-in-law! The forbidding, the unapproachable Prince Gregory . . . He had taken her virginity, had said that he was bestowing a great honor upon her by casting his eye in her direction, and she—his serf—had submitted silently—for wasn't she his personal property to do with as he pleased?—and although she accepted his advances with shame and reluctance, she had harbored the naïve hope that she would receive a good dowry from her master upon her marriage to Ossip. But the good Lord had judged otherwise—she sobbed bitterly—and now she was with child, her master's child. She had begged Prince Gregory to let her marry Ossip immediately, assuring him that since Ossip was learning to read and write, he was more enlightened than other muzhiks in the village, would understand her position, and would accept the child as his own.

"So what is the trouble now, Agasha?" Irina interrupted. "Is Ossip angry with you? Do you want me to talk to him?"

Piteously Agasha began to weep again. No, it wasn't Ossip at all. Ossip didn't know anything yet. But Prince Gregory said he didn't want to have his bastard child on his estate, that he wasn't even sure it *was* his child— imagine that!—and that he had sold her to another landowner 100 versts from here. She was to leave Dolovino and all her family and go to her new master.

Appalled, Irina sat down. Although she knew that sometimes serf families were broken up, no such sale ever happened on her family estate in Beryozovka, and those serfs who had been sold were surely never this abused.

Resolutely Irina rose from her chair. "Agasha, dry

your tears, and go to your room for a while. I won't need you today. I'm going to talk to Prince Gregory. After all, you have been assigned to me, and I'll ask him to change his mind."

Agasha grasped both of Irina's hands and showered them with kisses. "Oh, bless you, bless you, Barynia!"

But the interview with her father-in-law was not at all what she expected, for she had underestimated Prince Gregory's stubbornness and pride.

"You have no right to interfere in my private affairs!" he stormed. "That wench will pay for complaining to you!"

"She didn't complain, *mon père*! I ordered her to tell me, and she obeyed. After all, she is assigned to me, and I resent your selling her without my being consulted."

"Consulting *you*? Bah! You seem to have forgotten that this is *my* estate and these are *my* serfs to do with as I please! The fact that Agasha was assigned to you was through my graces, and mine alone!"

Irina tried another approach. "Please, *mon père*, I beg your don't send Agasha away! I'm willing to give her up and not have her around the house."

"I don't want her on my estate at all."

"She can stay in the village and marry Ossip right away," Irina persisted.

Prince Gregory shook his head. "I have already sold her for two hundred rubles. The deal has been made, and I'm not going back on my word!"

A ruined life for two hundred rubles, Irina thought dismally. Aloud she said, "*Mon père*, think of the misery you are inflicting on the unfortunate girl! Her whole life will be ruined!"

"She will adjust. Her new owner will find her a husband among his own muzhiks. And now I don't want to hear another word about this! Keep to your personal affairs, Irina, for your own good, and don't meddle in matters that do not concern you. Above all, never interfere in my private business."

He has turned the conversation around, Irina thought in amazement; *he has made me the one in the wrong.* Though she could not bring herself to concede defeat, she nodded curtly to her father-in-law and hurried out of the room.

Alexander would be coming home for a visit soon. Perhaps he could intervene on Agasha's behalf and persuade his father to buy her back. She had to hold on to that thought. Her stomach fluttered, and another wave of sickness rose to her throat. In her bedchamber she lay down on the chaise longue. For the moment there was nothing more she could do.

The next day Agasha flew into her room and threw herself at her feet. "Barynia, Barynia, woe to me, woe to me! The village lads jeered at Ossip yesterday. I don't know how the rumor started. I swear I said nothing to anybody! They—they called Ossip a cuckolded groom, and Ossip got mad and started a fight. The village elder tried to stop it, and Ossip hit him, too!"

Agasha wrung her hands, tears streaming down her face. "Oh, Barynia, they tied Ossip up, and you know what that means! They will lash him in public, and my Ossip is proud—so proud! What will it do to him?"

Agasha sobbed miserably. Irina put her arms around her. "Try to calm down, Agasha. Tears won't help right now. We have to think how to help Ossip. I promise I'll do what I can!"

Her pride tucked away, Irina approached her father-in-law again. Prince Gregory stared her down with an icy glare. "I see my warning fell on deaf ears. If I allowed my serfs to go unpunished for raising a hand against authority, I'd have a riot on my hands. I do not interfere when they get into a brawl among themselves, but when one of them touches a village elder he has to be punished publicly as an example to others. And to you I say once again: Stay out of my affairs!" His voice was menacing, and it was this menace more than anything else that triggered Irina's indignation. Leveling her gaze at her father-in-law angrily, she enunciated each word with care. "If you don't order Ossip to be set free, I shall tell my mother-in-law the whole despicable story. I shall spare her none of the sordid details."

"You dare blackmail me?"

"If that's what you choose to call it—yes!"

Irina watched as Prince Gregory clenched his fists at his sides so hard his arms shook, and for an incredible moment she thought he was going to strike her; but he restrained himself and waved her away. "I'll think about it. Now go!"

But Irina stood firm, aware that for the moment she had the advantage. "I won't go away until you give me your word that you will not punish Ossip!" Then, unable to resist a barb, she added, "That is, assuming that I can still trust your word!"

Prince Gregory, who had turned away from her, now wheeled to face his daughter-in-law. His face was purple with rage, and a muscle twitched by the side of his left eye. "Watch that you do not overstep your luck, madame. I'll give you my word only because I want to protect my wife's peace of mind and her frail health, but remember this: It doesn't pay to make me your enemy!"

The threat was implicit. How dare he say this to her, his son's wife. He was a formidable adversary, but she held the trump card and would not hesitate to use it if need be. For now she had won, and she knew Alexander would support her. Alexander. For a few hours she had forgotten her concern about him, but now she could hardly wait for his arrival.

Two days later Irina learned that Ossip had been set

free. That same afternoon she was attracted to the
window by a commotion. The outbuildings connected
to the main house by a narrow corridor formed a
courtyard which was a beehive of activity from dawn to
dusk. The kitchen, the laundry, the icehouse, the dairy,
and the stables adjoined the last building, a two-story
wing, called the Flügel, where the estate manager had
his office, and where the old *nyanya* as well as some of
the houseservants lived. It was here now that the noise
was concentrated, and as Irina watched, her eyes filled
with tears, blurring the scene before her.

Several *dvorniki*—yardmen—were loading a one-
horse cart that stood at the door. Protected from rain
and snow by a bast mat fastened to curved splints, it
was already full of pots and pans and bundles of
personal effects. Agasha stood weeping by its side as
the *nyanya* and other women servants were kissing and
hugging and blessing her between wails of woe.

Irina turned away. A human being was being torn
from her roots and thrown among strangers against her
will. Man's atrocity to man, and she, Irina, stood there
in impotent fury yet helpless to defend her Agasha. Oh,
God, someday somehow she would correct this injustice. If only Alexander were here, he might have
averted this tragedy!

By the time he returned two weeks later she had
momentous news to tell him, but first, there was
something she needed to ask him.

In the privacy of their bedchamber, encircled in his
arms, Irina could not make herself look into his eyes as
she asked the painful question.

"Alexander, is there still a—shadow between us?"
she whispered, and felt his arms tighten around her. He
did not answer her at once, and in the silence that
followed her heart beat so!

Slowly he raised her chin. "Shadow?" he repeated,

"No, my beloved wife. There is no shadow between us. You are the only one I love!"

It was a strange answer, an oblique one, but she realized that she did not want to hear any details of what had gone on in St. Petersburg, that if he tried to tell her, she would hate it, and something would die inside her.

But he said nothing and held her close, showering her face with insatiable kisses, and she forgot everything except the one enormously important, enormously wonderful bit of news.

He held her so tightly she had trouble pulling herself away, for this time she wanted to see the reaction on his face when she told him.

"Alex, my love, I have kept a secret from you. I didn't want to write it, for I was selfish and wanted to look into your eyes when I told you."

Alexander raised his eyebrows and waited.

"If I don't bring you a son," Irina said mischievously, "will a little girl do?"

He stared at her for only a second, then, with a cry of joy, swept her back into his arms. "Oh, my love, what happiness!"

He smiled self-consciously. "I'll be a father!" Then a torrent of anxiety: "Are you well? Have you seen our doctor? Are you following his instructions?"

Irina laughed. "So many questions! I can assure you everything is fine, and I am well. A little sickness in the morning, but then that's to be expected!"

There followed a fugue of such passion, such mindless flight into rapture that all her fears and all the questions she had wanted to ask vanished, and she abandoned herself to this happiness. An aching of limbs, a tension of muscle, a mingling of essence . . . She thought: *There is no moon tonight, but the thousand stars in the velvet above are the gems that are*

*mine to enjoy, as is this precious moment—all silk and
softness and warmth—a respite from tomorrow's concerns.*

She awakened as the first pale light of dawn con-
toured the diffused shadows, bringing back her anxiety
and flooding her mind with things yet to be discussed
with Alexander: the Secret Society, Agasha's misfortune and Prince Gregory's behavior.

Alexander stirred beside her. Half awake, he pulled
her toward him, his hands asking for love, but Irina
moved gently away. Fully awake now, Alexander sat
up and peered at Irina. "Is anything wrong, *golubka*?"
he asked, and leaned over to take her hand.

Irina hesitated, then said, "Alex, the day you left, I
found a note in your morning coat." She waited, but
when Alexander remained silent, she went on. "It was
from a Colonel Paul Pestel, and after I had read it, I
was frightened. Is it true? Are you a member of that
secret society?"

Alexander pulled her toward him, and this time she
did not resist. "Yes, my love. Does it shock you
terribly?"

Irina bit her lip. "It does. I would be dishonest if I
said no. But perhaps not for the reasons you think. I
can't accuse you of betrayal, for Lord knows, I feel as
you do. We both know that there has to be a change,
but—but getting involved in subversive activities . . ."

Alexander did not let her finish and crushed her
against him. "*Golubka,* this is the reason I kept it from
you! I was so afraid you would condemn me for plotting
against the tsar. You see, I firmly believed in the Union
of Welfare and was afraid you'd ask me to withdraw."

"Why do you protect me from life?" Irina cried. "I'm
your wife, not a parlor decoration! I thought we both
knew this when we married!"

Then she clung to him. "But, Alexander, I am so

afraid for your safety! There are traitors everywhere, and sooner or later someone will betray you to the police. You know what the consequences will be!"

"Don't worry, darling. The meeting in Moscow convinced me that it is unlikely the Northern and the Southern Societies will come to a mutual agreement on their policies, and without unity the whole movement is doomed. And so I have resigned."

"But if the movement becomes exposed, how can you prove that you no longer belong to it? Who will vouch for you?"

Alexander averted his gaze. "There is no reason to worry about it right now," he said evasively.

Irina shuddered, suppressing a nagging premonition. There was one more thing she had to tell him. "Alexander, it's not going to be pleasant news to start the morning with, but something else happened while you were away."

He listened silently as she related the events of two weeks ago, when she had learned of Agasha's tragedy and Prince Gregory's behavior. "I thought you might succeed where I failed in persuading your father to buy Agasha back and to marry her to Ossip," she concluded.

"I can try," Alexander said after a moment's reflection, "but I'm afraid Papa is in his rights to do as he pleases. These things do happen, you know!"

He paused, then chuckled. "The old rogue! I hadn't expected this of him. I guess he still clings to the idea of the droit du seigneur."

"How can you make light of it?" Irina cried, shocked. "Droit du seigneur, indeed! That belongs to the Middle Ages, not to this progressive year of 1825!"

"I know, I know, but that's the way he thinks. And that's why our secret society was formed. To do away with just such injustices."

"You mean you don't think you can make your father change his mind?"

Alexander shook his head. "No."

"What if you threaten to tell Maman about it?"

"It won't help, Irina. Papa will call my bluff. He knows I'd go to great lengths not to hurt my mother."

And so it was that Alexander's talk with his father came to nothing and Agasha was to remain with her new owner. Irina prayed that she would not be forced into a marriage with someone she did not care about. To Alexander she said, "I am glad that at least Ossip has been spared his punishment and public humiliation."

Alexander nodded. "It was easy for Papa to pardon him because the village elder told him that he holds no grudge against Ossip." Alexander paused, then added pensively, "It's curious that the elder's younger brother, Igor Panfilov, who is visiting him from Kyakhta, persuaded him not to press charges."

Irina frowned. "Where is Kyakhta?"

"It's on the Siberian-Mongolian border, about six thousand versts from Moscow and about three hundred versts south of Irkutsk. The elder explained to Papa that his brother, who is a Kyakhta merchant and trades with the Chinese in their border town of Maimachin, told him how the loss of face among the Chinese foments vengeance and tragedy, and it influenced him to forget the whole incident."

Later in the morning Ossip was announced, and when he came into her study for the first time in two weeks, Alexander was just leaving to go hunting with Prince Gregory. After bowing low to Alexander, Ossip knelt slowly before Irina and, taking the hem of her skirt, brought it to his lips. "Thank you, Barynia," he mumbled, never raising his eyes.

Irina's heart ached for him, and she was about to

raise him from his knees when Alexander said sharply, "Get up, Ossip! There is no need to grovel! You should have known better than to hit the elder and I'm sure you'll be more prudent in the future. Right now Her Grace is indisposed. Go back to the village, and we shall let you know when to return."

Ossip rose to his feet, his face crimson and sullen. Bowing stiffly to both of them, he left the room without a word.

Irina wheeled on her husband. "Alexander, that was so unkind! Why did you send him away? I feel perfectly fine!"

"He shouldn't be coming in here without being summoned."

"But, Alex! Ossip has been instructed to come here on appointed days for his lessons. I am surprised at you! On one hand, you risk your life by joining the Secret Society to help the serfs, and on the other, you order Ossip out of the house without due cause."

Alexander took Irina's hand, kissed it, and said, "I'm sorry, *golubka*. I guess the whole unsavory affair has affected me more than I realize, and I took it out on Ossip."

He kissed her cheek and left. For a long time she stood by her chair. The skies were rarely totally clear, were they? So it was with life, she reasoned. Clouds gathered, dispersed, gathered again. Right now the room had darkened from the heavy overcast outside. She walked to the window and looked out. The earlier wind had subsided, and nothing seemed to move. Moments later it began to snow.

Chapter Seven

On November 19, 1825, Tsar Alexander died in the remote town of Taganrog on the Sea of Azov, and the unexpected death of the sovereign who had been in good health, shocked the country.

Shortly thereafter, somewhere in the far corners of the land, a rumor started, grew, and enveloped the country: "The tsar did not die in Taganrog," the people whispered. "He was well, still young . . . he couldn't have died!" Their beloved tsar, Alexander the Blessed, had simply decided to withdraw from public life and become a hermit to expiate his sins. He was pursued by the specter of his assassinated father, who fanned his guilt. What guilt? Imaginary, of course, for the tsar surely was not implicated in the plot to murder his own father . . .

Rumors burgeoned. Who would take the throne after the childless Alexander the Blessed? The next in line was his brother Constantine, but Constantine lived with his morganatic wife in Poland and was reportedly a reluctant heir to the throne of Russia.

Poor Mother Russia. Who could protect her now? Who could lead her? The next brother was a much younger man, only twenty-nine, whose Prussian military training made him a stern taskmaster. If Grand Duke Nicholas became Tsar Nicholas, the rigid discipline he imposed on military ranks would then be

extended to the people of Russia. Woe to the mother-
land and her Russian soul!

And so it went, hour after hour, day after day.

At Dolovino Alexander and Irina heard the news on
one of those quiet afternoons when the sun sprayed like
brilliants on the fresh snow, when the wind idled and
smoke coiled from chimneys into the purity of a
cloudless sky. On such a lovely afternoon, when the air
smelled of frost and pine resin and burning birchwood,
promising cozy, peaceful hours by a warm fireplace, the
forty-eight-year-old tsar couldn't be dead!

Two days after he had heard the news, Alexander
was on his way to St. Petersburg. He didn't want Irina
with him. In her condition, he told her, she should not
be traveling in cold weather but should remain in the
comfort of their family home. The other reason remained unspoken: He suspected that members of the
Union of Welfare would stage their uprising before
the new tsar was crowned, and he was rushing to
St. Petersburg to find his friends and try to avert a
disaster.

There was yet another reason why he wanted to leave
Irina behind, one that he was ashamed to admit even to
himself. He hadn't yet broken off his liaison with
Marianna. After attending that joint meeting of the two
societies in Moscow, he had been so distressed by his
findings that he wanted to share his doubts and worries
with someone, and he had gone to Marianna. After she
had listened to him and calmed his anxieties, he could
not bring himself to make the break.

This time, though, he was determined to end the
relationship. His wife was with child, he adored her,
and the memories of his intimacies with Marianna
brought a flush of hot shame to his face.

As his covered sleigh—the kibitka—stopped at
villages along the way to change horses, he heard the

rumor that Tsar Alexander had not died in Taganrog. The peasants, whose religion and superstition blended into one, embellished the story until they firmly believed it. Alexander was appalled. When on December 10 his kibitka reached St. Petersburg, and the Admiralty's golden spire loomed in the distance, his foreboding mounted.

At Kondraty Ryleyev's flat he found pandemonium. There he learned that Constantine, to whom the army and the Imperial Guards had sworn allegiance only two weeks earlier, had categorically refused the throne and declared his loyalty to his younger brother, Grand Duke Nicholas.

There was no time to lose, and debates lasted through sleepless nights.

"You're not ready! You're not prepared for a nationwide revolt," Alexander argued heatedly. "You have yet to secure the army's support! How do you propose to accomplish it?"

"I know, I know!" Ryleyev conceded, speaking with difficulty because of a sore throat. "But unless we do something now, posterity will call us irresponsible and weak!"

"The devil with posterity," Alexander cried in exasperation. "Do you want to commit suicide to please your grandchildren? Dreamers!"

Prince Sergei Trubetskoy raised his hand to silence him. "We can't miss this opportunity, Prince Dolovin," he said evenly. "The army has already taken the oath to Constantine, and now, with Constantine having renounced his right of succession, the army will be required to swear allegiance to Nicholas, and you know what Nicholas is like—a despotic disciplinarian who demands strict subordination. He's hated by the soldiers and is disliked by his officers. This interim time is our only chance. Once the army swears allegiance to

Nicholas, it will be much more difficult, if not impossible, for us to do anything."

Alexander was not convinced. "Then what exactly is your plan of action?" he asked.

"Our immediate aim," Prince Trubetskoy answered, "is to prevent the Senate and the State Council from giving the oath to Nicholas. That done, we'd force the Senate to convene an assembly in preparation for a constitutional monarchy."

"Tsar Alexander's death caught us by surprise," Kakhovsky said, nodding at Ryleyev. "Kondraty has caught a bad cold going around talking to the soldiers about the changes that should be made in the government. They listen; but the issues are too complex for them to absorb, and there's no time to convince the masses that we must rise against the tsar for the sake of democracy. The only way left us is to call on the army to demand Constantine and a constitution and refuse to swear allegiance to Nicholas."

Alexander looked around the room. "And whom have you chosen to lead the revolt on this crucial day?"

All heads turned to Prince Trubetskoy.

"Sergei is the natural choice," Ryleyev pointed out. "His family name will add authority to the cause, and he is a military man who will command the respect of the army."

Alexander pressed his lips into a thin line. Disaster! These men were flirting with disaster, and he wanted no part of it. He hadn't forgotten that at the Moscow meeting Prince Trubetskoy was horrified at the thought of harming the tsar, so how was this member of the ruling class going to translate military bravery into political courage? Alexander shifted from one foot to the other to shake a sudden chill from his body. Well, *he* was not going to be a party to this childish but lethal game. If all of them in their romantic delirium thought it an act of patriotism to sacrifice their lives for a cause that was doomed from the start, *he* had a responsibility to stay alive. Dead or exiled into a living death, there wasn't much he could do for his country!

Three days later, when the new tsar, Nicholas, announced that he had set December 14 as the day for the Senate and the guards to take the oath of allegiance, Alexander made one last effort to dissuade the society from acting impulsively.

Ryleyev leveled a penetrating look at Alexander. "You've resigned from the Union of Welfare, Prince Dolovin," he said quietly, his large, brilliant eyes burning feverishly.

Alexander flushed at the formal use of his name but remained silent.

"For your own protection you should not be frequenting our meetings," Ryleyev continued. "Perhaps you are not aware that we're being watched by the police." He paused, then went on. "One of our sympathizers, Yakov Rostovtsev, after attending only one of our meetings, denounced us to the tsar. We don't know if he listed our names; but all of us in the society are now suspect, and we have no alternative but to act. We're going to be arrested whether we revolt tomorrow or not, but at least if we do, we'll have the satisfaction of having tried."

"Do you have the support of any of the regiments?" Alexander asked, fearing the answer.

Ryleyev hedged. "A few; we plan to rally the rest to our side."

"How?" Alexander's voice rose.

Prince Trubetskoy answered for Ryleyev. "By leading our loyal men to the square to force the Senate to declare the establishment of the provisional government, then on to seize the palace and to arrest the royal family."

His voice lacked assurance, and Alexander thought: *My God, this is a military man talking! He's carried away by political issues instead of planning a strategy of how to win a battle.* There was nothing left to do but to leave and lengthen the distance between himself and this group of disorganized, foolish men.

In his bachelor flat Alexander found a note from Marianna. News of his return to the capital had spread fast, and she was asking why he hadn't been to see her. He crumpled the letter in his fist. Might as well see her and bring the relationship to an end once and for all. He should have done it on his last visit.

He thought about it. There was no doubt that Marianna had fire and insouciance and a touch of impertinence that had charmed him initially. And later, when their liaison started, she had become a chameleon who adapted to each of his moods, thus strengthening her hold over him. Who was the *real* Marianna? The last time he saw her, he mused, she had reawakened passions in him that he foolishly thought were now reserved for Irina. But his naïve, innocent wife was no match for the experienced courtesan, and lonely without Irina and hungry for love, he had pocketed his conscience and succumbed to Marianna's waiting arms.

This time, however, Irina's pull was the stronger, his conscience dominant, and today's revelations were so devastating that the idea of spending a night with the courtesan shamed him, and he was determined to make the final break much as he dreaded the emotional scene awaiting him.

But there was no emotional scene. He was surprised, relieved, yet a little piqued when Marianna reacted with dignified equanimity, not at all like a woman in love. The only signs of emotion were a flicker of eyelids, a pressure of lips, a sudden busyness of hands. Abruptly she turned her back to him and stood smoothing the tablecloth, picking up the bibelots, and putting them down in the same place.

"This doesn't come as a surprise to me, Alexander, my dear," she said without turning around. "As a matter of fact, I anticipated this and have already planned my future without you."

Was she too proud to show her humiliation, or had she really found another protector, as she implied? He did not know and did not wish to know. All he wanted was to leave her house as quickly as possible and never see her again.

At the door, as he bent over her hand for a farewell kiss, she said casually, "I'm glad for you, Alexander, that you are no longer involved with the Union of Welfare. This is the time of great decisions, and traitors exist everywhere."

Alexander raised his head. For a long silent moment their eyes locked, but there was nothing he could read in her veiled, enigmatic look.

Outside, he sighed deeply, welcoming the cooling air that filled his lungs. Now for the ride home and a glass of brandy to relax his nerves!

But at home his younger brother was waiting for him in the parlor. The blond, fair-skinned Nikita was quiet and studious, and Alexander remembered him as a child, spending hours in his room with books. After graduating from the lyceum at Tsarskoye Selo, Nikita had entered the tsar's service and was fanatically loyal to the monarchy. When he learned about Alexander's membership in the Union of Welfare shortly before his brother's marriage, he had tried to voice his disapproval, but Alexander had refused to listen. Now, facing Nikita across the room, Alexander sensed why his brother had come to see him.

How refined his features are, he thought irrelevantly, watching his brother's obvious discomfiture.

"What may I offer you, Nikita? Will you join me in a glass of brandy?"

Nikita shook his head. "No, thank you. I can't stay long. I—I came to tell you that Tsar Nicholas knows of the existence of the Union of Welfare; he also has a detailed list of its members."

"And are you here to tell me that my name is on that list?"

"I haven't seen the list. But there are rumors——"

"About what?"

"There are rumors that something is going to happen tomorrow on the Senate Square . . ."

"And?" Alexander prompted.

"And the tsar is well prepared for any eventuality."

"So you came to warn your erring older brother to stay away from the square tomorrow morning. Is that it?"

Nikita flushed. "You needn't be sarcastic, Alexander. Whether I approve of your political activities or not is beside the point right now. I'm here because you *are* my brother, and I feel dutybound to warn you."

Alexander walked over to Nikita and offered him a glass of brandy in spite of his earlier refusal. "How did I get such a wise and loyal younger brother?" he said, smiling indulgently.

Nikita was not amused but took the glass with a shaking hand. "I wish I could convince you how serious this is. I fear for your life!"

Alexander nodded. "I know. Don't worry about me, little brother. I appreciate your concern, and you can sleep peacefully tonight. You see, I've resigned from the Union of Welfare, and don't intend to participate in their—er—activities tomorrow."

"Thank God! I'm so glad that you've finally realized that it will never work!"

"Not quite, Nikita. I still believe in the Union of

Welfare, but unless the men settle their differences, the society is not strong enough to survive." For a few moments Alexander was silent, tracing the carving on his mahogany desk with absentminded care. "Therein lies the whole tragedy, little brother."

"Well, whatever reasons prompted you to resign, I'm glad you did," Nikita reiterated stubbornly. "I wouldn't want Papa to hear about this, and as far as I'm concerned, my lips are sealed."

The night hours crawled on a tortuous path through Alexander's restless mind. Conflicting thoughts taxed his brain; confusing issues taunted him. Where did his loyalties lie now that he was no longer a member of the Union of Welfare: with the tsar or with his former colleagues, misguided as they were?

Nothing made sense. Blast these endless winter nights! But would the morning be bright enough to clear his befuddled mind and help him make a decision on what, if anything, he should do? And so the night went, slowly, slowly, making him thrash in bed in a futile effort to escape the drumming questions.

In the morning—the clock told him it was morning—before the dawn's miserly light began to probe through the shuttered window, Alexander was up and dressed. Suddenly it was no longer necessary to think or rationalize or be cautious. No longer in doubt about what he had to do, *needed* to do, he put on his greatcoat and went to the Senate Square, where Prince Trubetskoy told him the rebels would assemble. How glad he was that he was not yet expected back in St. Petersburg and did not have to report to the Winter Palace this morning for the oath of allegiance!

Light began to filter through the overcast, gloomy sky shortly after nine o'clock, and when Alexander reached the square, it was still empty. A few spectators milled around the base of the granite block on which Falconet's equestrian statue of Peter the Great reared as if in warning to those who dared defy the Romanov dynasty. A few women bundled in padded wool coats were brushing the snow from the ground with brooms of birch twigs. It took only two or three questions for Alexander to discover that the new tsar had outwitted them all by having the Senate swear allegiance at seven o'clock that morning. Prince Trubetskoy, the chosen rebel leader, had bungled the first, the most important, plan of the day. Where was he? Alexander stood with his back to the Senate Building and watched the activity on the square.

An hour passed. He was cold and weary from lack of sleep. The risk he had taken in coming here to dissuade his friends from going through with their plan seemed in vain after all. At the last minute Prince Trubetskoy must have had a change of heart. A brisk walk to Ryleyev's flat would dissipate the chill and clear up the mystery. Alexander turned and was about to leave when a rhythmic beating of drums sounded in the distance. Faint at first, it grew in intensity, and as Alexander watched, the first ranks of the Moskovsky Regiment, dressed in green and white uniforms with gold piping, appeared from around the corner of Gorokhovaya Street and marched toward the square. Prince Trubetskoy was not with them, and Alexander saw only Michael Bestuzhev, whom he recognized instantly as one of the members of the society present at Ryleyev's flat a few nights before. As the soldiers began to fill the square, other insurgents joined them, and the ranks began to spread in battle-ready position to the four sides of the square, facing St. Isaac's Cathedral, the Admiralty, the Senate, and the statue of Peter the Great.

Alexander hurried over to Michael Bestuzhev. "I've

been waiting here for more than an hour," he said. "What happened this morning?"

In crisp, laconic phrases, Bestuzhev related the appalling facts. He and his brother Alexander had been successful in rallying to their side 700 men of the Moskovsky Regiment, but only small sections of Grenadier and Marine Guards regiments, the total count coming to no more than 3,000 men against the tsar's 12,000 loyal troops, now assembled on the Palace Square not ten minutes away. Blood had already been spilled. As the Moskovsky Regiment left for the Senate Square, the commander, Baron Fredericks, tried to stop them, but one of their company commanders, Prince Shchepin, agitated by rebellious fervor and enraged by the delay, swung his saber and killed him.

Alexander listened, scanning the crowds for any sign of Prince Trubetskoy. "Where is your leader?" he finally asked the distraught Bestuzhev. The pale, thin officer shook his head. "We can't find him anywhere! We don't know what happened. There was no time to lose, so we asked Prince Obolensky to take command. There he is!"

Alexander's heart sank. In a city of more than 400,000 inhabitants, Prince Obolensky, a staff officer, was leading an uprising with only 3,000 men! As he stood there absorbing this distressing news, the cherubic-faced Prince Eugene Obolensky appeared by his side and saluted him.

"What are you doing here, Prince Dolovin?" Obolensky asked. "You're no longer a member of our society, so why risk your life?"

"I'm here to make one last effort to dissuade you from going through with this insanity. You don't even have the minimum number of men Trubetskoy estimated you'd need to succeed. You're rushing headlong into suicide!"

"It's too late to turn back now." A voice sounded from behind, and Alexander wheeled to face Peter Kakhovsky, brandishing a pistol and looking at him with a sardonic smile. "We're waiting for reinforcements, and if they don't come, time will be in our favor; when darkness falls, we can rally government troops to our side."

Alexander turned and threaded his way through the crowd toward the adjacent Palace Square. There an awesome sight greeted him. The crack Preobrazhensky Regiment, together with other loyal troops, stood waiting for the tsar's orders. The tsar himself, dressed in the Izmailovsky Regiment uniform, a blue ribbon across his shoulder, sat astride a horse, regal and fearsome. Alexander went back to the Senate Square. It was obvious that neither side wanted to open fire first.

Thus they stood, minutes and hours slipping by without action. *This is going to be a standing revolution,* he thought, watching the men, cold and hungry, wait obediently for orders. Mobs of civilian sympathizers pressed around them, and occasionally he heard a shout: "We want Constantine!" and that was seconded by a muffled cry: "Yeah! And his wife, Constitutsiya!"

Good Lord, Alexander thought, *did I hear them right? These ignorant people don't even know what they are revolting against! Just because "constitution" is of a feminine gender, they think it's Constantine's consort!* Surely he must have misheard them!

Suddenly he was distracted by a commotion; the governor-general of St. Petersburg, Count Miloradovich, was galloping into the square. The hero of the Napoleonic war, he was revered and respected by the military, and his appearance was an unwelcome sight to the insurgents. Prince Obolensky must have thought as much, for he blocked the general's way and asked him, for his own safety, not to address the soldiers.

"Why shouldn't I?" cried the count. "There isn't a single officer here, not a single soldier, who is not a traitor to our tsar and to our fatherland! You're a blot on Russia, all of you! Criminals before God and before the world! On your knees before the tsar! Follow me, men!"

With lightning speed, Prince Obolensky grabbed a bayonet from the nearest soldier and pushed the count's horse away, wounding the count in the leg as he did so. Out of the corner of his eye Alexander saw a brisk movement behind Count Miloradovich as Kakhovsky raised his pistol. Without thinking, Alexander pushed forward and grabbed Kakhovsky's arm. He was too late. The shot rang out, found its mark, and Count Miloradovich toppled from his horse, mortally wounded.

Choking with anger, Alexander could only whisper, "Why? Why, Kakhovsky?"

Obolensky answered for him. "He wouldn't listen. He wouldn't go back! We couldn't risk his staying any longer and influencing the troops."

Horrified, Alexander backed away from the bloody scene and pushed his way through the mob of gawking civilians to the edge of the square, where the tsar's loyal troops were lining up in a small area between Peter's monument and the Neva Embankment. Mounds of granite blocks, brought on wooden barges for the reconstruction of St. Isaac's Cathedral, now served as a convenient bulwark for the tsar's cavalry. A crowd of civilians climbed onto the roof of the Senate and started throwing logs and stones at the troops. A hasty order to advance thrust the cavalry forward, and Alexander barely had time to jump out of the way. But the ground was icy, and the horses slipped and slid. Laughing and jeering, the rebels pelted them with snowballs. The humiliated troops were ordered to retreat.

Alexander watched, stupefied. The scene was unreal. Those soldiers were playing games, it seemed. Did they think it was all in fun?

More threatening than the cavalry on the Neva side were the men of the Preobrazhensky Regiment positioned on the corner of the Senate and Admiralty squares. The noose was tightening, and still the mutineers vacillated! Alexander started to look for Eugene Obolensky, who was probably on the opposite side of the square by now, but halfway across, he was blocked by a moving sleigh. He looked up. The metropolitan of St. Petersburg, Father Serafim, and his deacon were inside. The prelate stood up and called, "Soldiers, calm down! Swear allegiance to the tsar and go back to your barracks!"

The soldiers were cold, hungry, and weary, and their mood began to change. No more laughter, no more thrown snowballs at the tsar's slipping and sliding cavalry. Instead, angry voices rose among them.

"You're a deserter yourself!" a soldier shouted. "Traitor! You swore allegiance to two tsars in two weeks! Go away!"

The thudding gallop of a single horse drew Alexander's attention away from the priest. Turning toward the Preobrazhensky Regiment, Alexander gasped. The tsar's younger brother, the grand duke Michael, had entered the square, heading toward the rebels. Frantically Alexander looked for Kakhovsky. A few paces away there he was, standing beside another member of the society, the radical Wilhelm Küchelbecker. A sixth sense warned Alexander that yet another assassination was about to be attempted. He moved quickly toward the two men. At that moment Küchelbecker raised his pistol and aimed it at the grand duke. Alexander threw himself against the man with full force. The deflected shot pierced the air with a single explosive sound, causing the grand duke's horse to rear, sending it into a gallop. Enraged, Küchelbecker swung and hit Alexander with the butt of his pistol. Momentarily blinded by pain, Alexander reeled and moments later felt the blood trickle down his temple.

Holding a handkerchief against the wound, disgusted and saddened by the unleashed passions around him, Alexander began to work his way out of the square into a side street. There he leaned against a wall, still loath to leave the scene.

The impasse dragged on. At three o'clock the short winter day began to wane, and the tsar, suspecting perhaps that under cover of night loyalties were prone to shift, dared not wait any longer. Alexander held his breath when he saw the gaping mouths of cannons being leveled at the insurgents. Then he heard Alexander Kornilovich, one of the rebels, give orders to seize the cannon. The soldiers shifted their feet and shook their heads. "No! Those are our *bratsy*—our brethren! They're not going to fire on us!"

Anxiously Alexander looked at the tsar's troops and heard an echoing "Aim! Fi-i-re!"

The first shots went above the rebels' heads in warning. Their mood now shifted abruptly. With their bayonets at the ready, they aimed for attack. Another order to fire, and this time the shots went into their midst, and the tsar's troops continued firing.

In a few minutes it was all over. Stunned, the rebels broke ranks and scattered for cover, leaving behind the dead and the wounded. Into the side streets they fled, and across the frozen Neva River, onto Vasilyevsky Island to hide. But the cannonballs pursued them, broke the ice, plunged them into the frigid water.

Sickened, Alexander watched from around the corner of the Neva Embankment. He lost sight of Obolensky and Bestuzhev and Kakhovsky, seeing only dozens of nameless bodies on the ground, soldiers and civilians alike, motionless and silent. In the darkening, damp cold a sizzling sound reached his shocked brain. He looked down. A bubbling rivulet of blood ran past his feet, melting the snow, slowing as it ran, and freezing into a crimson schist before his very eyes.

He didn't know how long he stood there, mesmerized, numbed, unable to function. It wasn't until he saw Alexander Shulgin, the St. Petersburg chief of police, appear on the square and order workmen to throw the corpses and what looked like near-corpses into the Neva under the ice that he turned toward the English Quay and fled from the Admiralty and the Winter Place.

He wandered aimlessly through the darkened streets, distraught by the turn of events, shocked by the violence unleashed by his comrades, until he found himself in the courtyard of Ryleyev's small flat. He knew he shouldn't go in, knew the danger of being associated with the society, but he had to find out if any of his friends were hurt.

Ryleyev's wife, Natalia, ashen and frightened, let him in, their six-year-old daughter, Nastenka, clinging to her skirt. Without a word she nodded toward the parlor, where he heard familiar voices talking all at once.

Nervous and agitated, Kondraty Ryleyev was hugging his comrades. "A miracle!" He laughed, his eyes shining with feverish brilliance. "Imagine, they say there were eighty people killed, yet not one of our members was killed or even wounded!"

Stupefied, Alexander thought: *These doomed men—for surely they knew they were doomed—are rejoicing over their failure!* Somehow, in their twisted logic, they thought it was a glorious success. Fools! What were they doing now, idling at home? Why didn't they flee? There was still time! In the general confusion and cleanup surely they could slip across the border into Finland, where they would be safe from the tsar's wrath. But even as he thought this, he knew the answer, for he himself would have stayed behind. His was the generation that could forgive a friend's betrayal, could understand even a desertion, but to leave their country—why, that was moral degradation!

Unable to listen any longer, he slipped out and rushed back to his flat.

He stayed in bed the entire following day, at times shivering with an imaginary chill, then burning with fever. He was confused and yes, for shame of it, relieved in being free and safe.

Toward evening he rose, ate sparingly, and, sitting by the fireplace, drank several glasses of cognac. The crackling fire, the warmth from the liquor, finally calmed his nerves, and he dozed.

A loud knock at the door startled him.

He watched as his manservant opened the door. There on the threshold stood Alexander Shulgin, the St. Petersburg chief of police.

"Prince Alexander Dolovin! By the order of His Imperial Majesty Tsar Nicholas, you are under arrest!"

Chapter Eight

When Irina was growing up, she invented a fantasy world into which she routinely escaped, however briefly, to avoid or postpone an unpleasant duty. In the summer she studied the intricate patterns of the Bukhara rug in her bedchamber, creating rooms and connecting corridors in which she lived and reigned alone, and in the winter she used the lacy patterns of frosted windowpanes to imagine a glen of fairies and benevolent goblins who took her into their world of dance and laughter.

Today, standing in front of such a frosted window, she tried to recapture her childish imageries by staring at a crystalline chrysanthemum fanning across the upper portion of the window. The shape was blurred by thick, falling snowflakes blanketing the garden outside. She followed the flight of one of them, trying to picture herself feather-light, carefree, happy.

It didn't work.

How could it? She was no longer a child, and Nikita's words were etched into her brain, shutting out any escape route.

"I came to bring you the news myself," he had said. "I wanted you to hear it from me rather than from another source, and I wanted to spare you having to tell Papa." Nikita paused and cleared his throat. "He—er—he's rather upset with Alexander. I thought it best to leave him alone till he becomes more rational.

"On my way down, I learned that Boris Radin has been arrested, too, and that they're rounding up other members of the two societies and bringing them all to St. Petersburg. Most of them are in the Peter and Paul Fortress, and the rumor is that the tsar is going to interrogate them all personally. I'm sure it won't be long before they find out that Alexander resigned from the society before the revolt took place. He just happened to be at the wrong place at the wrong time."

Nikita bent over Irina's hand. "I have to return to St. Petersburg immediately, my dear. I only wish I could stay by your side and lend you some moral support. I'll keep you informed as events develop."

Now, with Nikita gone, she was still standing by the window where two hours ago she had watched his sled disappear in the shroud of whirling white.

It all would be cleared up after the tsar had interrogated Alexander, of course. But why should Alexander have to remain in prison waiting to be questioned like a criminal? He was innocent. Innocent! Her father-in-law must see the tsar, explain what happened, and bring Alexander home.

The Peter and Paul Fortress—that ominous, forbidding prison on the Neva River, with its dark gray walls, its moat, its secret dungeons! She must go to Prince Gregory, ask him to leave for the capital immediately, tell him that since Alexander had resigned from the society, he wouldn't have, couldn't have participated in the revolt.

She was about to leave her study when Ossip came for his lesson. She had completely forgotten about him. She couldn't possibly teach him today!

"Barynia," Ossip said, "is it true that our young barin has revolted on behalf of us, the serfs, and that now we can hope to be free?" He crossed himself several times. "May the good Lord bless him!"

"Prince Alexander did not take part in the revolt, Ossip," Irina said, leveling an angry gaze at him. "He was falsely accused and will be released soon."

Ossip shot her a quick sidelong glance and bowed respectfully. "Forgive me, Barynia, but the revolt . . . it was to free the serfs, wasn't it? Surely our *tsar-batyushka*—our little father—is not going to punish them for trying to help us?"

Irina bit her lip. "Yes, they tried to help you, Ossip, but the tsar sees it as a revolt against his authority."

Kneading his cap in his hands, Ossip said, "Barynia, the village elder's brother wants me to go with him to Kyakhta, and help him in the tea trading business with the Chinese in Maimachin, seeing as I am able to read and write now." Ossip hesitated, brushed his hat vigorously, then said, "But Prince Gregory won't give me my freedom and won't even sell me to him."

Unaccountably irritated, Irina asked, "Why would you want to go so far away from home, Ossip?"

Ossip raised his head and for the first time looked boldly into her eyes. "What is there for me here, Barynia? Shame and servitude and memories I'd just as soon forget. In Siberia I'd be my own man, free to build a good future for myself. The elder's brother says the land is rich out there and the life is good."

"You'd need to study more before taking on such a job," Irina said. "As for today's lesson, I can't spend any time with you right now. I'll let you know when to come back."

Ossip hesitated, seemed to want to say something, then changed his mind and, bowing again, left.

Irina stood in the center of the room, trembling. Ossip should not have spoken to her about these things. Who gave him the right to question her, to pursue his probing with unabashed audacity? Freedom, he said, yet he could not free himself from his own imprisonment of pride, had stubbornly refused to talk about the unfortunate Agasha, and had kept a sullen silence whenever she spoke of her. And he dared ask about freedom!

She hurried toward her father-in-law's study. Ever since that day of the argument over Agasha, Prince Gregory had never spoken to Irina first, and she knew that he had not forgiven her for forcing his hand. Instinctively she felt that he was waiting for an opportunity to avenge himself, but surely his son's safety would take precedence over any personal vendetta he might be harboring against her!

When she entered his study, he was seated at his desk, his face purple with anger, his fingers interlaced and white from pressure.

"*Mon père*! I'm here to ask you to go to St. Petersburg! You must see the tsar personally and tell him that Alexander is innocent. Please, for your son's sake."

Prince Gregory glared at her. "What do you mean, innocent?"

"Didn't Nikita tell you that Alexander had resigned from the Union of Welfare and did not take part in the uprising?"

"That doesn't make him innocent! At the last minute he ran scared! At least the others, like Boris Radin, had the integrity to stand up for what they believed."

"But, Papa! Alexander didn't take part in any of the activities in the past. He only attended a few meetings, that's all!"

"What part he played in all this is immaterial. The fact remains that he *was* involved, and I shall never forgive him for betraying the family honor, for tainting our old and spotless name. I have no intention whatsoever of appealing to the tsar for clemency!"

"How can you"— Irina choked on her words— "how can you abandon your son in his hour of need?"

"My son is a traitor, that's why!" Prince Gregory shouted, slamming his fist on his desk.

Irina began to shake.

"Alexander's involvement, however slight," she said, controlling her voice with supreme effort, "was motivated by an unselfish desire to help those less privileged than himself. Surely you can't call that kind of idealism betrayal of family honor!"

"Your argument is dangerous rhetoric that I wouldn't want anyone else to hear!"

"I'll cry his innocence from the rooftops if need be!" Irina cried. "You—you accuse your son of disgracing your name, but if you had treated your own serfs better, perhaps he wouldn't have become involved at all."

Irina hadn't meant to antagonize him but realized too late that she had touched on a sensitive subject.

Prince Gregory narrowed his eyes. "You're a disrespectful daughter-in-law! You have no right—do you hear?—no right to question the head of your family! Instead, you should bow your head in shame at your husband's treason and pray that the child you're carrying will turn out more honorable than he!"

Irina's eyes stung with tears. "How can you do this to your own son?" Her words came out in a whisper. "I love Alexander; I'd do *anything* for him. Family honor, humiliation, are nothing compared to what possibly awaits him. He's in prison"—her voice rose in anguish— "and we're arguing over tainting the family name! The tsar must be told that your son did not take part in the uprising, that he's not a member of the society!"

"I have only one son left—Nikita."

So cold, so final were Prince Gregory's words that Irina's anger dissolved into abject fear so powerful she dared not argue any further. She turned and fled from the room, down the corridor, and directly into her mother-in-law's boudoir.

Princess Dolovina was reclining on her chaise longue, her maid placing a wet cloth on her forehead.

Irina rushed toward her, sank to her knees, and grasped her hand. "Maman, oh, Maman! Help me! Help release Alexander from prison!"

"What can I do, my child? Go to Prince Gregory, ask him! He's the only one who can do anything for our son!"

Tears flowing freely now, Irina repeated her conversation with her father-in-law. "So you see, Maman," she cried, "you're the only one who can still influence him; persuade him that he must go to St. Petersburg and see the tsar!"

Agitated, Princess Dolovina threw the wet cloth away from her forehead and sat up, wringing her hands. Irina rose from her knees and flung herself into a nearby armchair.

"If Prince Gregory refuses to help," her mother-in-law said, "he—he must have his reasons. I cannot question his judgment!"

"Maman, for Alexander's sake! You must!"

"No!" The princess's voice rose hysterically. "I can't! It's unthinkable for me to oppose Prince Gregory! You know that! I can only pray for God's mercy now!" She began to weep quietly. "Oh, why did Alexander do such a foolish thing? Why?"

Irina clasped her hands, pressing her nails into her palms.

"Maman," she said, trying to keep her voice even, "if you refuse to do anything to help Alexander, then I must go to St. Petersburg myself."

"You can't be serious, Irina! Surely you realize it's impossible in your condition. Ladies of our rank are not seen in public while they are *enceinte*!"

"Ladies of our rank don't have husbands who are languishing in prison . . . especially while they are *enceinte!*"

"We should pray for his soul! I'll ask the Lord to help him!"

"The Lord helps those who help themselves, Maman. My *nyanya* often told me, 'Trust in God, but don't fail to act yourself.'"

"*Incroyable!* An *enceinte* Princess Dolovina traveling in winter alone!"

Irina planted both feet firmly on the floor in front of her. Grasping the arms of her chair, she said, "Maman, aren't you reversing your priorities? Our concern now should be for Alexander, not whether or not it is proper that I travel alone to the capital."

Later that day Olga Radina came to see her, and the two young women wept in each other's arms. Olga told her all she knew about Boris's arrest. He had been apprehended en route to St. Petersburg and taken to the Peter and Paul Fortress along with the others. It was meager information, but Irina promised to find out anything she could when she got to St. Petersburg. Gratefully Olga hugged and blessed her for her courage.

Irina did not tell her parents of her plans to leave immediately for St. Petersburg. Why subject herself to yet another argument when she needed all her emotional strength for what awaited her? She had no illusions about the difficulties she would find there, but nonetheless she was determined to go. Thank God she was only three months into her pregnancy. Even if she started showing while in the capital, the current styles were in her favor, and it would be a while before anyone would notice. She did not stop to think whom she would see or what she could do when she arrived in St. Petersburg. She knew only that she would stay at the Hotel Demuth on the Moika Canal and would not embarrass any of

their friends by asking them to give shelter to the wife of
an imprisoned man.

On December 28, taking only her personal maid,
Frosya, with her, she left for the capital.

Chapter Nine

It took Count Lavale, the father of her friend Katasha Trubetskaya, whose own husband had been arrested, to tell Irina that Alexander's chances of release were slim. What hurt so much was the embarrassment and unabashed pity in his eyes as he reluctantly answered her probing questions. Quick to read between the lines, she painfully pieced together an ugly story. It was her husband's courtesan, Marianna Kosinskaya, who swore to the police that Alexander had spent the night of December 13 in her mansion and had told her that he intended not only to participate in the uprising the next day but to help Kakhovsky assassinate the tsar.

"At the last minute," Count Lavale said, "my son-in-law had second thoughts and decided against leading the uprising." The count turned and looked out the window, then added, "He sought sanctuary at the Austrian Embassy, but he was arrested nonetheless that same day."

Distraught by her own tragedy, Irina could find no words of comfort for the old count. She thanked him and returned to her hotel.

Marianna Kosinskaya. So that was her name. Was it the revenge of a woman scorned that had motivated the courtesan to seal Alexander's fate by bearing false witness? And what if it was not false at all, but true? She could scarcely stand to think about it. What was the truth? That Alexander had not resigned from the society or that he had not broken his liaison with Marianna . . . or both? It hurt. Oh, it hurt! The doubts, the suspicions, were worse than any truth. But no matter now. What was important, enormously important, was that somehow Marianna must be made to go to the police and retract her statement. But who would be able to convince the courtesan to do so? There was Alexander's brother, Nikita. But he was too young and too critical of the society as it was to be persuasive. Who else was there? Who else?

All along the answer was buried deep in her mind, but it did not surface until the morning light left her no place to hide.

She had to do it. She had to swallow her pride, humble herself before this detested and detestable woman, and plead for her husband. *Oh, God, what else will you ask of me?*

The address was fortunately not far from the Hotel Demuth, so that Irina could walk the distance without hiring a sleigh. The fewer witnesses to her mission, the better.

In reply to her written request to see Mademoiselle Kosinskaya, a curt note had arrived yesterday, setting the time at one o'clock in the afternoon. The façade of the house was simple and unobtrusive, but when a woman servant led the way into a parlor, Irina winced at the garish decor.

A quick step, a swoosh of a skirt behind her, and she was facing Marianna. A lovely creature stood before her, delicate with small features, blond hair, and sinuous movements. *Alexander had touched this woman, had loved her, and they had spent many secret nights together.* Irina's imagination taunted her. *What intimacies had they shared, what private tenderness and words*

exchanged would forever be in this woman's posses-
sion? With a stab of jealousy, Irina refused Marianna's
politely offered chair. She would remain standing; she
would not accept the other woman's hospitality. She
wouldn't, couldn't do otherwise.

"I am sure you suspect, mademoiselle," she began,
"why I am here. Since it is painful for both of us, I shall
come directly to the point."

It sounded wrong, she wasn't saying it right; each
word, each movement, must be calculated to win this
woman over, to disarm her!

Marianna remained silent, studying Irina with narrowed eyes. Irina bit her lip, then forced the words out.
"I came to ask you to retract your statement to the
police."

"You are asking me to lie, madame?"

"I'm asking you to tell the truth! You have nothing to
gain by condemning Alexander!"

By using his first name without his title, Irina knew
she was acknowledging the intimacy between her husband and the other woman, but it was a calculated
move, designed to lower the barrier, however, slightly,
between them.

"Do you seriously think that I would go back to the
police and voluntarily admit to false witness?" Marianna said. "The authorities do not look kindly on
perjury!"

Irina stepped forward and swallowed hard. "I beg
you to reconsider . . . to—to tell the truth!"

A touch of a smile curled at the corner of Marianna's
mouth. "I've already told the truth, madame. Alexander *was* here the night before the revolt, and he *did* say
what I have already repeated to the police."

Angry, desperate, feeling ill, Irina swept her arm
around the room. "Is this how you repay your benefactor for the luxuries he surrounded you with?"

"This luxury is but a fragile illusion dependent on the whim of my protector, madame."

"Then why did you help send him to prison?"

"Because Alexander was suspected of treason, and I couldn't afford to be implicated as his accomplice, however remotely. You see, having no influential family to defend me, I am forced to look out for my interests myself."

"And what are your interests?" Irina asked, controlling with difficulty a wild desire to scratch Marianna's delicate face.

"To be free of suspicion and to seek another protector in the event Alexander is convicted."

"How can you be so callous, so unfeeling?" Irina cried.

"Because I'm destined to live on the periphery of that respectable world that is yours by the accident of birth, madame, and I find it a precarious existence." Marianna pursed her lips and, moving around a small circular table in the center of the room, picked up a jeweled letter opener and tapped it gently over the back of her hand. Then she looked at Irina.

"For some of us life allows no room for sentiment. There's an old saying that your camisole is closest to your own skin."

"But that's so selfish!"

"I don't deny it for a minute, madame."

"It is not easy for me to do this, mademoiselle, but I am pleading with you humbly: Help me free my husband!"

"I am sorry, madame!" Marianna's voice was edged with steel, and Irina, desperate, cried out, "Why? Why did you betray him?"

It wasn't until after she had left the courtesan's mansion and was gulping deep breaths of cold air outside that she realized that not once had Marianna addressed her by her title. A subtle, pathetic barb! But a far greater hurt was the thought that on the eve of the uprising Alexander must indeed have spent the night with Marianna. . . .

Discouraged, weary, her vision blurred by tears, Irina thought: *What if, after I have succeeded in freeing Alexander, he forgives Marianna and goes back to her?*

Strangling a sob, Irina stumbled on. No matter. She would still love him.

She raised her head and found herself standing before Count Lavale's mansion. She would not go in. There was nothing to be gained by talking to the count again. After all, his own son-in-law had been arrested, too, and she could not intrude further on his sorrow. But she continued to stand in front of the imposing entrance, looking at its elegant façade, freeing her mind into a rush of memories: Katasha Trubetskaya's birthday, the ball, the dance with the grand duke Nicholas, that lovely, charmed night. . . .

A memory stirred. Grand Duke Nicholas had enjoyed dancing with her, had apologized for taking the mazurka promised to another, had gallantly said he owed her a favor. . . . Irina's breath quickened. Could so tenuous a thread be used to help Alexander? Did she dare remind the tsar that he had once looked upon her with kindness? A slim chance, but she had to try.

The tall windows of the mansion reflected the fading afternoon light with an opaque luster, hiding the outlines of the silk draperies inside, secretive, forbidding.

Tomorrow she would seek an audience with the tsar. Her last, her only hope . . .

She walked along the Neva Embankment, stopping occasionally by the iron railing, reluctant to return to her rented rooms at the Hotel Demuth, where, she knew, her faithful Frosya would be waiting for her. On the other side of the river a few pedestrians, bundled in wool, hurried along, their chins set deep into their fur collars. The frozen river was covered with a smooth blanket of snow, and as Irina looked at it, she tried to conjure up Alexander's face before her eyes. A pale outline appeared, fading too quickly to capture his expression. Did his eyes shine with love or sadness? She could not tell. She did not want to know the rest. What if his legs were in chains? . . . They would make a clanking noise as he walked. . . . Would the tsar allow her to visit him in prison? Count Lavale said that no one was allowed to see the prisoners. . . . How dreadful it all was, how tragic! She must return to the hotel; the afternoon was turning cold and windy, and she could not afford to catch a fever.

Running her gloved hand through a fluffy layer of snow atop the railing, she irrelevantly thought of how as a child she would make snowmen and give them faces and names. She turned and walked away from the river, away from the Lavale Palace and the memories that hurt so deeply.

She had never been inside the Winter Palace and was enormously relieved to find that she was treated with courtesy and—perhaps it was only her imagination— deep compassion by the officials who greeted her at the Neva Embankment entrance and led her through the Hermitage to the reception hall. There she was helped out of her sable-lined coat and offered a gilded straight-backed chair. Sitting stiffly, she hid her cold hands inside her muff and watched an adjutant who sat behind a large ornate desk, making notes. Above him a painting of Pope Clement IX drew her attention. Her mind drifted. A Roman pope on the wall, a collection of French and Italian paintings in the palace, a tsar with a German tsarina, a German mother and grandmother

—this was Russia? And this was the citadel from which the tsar was expected to understand his subjects, know the heart of his country, where serfs toiled in the fields and were bought and sold like inanimate objects? Suddenly chilled in her blue velvet dress, she clasped her hands tightly inside her muff. It was cold in the large reception hall; she must ask for her coat. But as she was about to do so, the gilded double doors were flung open, and she was ushered through them by an aide.

Dressed in the dark green uniform of the Izmailovsky Regiment, Tsar Nicholas stood in the center of the room, erect, his head high. Irina curtsied deeply, then waited for the tsar to speak.

"I see that the spirited young Countess Radina, who dances the mazurka so well, is now Princess Dolovina," the tsar said with a chilly smile that faded as quickly as it appeared. "How tragic for you, madame!"

The tsar pointed to an armchair and nodded for her to be seated, then went around his elaborately inlaid ormolu desk and sat down behind it. Irina lowered herself stiffly, carefully holding her hands in her lap. The forbidding person of the tsar certainly did not make her difficult mission any easier. *God, give me strength,* she prayed, meeting the tsar's icy, clear eyes, which looked at her expectantly from a regal, unsmiling face.

"Your Majesty," she began, choosing her words with great care, "I sought this audience to clear up a most unfortunate misunderstanding."

The tsar raised an eyebrow and watched her. How disconcerting it was to be scrutinized in silence by one's sovereign, a man whose awesome countenance belied his twenty-nine years! She forced herself to go on.

"You see, Sire, my husband, Prince Alexander, is being kept at the fortress unjustly! He is innocent!"

"Innocent? I call it treason!" The tsar's voice carried

a shade of sarcasm. "Your husband has disappointed me gravely, Princess!"

Irina flushed. "He's not guilty of treason, Your Majesty. My husband resigned from the Union of Welfare long before the uprising. He was at the Senate Square for the sole purpose of trying to dissuade his friends from going through with the revolt."

"That is not what my report says about him, Princess."

"The witness who reported him committed perjury. She did it out of revenge!"

The tsar raised his brows. "She?"

Irina felt a hot flush rise to her face; her eyes filled. It was impossible to look at the tsar's face. "Yes, Sire," she whispered, smoothing the heavy velvet folds of her skirt.

There was a moment's silence.

"Who was it, Princess?" Suddenly the tsar's voice softened. "Tell me everything, for the more I know, the better I can serve justice."

Her eyes level with the tsar's bemedaled chest, Irina told him of Marianna Kosinskaya's testimony and her refusal to repudiate it. After she had finished, the tsar studied her for a few moments with what she imagined was shaded admiration and surprise. Then he cleared his throat.

"You have spoken to this woman yourself, Princess?"

"Yes, Your Majesty."

"And you have reason to believe that her testimony is false?"

"I don't believe her testimony for a minute, Your Majesty!" Irina said heatedly.

"You must love your husband deeply to have done this. Prince Dolovin does not deserve such loyalty."

"Ah, but he does, Sire. He is innocent!"

"I disagree, Princess. The fact remains that he once belonged to the Union of Welfare and shared the traitors' views."

"He did not take an active part in the society, Your Majesty. He wanted only to help the underprivileged, to help change some laws concerning the serfs."

"He should have come directly to me."

"But—but such changes would have necessitated a constitutional monarchy, and he knew Your Majesty would not consent to it."

The tsar's eyes narrowed and flashed like steel.

"You are audacious, Princess. Do you also share these goals and ideals of your husband's?"

Irina raised her head and looked at the tsar's firmly set jaw. "I share his wish to help the underprivileged, Your Majesty. No person of compassion could help feeling the need to bring about some changes in our laws."

"And I say your husband and his friends should have started by coming to me first!"

"You're above the law, Sire. Your power is absolute, and this is why I'm here, pleading for my husband."

"Your husband and his friends acted before I had time to introduce my own policies. They never gave me the benefit of the doubt. Why should I show them mercy now?"

The tsar's voice was hard. Irina swallowed, then said, "Because, Sire, my husband came to the conclusion that he could not go along with what the other members of the union planned to do, and—and as I said earlier, he was falsely accused. Surely he should not be condemned along with the others!"

The tsar rose, indicating that the audience was over.

"Your husband resigned from the society not because he was loyal to the monarchy but because he did not approve of their methods. Even if he indeed did not take part in the revolt, he is still guilty of treason! I can only promise you, Princess, that I shall be fair and impartial. As for his being falsely accused by a—a— whoever it was that brought false witness against him, I assure you the accusation will be thoroughly investigated. Beyond that I make no promises."

As Irina sank into a deep curtsy, her skirt folding onto the Aubusson rug, she asked, "Your Majesty, may I have your permission to visit my husband?"

"Not at this time, Princess. I assume you will be remaining in St. Petersburg; I shall leave orders to keep you informed as the investigation progresses."

"I am with child, Sire, and must return to Dolovino at once. I had hoped to see my husband before I left St. Petersburg."

"My felicitations to you would be out of place at this time. Now more than ever I would not grant permission for you to see your husband. The Peter and Paul Fortress is not a place to be visited by a lady in your delicate condition."

The tsar looked at her for a moment in silence. For a fleeting second she thought she saw a gentleness in his eyes; but before she could be sure, it was gone, and the formidable sovereign stood before her again.

"In view of all you have told me today, Princess, I must say that I admire your courage and determination."

There was nothing for her to do now but leave.

Irina went home to Dolovino. She did not weep, or complain, or attempt to rally her father-in-law to her side. Some things were futile, and that was one of them. Besides, she felt that if she had been unable to persuade the tsar, surely Prince Gregory could do no better and he might even damage Alexander's chances of being found innocent. So she resolved to live one day at a time.

But the great house brooded through the long winter, the winds whistling around it, the snow deep and cold. To avoid facing Prince Gregory as much as possible, she chose to eat most of her meals alone in her bedchamber. But it seemed hollow and empty, and she would stand in front of an oil painting of Alexander, unable to take her eyes off his fine features, his luxurious wavy hair, his sparkling dark eyes, which seemed to smile at her.

She sought comfort in teaching Ossip, who was now able to read quite well. His was a silent expression of gratitude and loyalty, and under different circumstances a comforting friendship might have developed. Irina looked forward to his visits, when she was forced to concentrate on the lesson and temporarily put aside the gnawing anxiety.

Princess Dolovina continued to pour affection and solicitous care upon her, and for some strange reason Irina could not discern, she felt more at ease with her mother-in-law than in the company of her own mother. Countess Radina looked at her with such pity Irina could hardly restrain herself from saying something that she knew she would regret later.

Olga came infrequently. Her visits grated on Irina's nerves because Olga whined about her miserable fate, her loneliness without Boris, how bored she was. Irina suspected that Olga missed the glittering balls far more than she did Boris himself.

The only person with whom Irina was able to relax completely was her *nyanya*. Her practical, humble approach to life, her tacit acceptance of whatever fate meted out to her, helped Irina carry her own burden with more patience. During the day she supervised the nursery preparations, went over her lessons with Ossip, visited with her mother-in-law, and in the evenings she read or crocheted by the fireplace, all the while living from one message from St. Petersburg to another.

"You can't hurry Father Time," Nyanya sighed every time Irina's face was shadowed with disappointment at yet another day without news. "Brighten your hours with little comforts; search for them! You can always find something to please you."

But Irina fretted. "What nonsense you speak, Nyanya! What possible pleasures can I find without Alexander? I worry so!"

"You're chewing your worry like a cud," Nyanya pointed out. "Look about you! That fire has warmed your toes after your walk in the snow this afternoon. Doesn't it give you pleasure? And that book I see you reading—it must please your pretty head, or you wouldn't reach for it in your spare time. Now don't anger God by denying there's anything to be thankful for. Besides"—she chuckled— "one Olga is enough to spoil my day, so spare me the two of you with long faces."

Irina was comforted, however briefly. *Dear, wise Nyanya! What would I do without your simple philosophy? Soon, soon now, good news will come to Dolovino. It has to. It must!*

But the news that did come periodically was meager. Although Nikita wrote faithfully, his letters were becoming repetitive and no longer encouraging. The investigative process was maddeningly slow, and there was no way to tell if Alexander had been questioned yet. No one except the officials involved in the interrogation was allowed to visit the prisoners. Irina steeled herself against the suspense, refusing to admit frustration into her consciousness. During the day she kept busy, and it was only during the nights, the long, empty nights, that she fought a deep panic rising within her.

As the snow turned to slush and the birch and alder tree buds burst into bloom, her time of confinement drew close, and still there was no word from the capital on Alexander's fate. Then, on June 20, she gave birth to a son, her little Alexander, her own precious Sasha.

The love and care surrounding her at the first sign that her time had come sustained her during the ten hours of labor. Her mother-in-law remained by her side throughout, bathing her forehead with scented water and refusing to leave the room in spite of Nyanya's and the midwife's insistence that she rest. After the baby had been cleaned and wrapped in a blanket, Nyanya took him to Prince Gregory before Princess Dolovina had a chance to bring him into the bedchamber to view the child.

Relieved, exhausted, Irina gave in to the healing flow of tears.

What a blessing it was to devote her energies and thoughts to her child, a miniature of Alexander! A healthy wet nurse was brought immediately from the village to live in the house, and Irina welcomed the custom, aware that she might soon have to return to St. Petersburg. She would need all her strength and stamina to face the verdict that was about to be announced. She no longer had any illusions about Alexander's being found innocent, for had that been the case, he would have been released long before this. All she hoped was that his punishment would not be too severe.

Chapter Ten

The high barred window allowed little light to filter through, and in spite of the spacious cell's whitewashed walls, it was dark inside. Over the long months of solitary confinement Alexander had wished many times that the cell were smaller to give him an illusion of not being so alone. The worst thing of all was the total isolation from his comrades and his family.

From the beginning he counted days, then weeks, and finally months. A few packages of food and clothing had arrived from home, but he was allowed no mail and had no news about his family. It was July now. Irina's confinement was over, and he must be a father. A father! He fantasized. A tiny baby ruled the household at Dolovino, flesh of his flesh, a lusty, plump baby, with kicking legs and swinging fists, and he, the father, didn't know whether he had a son or a daughter.

It had taken several months of self-delusion and fruitless hope before he would admit to himself that he was not going to be found innocent. His interview with the tsar had gone badly. Returned to his cell, he went over and over every word, every nuance of the interrogation, weighing the tsar's questions and abrupt changes of mood and torturing himself with doubts about each sentence he had uttered. The presence of the adjutant general Levashev, who wrote down everything Alexander said, was unnerving, particularly when during the questioning it had become clear that someone had implicated him in the uprising. Alexander vehemently denied his involvement, stressing his resignation from the Union of Welfare, but over and over the tsar returned to the same question: Had he resigned because he condemned the society's ideology and was loyal to the monarchy, or had he resigned only because he felt that the two societies were not united and thus doomed to failure?

How easy it would have been to lie, to assure his sovereign that he was loyal to him, but had he done so, he could not have lived with himself, any more than he could have kept from going to the Senate Square on that fateful December 14. In the end he knew his interview had sealed his fate.

And so he waited.

One day in July, as he was led out into the minuscule courtyard for his twice-weekly exercise, he stopped to inhale the fresh air, feeling the warmth of the summer day course through his veins. His guard smiled. "Enjoy it, Barin!"

Alexander looked at him. Semyon was his name, and he had been kind to Alexander and surreptitiously fussed over him, bringing him on occasion an extra blanket or a double portion of soup.

Perhaps it was his weakened condition after months of solitary confinement, or maybe it was the tender warmth of the noonday sun, or simply a craving to talk to another human being; but Alexander touched Semyon's arm and suddenly found himself telling him about his childhood at Dolovino and how on a similarly lovely day he used to climb the cherry trees, sit in their branches, and eat the fruit by the handful.

"I know the feeling," Semyon said pensively.

The next day he brought Alexander a basket of raspberries.

"I don't have any money to pay you," Alexander said, his voice quavering as he looked at the luscious berries.

"Don't worry about paying, Barin," the guard replied good-naturedly. "They didn't cost me a penny."

"How come?" Alexander asked.

"I went to the Milyutin's shops and asked for a quarter's worth of raspberries. The merchant gave me a few on a small sheet of paper. I told him that if he knew who was going to eat these raspberries, he would add more. He wanted to know for whom I was buying them, and when I told him and said that you had no money, he returned the quarter and said to come back for more anytime. 'God will judge those noblemen better than we,' he said. After all, you are suffering now for our sake, Barin, and we, the common folk, thank you deeply. Truly!"

Shaken by this first expression of kindness from another human being in many months, Alexander sat on his cot, thinking. Seven months of confinement with leg irons; a lifetime . . . an eternity. . . . To be kept in solitary was bad enough; to be kept in suspense was torture. Unanswered questions scattered, darted, climbed over one another. Had Irina had a difficult labor? Was the baby healthy? What was its name?

Then: What was the tsar waiting for? Was there going to be a trial? In the eyes of his sovereign he was guilty; his own logic told him this was so. No matter that he had resigned from the Union of Welfare; what mattered was the reason for his resignation, and that he couldn't lie about. Alexander repeated this to himself over and over. So, in essence, he condemned himself, and the best he could do now was hope for a reduced sentence.

Then he thought: His comrades—who was incarcerated with him? Who was in the adjoining cell? And as he ate the precious raspberries (he took only a small portion from the basket and asked Semyon to divide the rest among the others), he took care not to stain the piece of wrapping paper they came in. That night, by the light of a single candle that Semyon had sneaked in to him along with a needle, because prisoners were allowed light and ink only if they wished to write additional testimony, he laboriously spent the hours puncturing a message to Boris Radin. Alexander was sure that Boris was somewhere near and asked Semyon to give it to him. The very next day Boris responded, and although the messages they exchanged were brief and innocuous, Alexander no longer felt so isolated and alone. The date was July 12, 1826.

So pleased was Alexander with the established contact that at first he paid no attention to unusual noises outside his cell. There were hurried footsteps, hammering, pounding in the prison courtyard. All at once cell doors clanged open, and the prisoners saw one another for the first time. They hugged and cried and slapped one another on the back, ignoring the guards, who were pushing them toward a room at the far end of the corridor. There a large number of officials sat behind a table covered with red broadcloth. Stunned by the number presiding, Alexander tried to count them, but in his anxiety and confusion he lost count after seventy. He saw senators, military and civil government functionaries, as well as church metropolitans, staring fixedly at the prisoners.

Alexander recognized the minister of justice, Lobanov-Rostovsky, who was dressed in parade uniform with a St. Andrew ribbon across his shoulder. The official did not return Alexander's nod and ordered the clerk to read the verdicts.

Verdicts, Alexander thought, what verdicts? He didn't even know they had been tried, much less convicted! How could they have done this? He listened, stupefied. The leaders of the uprising, Pestel, Ryleyev, Kakhovsky, Muravyev, Bestuzhev—men he knew and respected—were sentenced to death by hanging. The other 116 were divided into eleven categories with sentences of varying severity. All lost their rank and titles. Private correspondence was forbidden. Boris Radin's sentence was in the seventh category: four years at hard labor and then permanent resettlement in Siberia. At last Alexander heard his name called. His sentence fell into the eighth category: No hard labor, but in addition to losing his rank and title, he was to be exiled to Siberia for life.

For life! The words registered slowly. Surely there must be some mistake; surely the tsar couldn't have been this harsh!

He did not hear the rest of the verdicts as they were read, and after all had been announced, he was ordered with the rest of the prisoners into the courtyard. Several bonfires were burning around them. Forced to kneel, they were stripped of their shoulder boards and their decorations, which were then thrown into the fire. Their swords were brought in and broken above their heads in a symbolic sign of disgrace.

Alexander submitted to this humiliation in a daze, accepting the striped prison gown and following his comrades as they were led across the courtyard back toward the cells. To their right stood the wooden gallows with five dangling ropes. In front of it, dressed in a red shirt, an executioner paraded slowly back and forth. In spite of the warm weather, a tremor took hold of Alexander. His teeth chattered uncontrollably, and clamping his jaws tight, he walked quickly back to his cell. There he stood in the middle of the floor and waited until the guard closed the door behind him and pushed the large iron bolt with a scraping, grating sound. When Alexander heard the key turn in the heavy lock, he sat down on his cot and buried his face in his hands.

He didn't know how long he sat without moving, but after a while he rose and began to pace the floor. While he had escaped a prison sentence, the others had received harsh and arbitrary sentences. The shortest sentence of four years was given to Boris. Was this justice? Yet his own sentence carried a subtle and insidious punishment. Others would suffer at hard labor, but at least they would be together, gaining sustenance and mutual support in their moral and physical degradation. But *he,* deprived of his comrades, of any link with his past, untrained in earning a living, was condemned to exist alone and learn firsthand the harsh realities of survival.

Deep in thought, he jumped at the grinding sound of rusted hinges as the door opened, and Semyon walked in, carrying a basket of fruit hidden under a kitchen towel.

"Eat, Excellency," he said, "Lord knows when you will see such delicious fruit again!" He looked behind him, then bent closer to Alexander. "Don't grieve, Prince! I heard that originally the judges recommended much harsher sentences. They say that the five men condemned to death were to be quartered, but our tsar showed clemency and changed it to hanging!"

Semyon sighed and shook his head. "You're lucky, Barin!"

Alexander could only nod. His own exile for life, a permanent break with his wife and the child whom he had never known, paled beside the gallows he had just seen and the vision of what was to happen in a few hours. Where were the doomed men now? They had not been with the others in the courtyard. They must have been sequestered in their cells, preparing for death. Death! God, what were they doing? How were they holding up? They were so young, so idealistic, and so misled by their idealism! Bestuzhev was only twenty-three years old! The real crime was to snuff out such a life! Alexander rubbed his forehead, pressing his fingers into it until the physical pain deflected his mental anguish.

That night he could not sleep. For hours he sat up, tense, shaking, afraid to relax and break down. His comrades had hours or possibly only minutes to live. And he could do no more than pray for them.

In the morning Semyon brought him tea and for the first time avoided his gaze.

"Tell me," Alexander whispered, "is it over for them?"

Semyon nodded, brushed his sleeve over his eyes, then sniffed and said, "I heard that they didn't die at once, Excellency! Some of the ropes broke, and three of them fell to the ground."

"My God!" Alexander gasped. "Who fell?"

"Ryleyev . . . Muravyev . . . Kakhovsky . . . Oh, Excellency! It was shameful! Muravyev cried out, 'Poor Russia! Can't even hang people properly!' They were bloodied, and they broke their legs and had to wait on the bottom of the pit for half an hour, moaning until new ropes could be found to hang them again!" Semyon whimpered. "Oh, how terrible it was, Excellency! They helped them up to the gallows, but Ryleyev refused and climbed unassisted, blood over his face. . . . And then, just before they put the noose over his head, he said, 'I'm glad to die twice for my country!' God rest their gentle souls!" Semyon began to sniffle. "It was dreadful, Excellency. . . . Dreadful!"

Alexander shook him by the shoulder. "How do you know this is all true?"

Semyon crossed himself quickly three times. "That's what I heard, Excellency, I swear it!" Then, speedily, he shuffled out of the cell.

This time Alexander did not hold back. He buried his face in the pillow and shook with dry sobs.

Dawn broke, and then another, and one by one the prisoners were taken out of their cells past his door, their leg irons clanking, echoing in the corridor, and still he was not told when he was to be sent to Siberia. Then, two weeks after the execution, the door to his cell was flung open, and silhouetted against the mid-day's light, an angel stood on the threshold. It had to be an angel.

"Irina," he whispered. Spellbound, he moved toward her, and after Semyon had closed the door, she fell to her knees and, bowing to the ground, kissed his leg irons. Then she rose, and he looked at her face, contorted in a forced smile, tears running down her cheeks, and he looked and looked, memorizing every line of her beloved face to last him forever.

His mind screamed: *Why did you come, why did you come? It would have been easier if you hadn't, for then your face would have become a dream, a dream to nourish me in the years to come!*

Aloud he said nothing.

With her in his arms, the physical contact was a piercing pain, an unquenched, burning thirst, and he held her tightly to him, afraid to let go and break down.

"I wrote," she said, "but they told me only now that you weren't allowed to receive any letters."

Her mouth quivered. "Oh, my darling, we have a son. Our Sasha! He's a good, healthy boy. A beautiful little Alexander!"

"A boy! Sasha," Alexander whispered slowly. "You will bring him up not to hate me, I know!"

He hadn't meant to say it, but the words slipped out,

hung in the air. Irina backed away a little, reached up and took his face in her hands, and looked at him with eyes full of love and pain.

"You know I'll do my best with him." She spoke rapidly. "He will be my whole life. I'll tell him about you when he is old enough to understand. . . . About everything. And you, my dear . . . How are you? You must tell me what you will need when—when you get there. I'll send you food, money, clothes!"

"I won't need much for myself, *golubka*. I'm one of the luckier ones, for they told me I'll be resettled in Irkutsk, which is not as remote as some of the other places."

"How are you going to live? What are you going to do? I wish I could spare you this humiliation!" Irina's voice rose, and she blinked rapidly to hold back her tears.

"I'm not afraid of being humbled. Only my own dishonest or shameful deeds could ever destroy me. I thought I'd contact our village elder's brother in Kyakhta. Maybe he'll let me join him in the tea trading business with the Chinese in Maimachin. Remember how he saved Ossip from a lashing and then wanted to take him to Siberia? He told me then that the merchants run caravans regularly to Irkutsk. So you see, I have a link. I'll manage."

The words sounded hollow, and they both knew it. The most important, the most excruciating truth hung between them unsaid: They were seeing each other for the last time. A few more minutes, and she would be gone forever. Forever! He couldn't accept it. Not yet. The ache, the longing, would crush him, and he was sure that if he voiced his pain, he would not be able to bear it.

So he stood there, holding Irina in his arms, wanting to tell her how sorry he was for his actions, for the things he believed in—no, that was not true—for the things that had not worked out, for causing her such hurt, for leaving her to a life of pseudowidowhood with a husband disgraced and in exile, for their son who would not know his father.

But he said none of these things, only held her to him, clinging to the seconds and minutes that were slipping away. He was afraid to kiss her, to revive the taste of her mouth, to feel the delicate softness of her lips; but she sought his mouth, and he lost himself for a long moment, desperate to capture this memory for all eternity.

The awful reality would not go away. This was the last time he would hold her supple body in his arms, the final touch. Never, never again would he see this beloved face or brush the glistening tears from those loving eyes. Nor would he hear the music of her voice as she read a poem, nor laugh together, nor watch the shadow on her cheek below the lowered lashes, nor wake up in the morning with her silky hair spread across his pillow. . . . Never!

Maybe death was better after all—no more agony of separation, years of struggling to exist without her. . . .

A bleak and dreaded future stretched endlessly before him.

He could not bear to see her leave the cell, to watch the heavy, grinding door clang shut behind her. His arms lost their strength, and abruptly he released her. She did not question him but seemed to sense the reason for this sudden change. He turned, and the only sound in the cell was the heavy clanking of his leg irons as he moved toward the wall and, closing his eyes, leaned against it with his hands.

When at last he dared turn around, she was gone.

Irina didn't tell him she had petitioned the tsar for permission to follow her husband into exile.

Thank God his imprisonment was now over. When the one-legged fortress commandant, Sukin, met her at the entrance, she had sensed from his stern and disapproving countenance that the experience awaiting her would not be easy and that it would take all her emotional resources not to break down in front of Alexander. Still, she was unprepared for what she saw. He looked so haggard, so distraught, so thin, and the sight of his leg chains shocked her. Quickly she realized that her visit only intensified his longing for her and had disturbed a kind of forced resignation he must have developed during those seven months without her, and she felt selfish for having gone to see him.

The next day she left for Dolovino to await the tsar's permission and to plan her departure. Already Princess Trubetskaya, her cheerful, gentle friend Katasha, had received permission to follow her husband and had left for Siberia, and Princess Marie Volkonskaya, the strong, willful beauty, was waiting to hear from the tsar. If these wives, whose husbands were sentenced to hard labor, were allowed to go to Siberia, surely she, too, could join her husband in his resettlement. Besides, Olga Radina had surprised her by telling her that she, too, had petitioned the tsar to follow Boris. Irina did not think Olga had that much strength of character, but in response to her silent surprise, Olga shrugged and said half apologetically, "What is there left for me to do without him, Irina? I might as well be near him. It can't be all that bad, and at least in four years when he is released, we'll start building a new life together." She smiled. "Irkutsk must have its own social life. After all, it's not a small village!"

But the authorities were unpredictable, and already there were whispers of indignation in St. Petersburg and Moscow salons of how appallingly unjust the sentences were, for many who had been only remotely involved in the plot had been sentenced to many years of hard labor, while some others who had been deeply implicated in the Union of Welfare had been acquitted. How could Irina be sure that she would not be forbidden to go to Siberia because her husband was not in prison and was free to take care of himself? No. She did not want to tell all this to Alexander. It would be cruel, inhuman, to raise his hopes and then, possibly, have them dashed. Much as she yearned to tell him that this was not the final good-bye, she dared not.

In her unfailing optimism she was already secretly planning her journey and the life she would make for Alexander. They would rear their little son in a wholesome environment, away from the glitter and treachery of the capital. So her thoughts ran.

Only the faithful Nyanya was taken into her confidence, while she waited, and the serene, loyal woman understood. Tears flowed freely down her wrinkled face, but she said not a word and, picking up Irina's hands, kissed them in silent approval.

But no word came from the Winter Palace. Nikita wrote that the tsar was alarmed by the number of wives petitioning for permission to follow their husbands. Faced with the prospect of these aristocratic women who were ready to sacrifice everything and subject themselves to unknown hardships for which they were totally unprepared, the tsar vacillated.

Irina read and reread her brother-in-law's letters and busied herself with little Sasha. He was her joy and comfort, her plump and feisty baby, kicking his chubby legs and gurgling happily at the sight of her. Oh, how she adored him!

Weeks and months slipped by, and then, early in November, both Irina and Olga received the august permission to leave for Siberia. Irina read the official document with unconcealed excitement, tears of relief filling her eyes, until she came to the end of the page. There she stared at the words, and her breath caught in her throat.

A moment later she heard her own keening wail. "Aaaaah!" she cried. It came from the depths of her heart, wrenching her being with a fierce, primeval denial.

There was a condition. A terrible condition. By royal command, all the women allowed to follow their husbands into exile had to leave their children behind forever.

Chapter Eleven

There comes a point in human endurance when the mind refuses to accept any more stress, shuts out all outside impulses, and withdraws into an inner world.

And so it was with Irina. She spent hours by the side of her child's crib. Her agony was such that she found herself incapable of moving or talking or making decisions. No one in the household could understand the sudden change in her. Her mother-in-law wanted to call in the family doctor, for, the princess said, her listlessness and weakness were the first signs of consumption. Irina shook her head and stayed in the nursery with little Sasha. Only her *nyanya* knew and grieved with her, stroking her head and feeding her from a spoon as she would a child.

Over and over Irina tortured herself with arguments. Where could she find the courage, the strength to abandon her own baby? Never again to see his sweet smile, or hold him to her heart, or feel the plump arms circle her neck! She would be deprived of the supreme experience of her child's love as he grew up, and what about Sasha's deep hurt when he would ask about his parents and discover that his mother had abandoned him?

But then Sasha would never know his mother, and thus his hurt would not be as great as hers. He would enjoy his grandmother's love, which she surely would lavish on him in his mother's absence. She alone would carry the burden of loss. . . . And so these thoughts went around and around, without answers, without consolation.

It was either that or give up Alexander. But that was intolerable, unthinkable. He was alone, he needed her, and her love for him would overcome all obstacles along the way.

At last, she announced her decision to join Alexander in Siberia. Her parents knew the futility of trying to dissuade her from going, and Irina was grateful for their support. The strong, forceful Countess Radina held back tears, blessed Irina, and told her always to count on their moral and material support.

At home in Dolovino her news did not meet with equal acceptance. Princess Dolovina wept, begged, and finally appealed to Irina's sense of duty to little Sasha, hinting that her loyalty was misplaced and that she belonged near her son. When at last convinced that Irina's decision was irrevocable, she pleaded with her to wait at least until spring.

"Why such a hurry, Irina? Surely Alexander can manage without you for a few more months. Think of the hardships along your way, the long days that you must travel in a sleigh. The Siberian roads are primitive and dangerous. No woman of our milieu would venture to travel on them. There are versts and versts of snow-covered nothingness, and what if the sleigh breaks down in the middle of that vastness? I have heard there are packs of hungry, marauding wolves in the country-side in winter." The princess shuddered, her eyes shiny with unshed tears. "The temperatures are now forty, fifty below zero. Why not wait?"

But Irina could not bring herself to admit to her mother-in-law that the longer she stayed, the deeper her attachment to Sasha would become, and the harder it would be for her to leave him.

It was worse with Prince Gregory. Her father-in-law raged.

"You're placing a double stain of shame upon my head and the name of Dolovin! Not only did my son disgrace me, but now you think that it is noble and honorable to follow him into a life that can bring you only humiliation and degradation. You carry our name now, and your first duty is to atone for your husband's treason by showing your loyalty to the tsar, to your family, and, above all, to the new Dolovin growing up in our midst. What kind of mother are you to abandon your infant son and follow his irresponsible father?"

Irina listened silently. Strange, how unaffected she was by her father-in-law's words. She knew without a doubt that what she was doing was right, that following her husband was the ultimate, the highest, sacrifice of love. Nothing could shake her convictions now.

Against her silence Prince Gregory stormed. "I'll disown you! I won't send you a kopeck, and I'll forbid my wife to communicate with you! You and Alexander can rot in hell out there for all I care!"

"I'm not going to beg you for anything, *mon père*," Irina said. "As long as Sasha is well cared for and is protected by the loving arms of Maman, I shall be content. As for Alexander, I'll go to the end of the earth to be with him"—her voice rose—"I'll follow him to the moon and beyond!"

"You're being melodramatic and childish, Irina! I wash my hands of you!"

Irina fought for composure. "Let God and your conscience be your judge!" she cried, and walked quickly from the room.

Toward the end of December, as she went on with the preparations for her departure doggedly, methodically, and it became obvious that nothing would change her mind, Prince Gregory relented. One day he called her in to his study and announced coldly, his eyes focused on some point above her head. "Contrary to what you may think, I do have a conscience and even a sentiment. You are a misguided fool to go ahead with your plans, and I consider your motives immature. But I cannot let you suffer greater hardships through my neglect. Because of that, I shall be sending you money regularly until you establish yourselves in Irkutsk. I want to make one thing clear: I'm doing this for you, not for Alexander. He is lucky to have escaped hard labor, and I hope he will be grateful to the tsar for his clemency. As for myself, I shall never forgive him, and you may tell him that."

He lowered his eyes and met her glance for the first time since she entered the room. "As for you, I have done this: I'm sending Ossip with you to Irkutsk."

Irina stiffened. "Not unless you make him a free man first. I won't have him with me as a serf."

Prince Gregory pursed his lips. "You drive a hard bargain, daughter-in-law. But . . . have your way!"

Irina could not bring herself to show gratitude to her father-in-law beyond a whispered thank-you. Too much bitterness had passed between them for her to feel anything more than sadness at the irreparable rift that her father-in-law had created between them. But in her heart she was relieved that at least the financial burden was lifted from her and that dependable, loyal Ossip was going to accompany her on the arduous journey.

At last, all preparations were finished, but there was one more thing she wanted to do. Because Ossip was going to Siberia, because he was now a free man and Agasha was still a serf living among strangers, Irina wanted to see her.

To Irina's surprise, her mild-mannered, gentle mother-in-law objected.

"It's below your dignity, *ma chère*," she said quietly, "to make the trip to our neighbors' estate for the specific purpose of visiting a serf girl. What will our friends think? In the summer you could use going for a ride as an excuse, but the weather now is such that one avoids going out. There's enough disgrace on our roof already without adding to it!"

"Maman, how can you worry about this minor embarrassment when your son has been in prison and in leg chains for seven months? He's been sent to Siberia for life, you'll never see him again, and you speak of shame?" Irina's voice shook with anger, but the older woman stood firm.

"My dear child," she said sadly, "there's nothing I can do about Alexander. You see, I learned years ago that it is easier on my nerves to dismiss a problem that I'm unable to solve than to agonize over it. Inability to suppress heartache is the worst kind of agony."

"I'm sure I don't understand your kind of philosophy, Maman," Irina said. "To shut out my problem would mean abandoning the man I love, condemning him to loneliness and hardships and Lord only knows what mental anguish. I couldn't live with my guilt. I'm his wife, and it's my duty to be by his side and lighten his burden in whatever way I can."

"Alexander is reaping the fruit of the seeds he himself has sown. It was his own choice. What about the child you are abandoning? You speak of duty and guilt; those are strong words. Shouldn't you feel an even greater sense of guilt for condemning your child to a life without his mother to love and guide him?"

"I know, Maman! The choice was dreadful." Irina's voice broke. "Surely you must know that. But by the same token, I cannot understand your rejection of Alexander. He's your child, your firstborn. Does the parable of the prodigal son have no meaning for you then? The church and the prayers we say—are they all a farce?"

Princess Dolovina rose from her chair and straightened up very slowly. Irina thought: *She has become so thin, so fragile and shaky. Like a willow reed. But the reed does not break. Whipped by the force of the wind, it only bends!*

In the soft light of the overcast morning the princess's face was drawn and sallow. "What do you know about my heart, Irina? How can you possibly know what goes on inside my soul? Do you think I dismissed my son from my life with a snap of my fingers? Do you? Answer me, do you?"

Slowly, piteously the older woman's shoulders began to shake. "I've dismissed him from thoughts, I told you. I *had* to, to keep my sanity. What else could I do? My spirit is vanquished."

Princess Dolovina paused. Her eyes came around and fastened on the miniature of Alexander hanging on the wall by her bedside. Irina waited, and for a few moments neither spoke. Then her mother-in-law turned to Irina, tears streaming down her face, her lips quivering. "You know, I—I'm glad you'll be with Alexander! I tell you, the heart remembers, and at night sleep is elusive. So I guess we must grapple with our problems in our own special ways."

In one impulsive movement Irina was by her mother-in-law's side and embracing her. "Maman, oh, Maman, why were we born women? Appendages to men, subordinate to their wills, unequal in the partnership of marriage!"

Princess Dolovina pulled away. "Shhhhh! What are you saying, child? We mustn't question God's laws! And this is why I asked you not to make the trip to see Agasha. What is to be gained by it? Only more pain . . . more pain!"

"I want to go, Maman. I *must*. Don't make it harder for me than it already is. Please! In my small way I feel I am doing something."

For a few moments the two women looked at each other in silence. Then Princess Dolovina nodded her head slowly and sighed. "I do understand. We older mothers think we can save our children from pain, protect them. We think we are wiser, more experienced. But in truth, are we? Just because we've lived longer doesn't make us wiser. You're young, resilient, and perhaps when you see Agasha, you will gain some insight into the scheme of things, and the pity you feel for the girl will balance your own pain."

The older woman put her arms around the younger one and pressed her gently to her chest. "Go then, Irina, do what you feel you must do. Just remember: Sort things out in your heart; weigh them and put them in their proper perspective; otherwise the burdens you invite will overwhelm you."

Agasha lived with her infant son, Vanya, in the Flügel adjacent to the manor, together with other servants of the household. Thank God she was not in the village, Irina thought as she sat in Agasha's tiny room. Aloud she said, "I'm glad you're working in the main house, Agasha, and not out in the fields and living with a strange family in an izba."

Agasha nodded and smiled. "I'm glad, too, Barynia; it makes my loneliness a little easier to bear. I miss everyone at Dolovino. It was my home since I was born. I knew nothing else. . . ." Her voice trailed, then picked up again. "But it could have been much worse. My masters are kind and have not forced me to marry anyone. I am glad for that."

"I came to tell you again, Agasha, how sorry I am that I could not keep you from being sold."

"It would have made no difference, Barynia. Ossip has turned away from me, and in a way it would have been worse if I had stayed at Dolovino."

"Ossip was hurt, Agasha, that's all. He would have gotten over it in time."

Agasha shook her head. "No, Barynia. Don't you see? I'm damaged goods now."

"How can you be so calm and meek about the injustice dealt you?" Irina asked.

Agasha spread her hands. *"Shto dyelat?"*

And there, Irina thought bitterly, was the age-old Russian phrase of resignation, "What to do?" Was she, her former mistress, any better?

As if reading her thoughts, Agasha said, "And you, Barynia, can you accept the hardships awaiting you in Siberia?"

Irina nodded. "Yes, Agasha. I must. I guess in some ways we have much in common. The only difference between you and me is that I still rebel against injustice, even though I cannot change anything."

"God bless you and protect you, Barynia. Yours is a saintly mission, and I shall pray for you."

"Ossip has been given his freedom by Prince Gregory, and he is going with me to Siberia. Do you have any message for him?"

Agasha lowered her gaze and studied her hands. "Tell him that I wish him well, Barynia."

"I'm sure he still cares for you, Agasha."

The girl shrugged. "What good will it do, Barynia? He's now a free man who'll be living with you in Siberia, and I am still a serf in Russia. Besides, there is this muzhik here in the village who comes to see me now and then. I like him, and he likes me and my child. What more could I want?"

Agasha's simple logic was indisputable, yet Irina chafed at the girl's acquiescence to her fate. "Put things in their proper perspective," Princess Dolovina had said that morning. Yes, Irina thought, all other emotions would have to be subordinate to her first, her most important mission in life.

She could hardly dwell on the thought that she was leaving behind all reminders of her serene and carefree childhood and all too brief happiness at Dolovino. And before she left, there was one more ordeal to endure. Marie Volkonskaya's sister-in-law, Zinaida, had invited Irina and Olga to a farewell party she was giving in Moscow for Marie. Though Olga wanted to go, Irina felt it was a macabre reason to have a party. More like a wake, she thought, but she went because she didn't want to hurt Marie Volkonskaya's feelings.

Zinaida Volkonskaya's residence at 14 Tverskaya Street in Moscow was an imposing mansion with tall pillars and white marble steps leading to the grand entrance. As Irina climbed those steps, she wondered if Olga and Marie were as painfully aware as she was that this would be the last time they would attend an elegant reception, the last time they would enjoy the luxurious surroundings of a sumptuous home.

Alexander Pushkin was present, and Irina had difficulty holding back her tears as she looked at the familiar features of this famous poet with his reddish-brown curly hair and dark skin, which he had inherited from his Abyssinian ancestor Abram Hannibal, favorite of Peter the Great. She admired Pushkin's genius greatly, and as his brooding gaze found hers, she tried to smile.

"You may not believe me," he said earnestly, "but I envy you ladies. A life of self-sacrifice and heroism awaits you, and you'll be living among the best men of our times, while we—we'll be the poorer for it!"

Irina was afraid her voice would break and whispered a barely audible thank-you. Pushkin turned to Marie

Volkonskaya. "I've written a poem to the prisoners; it starts with these lines:

> In the depths of Siberian mines
> Guard your proud patience. . . ."

Irina didn't hear Marie's reply, for music and singing sounded behind her; their thoughtful hostess, aware of Marie's love of them, had invited musicians and singers to entertain her sister-in-law, and soon Zinaida herself began to sing. She chose the aria from *Agnese* by Paer, in which a tragic daughter begs her father's forgiveness.

How unfortunate is her choice of the aria, Irina thought. Zinaida must not have known that Marie's father had forbidden his daughter to follow her husband into exile and that Marie was leaving without his blessing or approval. Anxiously Irina looked at Marie. Tears trickled down the dark-haired beauty's cheeks, and abruptly Zinaida stopped singing and called for the others to join in a cheerful folk song instead. Irina's heart began to beat rapidly. She was suffocating. She had to get out of there. Pulling a reluctant Olga behind her, she slipped out of the mansion and down those white marble steps she knew she would never see again.

Two days later Irina and Olga accompanied by the faithful Ossip, left Moscow on their long trek to Irkutsk. They would travel by day and stay overnight at relay stations. At the rear of their kibitka a frame of poles, covered with a net of thick rope, supported their trunks, and they carried their own mattresses, for they were advised that the station beds were often full of bedbugs.

Bundled in fur-lined coats and boots, their legs wrapped in fur throws, the three travelers sat in silence as the sleigh pulled out of the Dolovino estate. Irina did not look back. She had said her farewells the day before and had asked that no family members see her off on the morning of her departure. She couldn't cope with any last-minute tears. Nor could she go into the nursery one last time. There would be Sasha's lace-covered cradle, his *mishka*—stuffed bear—tucked in the corner, his toys, and Sasha himself with his welcoming, toothless smile, reaching his arms toward her to be picked up. No. She couldn't go in.

She carried a tiny miniature of him in her locket against her heart, and someday, maybe, she would be able to look at it without crying. Right now she had to fill her mind with thoughts of Alexander, alone in Irkutsk, unaware that she was on her way to join him. She must concentrate on the happiness she hoped to bring him.

All else must wait.

PART II

THE VANQUISHED

Chapter Twelve

Everything in life was relative, Alexander concluded. It would have been laughable to tell him after his sentence that he would ever be resigned to his fate. But here he was, living in reasonable comfort in a large izba in Irkutsk, earning a living he never would have thought possible.

It had been terrible for him in the beginning. Of all the hardships and deprivations, the loss of his wife and child was the worst of all. There was no turning back, and he saw his future as one humiliating lonely experience after another.

Upon his arrival in Irkutsk he was taken directly to Governor Tseidler's office to receive further orders. Although the governor treated him politely, the absence of deference to his rank—a deference he had been accustomed to all his life—was glaringly obvious, and Alexander braced himself for further shocks after this encounter with a man who, under different circumstances, would have treated him with the respect due an aristocrat.

He listened in a daze to the long list of instructions of what he was and was not allowed to do, and while he chafed at being restricted in his freedom to travel wherever he pleased, he kept reminding himself that he was luckier than his comrades; they were living in leg chains in prison and working at hard labor in the remote Blagodatsk mine near Nerchinsky Zavod, some 900 versts east of Irkutsk. Perversely, however, he wondered, as he had in his cell long ago, if they were not better off emotionally than he, for they had one another for companionship and a thread with the past on which they could feed their souls, while he had been thrown alone into an alien—to him—world, totally unprepared for the harsh realities of life there.

Once inside the log cabin which he was able to rent for three and a half rubles a month with the money he had been allowed to bring with him, he discovered that its interior differed little from that of the izbas of his father's serfs. Although officially stripped of his noble rank, Alexander had naïvely hoped that the governor would invite him to his home and accept him socially. After all, he reasoned, he was not a prisoner; he could move about and make his own living and, in a way, was a free citizen in that area. But no such invitation came, and soon Alexander knew that he would have to make his own way in Irkutsk. Very quickly he realized that before trying to reach his contact in Kyakhta, he had to get a housekeeper. He was told that the quickest way to find one was outside the city among the nomadic Buryats, who lived primitively in yurts tending cattle and would welcome extra income by giving up one of their unmarried girls into domestic service.

Alexander hired a droshky and rode to the Buryat camp. A dozen round-domed felt yurts were scattered on flat grassland. Sheep were grazing nearby, and a few children, dressed in loose pants and belted shirts, were playing on the ground. A canvas-lined felt flap covered the entrance to the nearest yurt, and while Alexander stood before it, perplexed about how to announce his arrival, the flap moved, and a dark-complexioned Buryat with deep furrows on his weather-beaten face came out and squinted at Alexander. He was dressed in a knee-length cotton gown, belted with a sash decorated with coral beads, and loose pants tucked into pointed felt shoes. His quilted hat had a turned-up brim and came to a peak in the center. On seeing Alexander, the man took off his hat and bowed. His black hair, pulled tight to the top of his head, was braided into a short and thin queue that now bounced freely as he bent his head.

"To what do I owe the honor of your visit, sir?" the man asked in slightly accented Russian.

"I need a domestic servant and was told to come here," Alexander replied, not a little surprised to hear good Russian spoken by the exotic-looking Buryat.

The man bowed again and, opening the felt flap, invited Alexander inside.

Alexander's first sensation upon entering was one of choking. In the center of the yurt a cast iron pot hung suspended from a tripod over a brazier of smoldering wood. The smell of cooking mutton combined with smoke was overpowering. Involuntarily he looked up at a small opening through which only a little of the smoke was able to escape. Almost immediately Alexander's eyes began to smart, and he squinted, curious to study the dark and crowded interior. A series of wooden trellises held together by braids of lambs, wool and horsehair were attached to wooden stakes and twigs that were bent into a semicircle to form a dome-shaped dwelling.

In one corner of the yurt stood an altar, a small red-painted multitiered chest, on top of which sat a few gilded Buddhist idols. Alexander noted that a number of brass bowls filled with water, grain, and flour cakes were placed on each tier. A bell rested by one of the bowls.

As Alexander blinked to keep his eyes from tearing, the Buryat man called, "Marya! Come over here!"

A short girl emerged from a dark corner of the yurt and came forward. Her shiny black hair was pulled off her face and braided tightly in the back, exposing a high forehead and dark, arched brows. Almond-shaped eyes sparkled boldly as she looked at Alexander with unabashed curiosity. There was something ingenuous and warm about the girl, and as he looked at her, the Buryat said, "She is my daughter and would welcome living in town. You can take her with you now!"

Taken aback, Alexander explained that he had only a modest izba with two rooms and had hoped that Marya could go home nights, but the Buryat said it would be much more convenient for everyone if Marya stayed with him in the izba even if it meant sleeping on the floor.

And so it was that Marya moved into Alexander's izba and slept on a cot near the big stove. She cleaned and cooked for him and stayed out of his way as much as possible. On the first day he watched as she took down the vigil light container that hung suspended from the ceiling in the right corner of the room before an icon of the Lord. She emptied it, cleaned and refilled it with water and oil, and put in a fresh wick. Alexander was curious.

"Marya," he asked, remembering the altar in her yurt, "aren't you a Buddhist?"

Marya, who was standing on a taboret, replacing the red container in its filigreed holder, stepped down.

"Yes, Your Grace," she said, wiping her hands on her apron and then showing him an amulet of coral that hung on a black ribbon around her neck. "I always wear this. But there are many of us who are Christians, so I am familiar with your customs and rituals."

"What is this red band you have across your shoulder?" Alexander asked.

"It is to show that I have given a vow not to eat unclean meat, such as pork and camel," Marya replied.

Her voice was soft and melodious, and suddenly, as Alexander looked at her cheerful, sparkling eyes, her smile blurred before him, and for a fleeting moment Irina's green eyes shone from the Buryat girl's face. A knot tightened in the pit of his stomach. With a soft moan he buried his head in his arms.

His life had ended. What sort of existence would this be in his peasant abode, served by a Buryat girl in a harsh world, living and working in a strange and unknown territory? Inconceivable. Given the circumstances, how could he possibly retain his identity? His birthright was now a farce. But he must not forget that his name was Alexander Dolovin. Nothing more was left to him.

As he shook his head in grief, he felt a delicate touch of massaging fingers on his neck, gentle at first, then pressing deeper, kneading tense muscles at the base of his head—soothing, relaxing. Almost without realizing it, he sensed that the past had to be pocketed, dismissed, and that it was time to think of the future. Alexander raised his head and looked at the girl standing beside him, her almond eyes watching him with compassion. She had been born and reared in this area; she might be able to teach him things he needed to know. Choosing his words carefully, he told her of the village elder on his father's estate whose brother, Igor Panfilov, was in the tea trading business in Kyakhta and needed a partner. Marya listened silently and then said that her uncle Stepan was a contact man in Kyakhta and had lived there for many years, trading with the Chinese.

"You should seek him out," she concluded, "he knows everyone in Maimachin."

A few days later Alexander set out for Kyakhta.

Marya told him where to look for Stepan and added, "There are no hotels in Kyakhta; my uncle told me once that no strangers are allowed to stay there overnight; but there are lodging houses in neighboring Troitskosavsk, which is only about three versts away, and they are registered with the police master. You pay for staying in these lodging houses as you would in any hotel."

Alexander found Kyakhta to be a small town of fewer than 1,000 people, a cluster of modest wooden houses in a sandy terrain. A five-spired stone cathedral stood on elevated ground, and Alexander turned toward the church. He stood on its hill and surveyed the panorama before him.

Houses and fences seemed freshly scrubbed and clean, and about 200 to 300 yards beyond he could see the curved roofs of the neighboring Chinese town of Maimachin, its tall gate towers colorfully painted with dragons.

After saying a prayer inside a richly decorated church, he went into town, only to learn that Igor Panfilov was away on vacation. However, he had no difficulty finding Marya's uncle, whose modest house stood at the end of the main street. It consisted of two small rooms, the front one sparsely furnished with wooden benches, a table, and a large cupboard.

A fat Buryat introduced himself as Marya's uncle Stepan and greeted Alexander courteously enough, but his narrow eyes shifted and blinked and never once lingered on Alexander's. A crafty man, Alexander thought. He told him who he was and what he wanted, but before Stepan could answer, the door opened, and a tall Chinese dressed in a long blue gown walked in. His bearing was erect, and when Stepan introduced him as Chien Yung-lin, a prominent merchant from Maimachin, the Chinese, whose arms were folded inside his wide sleeves, dropped them to his sides and bowed slowly.

As the Chinese began to barter with Stepan over an exchange of tea for articles of Russian manufacture, Alexander listened in fascination to Chien Yung-lin's slightly lilting but fluent Russian. After the deal had been made, Chien Yung-lin declined an invitation to stay for tea, and Alexander guessed that he was anxious to leave, for his slim hands were clasped tightly together the whole time he talked to Stepan.

After he had left, Stepan offered Alexander tea. As they sipped the hot liquid, the Buryat studied his guest with narrowed eyes. "You need to put money into this business if you want to be a merchant and not a go-between like I am, working on commission," he said slowly.

"How much would I need to start?" Alexander asked.

Stepan shrugged. "That depends. How much do you wish to buy? One chest of tea officially costs twenty rubles, but unofficially we pay about eighty rubles. Our customshouse is in Troitskosavsk; the officials there know of our transactions, but they look at it through their fingers. It's a lot easier to work for commission, I tell you. I make about one ruble sixty kopecks on each chest. Not bad, eh?" He winked and slapped Alexander on the shoulder.

Alexander suppressed a wince. "I didn't see you pass any money to the Chinese merchant," he said.

"Of course not! Our imperial law forbids any exchange of coins, and we aren't allowed even to melt them. So we get our silver directly from the mines and then cast it into various figurines and idols for the Chinese." Stepan guffawed. "They don't buy them for our artisans' work! They weigh the idols and trade the tea for the weight they get in silver. Clever, eh?"

Alexander was aghast. "But that's dishonest! What's wrong with trading in legal merchandise?"

"Because we need much more of their tea than they need our furs, just like we have little use for their cotton and silk or porcelain figurines. Who needs them? Anyway, they want silver, and we give them what they want."

"But then how do you get around customs?"

"Simple. We must show our trading goods first, and give them the price of twenty rubles a chest of tea. The real price is then traded by us in silver."

As Alexander absorbed this bit of information, another thought struck him as strange. "Do you speak Chinese as well as this merchant speaks Russian?" he asked.

Stepan dismissed the question with a wave of his hand. "Naw! They all speak good Russian. Let them study our language. Why should we bother to learn theirs? We do have a school here in Kyakhta to teach us Chinese, but no one finds it necessary to learn. Chien Yung-lin's visit today was unusual; you see, the Chinese merchants almost always come here in groups. They discuss their bargains between themselves, and those who don't speak too well have someone among them who can. As a matter of fact, Chien Yung-lin told me that only merchants who speak Russian are allowed to live in Maimachin."

Alexander thought for a moment, then said quietly, "Perhaps they are smarter than we are after all."

"What do you mean?" Stepan's voice sounded defensive.

"I mean that they understand everything you say, yet they are able to discuss prices among themselves in front of you without your knowing what they are saying!"

Stepan shrugged. "I get my commission and live well. Beyond that, who cares?"

"What happens when you go to Maimachin and are entertained in their homes by their families?"

"They have no families in Maimachin, and we are rarely asked there. As a rule, we are only invited to Maimachin during their so-called White Month festivities, when they celebrate their New Year. Their women live in Urga because their government is afraid that they would move over across the border and never go back!"

A sly smile played on Stepan's lips. "I guess their women's lot is not an enviable one. I understand they are never allowed to meet men outside their own clans and never leave their courtyards except in covered sedan chairs, so no one ever sees them."

There was nothing more to say, and Alexander left. He did not want to work on commission. He would return to Irkutsk and see how much money he could gather together to start modestly. Besides, he had to come to terms with trading in silver, a practice that was definitely designed to skirt the law. A whole new world it was, and he wasn't sure he could adjust to it.

Outside Stepan's house he saw a camel caravan move slowly along the street, its heavy load of chests covered in rawhide. Each one represented eighty rubles' worth of silver. Where would he get so much money to begin his business? he wondered. Deep in thought, he had started up the street when a familiar figure emerged from a neighboring house. It was Chien Yung-lin. Ceremoniously the Chinese joined his hands before his face and bowed. "What brings the illustrious nobleman to our humble trading towns?"

Surprised, Alexander asked, "How do you know who I am?"

Chien Yung-lin closed his eyes, and a gentle smile touched his mouth. "It is enough to look at the honored gentleman to know who he is."

Alexander flushed. "I am—I came to learn about the tea trading business."

Chien Yung-lin raised one brow. "There is much to learn. Stepan is experienced and knowledgeable, but a wise man must always keep his own counsel."

Alexander understood. Chien Yung-lin was warning him about Stepan. "Do you know Igor Panfilov?" he asked.

"A fine man. It is a pleasure to do business with him. Does the honored gentleman know him?"

In spite of Chien Yung-lin's foreign attire of blue silk gown with full sleeves, his slanted eyes, and the queue at the back of his head, Alexander felt a sudden kinship to this Chinese man, who had gentle manners and an aristocratic bearing. He wanted to talk to him, needed to talk to him. And as if the Chinese had sensed that need, he led Alexander through the crowded street to the edge of town, where they sat down on a bench and conversed.

The September air was cool and filled with laughter and the staccato sounds of Chinese voices. A homey fragrance of burning wood wafted toward them. Near where they sat, ten or twelve men worked at the open door of a warehouse, sewing rawhide around the packed tea chests.

"This is a good source of income for the local populace," Chien Yung-lin said. "The merchants feel—and rightfully so—that the best way to protect tea from the elements is to enclose the chests in rawhide, which they get from the Transbaikal region. Many merchants started in the trade business by earning money this way or through commissions from well-established tradesmen in Irkutsk."

"Do you know Irkutsk?" Alexander asked.

Chien Yung-lin inclined his head slowly. "Yes, I have many occasions to visit there on business. It is an important city and has many cultural events during the year."

"Have you lived in Maimachin a long time?"

"I left my clan in Urga seven months ago," Chien Yung-lin replied.

Alexander studied the Chinese curiously. "It must be a strange existence to live in a town populated entirely by men. Do you visit your family in Urga often?"

"When I was orphaned, my father's friend took me into his clan and reared me. He arranged my marriage, and a year and a half after my wife had died, he suggested I move to Maimachin and conduct his business here."

"I see. You must be happy to be away from sad memories in Urga."

Chien Yung-lin did not answer at once. With the pointed toe of his black silk shoe, he traced a hieroglyph in the sandy earth, then said, "What is happiness? A restless bird. One must keep it caged lest it fly away forever. My heart remains always in the courtyards of my clan in Urga."

"I understand fully. I, too, have lost my wife, even though she is still alive." The moment he said it, Alexander realized how strange it must sound to the Chinese. He hastened to explain. Chien Yung-lin listened in silence until he finished.

"Yours is a tragic story, honored gentleman, and the nobility of your spirit fills me with awe. My sorrow, on the other hand, is not for my departed wife, but for someone who is still living."

Alexander waited for an explanation, and when none came, he rose and thanked the Chinese for his company.

For the rest of his stay in Kyakhta, Alexander could not get the man our of his mind. There was a sadness about him, a hint of tragedy buried deep that he was not prepared to share, even though Alexander had told him about himself. But Chien Yung-lin impressed him as a man of integrity, and Alexander could not understand how the Chinese reconciled his honor with accepting silver idols as payment for tea.

Before he left, Alexander asked him about it. Chien Yung-lin looked at him for a while in silence, then closed his eyes for a brief moment and inclined his head. "It doesn't matter to us in what form we get our payment," he said at last, "as long as it is silver or gold. It is not our business to ask where or how our Russian colleagues get it."

Alexander accepted Chien Yung-lin's explanation without comment. Everything was so new and foreign he needed time to ponder such logic. He returned to Irkutsk without meeting Igor Panfilov but determined to avoid dealing with Stepan as much as possible.

Over the next few months Alexander made several trips to Kyakhta, but as the weather turned cold, the journey took longer. The sandy earth around Kyakhta absorbed the snow, leaving none on the surface, and before reaching town, the sleigh had to be replaced by a coach on wheels. But the trips were well worth his time. Igor Panfilov, a young and cheerful man, accepted him as his partner and was invaluable in introducing him to the intricacies of dealing with the Chinese. Soon Alexander was able to borrow money from a wealthy merchant in Irkutsk and, in spite of the steep twenty percent interest, invested his own share in the business. Gradually he familiarized himself with the commercial and until now alien—to him—world, rationalized the transactions in silver as necessary, and began to make a modest living.

Loneliness, however, haunted him more and more, and he wondered how Chien Yung-lin was able to cope with it. Russian merchants had their wives and mistresses, but the Chinese lived a celibate existence in Maimachin. He could not understand it.

Marya served him well, mostly in a silent and subservient way, and when she did speak, it was in quiet, barely audible monosyllables. One night, after a particularly idle day, when the hours seemed to stretch into infinity and the wooden walls of his izba moved in to choke him, Alexander escaped to his bed earlier than usual, hoping to blot out his longing for Irina in dreamless oblivion.

But sleep would not come, and he tossed restlessly until the darkness became unbearable. Finally, he reached to light the candle by his bedside, and as he raised his head, there on the threshold stood Marya in a long white nightgown with a lighted candle in her hand.

Slowly Alexander sat up. In the flickering light of a single candle, Marya's smooth skin glowed like satin. Her dark eyes shone, reaching out, bridging the distance between them with what seemed to him a simple acceptance of what was inevitable, natural, and so long denied. He had not noticed before how perfectly shaped was her oval face, how chiseled her nose, how full her dark and parted lips.

The shadows in the dark room softened. The single candle flame grew to warm the air and stir the blood. Muted night sounds whispered.

Loneliness inflamed desire and was appeased.

Days slipped by imperceptibly, taking on a different hue in Alexander's life. Irina was lost to him forever, and he felt no guilt about his relationship with Marya. She made no demands on him, and he was comforted. Chien Yung-lin came to Irkutsk frequently, and the two men, their backgrounds so different, yet bound by a common bond of trade and loneliness, became friends, although neither confided in the other. Alexander found the Chinese reserved, and his manner invited no confidences. So be it, he thought. Perhaps it was easier not to talk about his personal tragedy, not to bring up Irina's name to the man who had never met her and possibly would not understand his inability to break with his past completely when there was no hope of a reunion.

He should not think about Irina, but her sparkling eyes, her carefree laughter, her teasing humor haunted him at the most inopportune times. In those moments he tortured himself with unanswered questions: How was she getting along without him? How long would she continue to love him before her heart would admit another? Then shame pierced his thoughts. What right did he have to think these things when he himself had another woman offering him a measure of comfort? But then, he was a man, and he didn't love Marya. Irina would always be his only love. Did she think about him as often as he did about her? How was she getting along at Dolovino?

The questions came, and there were no answers.

Chapter Thirteen

Irina and Olga had crossed the Urals and had started on the seemingly endless expanse of the Siberian steppe. As they passed through the narrow valleys of the gently sloping mountain range, Irina tried not to think that they were leaving behind European Russia, that the Urals were a dividing line between Russia, where everything was familiar, and Siberia, where everything was strange and unknown. The last sizable town had been Kazan, where they stayed overnight in a courtyard hotel, surrounded by several buildings. One of these was a clubhouse for nobility, and that night Irina watched with a twinge of envy as festively dressed couples entered the brightly lit building to attend a masquerade ball. Would she and Alexander ever dance again? How could she ever be carefree and gay when she had chosen a life without her child? How was her little Sasha? The gnawing guilt followed her relentlessly.

Travel was arduous, and their kibitka slid and bumped over the frozen ruts in the track, covering the versts between relay stations that were nothing more than tiny hamlets.

Ossip's concern for Irina's comfort was constant. He reacted to her every wish instantly, as though her life depended upon his prompt response to her requests. After the first few days it became apparent that Olga chafed at Ossip's presence.

"He should be riding outside with the coachman," Olga remarked, but Irina reminded her succinctly that Ossip was now a free man and, as such, was entitled to ride with them. "Remember," Irina added, "he didn't *have* to come with us. He sacrificed everything voluntarily to go to Siberia."

"Accompany *you,* you mean," Olga sniffed disdainfully, and Irina felt it wiser to drop the subject. Could it be that Olga was envious of Ossip's devotion? Well, so be it.

Over Ossip's objections, Irina insisted on traveling every day without taking a break. "We rest every twenty versts while we change horses, so why waste a day in between? Anyway, the best those hamlets have to offer is barley soup and black bread!"

Olga looked at her with an amused smile. "Your snobbery shows through, my dear. We're lucky to be fed at all!"

Irina flushed, realizing her blunder. The kibitka was sliding over some rough spots on the road, the jolts violent and frequent. "I see no reason to be on this wretched track any longer than we have to!" she said defensively.

Even in daylight, there wasn't much they could see along their way. Freezing winds blew frequently with such force that mounds of snow piled high between the cab and the coachman, and Ossip had to lower the bast flaps from the top of the kibitka to protect them from the fury of the gusts.

Somewhere in the depths of this hostile wilderness they stopped in the middle of the day to rest and have hot food at a posting station. In European Russia these buildings were pillared and well kept, and it seemed to Irina that the deeper they traveled into Siberia, the worse they became. This one was a small wooden house in a village with a handful of izbas.

Tired and weary, they savored the cabbage soup thick with buckwheat kasha and meat morsels, and after they had finished, a bureaucrat from the military governor's office in Irkutsk approached them. Fingering a greasy tobacco pouch dangling on his chest, he advised them to turn back before it was too late, for if they didn't, greater trials would await them. He told them that Princess Trubetskaya had been delayed in Irkutsk, waiting for permission to join her husband, that her personal belongings had been thoroughly searched and for months she had been subjected to harassment. She had been very lonely before she was finally allowed to join her husband.

Irina never thought that she would consider herself fortunate that Alexander was resettled in Irkutsk and that she would not have to be going any farther.

With their meal finished, Irina had risen to leave when the stationmaster recommended that they stay overnight.

"He wants to make money on us," Olga whispered to Irina. "It's still early in the day. I don't see why we shouldn't go on to the next posting station."

Irina agreed, but Ossip wavered. The stationmaster, a thickset man with a walrus mustache, shook his head. "Look at the sky, Princess. It is all gray, and the air is still. A sure forerunner of a snowstorm."

The coachman, a burly muzhik with merry eyes, who stood at the door, chuckled. "This doesn't look bad to me!"

Encouraged, Irina insisted on leaving. Every verst counted. Another few would bring her closer to her destination and Alexander.

Outside, there was nothing to see but the snow-covered steppe that stretched beyond the limits of her vision, into eternity. Both the overcast skies and the darkening blur of the earth merged in the distance, obliterating the horizon and coloring the world around them with a monochromatic hue. Ossip lowered the bast flaps again to keep the inside protected, and soon Irina dozed off.

She did not rest well, for the kibitka shuddered along the road, and a whistling wind whined, slapping the flaps against the sides of the coach. When she opened her eyes, it was dusk, and she could barely see Olga and Ossip.

"I guess the stationmaster knew what he was talking about," she said. "How far do you think to the next village?"

"It's hard to tell, Barynia," Ossip answered. "The horses have been slowing down, and I don't know whether it is because they are tired or because the storm is hampering their movements. Anyway, the stationmaster assured me that we have an expert coachman who knows how to handle the horses in a storm."

But even as Ossip was talking, Irina became aware that the horses had slowed to a walk. For a while no one spoke. The storm raged on, and the wind lashed at them for a long time before it finally subsided and then died down altogether.

Incongruously Olga giggled. "I'm so relieved the wind has stopped, Irina!" she said. "Frankly it frightened me. I thought we might have to stop in the middle of nowhere and we'd freeze to death. Wouldn't that be an ignominious end to our adventure?"

"Don't be silly," Irina said, trying to sound more confident than she felt. "I'm glad our coachman knows his way, though."

She turned to Ossip. "Ossip, could you take the coachman's place if for some reason he had to be replaced?"

She didn't know what prompted her to ask such a question, but Ossip responded immediately. "I'm sure we're not far from the next village, Barynia. Unless the storm has obliterated the road, I could certainly follow the track."

"Please lift the flap, Ossip. I want to see what it looks like outside," Olga said.

It was already dark, but the night was illuminated by the ethereal blue of a full moon. After the storm the stars seemed brighter and winked at them from a clear sky. A few stray clouds hung over the horizon, but they could have been mounds of snow in the distance—Irina could not tell—as she looked in fascination at the fluffy blue snow sparkling in the moonlight.

"How beautiful!" she whispered, loath to tear herself away from the luminous and virgin beauty around her. Olga tugged at her sleeve. "Irina, you'll get sick from this cold. The air is icy. Let's lower the flap. Please!"

But Irina kept looking at the awesome yet somehow serene sight. One giant aquamarine, she thought, crystal clear, translucent, untouched. Could such serenity ever enter where humans dwelled? She thought not. At last, reluctantly she sat back and let Ossip lower the flap. As he did so, a thin, distant sound reached her ears. So faint it was she wondered if she might have imagined it. She held her breath and listened.

A deep, plaintive wail came again, rising in its pitch, holding it, then dying in the air . . . only to be echoed by another wail . . . and yet another. A long-drawn-out, tremulous sound it was, piteous and rending and, in its very dolor, terrifying.

The howling of a pack of hungry wolves. Irina shuddered. How far away were they?

The coachman had heard it, too, for he was urging the horses on. Ossip raised the flap to look outside, and Irina looked over his shoulder. Somewhere behind them the howl intensified, grew louder and more restive. The beasts were getting closer. With rising panic Irina peered ahead, and there, on the horizon, blinked a handful of lights. Thank God, a village! Why, they were almost there! She sat back. They were near a village; they would soon be there . . . Surely they were almost there . . .

Olga whimpered. "Oh, God, we never should have left that last posting station!"

Irina grasped Olga's hand. Deafened by the blood pounding in her ears, she listened. The wolves were gaining on them, their howl now a guttural roar calling the chase. They had picked up the human scent. Terrified, the horses bolted and ran.

But the wolves ran faster.

In the hamlet the villagers had heard the wolves and had scurried to build bonfires. They talked among themselves and checked that no one was missing. What prey the wolves had caught was not of their concern. No human, they reasoned, would travel at night through the storm. So, they watched in amazement as the travelers' kibitka came into view; they crossed themselves and waited as it came to a stop at the first izba.

Frozen in horror, Irina had to be helped out of the coach. Olga sobbed and refused Ossip's supporting arm.

Behind them they had left the coachman to be torn to pieces by the hungry wolves, abandoned to death in the crimson snow. How could it have happened on that seemingly tranquil steppe?

Irina couldn't open her clenched teeth; if she did, she knew she would scream, echoing the screams she had heard back there. . . .

Dreadful it was, dreadful. The wolves had scratched at the sides of the kibitka, then rushed at the horses, but when a whip whistled through the air, the enraged animals yelped and snarled. A terrified scream came from the coachman. Ossip jumped out and, climbing the driver's seat, urged the horses on as the wolves pulled the coachman down. The kibitka shuddered, jerked forward, and the frightened horses took off, racing away from the beasts.

The coachman's screams had pursued them, piercing the air for a few rending seconds, then turned into a tortured howl that rose and fell and finally broke. It was then that Irina had clamped her teeth tight and covered her ears to muffle Olga's hysterical sobs.

Taken to a warm izba, Irina sat rigidly on a bench, her hands clasped on her knees, and watched as a peasant woman placed a bowl of steaming barley soup on the table. Face buried in his hands, Ossip ignored his food. Olga's cries, which had subsided somewhat, now started to rise again.

"Take yourself in hand!" the peasant woman ordered her. "You're no longer in Moscow to carry on in this fashion. Over here we fight for life the best way we know how, and if sometimes we lose, well—that's God's will."

But Olga continued to sob and whimper and was soon hysterical again. With a sudden swing of the arm the peasant woman slapped her. Olga's sob strangled in her throat. For a few moments she stared at the woman, then abruptly turned on Ossip.

"You!" she said, her eyes flashing. "*You* are responsible for the death of that poor man. Nothing is sacred to you except your precious mistress!"

Startled, Ossip raised his head. He started to say something, but Olga silenced him. "Don't you dare answer me back! You left the poor man to die, so you could save yourself. Coward! And you are stupid enough to think that I haven't noticed your arrogance and your attachment to Princess Dolovina. How dare you think of her in this way?"

Irina suppressed a gasp. Suddenly there was silence in the izba. The peasant woman stopped clearing the plates and, propping her sides with her fists, listened. Alarmed, Irina looked at Ossip. The young giant rose slowly to his feet. Towering over Olga, he clenched his fists and stared down at her.

An enraged bear, Irina thought. A dangerous, roused bear. He must surely want to strike Olga for her impudence. The poor man! His lifelong training of subservience was still holding his tongue and fist. She placed her hand on Olga's arm and patted it gently.

"Olga," she said, "we've all been through a terrible experience, but Ossip had to make a dreadful choice. It took tremendous courage, not cowardice, to leave a fellow human being behind, so others could live."

"Ossip," she said quietly, turning to him, "go ahead, say what you want to say. Remember, you are no longer a serf, and here, in this izba, we are all equals."

As she said this, she caught his grateful look, and for a few seconds he continued to look at her as if he had wanted to make sure he had heard her correctly. Then he turned to Olga.

"I may not have a way with words, Countess," he began, measuring his words slowly, "but I do know right from wrong, and it is wrong to offend another person. It is true that I worship my mistress. She is the purest of angels, who made me what I am today—a literate man, a free man. It is my sacred duty to protect her now, and what you say besmirches that duty. Your words are shameful!"

"I'm sure Countess Radina understands that, Ossip," Irina said. "She is in shock and confused. Let her be now. We all need to rest."

But Ossip continued to stare at Olga. "I ask in all fairness, Countess," he said firmly, "that you take back your words." His tightly clenched fists shook. "Right now!"

His voice was strong, resounding, his eyes narrowed, as he looked down at her. Olga slid sideways on the bench and lowered her gaze.

"I—I guess the princess is right, Ossip. I'm over-wrought and must have misinterpreted your actions. We're lucky to be alive!"

Ossip nodded and without a word moved to the far corner of the izba, where he spread his greatcoat on the floor and lowered himself onto it wearily.

Tears glistened in Olga's eyes as she watched him walk away from the table; then she turned to Irina, put her arms around her, and, burying her face in her shoulder, wept quietly.

Chapter Fourteen

After thirty-four days of travel they had finally reached Irkutsk. The capital of Eastern Siberia, it lay sprawling at the edge of graceful birch forests and along the crystal waters of the fast Angara River, now covered with ice. As they approached the city, Irina tried to remember everything she had read about Irkutsk before she left Moscow. Established in 1652 to collect fur taxes from the Buryats, it had become the capital of Eastern Siberia and its largest city. It was a fur trading center now, with the neighboring Lake Baikal region rich in seal, beaver, fox, and sable as well as squirrel and marmot. It had also become a social center of activities, with balls, dinners, and concerts filling the winter season.

Ossip had lifted the bast flaps, and Irina and Olga looked out. The streets seemed deserted. A one-horse sleigh passed, piled high with wood. Driven by a hunched, bearded muzhik in an enormous bearskin greatcoat, it squeaked slowly along the snow-packed road. Puffs of vapor drifted from the man's mouth, and he clapped his mittened hands together to keep warm. Three or four little boys or girls—it was hard to tell from their round, bundled bodies—played with snowballs on the street, spurts of gleeful shrieks greeting each throw that found its mark. . . . Much like children in Moscow; only these had no watchful nannies supervising them from a nearby bench.

In the distance a stone belfry, of what Irina assumed was the Irkutsk Cathedral, towered in front of the Jerusalem Hill. The streets were lined with wooden houses, their windows framed with intricate and colorfully painted fretwork. The smell of burning wood wafted from the snow-tufted chimneys and hung tauntingly in the air. The homey fragrance brought memories of, their faraway home, of crackling fireplaces and moving shadows on beloved faces . . . Better not to dwell on the past!

At the station they consulted with an official, a hospitable, bustling man who wouldn't let them leave until they ate a bowl of Siberian pelmeni—hot meat dumplings in bouillon beneath a baked bread crust. Thus nourished, the three travelers set out on a search for a place to stay and soon found what they were looking for: a couple of rooms for rent near the center of the town square.

What they needed now was sleep. They knew they would need all their wits for the meeting with Governor Tseidler, an old German reputed to be a faithful servant of the tsar, who scrupulously followed his sovereign's orders.

Yes, rest was a must, for Irina wanted to look fresh when she saw Alexander. But sleep did not come at once. Having come this close to him, she fretted. It had been more than six months now since she had last seen him. Where did he live? How was he getting along? Who was cooking for him? The worrisome thoughts kept her awake. Olga tossed in bed near her, and suddenly Irina's anxieties seemed minor by comparison. Boris was in prison, and Olga didn't even know where he was and how far she had yet to travel.

The next day they went to see Governor Tseidler. As they had expected, he used every argument he could think of to make them return to Moscow.

Undaunted, Irina said, "Governor, I suspect that you are not as much concerned with our future as with following the tsar's orders. I'm sure His Majesty fears that our presence here will arouse too much sympathy toward the exiles. Since they are forbidden to write their relatives, the tsar must hope that the prisoners will soon be forgotten in Russia. But our correspondence with our families in Russia will, of course, keep the memories of the exiles alive, won't it?" She smiled sweetly at the governor, a stern, reserved man of declining years.

He grunted and peered at Irina. "You are remarkably outspoken, Princess Dolovina. I wouldn't dare repeat your words to His Majesty. Hasn't it been his kindness and consideration that permitted you to follow your husband here?"

The none too subtle rebuke did not escape Irina. "I wouldn't be here today, Governor, if the tsar hadn't given me permission to come," she said. "It does not, however, keep me from speaking my mind."

For a few moments the governor seemed at a loss for words, and Irina, amused by his discomfiture, added, "As you can see, Governor, I could never qualify as a diplomat, but that's the way I am!"

Tseidler threw up his hands. "Oh, you young and foolish women! You are guided today by the romantic notion that love will triumph over all. Living in your husbands' barren dwelling, deprived of luxuries and even the basic comforts that you've been accustomed to all your lives, how long do you think it will be before you regret your impulsive decisions?"

"Never!"

Olga's quick answer startled the governor, and he looked intently at her pale face, accentuated today by her flashing eyes and shining black hair.

Irina shrugged.

"I'm practical enough to realize," she said, "that there

may be times when we shall long for our families and homes. . . ." She hesitated, then went on. "You may not know this, but I left my infant son—my only child— behind. With such a supreme sacrifice, I am determined to accomplish what I have set out to do, and that is to ease my husband's life, and I am prepared to accept all future heartaches as part of the bargain."

The governor bowed slightly. "I admire your fortitude, Princess. You have an indomitable spirit which will serve you well in the future."

He turned to Olga. "I hope you are strong enough, Countess Radina, to face what awaits you. Your husband is in chains and working in the Blagodatsk mine near Nerchinsky Zavod. It is beyond Chita and not far from the Chinese border." He paused, then added, "It is another nine hundred versts from here." He waited for her response, and when none came, he sighed and said, "You may continue on your journey as soon as you are ready."

Irina thought of a word the governor had said a few minutes earlier: "dwelling." *Not a house, but a dwelling. Oh, God, what kind of humiliating circumstances is Alexander being subjected to in Irkutsk?*

"Governor," she asked, "in what kind of *dwelling* is my husband living?"

"He is living in an izba, Princess. It is small, of course, but quite comfortable and adequate for his needs."

Izba. A log cabin. The aristocratic, elegant Prince Dolovin living like a peasant. She closed her eyes for a moment, imagining Alexander in his dress uniform and gleaming boots, a fur-trimmed dolman over one shoulder, moving among his peers in one of the imperial palaces in St. Petersburg. Oh, God, what was he wearing now, living in an izba like a muzhik?

"When may I go to him, Governor?" Irina asked.

"Let me prepare him first, Princess."

"No! I came all this distance without letting him know, and I want to surprise him!"

"I'm not sure it is a good idea, Princess. It will be such a shock for him to see you here."

"I know him better than you do, Governor. My husband is a strong man. Don't forget, he survived months of hardships and mental anguish while in prison. Surely this kind of shock would not hurt him now. Don't deprive me of this moment!"

The governor cleared his throat. "It may also be a shock for you, Princess—er—a rather unpleasant one."

"I'm not concerned about myself," Irina countered.

"He may be humiliated; he may not look his best."

The excuse sounded weak, and Irina looked at him closely. "Governor, I've never favored innuendos. What are you implying? Is he ill?"

The answer was quick. "Not at all, I assure you! I'm only trying to save your delicate sensibilities."

"My sensibilities have been blunted considerably in the past few months."

"What about his pride?"

"His pride can't be hurt any more than it already has been."

The governor spread his hands. "You're a force to be reckoned with, Princess. I concede! I shall have someone escort you to your husband's izba."

A row of log cabins was clustered on a narrow street several blocks from the town square. Some had intricate painted fretwork framing the windows, but most had plain shutters hanging loosely on rusted hinges. A chimney belched a coil of smoke through the thick mantle of snow at the izba where the coachman stopped. Someone was home.

Irina's heart struggled to leap out as she knocked on

the front door. What would his face look like when he saw her? What would she say to him?

But when the door opened, it wasn't Alexander who stood on the threshold, but a young woman, who eyed her curiously through narrow, elongated eyes. *A servant! He is able to afford a servant,* Irina thought, and smiled at the diminutive girl, who was hurriedly wiping her hands on a large apron. Irina took in her black hair, neatly pulled back in two braids, her high cheekbones and slanted dark eyes, which twinkled intelligently at her now. Must be a Buryat. She had heard, of course, of the regional natives, mostly nomads of Russian-Mongolian origin with their unique customs and language, but she had never met one.

"Do you understand Russian?" Irina asked.

"Of course!" the girl said. "What do you want?" Her Russian was unaccented, and Irina, embarrassed, ignored the brusque question.

"I want to see Prince Dolovin. Doesn't he live here?"

The girl nodded and stepped aside to let Irina in. The izba was large with a single square table in the center and benches running along the walls. A huge clay stove with a sleeping area on top dominated one wall. A man was sitting at the table with his back to the door, and when Irina entered, he rose and turned to face her. He was a young giant of a man, patrician in bearing, large of bone, and he bore distinctly Oriental features. He was dressed in a fur-lined blue silk gown, and his black, glossy hair was pulled into a thin queue at the back. With his hands stiffly at his sides, the man bowed deeply.

"Where is Prince Alexander?" Irina asked, not sure the man would understand her, and was surprised by the man's fluent Russian.

"I'm waiting for him. Marya here—" he nodded toward the Buryat girl—"says he is due back any minute. Allow me to introduce myself. My name is

Chien Yung-lin. I am a tea merchant from Maimachin, and I am in Irkutsk to transact business."

The man bowed and looked at Irina expectantly. Taking a deep breath, Irina blurted out, "And I am Prince Alexander's wife. I've just arrived from Moscow to join him!"

As she said this, there was a gasp and a quick movement behind her. She turned. The Buryat girl had dropped a tray and was picking up pieces of black bread off the floor.

If the merchant was surprised, he did not betray it, but a brief glimmer of concealed interest shone in his eyes for a moment. Then he bowed.

"The honored lady is most welcome to Irkutsk. May her life here be a happy and prosperous one."

The Buryat girl bowed deeply to Irina. "I shall leave now, Barynia," she said breathlessly. "I shall come back when you need me. The prince should be here any minute!"

"Where do you live, Marya?" Irina asked.

"My family lives in a yurt outside the city," the girl replied and turned to leave. At the door she suddenly spit on the floor and then was gone.

Shocked, Irina frowned and turned to Chien Yung-lin. "My heavens, why did she do that?" she asked.

Unperturbed, the merchant replied, "Marya is fasting. It is her religion."

In spite of herself, Irina smiled. "Is it her religion to spit on the floor?"

Chien Yung-lin did not smile. "I see that the honored lady is not familiar with Buryat religious customs. Marya belongs to the Lamaist sect of Buddhism and is required to fast once a year. During this fast she can eat sparingly on the first day; then on the second she has to abstain from food and drink and is not allowed to swallow even her saliva. Today is such a day for her. She can eat on alternate days and has eight two-day cycles in the fast."

For a few seconds Irina had to remind herself that she was still in the Russian Empire. Then she asked, "How is my husband? Have you known him long?"

Chien Yung-lin inclined his head slightly. "The respected prince is well. I have known him for several months now."

"Do you come to Irkutsk often?"

"Whenever the caravans make the journey, I sometimes come along."

"Is your family with you?"

He closed his eyes briefly and shook his head. "I have been widowered for two years, but I belong to a large clan in Urga."

Irina was perplexed. "Urga? But that's a good three hundred versts from our border! I thought you said you live in Maimachin."

Chien Yung-lin nodded. "I do. But a trading border town is no place for our women. Since they are not allowed to live in Maimachin, I make trips to Urga as often as my business permits."

No women in Maimachin! Irina was too polite to pursue the subject. Suddenly she felt a weakness in her legs. Perhaps it was the warm temperature in the izba after the cold sleigh ride or the disappointment of not having seen Alexander right away; but the reaction was setting in, and she reached out to grasp the edge of the table.

Chien Yung-lin's gaze followed, and he took a step forward. "If the honored lady will give me permission to leave, I shall go now and return later. My business is not a pressing one. It can wait."

Irina nodded, and moments later she was alone. She took off her fur-lined coat and hat and sat down on the bench by the table, wondering how long she would have to wait.

Seconds stretched into minutes, and those minutes seemed like hours before the door opened and Alexander walked in. He had taken only a couple of steps into the room when he saw her.

Much later she tried to remember the cadence of emotions that had played across his face and thought that nothing in her life had prepared her for his reaction. Stunned recognition and joy, then alarm, shame, doubt—all registered so fleetingly that she wondered if she had imagined them. Quickly he took off his greatcoat and stood before her in his peasant side-buttoned linen shirt and wide trousers stuffed into heavy leather boots. Without his elegant uniform he looked vulnerable and younger than his twenty-seven years. She whispered his name, and a sudden and unabashed joy softened his features. He spread his arms and rushed at her with a strangled cry. "Irina! *Golubka!* Oh, God, what have you done!"

They cried and laughed and talked all at once, interrupting each other, asking questions and answering them out of sequence, making no sense at all and understanding only one rapturous truth: They were together!

Alexander covered her hands, her face with kisses. "A miracle! Your love, your devotion, your determination! Oh, my love, what have I done to you? What have I done? Selfish man that I am, I cannot even say that I regret your sacrifice!"

A whirlwind it was, a madness that followed, a wild catharsis of tortured emotions that had built up through the months of suspense and of grief, through the days of despair and rejection.

A poem of whispers, a prelude of touch, a fury of limbs . . .

Loving like this, Irina thought, *surely comes only once in a lifetime, when joy and pain and shock of surprise all join to rise into mindless, unbearable tension, to an apex of rapture no words could adequately describe.* Nothing could better this hour. Nothing could spoil it. Nothing. Ever.

Later, in the peaceful aftermath of love, she told him about Sasha and her lonely fight against their family's opposition. She told him all: the good and the bad—about Prince Gregory's wrath and rejection; his mother's weakness; the care that would surround little Sasha; Ossip's loyalty. Only one thing she withheld from her husband.

She told him nothing about Marianna and her part in his imprisonment.

Irina stayed with Alexander in his izba and slept in the tiny bedroom adjacent to the living area. When the Buryat girl Marya had not come back to work, Alexander explained that she was needed by her family and had been planning to leave. Irina thought no more about it and hired a Russian girl, Anisia, happy to tell him that she had enough money sewn into her clothes to find a proper house for them now and that Prince Gregory had promised to send them a monthly allowance regularly.

"We don't need to live in an izba any longer," she said, and, looking at his peasant shirt, laughed apologetically. "And we don't have to look like peasants either!"

In a few days they said good-bye to a weeping Olga as she started alone on her journey to Blagodatsk. Saddened by their separation, Irina promised to write often and stood on the corner, watching the street long after Olga's sleigh had disappeared from view.

The next day Ossip, who had been living in a rented room in another izba, found them a large two-story house on a treelined street and asked if he could move into the servants' quarters. Irina tried to point out that he was no longer their servant and could establish himself in a separate house. Ossip demurred. "I would be more comfortable as a member of your household than living alone, Barynia. Now that I can read and write, I would very much like to be of help to the prince in any way he could use me, and I won't be any burden to you because I want to start working as a cobbler."

A few days later Irina was preparing to move from the izba and was clearing the tiny bedroom of her belongings, when she pulled a pair of shoes from under the bed. For a few seconds she held them in her hand, studying them. Of heavy pressed felt, they had thick soles and were flat and cone-shaped. They were also small enough to fit a woman's foot. Inside one of them was a broken piece of what looked like an amulet. Irina moved slowly. It seemed cold in the room, and her body felt stiff. She moved to the hammered iron coffer in the corner of the room and lowered herself on it slowly. "It may also be a shock for you, Princess—er —a rather unpleasant one." Governor Tseidler had said. Was this what he had hinted at? Straightening, Irina fought to control her pounding heart. It beat so painfully!

She was still sitting on the trunk, staring at the shoes, when Alexander walked in.

She swung to face him. "Whose are these?" she asked, lifting the shoes for him to see.

"Oh, God!" Alexander moaned, and sat down heavily on the taboret.

"I don't suppose I need an answer, do I, Alexander? It is pretty obvious that these belong to another woman, who felt quite at home with you in this izba. In fact, someone who *shared* your bed with you, right?" She felt herself trembling; a cold shiver took possession of her and would not go away. All the loneliness she had experienced, all the strength it had taken to stand up against the formidable opposition of her father-in-law and the tsar, all the willpower to swallow her pride and face the courtesan seemed now for naught in this shameful discovery.

"Like father, like son!" she cried. "No sooner do you leave Marianna's bed than you find yourself another! Shame on you, Alexander Dolovin, shame on you! Marianna knew you better than I! You deserve her betrayal! I've been a fool, an utter fool!" Irina threw her head back and laughed a loud, bitter laugh. She was out of control and could not stop it. "How she must have laughed behind my back when I humiliated myself and pleaded for your life!"

In one leap Alexander was beside her, shaking her violently. "What have you said? Irina, answer me!"

Sobered, she looked at him for a long moment and then told him, sparing him nothing. She told him in detail how she had found out about Marianna, how she had gone to see her to plead for his life, and how she had faced the tsar. And when she finished, Alexander went down on his knees before her and, taking her hands in his, said, "I know I ask too much of you to believe me, but I have no reason to lie about this: I didn't tell Marianna that I intended to take part in the revolt. I ended our relationship that night, and that must be why she betrayed me. She has had her sweet revenge."

He paused, then added slowly, "I suppose I deserved it!"

At the sound of the hateful name, the anguish of the past flooded over her, and tears stung Irina's eyes. The present vanished, and her bitterness over the courtesan's betrayal that had caused the suffering of the man she loved surfaced all over again. With fists clenched, she screamed, "What do you mean, you deserved it? She sent you into exile because she was a woman scorned! What did she expect—that you would continue your relationship? I despise her for what she has done! Don't you dare think you deserved her betrayal!"

She was choking and clawing at the air, reaching for the wall, which had begun to sway before her. Alexander caught her in his arms.

Gradually the past receded, and the present surfaced again with all its ugly connotations. She arranged her thoughts into proper channels. "Alexander," she said, "the past is gone. But it's the present that hurts. How could you? And with your own servant, that—that Marya, isn't it?"

Alexander shook his head. "Darling, she is only someone who helped me in my loneliness. You can't call it betrayal. I've been without you for more than a year. . . .Remember, I thought I had lost you forever and would never, ever see you again! Can't you understand that I considered myself a man without a wife or child or loved ones for the rest of my life? I beg you, try to see the situation, harsh as it may seem, in its proper perspective."

But jealousy and hurt taunted. Did the servant girl Marya know how to love him and comfort him better than she? She couldn't ask, of course. The less she knew, the less the hurt.

"Please, *golubka,* try to understand," Alexander coaxed.

She tried. Humiliated as she was, she did try. And trying, she went into his arms and wept on his shoulder, accepting his embrace and murmured words of comfort.

But the hurt and a perverse sense of resentment festered.

Chapter Fifteen

When the blanket of snow finally melted, and spring ventured forth to divulge its secrets hidden beneath, Alexander invited Irina to ride with him into the countryside. She accepted gladly, hoping that the beauty of the area surrounding Irkutsk would help soften her pain.

Her estrangement from Alexander was extending from the emotional to the mental chasm, a chasm that seemed impossible to bridge. Part of it was jealousy. She had to fight this most shameful of human emotions, but the hurt—the hurt was harder to overcome. Even her usual sense of humor, her ability to see the lighter side of things quickly, failed her now.

A distance had crawled between them, and into that distance moved an invisible shadow of the Buryat Marya. There was no use bringing it up again. What could he tell her except that which he had already explained? Her mind accepted it, but her heart refused. A perverse, womanly spite it was, to punish him for having found solace—however brief—in another woman's arms, while she—his wife—had agonized in loneliness and yearned to be by his side to comfort him, unaware that all along he had already been comforted. And now this shadow was tainting even their lovemaking. She could not bring herself to submit to him without restraint, pursued by the thought that a third presence was watching them in their bedroom, and she was filled with resentment and shame.

It was absurd to harbor such a feeling; destructive and threatening to erode their relationship and tarnish their love. Yet she couldn't conquer it.

One night a month ago, after several days of refusing him her bed under the pretext of being indisposed, she had finally given in. It was he who had suddenly lost his impetus and left her bed without explanation. It was obvious that he had sensed her frigidity, had tried to break the growing barrier between them and failed. The next few days he was embarrassed, or so it seemed to her, and after that night his demands on her were less frequent. She tried to dismiss the incident as of no importance, but then, a few days later, something that revived her suspicions happened.

One evening he didn't come home from his office. She was frantic with worry and wanted to send Ossip to the police, but Ossip persuaded her to wait until morning. "There may be many explanations, and we don't want to draw the attention of the police to the prince unnecessarily," he had said. "Let me look for him myself first."

Irina stayed up all night, waiting, and in late morning Ossip came to report that he had found the prince in the Buryat camp. Evidently Alexander had gone for a ride in the country after a busy day of trading, and his coach had broken down. He was forced to stay overnight in the Buryat camp before the broken spokes of the wheel could be repaired.

Ossip was sullen and curt as he related the story and then, mumbling something about his pressing work, disappeared into his cobbler's shop. When Alexander returned shortly thereafter, he told the same story and avoided looking at her. A nasty suspicion took hold of her and continued to nag.

Since that episode Alexander seemed more solicitous of her, more attentive, as if he were feeling guilty for having put her through that kind of worry, even though, according to his words, it was not really his fault. Or was it? Was he feeling guilty for another, more shameful reason? Whose yurt had he slept in? And why had Ossip behaved so strangely that morning and had remained uncommunicative ever since?

Irina was too proud to ask. But the Buryat custom of sharing wives and daughters with a visiting guest was known to her, and she tortured herself with these unanswered questions. She tried to suppress her feelings, reminding herself repeatedly that she should count her blessings and be happy in Irkutsk, where people accepted them with kindness, where new friends treated them with open, ingenuous warmth and showered them with the sincere hospitality legendary among Siberians.

In winter months heavily bundled peasant women wrapped in woolen angora shawls smiled warmly at her when she passed them on the street and frequently greeted her with a cheerful "Good day to you, Barynia. Cover your nose, or Father Frost will bite it off!" In a nearby produce shop, when she counted her twenty kopecks for the pud of flour, the fat merchant behind the counter chuckled good-naturedly and joked: "*Dovolno*, Barynia, enough! You don't need to count your kopecks!" No such simplicity of relationships could have existed in Moscow or St. Petersburg. Especially not in St. Petersburg!

In fact, she and Alexander were more needed here in Siberia than they would have been in Moscow. Irina had started weekly soirees, introducing readings from Pushkin's works and encouraging local musicales and dances. They were respected, sought after, admired. Irina's styles were copied, for she never permitted herself to appear in public any less than perfectly groomed. Even today, on her outing into the country with Alexander, she wore a wide-brimmed straw hat with a veil and carried a parasol.

She reveled in the beauty around Lake Baikal. "The best-kept secret in Russia!" she said in wonder as they rode the sixty-five versts to see the lake. It was her first trip outside Irkutsk since her arrival, and she was determined to enjoy herself and forget her mounting problems for a few short hours. She couldn't allow herself to dwell on them today. Not on a sunny day with a turquoise sky, when the shimmering air was redolent of a bouquet of fragrances from field flowers. And there were so many! Blue larkspur, columbine, yellow aconite, campanula, pink willow herb—they all were there in a bold splash of color at her feet. Whoever said that Siberia was grim and unfriendly? The sun was so bright she had to shade her eyes with her hand to take in all the beauty around her. For a while they rode along the Angara River, icy blue waters fed by Lake Baikal rushing away from its source. Soon they turned inland, and as they reached the edge of a birch grove, Alexander ordered the coachman to stop and then helped Irina down. They walked along a narrow dirt road, closely followed by the coach.

Bushes of crimson rhododendron grew along the road, adding a splash of color to the snow white bark of th birch groves.

Alexander stopped and pointed to a cluster of plants. "I want you to see how rich this country is. I've learned a lot from the local Buryats," he said. "See this mint and camomile? They use them, as well as sage, elder, and even rhubarb, for medicinal purposes. When the weather is stormy, Baikal spews out a kind of dark brown sea wax, and old *babushki* use it to treat rheumatism."

He knows so much about the Buryats, Irina thought. *Did he get all this information from Marya?* She tried to concentrate on what Alexander was saying, but the persistent thought ran on. *How do I know that he isn't still seeing her behind my back? Will I ever be able to trust him again?*

'. . . when I came here late in the summer last year," Alexander was saying now, "wild strawberries and cranberries were ripe and delicious—" Abruptly he stopped and looked at Irina. "You're not listening to me, Irina. Where is your pretty head now? In the clouds?" He looked up. "But there aren't any today!"

Irina could not even smile, and after a few moments of silence Alexander helped her back into the coach.

They had reached the lake. It shimmered and sparkled before her, this vast sapphire sea, its quiet waters gently breaking against the granite and porphyry cliffs on the shore. In the distance the columnar structures of basalt rock rose high above the water, and as Irina stood, awed by the grandeur of the lake, a child's laughter sounded behind her. She turned. A small boy was squatting by the edge of the lake, scooping a handful of stones into his hand. He couldn't have been more than five years old, and as his Buryat mother watched him with an indulgent smile, the child ran up to Irina and opened his small fist to show her the stones he had collected. She looked down at his plump pink palm in amazement. The boy held pieces of yellow opal, crystal, even a small aquamarine. Irina stared in fascination.

"Tyotenka—Auntie—" the child said, "which one would you like?"

In another four years her little Sasha would be five years old and running happily about Dolovino as this child was doing now. Her mother-in-law's letters were tearing her apart with details of Sasha's daily routine,

the sounds he was making, his cheerful disposition. She
wanted to tell her that she didn't want to read about
him, that she wanted to forget his little face, his plump,
dimpled arms. But does a mother ever forget? Even
one who has left her child forever? No! A mother's
heart remembers, hides the pain, and endures . . .
always.

"Tyotenka? Take one!" The child persisted. Tears
blurred Irina's eyes as she bent over and picked the
opal from the boy's hand.

"Perhaps we better start back," Alexander said. He
must have sensed her mood, must have guessed the
reason, for he did not even offer to stroll through the
birch groves to look for mushrooms. Irina looked at the
empty basket they had brought along for that very
purpose and then at Alexander.

For a few seconds neither spoke, and then she said
the first thing that came to mind. "We can always buy
mushrooms on the market. Speaking of markets,
Anisia bought a goose yesterday and cooked it for
Ossip." When Irina caught Alexander's surprised look,
she added, "Ossip may be doing fine as a cobbler,
Alexander, but I suspect that he still needs extra
income. As a matter of fact, I am wondering where he
gets such good rawhide."

"He gets it from the Buryats," Alexander said.

"So that's it! I was wondering why he spends so much
time in their camp. He is lonely, and I wish . . ."

"You wish what, *golubka*?" Alexander prompted
quietly.

"I wish somehow we could get Agasha to come
here!"

Alexander shook his head. "You know it's impossible. Besides, I doubt that Ossip would accept her with a
child any more easily now than he would back home."

Irina sighed. Ossip still lived in the small servants'

house in the courtyard of their home and had set up a cobbler's workshop in one of the rooms. Always ready to help around the house when minor repairs were needed, he nevertheless kept to himself and never spoke of the past.

They waited for fresh horses, then rode home in silence, each preoccupied with his own thoughts, the clear, warm day now touched with an imaginary chill.

At home Irina found a letter from Olga. She wrote frequently and copiously, and from her letters Irina was able to reconstruct the misery of Olga's life. She lived in a rented room in a large izba in Blagodatsk near Boris's prison, where he worked in the mine. As a convict's wife, Olga was not allowed to receive money directly from home. Her funds were in the hands of the local administration, and she was required to account for every kopeck spent to the commandant of the mines, Burnashev. Boris received a monthly pay of sixty-five kopecks, which, despite the low market prices, was still negligible, and Olga spent all her time mending his clothes and cooking extra cabbage soup and kasha for him. This left her so little money that at times she could afford only bread and kvass—a bread-based fermented drink—for her own nourishment.

One day an overzealous prison warden, Rik, deprived the prisoners of candlelight after they had returned from work in the mine and forbade them to communicate with one another. To be isolated in total darkness until daybreak was unbearable, and the prisoners went on a hunger strike. Alarmed, the administration relaxed the rules, but the incident only added to the wives' constant anxiety for their husbands' welfare.

Deprived of the basic comforts, forced to do menial work, Olga wrote letters that breathed bitterness. She envied Katasha Trubetskaya and Marie Volkonskaya, who shared an izba near hers and had found solace in each other.

Their only recreation was an occasional horseback excursion across the border into China, which lay only twelve versts away. There they watched local peasants trading their handiwork for tea and millet, in order to escape the high customs tariff. Olga wrote that all the local women rode horseback astride, and it was amusing to see the local officials examine her sidesaddle. Irina wondered how she got along with the other two wives, who were known to be strong in character, emotional, and fiercely loyal to their husbands. She worried.

Now she sat down with the letter but was in no hurry to read it, for Olga's letters made her feel guilty because she was the more fortunate of the two.

Irina looked around the room and realized all over again how lucky she was. Here, in their two-story house, she had used the money Prince Gregory had given her to fill the rooms with Oriental rugs brought with the caravans from China, tasseled draperies ordered in Irkutsk, and portieres to cover the unadorned wooden doors. She had furnished the house in walnut and Karelian birch, reminiscent of the furniture in her native Beryozovka, and she had to admit that she felt more at home in this house than she had in her husband's palatial Dolovino with its Louis XV gilded chairs and silk-covered walls. Alexander had let her decorate the house to her own taste, and she knew that no such freedom would have been permitted her at Dolovino.

Olga's letter still lay in her lap, and Irina forced herself to open it.

... A notorious criminal by the name of Orlov [Olga wrote] escaped with several other inmates from the neighboring prison and hid in the hills. Most were recaptured, but he disappeared without a trace. He's considered to be a kind of Robin Hood of Siberia. Escape, then, *is* possible here. I am restless, Irina; angry at Boris for what happened to us, and angry at myself for my naïve expectations about life in Siberia. . . . We are allowed to visit our husbands only twice a week. The men suffer dreadfully from bedbugs; even rubbing themselves with turpentine doesn't help. Boris says it's as bad as the torture in Persia, where they leave criminals to be eaten by insects. When we come home from each visit, we have to shake out our clothes thoroughly.

Katasha Trubetskaya's husband collects field flowers on his way from the mine and leaves the bouquet for her by the side of the road before reentering the prison compound. After all my sacrifices for Boris, why can't he do something equally thoughtful for me? . . .

Irina finished reading the letter and sat quietly for a long time, thinking. Something was brewing in Olga's mind, something dangerous and unworthy. But what could she write her? Words committed to paper were flat, devoid of animation, and lacked nuances that could influence and convince. A journey to Blagodatsk might not be such a bad idea. Olga needed someone to talk some sense into her, to set her mind into proper perspective.

There was another reason why she wanted to see Olga. She felt alone. In the beginning she had enjoyed going to the quiet country church, with its well-trodden Oriental runner in the center of the wide plank floor, the bent-over old *babushka* tidying the interior without so much as a glance in her direction, or the quiet stroll

through the graveyard, where modest tombstones re-
corded the names and the years of birth and death and
no epitaphs. But her frequent visits to the wooden
church at the edge of town no longer satisfied her, and
in spite of resentment in Olga's letters, she envied her
friendship with Katasha and Marie, her contact,
however brief, with other exiles in prison. They were
together, drawing and giving support to one another,
sharing memories that no new friends, no matter how
understanding, could share.

The next day, drawn by some hidden, irresistible
force, she ordered her horse saddled and went alone for
a ride to the birch grove she had seen the previous day
with Alexander. Surrounded by the beauty outside
Irkutsk, she would escape from disturbing thoughts
about Olga and would revive her inner resources by
communing with nature. She yearned to lose herself
once again among nature's gifts and forget, even if for a
brief moment, her restlessness and her hurt. Surrounded by evergreens with their pungent fragrance of
resin, the dew-washed grass sprinkled with delicately
nodding forget-me-nots, she longed to hear the lark
with its vibrant song, to watch the industry of a fluffy
squirrel.

Soft with summer languor, the air bathed her face
with a grassy fragrance, and as she stopped along the
wooded path to pick a bouquet of field flowers, she
realized, with a suddenness that startled her, that
perhaps she was ungrateful; not only did they have new
Siberian friends, but there was also Chien Yung-lin.

In spite of his alien background, Irina and Alexander
had developed a deep affection for this Chinese
stranger, who was more cultured and intellectually
stimulating than their new Siberian friends. He was well
mannered, enigmatic, disarmingly dependent on their
friendship. But there was an aura of sadness about him,

perhaps a weight of hidden tragedy that he carried alone. Although he was well established in Maimachin, he came to Irkutsk often enough to know and like it. If it was impossible for him to live in Urga, why couldn't he move to Irkutsk, marry and settle down? After all, there were quite a number of Chinese living in Irkutsk already. Of course! That's what Alexander should suggest to him.

Irina stopped picking flowers, surprised by the audacity of her own thoughts. Why, that would mean giving up his heritage; that would mean defying his adoptive father's wishes! Would he be willing to take such a step for the sake of personal happiness? She didn't know.

A rustling sound startled Irina. Immersed in her thoughts, she had forgotten for a few moments where she was. The clear morning air so full of nature's sounds only a few minutes ago now shimmered with silence, a taut, exhilarating silence that suddenly swept her turmoil away and filled her with a strange peace and an undefined joy. It had not occurred to her that someone besides herself might be walking in this bucolic birch grove.

She turned around.

A tall man in a long hermit's gown was walking slowly toward her. His high, smooth forehead was crowned with pale blond hair silvering at the roots and falling in rich waves to his shoulders. Round, brilliantly blue eyes seemed to blind her with their magnetism, their penetrating look. His hand was smooth and white as he lifted the staff he held.

"Good day to you!" he said, his resonant voice echoing through the trees.

"And good day to you, kind man," Irina replied, unable to take her eyes away from this stranger, who did not look like one of the pilgrims who roamed the country begging for alms.

"It is a surprise to meet a lady alone in this isolated birch forest. Are you lost, and if so, may I be of assistance to you?"

The man spoke in a cultured, modulated voice with the carefully chosen phrases of St. Petersburg parlors, not at all like the simple peasant speech of a wandering monk.

Recovering quickly, Irina replied, "Thank you, but I am not lost. I came here to enjoy the forest and the flowers and this beautiful day. It is strange to meet a gentleman in these remote Siberian parts who speaks with the gallantry of an aristocrat." She paused, then added with a smile, "In spite of the hermit's clothing."

When he did not answer immediately, she said, "I am Princess Irina Dolovina, and who are you?"

The man bowed slightly. "I am delighted to make your acquaintance, Princess," he said courteously. "To meet not only a member of the illustrious family in this remote part of the country but a courageous woman as well."

Irina felt herself flush. "What makes you think I am courageous? Surely there is no danger in being here in broad daylight!"

The man smiled, but his eyes held a shade of sadness. "I was not referring to your presence here, Princess. I meant your courage in following your husband into exile."

Irina was stunned. Who was this man who knew so much? Aloud she said, "Every loyal wife would act the same in similar circumstances, especially since my husband was falsely accused."

"Indeed. Some of us expiate our sins by choice, but others are forced to suffer innocently. I promise you that your husband will be vindicated, for the hand of nemesis reaches far and never misses."

"I—I don't understand. On whose authority do you say these things?"

"Let us say that I am privileged to know more than an average person. Remember my words, and you will find that I am right."

"Who are you? You haven't told me your name!"

The man straightened, his patrician head tilted gracefully to one side. "I am sometimes called Fedor Kuzmich. It is enough for me to be known as that."

"Thank you for your kind words, Fedor Kuzmich. I shall remember them!"

Irina felt dazed all the way back to Irkutsk. The image of the tall stranger haunted her. There was such serenity, such peace emanating from him that she wondered if she had been privileged to catch a rare glimpse of a hermit saint. But when she described him to Alexander, her husband paled and stared at her.

"Do you realize that you have just described Tsar Alexander the Blessed?" he asked. Irina was shocked.

"But Tsar Alexander died in Taganrog!" Irina cried, suddenly frightened.

"Yes, and after he had died, we heard all those rumors that he did *not* die . . ." Alexander said pensively.

"Are you implying that this Fedor Kuzmich—the man I met in the forest—and Tsar Alexander are one and the same?"

"I am not implying anything, Irina. I'm only saying that it was certainly a strange encounter, to say the least."

They lapsed into silence, each preoccupied with his own thoughts. What did this strange encounter mean? Alexander thought. Was the hermit really Fedor Kuzmich, or was he truly Tsar Alexander? And if so, did he now possess some mystical power to foresee the future? Alexander dared not hope.

Chapter Sixteen

In the past few months so many of Alexander's hopes had been dashed, so deep a gulf existed between him and Irina that he wondered if he would ever be able to regain a measure of his previous happiness. True, much of it was his own fault, and he was guilty of—of what? Of being human in the face of loneliness? He couldn't accuse himself of infidelity during those early months without her when he thought he had lost her forever.

But what about now and the time since Irina had joined him? What about that day a month ago, when everything had gone wrong and he found himself in the Buryat camp?

The day had started badly. Igor Panfilov, his partner from Kyakhta, had come up to Irkutsk with a current shipment of tea and told him that Stepan had been hurting the market by producing extra silver idols in payment for additional supplies of tea, which he was then selling to other Russian merchants at higher prices.

"I don't know what we can do about it," Igor said, "except confront him and threaten to expose him to the authorities. The trouble is, many Irkutsk merchants use him as their go-between, and unless we can persuade him quietly to curb his illegal dealings, our Russian colleagues will be unhappy."

Alexander had trouble concentrating on what Igor

was saying. Thin and pale with a neatly combed bronze beard, Igor was a quiet young man who took his work seriously, had taught Alexander all he knew about the business, and Alexander envied him his dedication. To some, this work was a life's career, Alexander thought, and to others like himself, it was a tedious and necessary means of survival.

"I don't know what to advise you," he said finally. "What I don't understand is how he smuggles all that silver and gold past the customs officials."

Igor threw his hands up. "Easy! The smugglers have worked it out to perfection. There are coaches with double bottoms; even the wooden horse yokes and shaft bows are hollowed out. He's getting careless, though. Not long ago he boasted about it to one of his friends, and shortly thereafter a band of marauding Buryats attacked and robbed one of the caravans."

"Then we should inform our colleagues in Irkutsk about him. After all, their profits must suffer as well."

"It is unwise to antagonize anyone in this business. So many people are involved. I guess the best thing to do is to watch Stepan closely for a while, and if things get out of hand, then we can take action."

After Igor had left, Alexander stayed in his office for a while. He hated dishonesty of any kind, had often thought that many of the rich merchants acquired their wealth by dealings that stretched the edges of the law, and now his suspicions were confirmed. The devil of it was that he, Prince Alexander Dolovin, the scion of an old and noble name, was now swallowed in the boiling pot of such a commercial world and was expected to bend his high principles, his very ideals for which he had sacrificed so much. He had come a long way from those days of idealistic rhetoric with Kondraty Ryleyev and other Decembrists. How naïve and unrealistic they had been, and what a price they all were paying for their folly! Utopia was what they'd been after, he realized now, a utopia that did not exist in this material world, and the best he could do, *had* to do was to find that gray area between his uncompromising integrity and common sense that permitted stretching the law for the good of the commerce. It was the boundaries of these limits that he had to come to terms with.

It was humiliating, and he couldn't even share his feelings with Irina. After what she had gone through to join him in Siberia, and the hurt she was still harboring, he could hardly tell her that he wished for something that was unattainable. In the final analysis, he should count his blessings and not complain. But rationalizing in his small office room full of dark furniture and bourgeois trappings with papers and abacus strewn on his desk did not help, and he wanted to get out, to take a ride and clear his mind.

When he came out on the street, the late-afternoon sun was warm, and the smell of dust in the air oppressive. He hailed a coachman and told him to ride out into the country until he told him to stop and turn back.

He couldn't anticipate—could he?—that the coach would break down and he would find himself at the edge of Marya's camp? The spokes on the wheel had rotted and splintered, and new ones would have to be fixed. He would have to stay overnight. As the coachman promptly disappeared into one of the nearby yurts, there was nothing for Alexander to do but go to Marya's yurt and ask her father for help. When the Buryat invited him to spend the night, Alexander hesitated; but he had been treated with courtesy and warmth, and it would have been unseemly for him to refuse their hospitality.

Marya cooked him a rich meal of mutton in the smoky caldron, served him in silence, and never once looked directly into his eyes, while her father, his

weather-beaten, sun-bronzed face crinkling from obse-
quious smiles, talked of the honor that had been
bestowed on his insignificant yurt by such an honored
guest and filled Alexander with vodka.

Tired, warm, his eyes smarting from smoke, Alexander thanked his host, who had given up his bed to him,
and fell quickly into a fretful sleep. A series of sha-
dowy, diffused tableaux was drifting through his mind
when all of a sudden he was dreaming about Irina—his
lovely Irina, who appeared to him in flashing vignettes
of the early days of their happiness.

One moment she was running toward him through
the lanes of Dolovino, waving a basket of flowers and
laughing, the blue ribbons of her straw hat floating
gaily behind her; the next moment she was sitting
beside him in the park gazebo, stroking his cheek
tenderly and whispering gentle endearments; and then,
suddenly, she was lying beside him, her warm, volup-
tuous body soft and pliable and moving against him.

He took her in his arms, struggling to force her name
out of his throat and unable to voice it, but holding her,
wanting her, needing her beyond reason, beyond comprehension of what was happening, aware only that at
last he had recaptured their early passion, the total
abandon of their mutual rapturous love. And in that
final moment of ecstasy, when the pinnacle of his
happiness seemed within his reach and when nothing
could stop him, he suddenly, cruelly awoke.

The smell of mutton and smoke, the oppressive heat,
the burning taste of vodka, were still with him in the
yurt.

And Marya.

It was Marya whom he held in his arms. Marya, who
had come to his bed under cover of night after her
father had moved to the neighbor's yurt. Marya, who
was lying beside him, responsive and tender and eager

to please. It was she whom he was caressing and upon whom he was pouring his love—the love that belonged to Irina.

Driven by unendurable passion and aroused beyond control, he cursed the Buryat custom, his taunting dreams, the world around him, and plunged his mind into oblivion. Banishing reason and guilt, his body on fire, he took Marya with all the force of his emotional and physical anguish.

In the morning, when he awoke, feeling drugged from vodka and smoke, alone in his bed now, the memory of Marya's lovemaking was both a shame and a release. He heard voices at the entrance to the yurt and, fully awake now, saw Ossip talking to Marya and looking at him with mingled accusation and suspicion.

"The princess has sent me to look for you, Excellency. She was worried when you didn't come home last night,' Ossip said sullenly. "I understand your coach will be ready shortly."

Without waiting for a reply, Ossip turned on his heel and left.

Why, Alexander thought, *he's in love with Marya! That's why he's been spending so much time here. I must explain*—he did not finish the thought. No! To explain himself to a former serf would be demeaning, would sound like an apology and an admission of guilt. After all, Ossip had seen no evidence of wrongdoing, and surely Marya was smart enough not to admit to anything. Surely . . .

When he returned home, he found it impossible to look into Irina's eyes and hoped only that his story sounded sincere.

In the weeks that followed he tried unsuccessfully to forget the incident and was relieved when Ossip kept close to his workroom and stayed out of his way. To amuse Irina and perhaps to minimize his feelings of guilt, he took her for a ride to Lake Baikal, but even that trip seemed to work against him when he watched her reaction to a Buryat child at the edge of the lake. It wasn't until after she had returned from her own ride to the birch grove and described the hermit, repeating his mysterious words, that he dared hope for a brighter future.

The next day Chien Yung-lin came to see them. He had become a frequent visitor to their house, and in spite of his unfailing formality, a warmth shone through his stilted, flowery phrases, and Alexander sensed that the attraction between them was mutual.

As Anisia served tea, Ossip came to the door.

Alexander looked up. "What is it, Ossip?"

"I beg your pardon, Your Grace, but there is an official from the governor's office in the entry, asking to see you immediately."

When Irina saw the imperial seal on the papers that the official had brought them, her heart stood still, and at first his words did not make sense. Then, finally, she understood. Alexander was free! Free to return to Dolovino with all his privileges and rank restored. He was exonerated!

Darting embarrassed glances in Irina's direction, the official, a slight rheumy man in an oversize frock, shuffled from one foot to the other and stumbled over his words. It seemed that a consumptive woman in St. Petersburg had confessed that she had falsely accused Prince Dolovin, was then imprisoned for perjury, and died shortly thereafter. The tsar, in his merciful wisdom, felt that Alexander had paid for his minor involvement in the events of December 14 and should be fully pardoned.

There was no doubt in Irina's mind, of course, who the consumptive woman must have been, and in spite of Marianna's death, she could find no pity for her.

Would she have been this remorseful if fate had treated her kindly and death had not threatened so soon? Or was there another reason for her confession? Irina thought not.

The rest of the afternoon became a blur in her mind, a storm and a rainbow of emotions that swept her into a vortex of excitement. Sudden happiness washed over her. She was going to regain her child. Her Sasha! What happiness, what complete rapturous happiness! Back in Dolovino her toddler son would smile at her again, and they would be a family reunited. Her own parents, Alexander's parents, her *nyanya*, her home! She remembered the saintly hermit's words. They were prophetic! Unable to restrain herself, Irina picked up her skirts and whirled around the room, throwing her head back and laughing aloud—a carefree, childlike laugh of total abandon.

Dizzy, she stopped and was suddenly embarrassed. Although the official had left, Alexander was smiling indulgently, and Ossip was still standing by the door, his eyes downcast, his face somber, his hands clasped tightly. And to her left was Chien Yung-lin, risen now from his chair, a strained smile on his face, and still holding his cup of tea that clicked on the saucer in his unsteady hand.

Irina stopped laughing. With her hand outstretched toward Ossip, she cried, "Ossip, can you imagine it? We all can go home now! Isn't it wonderful? All three of us will be going home!"

Ossip lowered his head, unclasped his hands, and studied his palms. "I wish you all the happiness in the world, Your Grace, but most respectfully, I don't want to go back to Dolovino. There I have nothing but bad memories. Here I'm a free man and live better than I ever dreamed possible. I thank you for thinking of me, but my home is in Irkutsk now."

The arguments she wanted to give him stuck in her throat. She knew he was right yet resented his wanting to stay behind.

Then she thought of Olga. Nine hundred versts away in Blagodatsk, but not so far away that she could not see her occasionally if they remained in Siberia. Never overly fond of her, Irina now felt a perverse sense of kinship to her cousin's wife. Inexorably she and Alexander were now changed, and Irkutsk had become a second home with memories to reckon with. They were not going back to Moscow with ties totally severed behind them. Happiness for her was ever so, wasn't it? she thought with annoyance. Never a complete, unblemished joy.

She looked around her again. Alexander took her hand and kissed it tenderly. "My dear, what glorious news!" he said, smiling. "I can't wait to see my son, to hold him, to be a father to him! Oh, to be truly home again!"

"Sasha!" Irina said with wonder. "Our own little Sasha. We're going to have him with us and never part from him again!"

Out of the corner of her eye Irina saw a movement on her left. Chien Yung-lin put his cup of tea on the table and, placing his hands stiffly at his sides, bowed deeply.

"I shall be leaving now. My felicitations to you both on your happy news. I hope I shall see you again before you leave. Your joy is now my sorrow."

Formally he inclined his head and backed out of the room.

Irina winced. "Oh, Alexander, I wish we knew what is the mystery that surrounds him. He's so sad! I want everyone we know to share our joy. But it isn't possible, is it?"

"No, dear, of course not. All we can do is be grateful for our own good fortune."

"Well, we're not saying good-bye to Chien Yung-lin forever. He is free to travel. Someday he may come to Moscow!"

Alexander took her in his arms, and for the first time in many months Irina was able to respond to his embrace with gladness. This was no time to dwell on the sadness of leaving Irkutsk. The happiness of what awaited them at Dolovino was the most important, the most wonderful thought to enjoy. Everything else would have to take second place.

PART III

THE VICTORIOUS

Chapter Seventeen

They decided not to sell their house but to leave it in Ossip's hands to lease after they were gone. "It would be a good investment for us," Alexander said, and Chien Yung-lin, who stayed in Irkutsk to see them off, agreed.

"Who knows? You may come back someday and visit us here," he said with a polite smile, but his eyes remained watchful. He stood erect, arms hidden in the folds of his wide sleeves, black, almond-shaped eyes half closed in his lean saffron face.

When the loaded kibitka pulled away, and Alexander and Irina leaned out to wave good-bye, Chien Yung-lin did not wave back but bowed deeply in a slow farewell, then remained standing with his arms folded and watched as the kibitka stirred up a cloud of dust and disappeared around the corner.

His new friends were gone, and he was alone again.

No sooner had he allowed himself to be drawn into a friendship than it ended. He should have known better than venture onto the risky ground of emotional attachment. It was bound to ripple the outwardly tranquil waters of his existence, disrupt the carefully cultivated image of an unruffled Chinese merchant, a respected emissary of his adoptive clan. With time he had almost begun to believe in this tranquillity himself and relied on his years of practice in sublimating his loneliness.

Though surrounded by people since childhood, he had been lonely in adolescence, lonely in adulthood, lonely in marriage. There had never been anyone for him to love, and his heart yearned to love. His father's friend Lo Chia-li took him into his clan after his parents had been killed in an ambush by marauding bandits, and although he was kind to Yung-lin and never made any distinction between him and the members of his own family, he was nevertheless distant as the patriarch of his clan, and it was unthinkable for Yung-lin to approach him with his childhood trivia. The women tended to his physical needs and disciplined him, but he would lose face if as a young male member of the clan, he were to confide his emotional needs to a woman. So he grew up in the wealthy clan's courtyards in Urga and studied diligently with an old family tutor.

When the time came, Lo arranged an appropriate marriage between Yung-lin and a friend's daughter, Chao Shu-lan, whom Yung-lin had never met because according to custom, he was permitted to see only the women of his own clan.

Dutifully he married and for two years lived through a loveless marriage. When his wife died in childbirth, he grieved more for his stillborn child than for his meek and obedient wife. For a while freedom seemed a welcome respite. Then, insidiously, things began to change.

He was not a religious man, but he had to concede that Buddha was right when he taught that most suffering was caused by desire. Deep in his heart, desire grew and smoldered and finally flamed. In the courtyards of his clan, his benefactor's only daughter blossomed into a delicate flower of exquisite beauty. Shu-hsien was her name, and it meant "pure and excellent." Studious, she read the poems of Li Po or the wisdom of Lao-tsu as she sat in the inner garden of the courtyards. He remembered her shiny black hair braided tightly over her ears, her high-collared dress of pink silk neatly folded around her knees, small feet in red embroidered shoes tapping impatiently as she struggled to understand the intricacies of hieroglyphs.

What an exquisite picture she presented, sitting on the marble bench in that garden or moving gracefully along the red-columned gallery toward the family quarters!

He should have realized then that she was special in her father's heart, for he had never before met a girl who had been taught to read and write. Quiet and elgant, she was also bold. She was studying with the same tutor who had once taught him, and one day she sent her servant to his quarters requesting that he see her, and when he met her on the connecting bridge between two courtyards, she asked him to help her with her reading. He was twenty-eight, and she seventeen.

What a mistake that was to agree! But he didn't know it then, didn't dream that before his mind would admit it, his heart would long for this exquisite creature, and he looked for reasons to be with her more than the studies required. He ordered a deep porcelain bowl to replace the ceramic one she had owned for the cricket fights, and when it arrived, he presented it to her ceremoniously and stayed to watch her use a bamboo stick with delicate hairs attached to its end to tickle the crickets in the bowl and watch them fight. After that he had noticed that she had discarded the ceramic bowl and used only the one he had given her.

On a clear afternoon, after they had finished reading and had risen from the bench, she stood without moving, her lovely face tranquil in the golden light, her arms relaxed by her sides. A tiny vessel throbbed at her temple, and as he looked at her, a door opened slowly somewhere in his mind, letting in a ray of brilliance; a myriad of stars cascaded forth.

"Shu-hsien," he said, "oh, Shu-hsien, I have been blind these many months. So blind!"

"And you are no longer so?" she whispered.

"I am no longer so, Shu-hsien."

"What do you see then?"

"It would take many moons to tell you."

"Then start telling!"

"I see a happiness that is within my reach."

"Then reach for it, Yung-lin. Please reach!"

Her hands moved—a fluttering of graceful fingers, a cupping of dainty palms to meet his burning hands. He took a step toward her; she moved against him, a sweet fragrance against his heart.

"Yes, Shu-hsien, it would take many moons to tell you. Can you not guess?"

Shu-hsien raised her eyes to meet his and said simply, "Why should you ask? I can tell you what is in *my* heart. There is no room for anything else but thoughts of you, Yung-lin."

The air shimmered with a song of hope and promise. But Shu-hsien drew back after a moment.

"Yung-lin," she said, "I fear that my father will not agree to our marriage right away."

Yung-lin took her hands in his. "Because as a widower I would be taking you as my wife number two?"

Shu-hsien nodded. "I am my father's only child, and he often says that he wants me to be number one wife in marriage."

"I shall convince him. After all, I am a member of the Lo clan and have been dutiful and obedient to him. I know that he has special affection for me. It shouldn't be too difficult to persuade him."

So, naïvely, trustingly, he went to her father, who presided, as custom demanded of the patriarch, in the exact center of the room. Yung-lin kowtowed.

"Adoptive Father, I have sinned!" he said, and when the patriarch asked him how he had sinned, Yung-lin confessed his love for Shu-hsien. Lo Chia-li, a thin, tall man with folds of skin reposing beneath his wary eyes, listened to Yung-lin's request for permission to marry.

"Shu-hsien's marriage was arranged before she was even born," the patriarch replied. "Her mother and her cousin were expecting their children at the same time and agreed that if they were of different sexes, they would be betrothed. The youngest son of the Woo clan is to be her husband, and even though he is a few months younger than Shu-hsien, I cannot break a promise. But even if there were no promise, I would wish my daughter to be her husband's first wife, and since you are a widower, Yung-lin, I would not have permitted the marriage between you."

Yung-lin bowed and backed out of the room. His mind was on fire. Shu-hsien, a delicate flower; Shu-hsien, an exquisite, precious jade, and the youngest son of the Woo clan . . . Yung-lin knew him. For years the Woo boy played in the Lo courtyards, careful to stay away from the women's quarters. He was scrawny and sickly, with a pockmarked face, but he was rich. His father dealt in silk and cotton and tea, and rumor had it that he had accumulated a large collection of silver and gold idols from Siberian craftsmen.

Soon thereafter Lo Chia-li sent Yung-lin to represent him in the tea trading business in Maimachin.

That was seven months ago, and in that time he had gone back to Urga only once, to hear Shu-hsien vow that she would never marry anyone else.

Now, as he thought of her, Yung-lin knew he had to see her again. It was summer, travel would not be hard, and he needed to look into her gentle eyes, touch her glowing skin. They had exchanged a stolen kiss before he left the last time, and the memory of that kiss burned into his brain with unquenched fire.

Yes. He would go home to Urga. The fastest way to cover the 600 versts from Irkutsk to Urga would be by relay coach. He would have to pretend to Lo Chia-li that he had come home on business and then return to Maimachin with the camel caravan, after which he would join the horse caravan from Kyakhta to Irkutsk. He hated the slow-moving caravans, especially the horse carts that transported tea from Kyakhta to Irkutsk. They moved at a walking pace sixteen hours a day, one horse pulling a cartload of six or eight tea chests, with only one indolent driver to every four carts, who slept most of the way on top of the chests on a makeshift bed. Yung-lin often marveled at the horses' sharply honed instinct for knowing their way.

This time he didn't think he would mind the tedious return to Irkutsk, for his Russian friends were gone and it would be yet another business trip. But the journey down to Urga—that was a different matter. Ah, to have the wings of a bird, to soar into the heavens and fly, unimpeded, into the courtyards of the House of Lo!

After the relative quiet and cleanliness of Maimachin, the affluence of its merchant residents, the total absence of beggars, Yung-lin winced at the noisy crowds of Urga when he entered the city. Much had changed since it was built in 1649. Too bad it couldn't have remained a quiet, picturesque monastery town on the Tola River, nestling at the foot of the Po-ko-to Mountain, instead of becoming a busy trade center in Chinese-occupied Mongolia. With its mixture of Mongols and Chinese, the coolies, the singsong voices of the vendors, the mendicants whining for alms, the odiferous Bactrian camels undulating through the dusty streets as if they owned them, Urga was a beehive of activity.

Yung-lin dismissed his coach and took a palanquin through the narrow, crowded streets, past the monastery section in the center of town with its resident *Kutukhta*-lama—and on to the House of Lo at the edge of town.

Once through the lacquered red and green dragon gates, he made his obeisance to the patriarch, explained the unexpected purpose of his visit, and although Lo Chia-li showed no surprise, Yung-lin feared that the patriarch suspected there was another reason that had brought him back to the clan. He suffered through the ritual of taking tea with the elder aunt of the clan, discussed the changing seasons and the state of health of the youngest nephew, and finally withdrew into the inner garden he knew so well.

There, on the marble bench, sat his beloved. Deeply immersed in a silk-covered prayer book she held in her hand, Shu-hsien did not see him right away. Yung-lin was surprised, for he had never known her to be religious. The books he had seen her read were books of poems and philosophy, never religion.

Sensing a presence, Shu-hsien raised her head. Surprise, joy, and deep pain registered in her eyes before she quickly lowered them. Slowly she rose, placed her two fists on top of each other over her left hip, and dipped briefly in obeisance.

"Welcome home, Yung-lin. The clan was not expecting you back so soon," she said quietly, her voice strained and flat.

Alerted by the unexpected formality, Yung-lin raised an eyebrow and caught a warning in her look. Quickly she glanced at the opened door of the women's quarters, and then her eyes came around to fasten on his face. He understood.

"I have unexpected business in regard to the next caravan leaving for Maimachin, and there was no time to inform the venerable patriarch of my arrival," he said, following her lead and aware of a dozen ears listening behind the blue lacquered door. Unhurriedly Shu-hsien moved away from the entrance and strolled toward the opposite side of the courtyard, toward his own study. Yung-lin followed. Once inside, she carefully closed her prayer book, placed it on the ebony carved armchair that stood by his desk, and, joining her hands under her chin, bowed her head.

"Oh, Yung-lin, how many moons have I waited to see you again! My heart overflows!" She took his hand and pressed it to her cheek. "My father says that he is patient, that he will wait until my cousin is more mature before we marry, and by then I should be free of my desire to marry you. Time and distance between us, he says, will take care of that. He doesn't know how wrong he is, my father! He is not going to be happy about seeing you here. He has forbidden us to see each other at all."

Yung-lin's glance traveled to the prayer book on the chair. "I see you have added to your reading material. Do you pray often?"

She closed her eyes and nodded. "Yes, I find prayer helpful. The same nun who brought ginseng root to treat my mother before she died still comes to visit, and we often talk." Shu-hsien picked up the prayer book and, turning it over in her hands several times, added, "Prayer is comforting; it wiles the time away." Suddenly Shu-hsien looked around her furtively. "We must not be seen together, or Father will be angry. I shall come to your chambers tonight after everyone has gone to bed, and then we can talk."

"It may be dangerous for you," Yung-lin said.

"No one will see me, I promise."

"I meant another kind of danger . . . from me!"

Shu-hsien smiled sadly. "I am not afraid of you, Yung-lin. Even if anyone sees me and I am compromised, it will only hasten my father's decision to grant us permission to marry!" And before he could tell her how foolish was her intention, she was gone.

That night the moon played hide-and-seek with the clouds in the heavens. It peeked out to flood the courtyard with a cool blue light, to pour silver over the garden pond, to change daytime hues into undine colors of nighttime magic. But even as the garden outlines sharpened into focus, the restless moon swam away and dived into a feathery cloud to throw a dark shadow over the courtyard.

In his black ebony chair Yung-lin leaned forward on his desk and tried to read by the flickering light of a taper. From where he sat, he could see familiar objects he loved so well—a precious Ming vase, a couple of Ch'ing paintings on the wall, a polished rosewood chest with brass locks, a few brocaded pillows on his kang, a rich blue rug at his feet—but his gaze returned again and again to the door, which he had left open to let the fresh air come in and have the night bathe the room in its gossamer light. When the crickets chirped to test the silence of the garden, Yung-lin heard other sounds. Hurried footsteps, a hesitation, a movement, and there on the threshold, silhouetted against the opalescent light, stood Shu-hsien.

He rose slowly from his chair. Was this a dream or a reality? Her quiet elegance, her fragile beauty. She stepped into the room and closed the door behind her. They stood a long time looking at each other.

"Shu-hsien," he said at last, "why did you come?"

Boldly she raised her chin. "You ask me that?"

"You have to marry your cousin."

"For me there shall never be another!"

Her words rang in the room, and then a quiet came between them. He tried to think of what to say but could only look at her shining eyes, her parted lips. He tried again. What was there left to say? A trite exchange to veil the truth? And would he ever realize his dream? Tonight that dream was his to have.

As if in answer to his thoughts, in one fluid movement, Shu-hsien unfastened her embroidered dress and let it drop in graceful folds around her pedestal shoes.

A whispered rustle of silk filled the silence; a timid step bestirred a puff of air; it brushed against his cheek without haste, its tender touch intolerably sweet. He bridged the space between them and took her in his arms.

All night the moonlight frolicked with the shadows in the room. The sounds were soft—a sigh, a murmur. The perfumed air—a heady wine.

Chapter Eighteen

Yung-lin returned to Irkutsk, stopping in Maimachin long enough to let his two colleagues, with whom he shared a house, know that he would be gone for several months. Intolerable were the men's questions about his visit in Urga and their raucous voices and insinuations about the women they missed so much in Maimachin.

In Kyakhta he closed the deal with the go-between, the Buryat Stepan, gave the silver idols to his colleagues to be taken back to Maimachin, and gave a vague answer to Stepan's curious question as to why he wanted to return to Irkutsk so soon. "I have some unfinished business in the city," he said casually.

"Then do me a favor, Chien Yung-lin," Stepan said.

Yung-lin inclined his head politely and waited.

"It's my niece Marya. She was working for Prince Dolovin until his wife arrived, and now she has quit and is back in the family yurt. Her father, my brother, was never able to control her, and now he has sent me a message that he is concerned about that man Ossip, whom she's been seeing a lot. You know, the one who came to Siberia with the Dolovins."

Stepan paused; his crafty glance darted toward Yung-lin, then moved away. "My brother, uh," he went on, "says that Marya was a fool to quit working for the Dolovins while they were in Siberia and that as long as she is back in the Buryat camp, she should be looking for a husband among her own people." Slipping his thumbs through the leather belt of his bloused shirt, he added, "Marya has always minded my words, and I want you to take my message to her."

These Russians indulge in too much vodka and pelmeni, Yung-lin thought, watching how the extra pressure from Stepan's thumbs bulged his potbelly.

". . . and tell her"—Stepan's voice rose a pitch—"tell her that she is a fool not to listen to her father. Tell her that her uncle Stepan says so!"

Yung-lin promised to deliver the message, although he could not see why Marya's father objected to her seeing Ossip. The young cobbler was an industrious man, and if a friendship was developing between him and Marya, he could see no harm in it.

As for himself, he wasn't sure why he was so eager to return to Irkutsk. The unfinished business he talked about was in reality, only a vague idea, perhaps opening a trading office in town and buying more silver from another source. Why then? Could it be that he missed his Russian friends so much he wanted to see Ossip again and hear news of the Dolovins? Whatever the reason, Yung-lin was impatient to get back.

But the horse caravan from Kyakhta was not ready to leave. Exasperated, he watched as men took their time soaking willows in hot water to bend into hoops and then arch them over the horse's neck to be connected to the harness's tugs. It was a slow process, and Yung-lin lost patience. A robust Russian coachman with a forked beard and a cheerful smile called to him, "Come on! I'll get you to Irkutsk in half the time!"

Yung-lin decided to take the coach and waved good-bye to Stepan.

He was glad to leave. Deep in his heart was a sequestered memory of one night of love. Shu-hsien . . . A delicate, fragrant flower was now his, and his alone. Surely Shu-hsien's stubborn father would relent within the year and allow them to marry. It couldn't be otherwise. It *had* to be.

Once in Irkutsk, Yung-lin changed into a fresh gown in his rented two-room flat near the center of town and went to see Ossip. A sadness enveloped him when he entered the courtyard of the Dolovins' house and knocked at Ossip's door.

Seated in the cobbler's modest room that was permeated with the smell of raw leather and wax, they talked. A Russian family with three boisterous children now occupied the Dolovin home, and although Ossip had never been invited to enter the house, he collected the rent promptly and was proud of the trust the Dolovins had placed in him.

"Has there been any news from them?" Yung-lin asked.

Ossip's answer was vague. "Only one letter so far. They are glad to be reunited with their son, and I am sure their families are happy to have them back."

Yung-lin glanced at him. "We shall miss them here. I suppose it is too early to inquire if they would ever consider coming back here for a visit."

"With time, I hope they would come to see their property, if nothing else."

For a while both were silent; then Yung-lin changed the subject. "The last time I saw Stepan in Kyakhta, he asked me to deliver a personal message to his niece Marya."

Yung-lin watched with amusement as color rose to Ossip's face at the mention of the girl's name. The young cobbler rose, lifted a pair of high leather boots that stood near his chair, and showed them to Yung-lin.

"I've just finished these for her father. Tomorrow I shall deliver them. Would you like to come with me?"

"The young Marya is a fine woman, isn't she?"

Yung-lin said, and watched with surprise as Ossip's lips closed in a tight line. He busied himself brushing the imaginary dust off the boots.

"Is she? I wouldn't know."

Yung-lin raised his eyebrows. "I was under the impression that you had a special interest in the Buryat girl."

Ossip shot him a quick glance and then bent over to put the boots down. "I'm interested in finding a wife," he said evasively.

"And Marya does not qualify?"

"The girl I marry must be pure."

"And Marya is not?"

"I can't accept the Buryat custom of sharing wives and daughters with overnight guests."

"Not all Buryat women do this. What makes you think that Marya is not pure?"

"She has admitted it to me recently. Evidently she doesn't see anything wrong in this." Ossip straightened up and shook his head. "As a matter of fact, she thinks it is a charitable thing to do. Imagine that!"

"I see your point of view, but there is a redeeming point in her candid admission."

Ossip frowned. "What do you mean?"

"She does this according to the customs of her people and not because she is dishonorable."

"This particular custom of her people is not acceptable to me."

Yung-lin said no more. After all, the customs of his own country were just as rigid and uncompromising in regard to virgin brides as those of Ossip's.

The next day he found himself sitting on a rug-covered low cot inside Marya's yurt, eating out of a wooden bowl a meal of lamb and cabbage prepared in the caldron. Since the autumn days were already cold and snow had covered the ground, Yung-lin was dressed in a polar-bearskin coat and fur-lined boots and was uncomfortably warm now. His eyes were tearing from the cooking smoke that had little chance of escaping through the small opening at the top; but he was an honored guest in the Buryat yurt, and it would be unthinkable to complain.

He noticed that Marya was festively dressed and suspected that all her finery was for Ossip's benefit. Her hair, plaited into several thin braids, was intertwined with coins and coral beads, and around her head she wore a black velvet band similarly decorated with coral. Her bright green brocaded dress was offset by the significant red ribbon across one shoulder, tied in a long sash at the waist. Yung-lin wondered if her father's objection to her friendship with Ossip was based partially on their religious differences, but in view of what Ossip had told him, Marya's father and her uncle Stepan no longer needed to worry.

Although Marya was small, her frame was firm and full, not at all like the dainty figure of his beloved Shu-hsien. Marya was sturdy, conditioned to the hardships of nomadic life, and it could be that this very quality was what had originally attracted Ossip to the quiet, high-cheekboned girl. Ossip had told him that after Marya's mother had died and she had been left alone with her father, she had to learn early how to adapt to her male-dominated world. Was it her lifelong servitude, then, that had struck a responsive chord in Ossip? Yet, according to Stepan, she was able to have a mind of her own. As he studied her through his stinging, half closed eyes, she offered him a bowl of brick tea, seasoning it with salt and sour cream.

"Marya, I've seen your uncle Stepan," Yung-lin began cautiously, wondering how he was going to deliver his message without Ossip hearing him.

Pitcher in hand, Marya paused and smiled. "How is

my uncle? I haven't seen him in a long time. I miss him!"

"He's fine and sends his greetings to you." Yung-lin glanced at Ossip, who had raised his mug toward Marya for more tea, studiously avoiding her eyes. There was no doubt that the young cobbler had been smitten by the Buryat girl and was now having difficulty coming to terms with what he had discovered about her. Would he eventually accept it and marry the girl, now that the Dolovins were gone and he was lonely? And was he aware of her father's opposition, which would now only add to the insult to his pride?

When the meal was over and they had gone outside, Yung-lin took several deep breaths of brisk, fresh air to clear his lungs, before touching Marya's arm.

"I'd like a word with you," he said quietly, moving aside while Ossip and Marya's father walked toward the sleigh waiting to take them back to town.

Marya waited patiently for him to begin. With her long sheepskin coat trimmed with beaver and a fur hat covering her dark hair, Marya's face seemed small and vulnerable.

As he met her questioning eyes, Yung-lin regretted that he had agreed to deliver Stepan's message. After all, it was a personal matter, and he was not accustomed to interfering in another's family affairs.

"Marya," he began, "your uncle is concerned that you are not looking for a husband among your own people."

To his surprise, Marya smiled. "I see that my father has lost no time in sending messages to Uncle Stepan. He was never able to control me."

Yung-lin was stunned. He was not accustomed to such audacity from a woman. "Is there reason, then, for your uncle to be concerned?"

Marya shrugged. "That depends. I don't see why I

should want to marry only a nomadic Buryat. I have lived in Irkutsk long enough to appreciate a more settled life."

"Are there many Buryats you know in the city?"

"Why should I limit my choice to a Buryat? There are eligible Russian men to chose from."

"What about your religion? You seem to be a devout Buddhist."

"I am, but husband and wife can worship their God in different ways and still love each other."

"Your uncle is particularly worried about your friendship with Ossip," Yung-lin said reluctantly.

Marya tossed her head back. "Uncle Stepan has never met Ossip. He listens to my father too much."

Having said that, Marya looked at Yung-lin searchingly. "I see you don't approve of my friendship with a Russian either, is that right?"

Yung-lin inclined his head slowly. "It is not my place to voice what I think, Marya. I am only a messenger from your uncle and as such withhold my opinion."

"But I value your opinion, Chien Yung-lin."

"My thoughts are that should you marry a Christian and a Russian, you may find unexpected problems in your life."

Marya flushed. "All this is speculation, for Ossip has not committed himself to me." She hesitated for a moment, then went on. "As a matter of fact, ever since Prince Dolovin stayed overnight with us and Ossip came looking for him in the morning, he has changed. Who knows? I may yet end up like my poor overworked mother—putting up yurts and breaking them down to move to yet another camp, cooking in the smoky interior, and condemned to look at the world through inflamed eyes."

There was such bitterness in her words that Yung-lin chose to remain silent. So that was it, he thought. Not only had Ossip discovered that Marya was not pure, but it was Prince Dolovin who had stayed overnight in Marya's yurt. The implication was devastating, and Yung-lin felt deep compassion for the former serf whose sense of honor had been so cruelly violated. But in all fairness to Prince Dolovin, he probably hadn't known that Ossip was falling in love with Marya and must have had his reasons for being unfaithful to his wife.

What words of comfort could he give this Russian cobbler, he—a Chinese man with his own code of ethics that were deep-rooted in tradition?

He rejoined Ossip and told him he was ready to return to town.

When they were back in Ossip's room, the young cobbler busied himself at the table, placing coals in a copper samovar, and when tea was ready, Yung-lin accepted the cup with a small bow. Blowing at the hot liquid, he said, "I think Marya is well into marriageable age. I wonder why her father hasn't found her a husband yet."

Ossip glanced at him quickly and then turned away. "I think Marya has a mind of her own and will choose a husband herself. I wish her luck."

Yung-lin looked at him reflectively. A hardworking, candid man sat opposite him, not at all like Marya's crafty uncle, whose shady dealings in silver and gold earned him scorn from all the Chinese merchants. Marya and Ossip were well suited to each other, and it was too bad that they all were victims of their traditions. His own problem with Shu-hsien's father was a case in point.

His reflections were abruptly interrupted when Ossip suddenly slammed his forehead with the palm of his hand. "Oh, I'm such a fool! A letter came for you this morning from Moscow, and I forgot to give it to you!"

He searched in the corner of the room among his cobbler's tools, strips of leather, boot wax, and finally pulled out a long envelope secured with a red seal. Yung-lin accepted the envelope and then, as soon as he gracefully could, thanked Ossip for his hospitality and hurried home.

There he broke the seal and read the letter slowly. Although his spoken Russian was excellent, he read the script with difficulty, trying not to miss any of the thirty-six letters of the Russian alphabet.

My dear, respected Chien Yung-lin [Alexander wrote in his sprawling handwriting]! Our greetings to you, our good and faraway friend. We are not sure if you are in Irkutsk at the moment and are sending this letter to Ossip to be sure you get it. Although we are happy to be reunited with our son and our families, we do miss our friends in Siberia and are eager to hear of your news. We do hope things are working out for you.

I have not yet decided what I shall be doing from now on. My father died suddenly before our return, and my younger brother, Nikita, who had lived in St. Petersburg, has come home to take care of my ailing mother and the Dolovino estate. Although I have been reinstated and can return to St. Petersburg and my duties at the Winter Palace, I am not sure I am ready to resume my previous career. So many of my dear friends are gone. . . .

Do let us know how you are getting along. Princess Irina sends you her greetings. . . .

There followed a few innocuous comments on the weather, and the letter ended.

Yung-lin pondered over it. The tone of the letter was courteous, warm, but he missed the expected exuberance that should have spilled onto the pages of a letter from a man reunited with his family, a man who had regained his honor and his home.

After he had folded the pages carefully, Yung-lin's mind drifted a great distance away. He would answer Alexander's letter later on. Right now winter with its storms and fierce temperatures was not far off, and he knew that he had to return to Maimachin for the Chinese New Year's festivities of the White Month. His adoptive father, Lo Chia-li had informed him that this year he would come to Maimachin to celebrate the New Year with him.

The holiday was good for the trade. During the first week of the White Month the Maimachin gates leading into Kyakhta remained open until ten o'clock at night instead of the usual sunset hours, and Russian and Chinese merchants exchanged visits to entertain and be entertained lavishly by their respective hosts in both towns. Perhaps it would do him good this year, Yung-lin thought, to throw himself into the festivities with vigor and forget even if for a brief few days his longing for Shu-hsien and the void he felt without his Russian friends. In China he was bound by tradition and protocol to yield to the head of the clan, to withhold his opinions, and, encumbered by the florid façade of required verbal courtesies, was restricted in sharing personal confidences. But in Irkutsk, in the home of hospitable Prince Dolovin, he had learned to admire and enjoy the gregarious personalities of Russians, their ready acceptance of themselves, and their willingness to let others see them as they were. No such simplicity was possible in the courtyards of Urga or the merchant homes of Maimachin.

He chuckled, remembering how the year before, thoughtful Russians prepared delicious hot glühwein for them in Kyakhta, unaware that he and his Chinese colleagues loved champagne. However, the hot wine was as potent as their own, and in one of the hospitable Kyakhta homes Yung-lin ended the evening by drinking sherry afterward, with the result that he had to spend the night in Kyakhta, to the great merriment of his colleagues, who teased him the next day.

This year he would concentrate on reciprocating to his Russian hosts and at the same time showing his adoptive father how much enthusiasm went into celebrating the New Year in Maimachin. Difficult it was to admit that no matter how hard they tried to make the holiday a happy celebration, it was a sad compensation for the absence of their families.

The streets of Maimachin were brightly lit the evening Chien Yung-lin, and Lo Chia-li went strolling through town. Colored lanterns and multicolored paper flags hung on tightly strung lengths of cord that were pulled from one side of the street to the other. A frosty breeze moved the decorations as the two men walked toward the end of the street, where a large pagoda shrine was filled tonight with colored candles lit before a huge figure of Buddha dressed in purple, yellow, and red brocade. They did not linger here but moved on to an open-air theater, where they sat down under a canopy and watched the performance.

Horns, tambourines, and kettle drums blared incessantly, and although Yung-lin tried to watch the play, he could not concentrate on what was happening onstage. A parade of male actors, taking the parts of both sexes, enacted a militant drama. They were dressed in the lavish costumes of medieval princes with bunched arrows at the backs of their long gowns, and their wide sleeves flowed as they raised their whips at imaginary horses. They strode across the stage in deliberately long steps, shouting at one another in a violent exchange, but the substance of the play eluded Yung-lin. Even when an actor lost his tiger's mask and his embarrassed face emerged from the striped animal's costume, it failed to amuse Yung-lin.

Shu-hsien's voice and presence hovered above the din, permeating his every thought. How was she? He dared not ask Lo Chia-li anything beyond a polite inquiry about the clan's welfare, especially after he had received a cursory reply that everyone was prospering well. The older man had been in Maimachin two days now and never once had mentioned his daughter's name.

After the play they stopped in at one of the open houses where long tables of food were set up to entertain visiting Russians. Yung-lin was not hungry as he surveyed the lavish display of food. There was pheasant in sour cream, salt pork, steaming millet, soybean cake, plates of *yi-ts'eh*—mustard greens—and the pungent fragrance of vinegar and garlic spices. He ate sparingly with the ivory chopsticks he carried with him, and he listened absentmindedly to the high-pitched voices around him.

After a few cups of glühwein, Lo Chia-li's face grew red and shiny, and with one of his rare smiles, he raised the cup and nodded to the merchant sitting across from him.

"I drink tonight to the betrothal of my only daughter, Shu-hsien, to the eldest son of the Woo clan!" he said clearly. Loud cheering followed his words. Yung-lin forced himself to raise his cup politely; he inhaled the fragrance of the hot wine with closed eyes. To meet his adoptive father's glance would be intolerable.

Angry, shouting voices interrupted the toasts. The noise was coming from the street, and as Lo Chia-li rose and put his greatcoat on, Yung-lin followed him outside into the courtyard.

A fistfight was in progress in the street. Six or seven men punched one another with gusto, shouting insults into the air. At any other time Yung-lin would have watched the drunken brawl with amusement, but now he stood shivering nervously in his coat, acutely aware that in the absence of women, these fighting men had found an outlet to vent their frustrations.

Suddenly Yung-lin became aware of a Russian invective. "Slant-eyed accursed devils you are! I'll show you! Here! Take this . . . and this . . ."

Peering more carefully now through one of the openings in the pyramid-stacked bricks of the fence, Yung-lin recognized Stepan. With determined strides he worked himself into the crowd of fighting men. Fending off a few aimless punches, Yung-lin grabbed the nearest man's wrists.

"This man is from Kyakhta and, as such, a guest in Maimachin," he said firmly. "We must not lose face by insulting our guest." With incoherent grumbles, the men shuffled off, leaving Stepan rolling from side to side like a ship in rough waters.

"Some hosts you have here," he mumbled, setting his fur hat in its place. "All I tried to do was pull a handkerchief from one of those fellows' pockets to wipe some wine I spilled. You'd think I was stealing something valuable from him!" Stepan turned to the side and spit onto the frozen ground, then looked at Yung-lin, one eye swelling shut.

"I need to have a word with you," he said, winking at him with his uninjured eye.

Yung-lin bowed to Lo Chia-li. "I shall presently be with you, Adoptive Father," he said, and, pulling Stepan by the sleeve, moved away.

Stepan took a few deep breaths.

"*Chort vozmi*—devil take us! That wine of yours is potent stuff. Whew! Let me budge my brain a bit. . . .

What was it I had to tell you? Ah, yes, I have a message for you . . . a strange message from one of your own laborers. He delivered a few chests to me yesterday and said he had to return to Urga immediately . . . said he could not see you privately while you were with your father. . . . A strange fellow, that one! Kept looking over his shoulder all the time, as if someone were after him!"

Yung-lin closed his eyes. In the frosty outside air his throat suddenly felt raw. Carefully measuring his words, he asked, "Who sent the message?"

Stepan scratched the back of his neck. "Let me think . . . fog has temporarily clouded my brain." He chuckled. "It's a strange name. Something like Shu-shu?"

Yung-lin prompted: "Shu-hsien maybe?"

Stepan's face spread into a grin. "That's it! Shu-shu!"

Yung-lin did not correct him. "What is the message?" he asked, spacing his words carefully.

"The message is to tell you that when the summer comes, Shu-shu will leave Urga forever and come to Irkutsk." Stepan narrowed his eyes and looked at Yung-lin with sudden alertness. "Who is this Shu-shu? A friend of yours? And why is he leaving Urga in such secrecy?"

Yung-lin looked at Stepan for a few moments in silence. That Stepan did not recognize a Chinese woman's name was that much to his advantage. But could he trust him at all? He had no choice, for he certainly could not confide in any of his Chinese colleagues. Stepan was a Russian citizen and a crafty businessman knowledgeable in border affairs. Paid a handsome cumshaw, he would be the one to help Shu-hsien in her risky and dangerous plan.

"Shu-hsien is a good friend," he said to Stepan. "This friend doesn't want anyone to know about the secret plans to come to Siberia. In a few days, when I come to

Kyakhta, we shall talk about these plans, and maybe you can help us."

An avaricious gleam appeared in Stepan's eyes. He rubbed his hands together. "Always ready to help a needy friend. Just call on me!"

Yung-lin nodded and, gesturing Stepan to rejoin the feast inside, turned and looked into Lo Chia-li's questioning face.

"Who is that man?" he asked, and when Yung-lin told him, he shrugged. "It is our holiday, and for the good of our business, I guess we have to entertain them all!"

Yung-lin did not answer, grateful that Lo Chia-li had not asked what Stepan wanted to tell him. He needed to digest the startling news.

Fragile Shu-hsien with a will of steel. She was contemplating an arduous trip with a camel caravan, disguised as a boy, for no woman would join a trade caravan. His heart beat fast. She loved him enough to give up her home and family, to join him in a strange and foreign land.

There would be no turning back. Such a move would bring disgrace upon her head and upon the clan of Lo.

This also meant that he would have to leave Urga and Maimachin and never return to China. It was a good thing that he had thought about establishing an office in Irkutsk and continuing the trade from there. His heart beat faster. When the New Year's festivities were over, he would quietly gather his belongings and leave Maimachin forever. It would be a long and difficult wait, all those many months until they were reunited. But he would be living in Irkutsk, a city where many warm memories would sustain him. He would see Ossip often and hear about the Dolovins. How were they getting along in Moscow now? Were they so happy that they would soon forget their new friends in Siberia? Not according to their first letter. Perhaps he would hear from them again.

In the meantime, he would wait for his beloved. He needed her. He wanted her. Many Maimachin merchants had concubines both in Urga and in Irkutsk.

Perhaps while he waited these long months for Shuhsien, it would do no harm if he did the same.

Chapter Nineteen

Moscow in the spring. Flowers everywhere. Graceful birch leaves fluttering in a warm, languid breeze. Peals of laughter wafting from the Moskva River to bounce against the Kremlin walls. A cheerful, happy time.

At the Dolovino estate the household servants were busy with spring cleaning in preparation for the most festive, most solemn celebration of Easter holidays. This year especially, in spite of Prince Gregory's sudden death from a heart seizure the previous summer, there was much to be thankful for. He was not missed by the household, not mourned by his sons or daughter-in-law.

Perhaps the only person who grieved over him in resigned silence was Princess Dolovina, aging, fragile, and melancholy. Even the joyous news about her firstborn son failed to make her happy. She crossed herself when she first saw him and mumbled something about the grace of God and then returned to her introspective world, which, in the absence of her husband, had given her the only security she wanted. Her second son, Nikita, was there to take over Dolovino.
. . . Her Nikitushka was there to run things. . . . Alexander and Irina were saddened to see Princess Dolovina so withdrawn and hurt by her apathy to their happiness.

Little Sasha, however, made up for everything else

that was lacking. When they first arrived at Dolovino and were nearing the front entrance of the house, Alexander jumped out of their kibitka to race up the steps and scoop Sasha out of Nyanya's arms. The fifteen-month-old toddler burst out into a lusty cry, terrified by this stranger who had kidnapped him from his sanctuary.

Irina, on the other hand, approached her son cautiously, afraid to burst into tears and frighten him further, yet aching to hold him to her heart and smother him with kisses. And as she fought her own tears, she watched Alexander weep through a happy, nervous laugh, tears flowing copiously and unrestrained. And when at last she held her baby in her arms, plump and squirming, she thought no greater happiness could have happened in her whole life.

She couldn't tear her eyes away from her son's little face. Although he had her rich golden brown hair, he was a miniature of Alexander with his dark eyes and ready smile and he was so full of baby smells—the milk, the soap, the freshness of his baby skin. . . . Oh, her arms trembled for fear she might squeeze too hard and hurt him!

In the days that followed, Irina devoted most of her waking hours to Sasha, showering him with love, everything else set aside to make up for the time she had spent away from him. The child responded with hugs and happy laughs. For Sasha's sake, she was glad to see Alexander become acquainted with his son, even though it did not diminish her own estrangement from her husband.

Soon after their arrival she had demanded to know about Marianna Kosinskaya, and although Alexander, embarrassed by her questions, avoided the subject, Irina insisted on knowing how and why Marianna had confessed. Surely it was human to want to hear the details of her adversary's humiliation after her own—when she had humbled herself and begged Marianna for her husband's life.

At last, Alexander told her that from what he had been able to learn, Marianna had married a young engineer from a bourgeois family and soon afterward sought an audience with the tsar.

"It was an unprecedented move on the tsar's part, to grant it to a courtesan," Alexander mused, but Irina understood, recalling the tsar's sympathy when she had told him about Marianna's betrayal. He had not forgotten, then, the anguished plea of a wronged wife and had enough compassion to see justice done.

Marianna's conscience evidently would not let her start married life based on a lie. After she had told her husband of her false testimony, he insisted she go to the authorities and confess. But Marianna must have known that the quickest way to right the wrong was to seek, if possible, an audience with the tsar. When it was granted, there were no witnesses, but soon afterward Marianna was given a three-year prison sentence for perjury. After serving only a few months of her term, she died of acute inflammation of the lungs.

The memory of Marianna's intransigence at the time when she could have saved Alexander's suffering was too strong for Irina to feel anything but bitterness against the woman. Although she was now dead, she had left a legacy of tragic events that involved them all and had changed their lives irrevocably.

Almost from the very beginning of their return it had become a time of growing disappointments and petty hurts. Irina's parents were kind but distant, as if they had been hurt so deeply that they were afraid of being hurt again. Countess Radina mentioned casually that they had seen little Sasha only in the presence of the *nyanya* and the other grandmother, and Irina, sensing that her mother had been deeply hurt and now wished to be left alone, curtailed her visits. The only person who seemed genuinely happy to have them back was the old *nyanya*. She cried and kissed and blessed them both and took it upon herself to become their surrogate parent, treating them and little Sasha as her three children.

In truth, they discovered that Alexander was not received as a wronged hero by the few friends they had left, but rather his reappearance was looked upon as an embarrassment to their established and orderly lives. Irina's enthusiasm in describing Siberian life, its hospitality and freedom, the absence of serfdom, was treated with skepticism and a haughty tolerance toward an unfortunate friend who had gone through so much.

Dismayed by the Moscow society that now treated them with such indifference, Irina was further taken aback by their reaction to her mention of Yung-lin. "A tea merchant?" they had repeated with a deprecating shrug. "Now really!" She could almost hear them ask, "Wasn't there something more appropriate to do for a prince?" So it would be unseemly—wouldn't it?—to discuss their Chinese friend and the tea trading business that Alexander had joined.

It didn't take long for Irina and Alexander to realize that their closest, their best friends were those who were languishing in Siberian prisons, and their initial joy upon returning home began to wane, eroded by a slowly growing sense of guilt at having abandoned, however innocently, their comrades in need.

Then, two months after their arrival, a letter from Olga upset Irina. Olga wrote that in September 1827, shortly after Irina and Alexander had left Irkutsk, the Decembrists were transferred to a prison in Chita, an oversize village with a single street flanked by a few dozen wooden houses and dilapidated izbas. Although the men no longer worked in mines, they were required to do menial work, and Olga chafed at it.

> Our noblemen [she wrote] are cleaning stables, cattle sheds, digging ditches, threshing grain on a handmill. Imagine, my Boris and Princes Volkonsky and Trubetskoy sweeping streets! Eighty-two men are crowded in four rooms with no privacy whatsoever. And you know what? They are still in leg irons day and night! It's grossly unfair, I tell you! Only second-offense criminals are treated that way.

After reading the letter, Alexander slammed his fist on the table. "That's inhuman! Why don't they complain to Adjutant General Benckendorff? He's one of the closest associates of the tsar and the head of the so-called Third Department, which oversees all petitions from the Decembrists. He may not even be aware of the situation."

Irina shook her head. "By the time their petition goes through censors and reaches Benckendorff it may take months before any action is taken. We should appeal to the tsar directly."

Alexander raised his brows. "We?"

Irina nodded. "Yes, we. And more specifically, *you.* I've been thinking about going to St. Petersburg to see Katasha Trubetskaya's family. Count Lavale was so kind to me on my last visit there, and I'm sure he would appreciate any additional news I could give him about his daughter. It would expedite matters if you went to St. Petersburg with me and saw the tsar yourself. After all, you haven't paid your respects to him since you came home or thanked him for reinstating you."

"It may prove extremely awkward. What am I

supposed to tell him when he asks why I have resigned from my duties at court and retired to my estate? And he is sure to ask that!"

"You have a legitimate excuse. Your father is dead, and you are now the head of the family and must remain at Dolovino."

"But the tsar knows that Nikita is already living at home, and he may offer me a new position at court. You realize—don't you?—that I could never serve the tsar again after what he has done to my comrades."

"Alex, in all fairness, you must see it from the tsar's point of view: Our friends *did* rise against him, and they *are* guilty of treason. You blame the tsar for their suffering, yet in the same breath you refuse even to try to ease their plight. You can't bring yourself to pocket your pride! Well then, *I* shall go to see the tsar. I did it once in much more traumatic circumstances, and I can certainly plead for my cousin's welfare now."

"You shall do no such thing, Irina! It will look as if I were hiding behind my wife's skirts! I can't permit you to go. Can you understand this?"

Irina inclined her head and said nothing. It hurt to see Alexander's moral conflict, but it hurt more to think of Boris's degradation.

She took one servant with her and went to St. Petersburg. Count Lavale's palace brought many memories back, and Katasha's family wept on seeing her. What could she tell them? That the letters Katasha wrote home told the truth about her contentment at being near her husband? Irina tried to console them as best she could and then left the palace before breaking down in tears herself.

Out on the streets, it was a déjà vu experience, but a much more pleasant one: Before, she was the wife of a prisoner, a supplicant for his life; now, she was once again Princess Dolovina, a member of an illustrious family with an entrée to the court.

Her sleigh glided smoothly over the snow-packed streets of the capital. Strange, how the mind interpreted the sights to fit the mood! The last time she had feared the majesty of the snowbound city, its monuments and church spires seemingly somber and disapproving of her presence. Yet now the same tall spires and gilded domes shone with a light of welcome; the palaces and the statuary were serene in the clear winter day. Even the forbidding towers of the Peter and Paul Fortress stood unobtrusively behind its gray walls on the banks of the Neva, as if trying to efface themselves from her view.

She had forgotten how elegant people looked on the English Quay as they raced by, wrapped in sable, in their private sleighs of shining ebony, their coachmen dressed in gold-braided red coats and fur-trimmed hats. A beautiful city it was, full of dignity and exquisite taste and wealth—wealth for the privileged few. While these seemingly carefree people indulged themselves in luxury, her cousin Count Boris Radin was debased in leg irons.

Secretly defying Alexander's wishes, she had requested an audience with the tsar, and it was scheduled for this early afternoon. Already the sun, hazed by winter mist, had crossed the sky and would soon disappear behind one of Rastrelli's and Rossi's architectural triumphs.

At the entrance to the Winter Palace she was met with deference and escorted to the tsar's private office. She curtsied deeply before the august figure of Nicholas standing before her again in the green uniform of the Izmailovsky Regiment. Ramrod straight and unsmiling, his hands behind his back, he was anew a forbidding majestic presence. She had forgotten how intimidating the tsar could be and fought a sudden tremor spreading to take hold of her limbs.

But as the doors closed behind her, an unexpected metamorphosis took place. In one quick movement he was beside her and, taking her hand, helped her rise. To her surprise, he kissed her hand and led her to a gilded Empire chair, then sat opposite her, crossing his booted legs. A gracious smile illuminated his face, softened his features, and endowed his eyes with a twinkle.

"The last time we met was in most unfortunate circumstances, Princess, and I am delighted that you have come back to St. Petersburg. It is indeed a pleasure to see you again."

For once Irina was at a loss for words. The totally unexpected approach, the warmth, the informality of the tsar's gestures touched a sensitive nerve. Was he trying to throw her off guard? She had heard that the tsar had been mercurial when he questioned the Decembrists, disarming some, threatening others, and never divulging his true self. Who was the real man? Although reputedly a concerned and tender family man, he was harsh and uncompromising with his subordinates.

The tsar tapped his fingers impatiently on the arm of his chair. "Princess?"

No annoyance, only a touch of amusement in his voice.

Irina regained her composure.

"I beg your pardon, Your Majesty, I was thinking how good it is to be back in the civilized world again."

"Oh? Am I to understand then, that you have found people in Siberia—er—somewhat uncivilized?"

"Not at all, Your Majesty," Irina replied quickly. "I was referring to the physical grandeur of St. Petersburg as compared to the rather primitive housing in Siberian towns."

"Well now, we could hardly have expected the Italian masters to build the whole of Russia, could we?"

Irina flushed. "Of course not, Your Majesty, but even in a large city like Irkutsk, primitive structures predominate. As for the people, perhaps it is to their advantage, for the classes are not so sharply delineated. We were treated with good-humored deference by the simple folk—no servility, no fear."

She paused for a moment, remembering the warmth and openness of the Siberians, then added pensively, "It was rather nice."

The tsar joined his hands at the tips of his fingers, then leaned his chin on them. For a few seconds he studied Irina silently, and she squirmed inwardly under his scrutiny. Then he said, "Tell me, Princess, you live in Moscow, yet you have come to St. Petersburg and have sought an audience with me. To what do I owe the pleasure of seeing you again?"

"My cousin Count Boris Radin is now in the Chita prison, and we have learned that their commandant, Major General Leparsky, is keeping the prisoners' leg irons on day and night. I am here, Your Majesty, to ask you, most respectfully, to have the commandant remove them. Those men work hard and suffer dreadful privations as it is, without having their legs in irons like common criminals."

"You are bold, Princess! But I do understand, however, your eagerness to help your cousin and others who are paying their penalty. As a matter of fact, one of the Decembrists, Alexander Kornilovich, has just submitted the same complaint. I shall look into it immediately, and as you know,"—he smiled frostily —"I do keep my word. I am curious about something, though. Tell me, why are *you* here, not Prince Dolovin? It is he who should have come to petition." The tsar raised a brow and gave her another of his cold smiles. "Although I must admit," he added, "I'd much rather grant an audience to you."

"My husband doesn't know that I have asked for an audience, Your Majesty; but it is *my* cousin who is in leg irons, and I felt it was my duty to plead with you on his behalf."

Frantically she thought: *Well, at least it's part of the truth, isn't it? I didn't tell Alexander about the audience!*

"Speaking of your husband, Princess, why hasn't he come to see me since his return? I understand that the reason he gave for his resignation was his duties as the new head of the Dolovino family estate, but should he ever wish to return to court, we can always find him a position here. I am sure that his younger brother, Nikita, would be willing to take over the running of the estate, which, incidentally, I understand he is doing splendidly already."

Irina bowed slightly. "Yes, he is, Your Majesty."

The tsar shot her a quick glance. "Then why is Prince Dolovin using such a weak excuse to stay away from the court?"

Irina bristled. "My husband is not using an excuse, Your Majesty. The reasons for his decision to remain at the Dolovino estate are complex but valid."

"Then permit me to guess them. Although your husband was proved innocent in the complicity of the Decembrist plot, his sympathies still lie with his comrades, and he cannot bring himself to serve his sovereign, who saw to it that justice was done to him. The trouble with your husband, Princess, is that he is rigid in his convictions and refuses to accept another point of view, a lamentable trait of character, especially if that point of view happens to be his sovereign's. The oath of allegiance demands absolute loyalty, and I must say I am disappointed in Prince Dolovin."

"Your judgment of my husband is harsh, Your

Majesty." Irina paused, then looked boldly into the tsar's eyes. "With all due respect, permit me to point out that not everyone is able to overcome his rigidity and consider another point of view."

The hint was pointed, and the tsar looked at Irina sharply. She was mortified. *My God, will I ever learn to hold my tongue?* she thought. *What made me think I could speak to my sovereign this way?*

But the tsar only shook his head. "I have never met anyone like you, Princess. After our last meeting a year ago I could not forget you. Yours was a tragic and wronged figure, yet one sustained by a courage rarely seen in an average woman. Thus, when the truth came to light, I acted promptly."

Irina inclined her head slowly. "And I thank you for it, Your Majesty, although my experience in Siberia has strengthened me further and taught me a valuable lesson."

"And what was that, Princess?"

"That one can search for happiness in many places."

The tsar studied her with narrowed eyes, then smiled and nodded formally. "I respect your philosophy, Princess, even if I fail to share it. I promise you, however, that I shall look into the business of leg irons immediately."

The tsar rose. The audience was over.

Irina curtsied deeply and withdrew from the room. There was nothing more to do but return to Dolovino and hope that the tsar would take action.

Chapter Twenty

Irina didn't tell Alexander about her audience with the tsar—she didn't want yet another argument—but privately she was gratified that in spite of her verbal fencing with the sovereign, the audience seemed to have left a positive impression on him. She had been uncomfortable in his presence and still considered him an enigma. Grateful that she did not have to live in St. Petersburg, she was nevertheless acutely aware that things at home were not what they should have been. Minor incidents took on larger proportions in her mind. She became annoyed, for instance, whenever she caught Alexander lying on the floor in the nursery, a willing victim to his son's vigorous bouncing atop his father.

"You're spoiling him, Alexander. Discipline must begin from the first day!"

"What else have I to do?" he answered spontaneously, ruffling the child's curls.

There's the problem, Irina thought. Alexander had difficulty adjusting, and they both felt out of place in an already established household run by a younger brother who obviously resented their presence. Nikita's actions were causing friction between the two brothers. Irina knew that as an older brother, Alexander should have been allowed to take over the reins of the estate on his return, but Nikita had entrenched himself in his father's apartments and was ruling the household with an iron fist, much in his father's egotistical tradition. Irina chafed at his unconcealed disregard for his older brother's place in the family. A young man like that, Irina thought with alarm, would turn into a true despot if allowed to continue uncontrolled.

One evening, as they sat in their apartments, sipping an after-dinner liqueur, she mentioned this to Alexander.

He shrugged. "Nikita knows how to run the estate by now far better than I. Besides, I don't have my heart in controlling the lives of the serfs we own. I wish . . ." He sighed and did not finish the sentence.

"You wish?" Irina prompted, already guessing what he would say.

"I wish we could free all our serfs and have them work for us as free men and women. I realize, of course, that I'm wishing for a miracle, but I wish it nevertheless!"

Irina nodded. There was nothing to say, for she dreamed of the same thing and, dreaming, knew that while Tsar Nicholas was on the throne, no such miracle could take place.

As they talked, peals of a woman's muffled laughter sounded nearby. Startled, they looked at each other and realized that the sounds came from Nikita's apartments. Alexander raised an eyebrow and smiled.

"It sounds as if Nikita has company!"

The laughter continued, interrupted by sudden cries and running feet.

"I'm sorry, darling, but Nikita is young and unmarried and is certainly entitled to freedom in his own apartments. I'm only sorry that the private sounds of his amusement are reaching us here."

Alexander's words sounded apologetic, and Irina was irritated. *Why is it*, she thought, *that blood always talks loudest of all? Just because they are brothers, he feels dutybound to excuse him.* She could not bring herself to say anything, and as the silence deepened in the room, the laughter continued at a sustained, unaltered pitch. There was something unnatural in the quality of that laughter, an artificial, painful strain. Irina listened. Imperceptibly it began to change to a forced, hiccuping sound with a touch of hysteria.

Their eyes met, held, and then Alexander's narrowed. Slowly, deliberately he replaced his glass of liqueur on the silver gallery tray.

"I think I had better take a look," he said without looking at Irina.

Irina rose. "I'm coming with you."

He barred her way. "It's a man's job, my dear. Whatever is going on in Nikita's bachelor apartments, there is no room for a lady there."

Irina raised her chin. "I'm no ordinary lady, remember? After facing the tsar while you were in prison, after fighting off the wolves in Siberia, nothing that Nikita is doing can shock me."

Alexander sighed and shook his head. "I've got myself a determined little wife, haven't I?" He offered her his arm. "Let's see, then, what's going on!"

As they neared Nikita's rooms, the laughter grew louder, more hysterical; there were sounds of scuffling. Impatiently Alexander rapped on the door, and when no one answered, he threw the door open and walked in. Irina followed.

The scene inside Nikita's study turned Irina's stomach. A strong smell of brandy hung in the air as she tried to sort out what was going on before her.

A plump servant girl, dressed only in an undershirt, her gauzy white blouse and red *sarafan* lying crumpled on the floor, wriggled in Nikita's arms as he held her from behind, digging his fingers into her ribs and tickling her. His ordinarily pale face was red and shiny with perspiration, his gaze clouded with drink and lust, as he nibbled at her ear. The tortured girl's bare feet shuffled frantically, clawing at the rug, but in Nikita's viselike grasp, she succeeded only in thrashing around, her body contorting in a paroxysm of agonized laughter.

Unable to hold her eyes on the girl, Irina glanced at the rest of the room. An almost empty bottle of *zubrovka* vodka stood beside a half-full decanter of brandy; shards of broken goblets were spattered near the fireplace; burgundy red pillows, lovingly embroidered by Princess Dolovina, and the girl's crumpled white apron lay trampled on the floor near the leather divan.

"Nikita, stop it at once!"

Alexander's angry voice cut through the girl's hysteria with instant effect. Nikita froze in motion, and the girl, taking advantage of the momentary slack in his grip, broke away and dropped to the floor, rolling her body in rigid spasms, her dreadful gasps of laughter turning to sobs.

Nikita looked up with bleary eyes. "Well, well"—he leered—"where did you appear from? Want to join in the fun? Matryoshka here is a good sport! She loves it when I do this to her!"

"The girl is hysterical!" Alexander shouted. "You can tickle a person to death, Nikita, don't you know that?" He stooped to help the girl up, but she flinched and cowered into the corner.

"Don't be afraid, I won't harm you," Alexander said gently.

The girl continued to cower; but her hiccuping spurts of laughter gradually subsided, and she began to tremble. Beads of sweat glistened on her face; moist wisps of hair lay limp on her forehead. Large blue eyes, now filling with tears, stared at Alexander in terror.

"Please, Barin, don't touch me now!" she whispered hoarsely. "I can't take it anymore! Not tonight!"

Irina held her hands behind her back, for the urge to scratch her drunken brother-in-law's face was strong. As she watched Alexander help the girl to a nearby chair, Nikita moved into her line of vision.

"So! My sanctimonious older brother comes again to the rescue of the underprivileged and brings his saintly spouse along for moral support. Ha-ha! Look where it got you the last time—chains and the steppes of Siberia. This time, though, you are trespassing on *my* domain. Matryoshka is my property, and mine alone!" His voice rose angrily. "Do you hear? Mine!"

Abruptly he turned on Irina. "And you! You have no business being here. No right to stand in righteous judgment . . . for that's what you're doing, aren't you? Aren't you?"

In one stride Alexander was between him and Irina. "That's enough, Nikita! You're drunk and disgusting. Don't you see what you've done to this unfortunate wench? Look at her, she's in dreadful shape! Let her go, and we'll talk tomorrow, when you're sober."

Tenderly Irina took the weeping girl, hastily helped her dress, and led her out into the hall.

"He'll have me whipped tomorrow, Barynia," the girl whimpered. "He will! I made too much noise. I know it!"

"No, he won't," Alexander said firmly. "I'll see to it that he doesn't. Now go to your quarters and rest."

The girl wiped her nose with the full sleeve of her blouse, curtsied, and darted into the darkness.

Back in her boudoir, Irina sank onto her chaise longue. She felt a weakness spread through her limbs. "Alexander, how could this happen to a young man like Nikita? I can't believe he's your brother! What's happening to our society? Do things like that go on in other households, too? How revolting, how shameful!"

"I'm sorry you had to witness this degrading scene, Irina. I'm ashamed of my brother's behavior. I had no idea that power would corrupt him so fast, and in such a way. Believe me, I've never known him to be this cruel even under the influence of alcohol. He was always fanatically proud of his name and title, but it seems that it has all gone to his head in the most despicable way. I'm glad that I am the older brother. He has to listen to me!"

With the emphasis on the last phrase, Alexander's voice shook, and Irina glanced quickly at her husband. Was there a shade of uncertainty? Did his voice lack conviction? She didn't want to think so. Certainly there should have been respect for the older brother in-grained in Nikita from childhood. Or had that been twisted around to justify his taking over Alexander's position as the new head of the Dolovin family?

Deep in thought, she started violently when Alexander tried to take her in his arms.

"I'm sorry, darling, for startling you," he whispered. "Let's forget this sordid affair for tonight. I love you so!"

Irina let him hold her for a few moments. "It's all so dreadful, Alexander. That poor girl! It brings back memories of your father and Agasha. But this is even worse, for Agasha never mentioned being treated like this. It's so revolting and horrible!"

Alexander didn't answer, only tightened his embrace. In a few moments Irina became aware of a slow, sinuous movement of his hands signaling his intent, and suddenly she pushed his arms down and backed away.

Alexander frowned. "My God, Irina, what's wrong with you? Why take it out on me?"

"I don't understand how you can approach me with your—I mean—after what we have just seen."

"Nikita's behavior and my desire for you have nothing at all in common."

With her lips pressed tightly together, Irina stood staring at her clasped hands. A few seconds later Alexander pulled her roughly into his embrace again.

"I don't deserve your rejection!" he whispered, reaching for her lips.

Instinctively Irina knew that to reject him now would be a wound to his pride creating an even deeper rift in their already threatened marriage. Reluctantly she submitted to his lovemaking. Passive at first, she gradually responded to his kisses and was caught up in his passion that, in spite of her stubborn will, revived exquisite memories of the past.

For a blissful, unhurried time, his feathery touch strained her nerves to an intolerable pitch, sending waves of tension through her whole being; then a strong muscular arm entrapped her waist, forcing submission, and her body responded willingly—a vibrant vessel yearning to receive his intimate power of thrust that would deliver her, even if for a brief ecstatic moment, of all the past and future hurts. She clung to him, her own, imperfect man, and loved him now with all the love of her tormented soul.

Later she was unable to fall asleep. Was it possible, she thought, that all men's carnal urges were involuntarily aroused by scenes that revolted a woman? Alexander's reaction tonight seemed to confirm her suspicion. And what about other women in his life? She squirmed, remembering.

Undeniably Alexander's early affair with Marianna had compounded Irina's jealousy and pain in Irkutsk, had fanned her imagination about his relationship with the Buryat woman, creating a barrier between them that had restrained her love. Her common sense had dictated that she must forgive him, and in essence, her mind had done so. But the heart remembered. "Forgive and forget," the axiom stated. Could it be that she had only *thought* she had forgiven him but in truth had not? Or was it possible to forgive yet to harbor an unwanted memory in a kind of masochistic torture?

Irina rose from her bed and paced the room. Perhaps she was unrealistic to expect any other behavior from Alexander. After all, he was a man, and men think and act differently from women. She had a son to love and cherish now.

A son. She shivered, stood still for a moment, and then walked briskly to the nursery. There she tiptoed, careful not to awaken the snoring *nyanya*, then bent over the sleeping child and gently stroked his downy hair. Another Dolovin was growing up. Another male in the family to assert himself, to be a *man*. This, then, would be her goal in life. If her untainted love for Alexander could not be restored, she would dedicate her emotional resources in molding her son into a different man from his father, one who would . . .

Irina did not finish her thought. It was nebulous and she was confused. Time would heal everything, would make her forget. It must. . . .

The Easter holidays were over, and May had arrived to bewitch. Cherry trees covered with white blossoms—a snow of fragile petals giving promise of delicious black cherries to follow—dressed the Dolovino park. Pansies, forget-me-nots, violets, lilies of the valley, abounded in the gardens and surrounding meadows, their intoxicating fragrance permeating the air.

A beautiful time of the year, Irina thought, a time for love. But she no longer felt love the way she used to. Her energy, her enthusiasm for life, were waning. What had happened to her desire to teach the village children?

Alexander's frustrated attempts to take over the running of the estate pained her. His arguments with Nikita grew daily, and she chafed at Nikita's ability to have the last word. Although Alexander had saved Matryoshka from a whipping after they had discovered the drunken scene in Nikita's room, the larger debates ended in the younger brother's favor. Undoubtedly he was more aware than Alexander of the mood and the needs of the local serfs. He was also more knowledgeable about the management of the estate. Moreover, Irina realized that Alexander had been impressed by the Siberian peasants' freedom and that he could not, would not exercise the harsh discipline so necessary in keeping the upper hand over the thousands of "souls" for whom he would be responsible. Although she was incensed that Alexander had not asserted himself right from the beginning, she knew that he would have been a reluctant master of his serfs.

Gradually, insidiously the world around her began to pale. A fragile, tenuous idea nagged at the back of her mind.

How would it be to return to Irkutsk?

Here at Dolovino, her sphere of activities was narrow. She had taken over the running of the household from her mother-in-law, for Princess Dolovina spent most of her time in her rooms now, frequently refusing to change her silk peignoir for days at a time and reclining for hours on her chaise longue. Nikita addressed himself more and more to the business of hunting and riding, devoting only enough time to the overseer and the manager of Dolovino to deprive his older brother from becoming actively involved.

What was the answer?

The birch groves near Lake Baikal would be in leaf now, their green, silvery petals shimmering in the sun. Was Yung-lin in Irkutsk? Had he finally found happiness? Letters took so long to reach them from Siberia. . . .

Here in Moscow receptions and balls continued as always, frequent and socially sought after, but Irina shunned them. Better to read at home than be bored by inane conversations. Whether she was with a book or an embroidering needle, talking to Nyanya or the housekeeper, the daring thoughts clung tenaciously.

How was Olga managing? Her letters begged for sympathy, complained of loneliness and boredom; she was envious of their return to Moscow. Irina thought: If they were back in Irkutsk, they could ask her to visit them, or they could go see her in Chita. . . .There was only one thing that kept her from saying anything. Back in Siberia there would again be the Buryat girl's specter between them. . . .

What would Alexander say if she voiced her thoughts?

Then, at the end of May, another letter arrived from Olga, and after she had read it, Irina ran to Alexander's study and handed it to him without a word. Olga wrote that she had decided to leave Siberia and return to Moscow. Not a word about Boris, about his reaction to her decision, his frame of mind.

Slowly Alexander rose from his chair and faced Irina.

"It is time we were truthful with each other," he said. "I know you have been unhappy. Ever since our return home you have spent all your time with Sasha, and it is not healthy to be wrapped up in the child this much. Do you want to tell me what is disturbing you, or shall I guess?"

Irina looked at him directly. "It is time we were truthful," he had said. She would try. What could she tell him? That she was unhappy in Moscow, that she wanted to return to Siberia yet feared a Buryat woman? How childish!

"I miss Irkutsk," she said quietly. "Life was different there, more meaningful. I felt useful. Chita is only six hundred versts from there. The Trubetskoys, the Volkonskys, Olga—they all are there."

Without a word, Alexander nodded. "Darling, I wondered—I suspected that this was partly what was bothering you, but I dared not broach the subject. I did not want to appear selfish in case I was mistaken. I, too, have changed. I no longer belong here. I cannot serve the tsar directly anymore, yet I suffer to see our serfs in continuous servitude. What would you say if we moved to Siberia permanently?"

Irina hesitated for only a moment. "It would certainly be an improvement over living at Dolovino," she said slowly. "After having a home all my own in Irkutsk, I don't feel at home here anymore."

They hugged each other, and for the first time in many months Irina felt the warmth toward her husband seep through her veins.

In a moment Alexander pulled away. "There is one thing I would like to do, though, before we leave," he said hesitantly. Irina waited.

"Off and on my conscience has been bothering me about my father's bastard son, my half brother. Shouldn't I take over his upbringing, give him more than what he has now as an illegitimate son of a serf girl? If we took him with us to Siberia and reared him along with our Sasha, he would have better opportunities in life."

Irina nodded. "Very well. Let's go see Agasha. It's only a few versts from here, and when we see her and the boy, we can tell her what we have in mind."

The next day they went to see Agasha and were pleasantly surprised to learn that she had married a hardworking muzhik from her village and lived in a clean, cozy izba near the main mansion.

When they knocked on her door and Agasha saw who it was, she paled and, without asking them to come in, dashed to the back of the room, where a tousled dark-haired little boy stood by the large clay stove. She swept him into her arms and held him tightly. Her once sparkling eyes, now clouded by pain and wide with fear, stared at Irina and Alexander.

"We came to see you and your little boy, Agasha," Irina began gently. "It's been a long time. How are you getting along?"

Agasha's face turned sullen. "I'm fine, Barynia, and I'm glad for you and His Grace."

"Are you happy here, Agasha?" Alexander asked. "Do you want for anything? We hear you are married now. Does your muzhik treat you well?"

Agasha nodded. "I have a kind muzhik. Although he doesn't beat me when he is drunk, he tells me that he loves me anyway."

Alexander smiled. "So much for the beating theory. A muzhik does not have to beat his wife to prove that he loves her, right?"

Agasha stared at him without comment.

"Agasha," Irina said, "we came not only to see how you are but to ask if you would like us to rear your son in our family as a free man."

Instantly Agasha's eyes filled with tears, and she tightened her grip on the little boy. "Don't take him away from me, Barynia! Oh, God, it is cruel! He's my joy and life. I'll die without him!"

"But we want only the best . . ." Alexander began. Irina grabbed him by the arm and said quickly, "We want the best for *you*, Agasha. If you want to keep the boy, we won't take him."

Agasha's lips quivered as she looked from Irina to Alexander with fear in her eyes, and then, when Alexander said nothing, she whispered, "Thank you,

Barynia, thank you, and may God bless you! I know you could take the boy away from me. . . ." She began to cry.

"I promise you we will do no such thing, Agasha," Irina said firmly, and on an impulse kissed Agasha's cheek, then ruffled the boy's hair. "He's a fine-looking boy, and I can see you're taking good care of him."

Agasha lowered the child to the floor and, taking Irina's hand in both of hers, kissed it passionately. With her own tears threatening to spill over, Irina turned quickly and motioned Alexander to follow her outside.

On their way home Alexander voiced his doubts. "Didn't you give in too easily, Irina? After all, he *is* my father's son, and I feel responsible for the child. We want the best for the boy, but we left him to be another serf!"

"Who's to tell what's best for him, Alexander? Wouldn't we feel guilty tearing him away from Agasha, who has already suffered so much at the hands of a Dolovin? Wouldn't our guilt reflect in his upbringing if we took him along with us? Who knows? Things may change for the better by the time he grows up. We have to believe that."

Alexander took her hand and kissed it. "I love you, Irina, and am proud of you for many things but, most of all, for your optimism and hope for a better future." He paused, then added, "and speaking of the future, I'll do my best to make you happy again."

Irina caught the subtle hint, the sadness in his voice, yet could not bring herself to reassure him.

After a while he put his arm around her. "As soon as the roads are passable, we shall leave for Siberia."

Chapter Twenty-one

How different was the view of Irkutsk to Irina's eyes this time! What a joy to see the brightly painted wooden houses, Jerusalem Hill—purple in the distance, the golden belfry of the Irkutsk Cathedral towering above the city—all familiar and friendly now. If inanimate objects had voices, she was sure she could have heard their hospitable welcome.

As they turned the busy town square corner and drove into the shady treelined street where their house stood near the country church, Irina's apprehension grew. Although they had written to Ossip about their return, there had been no time to receive his reply and learn if he had been successful in having their house vacated before their arrival.

Her fears were groundless, for when they reached the two-story house, there was Ossip, waiting at the door with the maid, Anisia. He had thought of everything: He had hired a Russian nanny for Sasha—a buxom Siberian woman, Anushka, with a two-year-old child of her own. A cheerful woman in a gray cotton dress and a large white apron, she swept Sasha into her arms first, kissed him on both of his dimpled cheeks, and only then bowed to Irina and Alexander.

"Welcome back, Your Graces," she said clearly, without the servile effusiveness of Russian serfs.

"We are honored to see you again," Ossip said,

bowing low and touching the ground with the tips of his fingers.

Tears came to Irina's eyes when she entered the house and saw the rooms immaculately clean, all her furniture and the bibelots she had left behind intact. The first thing she wanted to do was to slip out and run to the nearby church, but Anushka blocked her way.

"The church will wait, Princess, but the empty stomach will not. I don't want you swooning on me. Sit down and eat first; then go."

Stunned by such irreverence from a servant, Irina looked at Anushka disapprovingly, but when she saw her twinkling eyes and kindly smile, she could only nod and sit down at the table. After a delicious meal of Siberian pelmeni and a braided poppy-seed *krendel*— sweet bread—Irina complimented Anushka on her cooking. The woman smiled and paraphrasing a proverb, said, "What we have is what we serve."

Once inside the country church, Irina knelt to pray. In no grand cathedral of the Moscow Kremlin had she ever felt such uplifting of spirit, such near-hypnotic state of detachment from the turbulent world as in this quiet, modest church. For a fleeting moment she knew the serenity and the peace that ancient Essenes must have achieved in their meditative quiescence.

It was early for services, and the church was empty except for a stooped crone she had seen before. Dressed all in black, a kerchief around her head, she darted with amazing agility, from candlestand to candlestand, removing the burned-out candles, then unrolling the Oriental runner down the center of the floor in readiness for evening vespers. There were no bejeweled icons here, only modest images of the saints, painted by amateur hands with reverent love and care.

Irina prayed fervently for a new and happier future, trying to forget the sad farewell from her faithful *nyanya*, who had wept through a smile, wiping her eyes with the palms of her hands. "I know I shall never see you again, but we shall meet in the next world. I am happy for you. You now belong to that other land, and you must go there with your prince." Nyanya blessed and hugged her. Then she took Irina's face between her calloused hands and, looking into her eyes with a twinkle, said, "Don't forget to laugh together."

Now Irina wondered if they could make a fresh start, forget the tragic past and remember only the carefree days of their courtship and honeymoon, when they had indeed laughed well together.

Hopeful, she went back to their house, hugged little Sasha, and told Alexander how happy she was that they were closer to all their unfortunate friends. Alexander shook his head. "Darling, because we've traveled so many thousands of miles, it may seem that we are practically next door to Olga and the Trubetskoys and the Volkonskys. Don't forget they are still more than six hundred versts from here."

Somehow Irina's elation was dampened. "It's still possible that we shall see them again," she said. "We're far closer than we were in Moscow."

But for now, she was content to reestablish contacts with friends they had made in Irkutsk. Her desire to teach children, dormant in Moscow, now surfaced again with renewed enthusiasm. As soon as they were properly settled, she wanted to send word to the local school that she would teach French to the children if their parents were willing to send them to her home, where she would do it free of charge.

That night, as Irina prepared for bed, she remembered that she had hidden a black lacquered jewel box in the bottom drawer of her wardrobe. She pulled it out to put away her string of pearls, and as she did so, she saw the broken piece of coral amulet she had found in the felt shoe under Alexander's bed when she first arrived in Irkutsk.

Her hands burned as she picked up the broken piece and studied it. It was smooth and polished and obviously had been worn a long time. Marya must be missing it. She should return it to her, but she couldn't make herself do it. "Jealousy and love are sisters," her *nyanya* had said before her wedding. But it wasn't jealousy she felt now, was it? A deep hurt it was, so profound she would have to struggle to overcome it, for otherwise she was destined to live the rest of her life poisoned by such a hurt. Just as she thought she had rediscovered her happiness and had attempted to heal the estrangement between her and Alexander, this broken piece of stone had surfaced to taunt her. And why should a Buryat woman, whose invisible shadow haunted her, become such a barrier in her relationship with Alexander? Was it because her pride had a perverted twist that would not permit her to give herself totally to Alexander until she had resolved her conflict and had overcome her hurt? How foolish! How vicious to punish herself that way!

Yet no amount of self-chastising helped Irina overcome her resentment against Marya, and when she saw Alexander reading in the parlor, she turned abruptly and reentered her bedroom. There would be no point in bringing up the past again; it would only reinforce the rift between them, and she so wanted their life to be happier than it had been in Moscow! So much! She would give herself time for the wound to heal, throw the amulet away, and never think about it again.

But even as she thought this, she carefully replaced the piece of stone in the bottom of the jewel box and, after closing it, put it back in the drawer. A small voice inside her, however, warned her not to show it to Alexander. He seemed happier now than she had seen him the whole year they spent in Moscow, and there would be nothing to gain by telling him about the amulet.

As the weeks slipped by, Alexander indeed was happier than he had been since the fateful December 14 two and a half years ago. He was pleased to learn that he could reopen his office and trade again with Maimachin merchants, using Igor Panfilov as his partner in Kyakhta. Although reinstated in his rank and now financially independent, Alexander realized that the commercial world beckoned to him, and the life of leisure, which he had tasted the past year at Dolovino, did not appeal to him. He chuckled, remembering how humiliated he had felt when he was forced to make a living as a tea trading merchant. Now that he had a choice, he felt entirely different. Human nature was ever so, wasn't it? he thought. Already he was making plans to contact Igor Panfilov and check on the Buryat Stepan's activities. Perhaps now that he no longer feared the loss of revenue, he could do something about the illegal dealings in which the go-between had been engaged.

On a clear day in September, Ossip sent word through Anisia that he would like to talk to them on an important matter.

"He can see us anytime, Anisia," Irina replied, pouring Alexander another cup of tea from a steaming silver samovar in the parlor. It hurt to think that while Agasha had found her happiness with another muzhik in Russia, Ossip was unmarried and lonely in Irkutsk. He might have chosen to leave Moscow of his own free will; but it had been through unhappiness that he had done so, and Irina nurtured a hope that those frequent trips that he had been making to the Buryat camp a year ago were in reality to see someone he had met there, someone wholesome and well suited to become his wife.

When Ossip entered their parlor, kneading his cap, Irina knew at once that something important was on his mind.

Hesitantly, stumbling over words, something Irina did not remember his doing before, Ossip told them that during the past year he had stopped buying his leather from the Buryats, and now his supply was running low, and he wished to borrow an advance from Alexander in order to establish credit with a local trader in town.

"Don't you get a much better deal by buying directly from the Buryats?" Alexander asked, and when Ossip nodded, he went on. "Then why have you stopped buying from them?"

Ossip did not answer and began to knead his cap again. Irina's eyes narrowed. A vague nausea started in the pit of her stomach, and she tightened her grip on her teacup. Her eyes riveted to Alexander's face, she asked quietly, "Whom did you deal with in the Buryat camp, Ossip?"

Ossip took a long time answering, and when he did, his voice was very low. "Your former servant girl Marya's father."

Why should Alexander's face redden now, so long after Marya had left the izba never to return again? But even as she thought this, the answer came. That night a year ago when Alexander had not come home . . . she had sent Ossip to find him. . . . And Ossip dealt with Marya's father. . . . He would have gone to their yurt first. . . . Oh God, the guilt on Alexander's face was more than she could stand. She had been trying so desperately to hide her hurt, and he had betrayed her again! And Ossip had found out about it and couldn't bear to deal with Marya's father. His pain was written all over his face. Was it because of his loyalty to Irina? Or was it something more? In a flash of insight, she understood the link between the many hours Ossip had spent in the Buryat camp and the bitterness with which he spoke Marya's name. Ossip had loved her, too, that strange Buryat girl.

Irina rose and carefully put down her teacup. Then she looked at Ossip. "I'm sure there would be no problem at all in advancing you the necessary sum, Ossip. You must have valid reasons for not wanting to deal with the Buryats any longer, and we won't ask you what they are."

Without waiting for a comment from Alexander, Irina left the room.

Later that evening, when Alexander tried to talk to her and she barely answered, he said, "Irina, we have to clear the air. This tension between us cannot go on forever. You're continuing to nurture your hurt, and you won't even try to forget. You're ruining our marriage!"

Incensed, Irina stared at him. "You dare say that *I* am ruining our marriage? What about you? Do you deny having spent the night in Marya's arms that time a year ago when I sent Ossip to look for you?"

She waited for him to deny it, to swear to her that the whole thing was an unfortunate coincidence, that it was not true, and because she wanted to hear him say it so desperately, she was stunned by his reaction.

"No, I don't deny it!" he cried angrily. "In the last eighteen months you've denied me your bed more times than I care to remember. You've all but emasculated me by your frigidity, by your righteous, all-suffering attitude toward something that I can't even feel guilty about! I've told you this over and over, that at the time it first happened, I thought I'd never see you again. Can you understand that? Can you?"

"There is no need to shout," Irina said, controlling her own voice with difficulty. "What about last year?

Did you think then that you'd never see me again? Did you?"

"Don't be sarcastic! It doesn't become you. As for that night last year, I could explain how it happened and why, but I won't debase myself by doing it. All I'm going to say is that I love you, and only you!"

"What about Ossip? He must suspect something to have stopped seeing her. What must *he* feel after being cuckolded twice, once by the father and then by his son?"

"You're using strong words, Irina, without knowing the facts. If you can't take me on my word, then we have no marriage. All I can say is that I love you madly, with all the passion we both enjoyed at one time, and you are putting me through a torture I don't feel I deserve."

"I see. So that's your excuse to find solace in another woman's arms?"

Alexander slammed his fist on the table. "Damn it, yes! Did it ever occur to you that I could have denied the whole thing and you would have had no way of proving otherwise? Why do you think I'm telling the truth? Only to show you that I'm a man with healthy desires and a deep, abiding love for you that is frustrated at every turn of the way!"

"You certainly have a strange way of trying to prove your love for me! If what you say is indeed true, I need time to be convinced of it."

"Then what would you have me do to convince you?"

And when Irina remained silent, he reached her in two steps and, swinging her around to face him, crushed her to his chest. Irina wrenched herself violently out of his arms and ran behind a chair. She grasped its back, holding it as a barrier between them.

His fists clenched, Alexander narrowed his eyes. "Very well," he said, his voice shaking with emotion, "if that's what you want, you shall have it! I promise you I shall not touch you anymore until you come to me yourself!" With that, he turned on his heel and left the room.

Alone in her bedchamber, she tried unsuccessfully to grapple with her feelings. Would her rejection of him tonight drive him back into Marya's arms? Oh, God, what had she done? Where was the answer? In spite of it all, she still loved him. Was it truly the hurt she could not overcome, or was it simply her wounded pride that wouldn't allow her to forgive him? She didn't know. Confused, distraught, she tossed in bed and did not drift into an exhausted sleep until the break of a new dawn.

The next afternoon Yung-lin came to see them. His courteous, reserved manner belied the irrepressible sparkle in his eyes as he bowed ceremoniously and went through the flowery, formal greetings of his countrymen. Impulsively Irina reached out and touched the sleeve of his purple gown.

"We have missed you these last few weeks, Yung-lin. Please join us for tea and tell us your news."

Yung-lin settled himself in a chair, smoothing the folds of his long gown, and folded his hands in his lap. He looked first at Alexander, then at Irina.

"Your kind interest honors me, Irina Ignatyevna," he said, "and I must say that I decided to live in Irkutsk because you and Prince Alexander endowed it with memories of our cherished friendship."

"Let us hope that this friendship, Yung-lin, has been renewed," Alexander said with a smile. "We returned because we found contentment here that was no longer possible in Moscow."

"Tell us your news now," Irina pressed.

Yung-lin inclined his head slightly. "I am deeply touched by your interest." He then told them about

Shu-hsien and their love and added, "I do have news, and while it is distressing from one point of view, from another, it holds a hope of great happiness for me."

Irina clapped her hands. "Oh, I'm so glad! Please tell us!"

"Shu-hsien's father has arranged for a marriage between her and another man. Shu-hsien sent a message, however, that she would not marry the man her father had chosen and would instead leave her home and join me in Irkutsk as soon as she could make arrangements to escape undetected."

Yung-lin paused, as if this momentous news needed time to sink in, then went on. "It is a dangerous journey for a young Chinese woman and may take a long time before she is able to start, but she is resourceful and, with Buddha's help, won't be recognized until she reaches Maimachin and Kyakhta. Once there, she is to contact Stepan, my go-between, who is on the lookout for her." Yung-lin hesitated, then added, "For security reasons, I told Stepan that it is a young boy cousin who is joining me here. No one else knows that it will be Shu-hsien."

"Your secret is safe with us, Yung-lin," Alexander said quickly. "I only wish there were something we could do to help."

"Waiting is a difficult lesson in patience," Yung-lin said slowly. "Yet silent patience I must employ, lest I endanger Shu-hsien's safe passage. Your presence here and your friendship are of great support to me."

"I understand fully," Irina said, "for I, too, had to exercise such patience once, while my husband was in prison."

Yung-lin looked at her for a few moments, then said, "You are a person of strong character, and I admire you. Prince Alexander is a lucky man."

*   *   *

A week later Olga Radina arrived from Chita, carrying all her possessions, determined to return to Moscow. Dismayed by Olga's decision to abandon Boris, Irina nevertheless was filled with pity at the sight of her cousin's wife. She had lost weight, and the pallor of her face made her dark eyes, now underlined with shadows, seem even larger than before. A defiant fire burned in them as she related how she had parted from Boris.

"All we wives do the whole day is mend their clothes and struggle with cookbooks to prepare extra meals, and all this with no privacy whatsoever. What a life! I could accept it if I knew that we were improving their lot or hastening their transfer to a better prison, but no matter how much we petition Commandant Leparsky, he turns a deaf ear."

"But you do improve their conditions," Alexander pointed out, "by doing what you have just told us. Not only do you give them physical nourishment, but you brighten their lives by being near them. Don't you realize how much it means to those unfortunate men to have their wives near them?" Alexander's voice rose, and he coughed to cover his emotion.

Olga shrugged. "The daily sacrifices we have to make and the hardships to which we are subjected far outweigh the benefit the men derive from our presence, believe me! Only recently did they finally remove the prisoners' leg irons. Look!" Olga pointed to a bracelet on her wrist and pursed her lips. "Boris made this link bracelet for me out of his chains. I didn't have the heart to tell him that it holds no sentiment for me!"

So, Irina thought, the tsar had at last honored her request.

"How did Boris react to your decision?" she asked, fearing the answer.

"He didn't like it, of course. I—I told him that after he had served his years in prison and was resettled, I would probably consider coming back if the place were at least a small town rather than some remote village. I just can't adjust to the idea of living my whole life as a peasant. Can't you understand that?"

Irina narrowed her eyes. "What I can't understand, Olga, is your selfishness in thinking about yourself first and your loved one second. He's the one who is suffering far more than you are. What about your conscience? When you are living in luxury back in Moscow, won't the memory of Boris's suffering pain you?"

"He brought it upon himself. Why should I be penalized for it? I'm totally innocent of any wrong-doing. You know, I came here of my own free will. I tried! Other wives may be self-appointed martyrs, but I am not one of them!"

"What exactly did Boris say to you when you told him you were abandoning him?" Alexander asked.

Olga winced. "I'm not sure I like your choice of words, Alex. I'm not exactly *abandoning* him—after all, he was in prison when I came here, and he remains in prison after I leave. As for what he said, he was highly emotional and perhaps even theatrical, as only Boris can be. He told me that if I left, he would escape and follow me!" Olga sniffed. "How childish can he be even to think such a thing!"

"Did he say how he proposes to accomplish that?"

"He told me that some of the other prisoners were plotting to escape."

"I hope he's not serious about it," Alexander said. "The hardened criminals may well succeed in eluding capture, familiar as they are with the local terrain, and they probably have friends in neighboring villages who could hide them. But what chance does Boris have, an aristocrat unaccustomed to surviving in the deep forests?"

Olga sighed. "I don't know what he is thinking, Alex; you know how impetuous he is. I hope it all will blow over, and he will come to his senses. As for me, the sooner I leave this accursed Siberia, the happier I'll be."

"I beg you to wait," Irina said quietly, taking Olga's hand in hers. "For the sake of all that is sacred to you, for the sake of the happiness that Boris has given you in the past, I beg you—wait! Stay here in Irkutsk until you see how Boris adjusts to living without you. You owe him that much, Olga!"

Olga picked up the tassel of the shawl she was wearing over her shoulders and played nervously with its threads. The black shawl was embroidered with red roses and green leaves, so out of place, Irina thought, with her own stylish gray batiste dress, which she had brought from Moscow.

"I suppose it wouldn't hurt to wait awhile," Olga said, and then smiled suddenly. "After all, it may be quite a shock for me to be thrown from a peasant izba in Chita directly into the elegance of my Moscow home! Maybe I need this transition—to go through the provincial city of Irkutsk, I mean!"

"You're welcome to stay with us, Olga," Irina said with restraint, chafing at Olga's deprecating slur on Irkutsk. "You may find Irkutsk not so provincial after all. We have literary soirees here, cultural events, and balls, just as they have in Moscow. As a matter of fact, you may find Siberians far more friendly and hospitable than some of our friends in Moscow."

Without waiting for a reply, Irina rose and gave instructions to have two rooms prepared for Olga on the second floor.

Yung-lin came to visit the next day, and when Irina

introduced him to Olga, he dropped his hands to his sides in a respectful greeting and bowed deeply. Irina watched uncomfortably as Olga's eyes sparkled with interest.

"Welcome to Irkutsk, honored lady," Yung-lin said in his lilting Russian.

"Thank you! I've missed contact with civilized people." Olga paused, then added with a smile twitching at the corner of her mouth, "I hadn't realized just *how* much!"

Yung-lin raised his head slowly and looked at Olga. In the seconds that followed, he kept his gaze on Olga far longer, Irina thought, than proper courtesy required.

"Any news about your fiancée, Yung-lin?" Irina asked, to break the awkward pause and to remind him that he was a committed man. If he caught the implication, he showed no sign of it. Neither did Olga, to judge from her continuing show of interest.

"Not yet, Irina Ignatyevna, unfortunately not yet, and my patience is being sorely tested." Yung-lin turned to look at Olga again and added pensively, "It is not easy for a man to live alone this long."

Irina changed the subject quickly and offered them tea.

In the ensuing days Yung-lin came for tea every day, something he had not done before, and Irina became increasingly apprehensive. It annoyed her that Alexander did not appear to notice anything out of the ordinary in Yung-lin's daily visits. But Yung-lin was never alone with Olga, behaved correctly in her presence, and Irina began to chide herself for her suspicions.

After one of his particularly lonely days Yung-lin dismissed his coachman and walked the streets of Irkutsk for hours. He didn't feel like visiting the Dolovins that day. Olga Radina intrigued him, but there were moments when he sought solitude, introspection. Under different circumstances, perhaps he could have asked her to be his concubine to fill the empty, aching hours at night when he hungered for Shu-hsien. But Olga Radina still had a husband, and he must not forget that.

The weather was cool, but his silk gown, so light always, suddenly felt sticky and weighty. He was tired. Everyone he saw on the street—sturdy Russian women laden with baskets of produce, children trotting beside them, old men shuffling along aimlessly in their linen shirts, their loose trousers tucked into their boot tops—seemed headed in the opposite direction, so that he had to maneuver his way carefully to avoid bumping into them.

It was like a new world to him—an alien world he had never stopped to examine fully before, except through his intentionally lyricized view. What was he doing here anyway? But then where *was* his household? Had he ever really had a household of his own? He had nothing to mourn, nothing to miss. No. Irkutsk was the place he had chosen as his future home, a place of hope, a place for his happiness. Where else could he be united with Shu-hsien?

Shu-hsien. The lovely flower, waiting for the right moment to run away from home and join him. A courageous woman, and for her sake, he must wait and be patient.

The tightening of his muscles, the clammy feeling at the back of his neck—signs of tension, impatience, lack of self-control. Was there a Buddhist temple in the city where he could meditate and regain some serenity of spirit? He didn't think so. The little shrine in his rented flat would have to do.

Resolutely he headed home.

But at the door to his flat a messenger was pacing the floor. On seeing Yung-lin, he looked around to make sure there was no one within earshot and then whispered the urgent message.

Shu-hsien had disappeared from her clan's courtyard, and Lo Chia-li, her father, had sent out an alarm all the way to Kyakhta to be on the lookout for her. He had offered a large reward to the first person to find her . . .

Chapter Twenty-two

Through the high and narrow window of her convent cell Shu-hsien could see the Po-ko-to Mountain, lacy clouds threading their way along the skyline. Although she was standing on a stool, its black claw feet were short, and it was difficult for her small frame to reach the window. Dressed in a novice's gown with full sleeves and a matching kerchief around her head, she felt the sackcloth fabric rub against her body, not at all like the silk and damask she had been wearing at home.

The only child of Lo Chia-li's first wife, who died giving her birth, Shu-hsien was the pampered one of the Lo family and, as such, enjoyed more freedom in the courtyards than other female members of the clan. Shy and introspective by nature, she spent much time in the garden of the women's quarters, sitting on a marble bench with a book. Withdrawn into her dreamworld, she often conjured up the figure of Yung-lin before her mind's eye and indulged in silent dialogue with him, listening to his answers and imagining his smile.

Other women of the clan, who spent much of their time with embroidery and gossip, had long ago dismissed Shu-hsien with a shrug and a shake of the head.

"A strange girl, that one." They sighed. "What's brewing in that head of hers? Our patriarch pampers her too much. Whoever heard of teaching a girl to read and write? No good will come of it! The sooner she is given in marriage, the better!"

When Shu-hsien's aunt, a stern middle-aged woman informed her she was to marry her cousin in the Woo family, she kowtowed and begged her to tell her father not to give her away in marriage. She was not ready, she said, not sure she could be a good wife; she needed time to mature.

Her aunt scoffed at her pleas. "What do you mean, you couldn't be a good wife? My own niece saying this? You seemed to be quite ready when Yung-lin asked for you. As for maturity, it'll come after marriage. Yield, my child, yield! Remember your obedience!"

And so, while she waited to escape, solitude was her precious companion, and she frequently confided in her slave girl who was in love with a servant in the courtyards and understood her heartache.

She knew nothing of the world outside her clan's courtyards and had promised her slave girl much of her jewelry if she helped her escape. Thus, when the time came, it was relatively easy for her to slip out of the Lo compound under the pretext of going to the convent. She traveled openly in a sedan chair, accompanied by her slave girl and the manservant. They had provided her with man's clothing and after she arrived at the gates of the convent, the two conspirators disappeared never to return to the Lo courtyards.

A frequent visitor to the Convent of Peaceful Pursuit, she was glad that in the past she had donated gold as a spirit offering, and now, as she confided her problem to Mother Superior, she was reasonably sure of her help. The nun, a tall Manchu woman with a shaved head and flowing ecru robe, listened with half-closed eyes, reciting her beads and saying nothing until Shu-hsien had finished.

"Your honored father is a wise man," Mother Superior began, "and has chosen a good and worthy man to be your future husband. It is a grievous plan you devised and it will bring great shame upon the clan of Lo. Besides, you would surely be recognized long before you reach the border. I am not certain I can agree to help you risk your honored father's anger. Are you aware that you can be buried alive for bringing dishonor to your clan's name?"

Shu-hsien felt her chin tremble. "Reverend Mother," she said, "I beg you to help me! I plead with you! All I ask of you is to give me a novice's gown and allow me to remain in your convent until the next caravan leaves for Maimachin and Kyakhta. I already have a workman's clothes. Traveling with the caravan in disguise, I should be able, with your prayers and the merciful Buddha's help, to reach Kyakhta."

The Mother Superior hesitated, darting sidelong glances at Shu-hsien. Then she sighed.

"I'm taking a grave risk on your account. If your father discovers the truth, the gates of the convent will be closed forever and all the nuns expelled. But—as long as you remain under the roofs of our temples, I shall protect you. As soon as you leave the gates of the convent however, I shall deny having seen you. Is that understood?"

"Yes, Reverend Mother. My gratitude is boundless!"

"I'll show you to your cell and after you change, join the other novices in the Hall of Worship for prayers, so that no questions would be asked as to who or why you are here." Mother Superior looked her over and added, "You'll have to leave your pedestal shoes and your silk dress here."

Shu-hsien nodded.

The cell was tiny with room enough for only a narrow bed, one table and chair, and a washstand. In a small chest she found the novice's clothes and, after changing into them, joined the other nuns.

The kowtowing figures of praying women in the Hall of Worship moved like floating shadows against the perpetual motion of flickering candles. The heavy fragrance of incense, emanating from a large brass holder, enveloped Shu-hsien as she knelt to kowtow before the figure of Buddha. Here, within the peace and serenity of the convent walls, in the hushed silence of the hall, she was suddenly calmed by a total submission of spirit, having transferred all responsibility for herself into a temporary dependence on the deity before her. *That is how a child feels,* she thought, *carefree and secure in the care of a parent.*

When the prayers were finished, she withdrew to her cell, grateful that the dirt floor was dry, and the quiet around her complete. An industrious field mouse scratched the silence in one corner of the cell, then disappeared into its underground domain. The tiny flame from the wick in the flat dish of bean oil spread grotesque shadows on the wall, and as she sat down on the hard bed, the full realization of what she had done suddenly became clear. Her eyes stung. Slowly, carefully, tears crawled down her cheeks, salting the corners of her mouth and falling into the folds of her gown.

What had she done? In one impulsive act she had severed all ties with her past and opened a chasm between herself and everything that was dear to her. She stood alone on the ledge of a precipice and could never contact her family or regain her proper place in the Lo clan.

By running away, she had brought shame on her father's head, caused him to lose face before his friends. He would not forgive her for this disgrace. He had been a good father to her, but he could not accept her spirit of independence, the defiance of her heart. It was more important to him that his daughter be someone's wife number one. A thousand times she would rather be wife number two to her beloved.

Women of her milieu were not expected to fall in love. They were required only to be obedient and to yield. Always yield. To the patriarch of the clan, to the matriarch, to the father. But to fall in love—it was not necessary. How could they? They never saw their husbands until after the weddings.

So how had this happened? She could not order her heart not to love. The heart was a mischievous bird with a mind of its own, beating its wings inside her chest when she stood before Yung-lin in the clan's garden and as she listened to his gentle words, she thought that surely it would burst out free and fly away, never to be caught again.

Maybe it would have been easier then?

No. For then she would not have experienced the secret rapture of *knowing* him. And she remembered everything about him and about that special night: his tender words, a haunting music to her ears; his long and tapered fingers, a silken pillow to her cheek; the sweetness of his breath against her neck, the song of poetry; his eyes, the arcane pools of love concealed from all but her.

How could she not have done then what she had done?

She could never marry another, especially now, after she had experienced the ultimate in bliss. She would rather stay here, in the sanctuary of the convent, surrounded by pious nuns, sheltered from the turbulence of the world, than submit to a man without love. While here, she would pray for a safe journey with the caravan; for reaching Kyakhta undetected; for seeing her beloved soon . . . very soon. . . .

On the flight of this thought, dreams overtook her, and she was out in the sunshine, gathering field flowers near Lake Baikal, that beautiful lake Yung-lin had so often described to her. Everything sparkled—the dew-washed grass: the silvery foliage of a nearby birch grove; the rushing waters of the Angara, clear and shimmering and vibrant. Then, gradually, a large shadow crossed the sun. She looked and recognized a bigger-than-life figure of Yung-lin. He was walking toward her—not really walking, but floating above the grass with a smile—his arms outstretched to touch her. She moved toward him timidly, but somehow he passed behind her, his purple silk gown swirling through the air so close it brushed against her skirt. Dismayed, she turned, but his figure receded into the shaft of golden sunlight that blinded her by its brilliance; she blinked, and in that instant Yung-lin was gone.

She awoke in her cell at sunrise, smelling the dust and crowded by the bleak, unadorned walls, her novice's gown still around her body, now wrinkled and damp. She reached for her prayer beads. Here, in this refuge, she was safe until the caravan was ready to leave Urga. Trained by years of obedience to be patient, she would wait.

A few days later the mother superior summoned her. A caravan was departing in a few hours, and in order to slip in unnoticed, she was to join it during its busiest time of preparation for departure.

"If I were you, I would pretend to be mute," Mother Superior said in parting. "Your voice is too soft, too high-pitched not to attract attention at some point in the journey. Here, take some of these taels of silver and hide them in your pocket."

The mother superior hesitated for a moment, then handed her a folded piece of cloth. "Here, be sure to put this on under your gown."

Shu-hsien thanked her and retired to her cell to change. There she unfolded the piece of cloth, which was like a small apron. She recognized a belly cover. She held it up to the light by the neck strap and examined its damask border. Absentmindedly fingering the tie strings, she hesitated. No woman or a young boy-child was ever without one, of course, for it protected one from the evil spirits that were said to enter the body through the navel. But what if someone discovered her wearing it beneath her disguise? The moment she thought it, she discarded the idea. Who would look under her gown? Silly!

The wide pants and the long, roomy gown were too big, but she remembered to wrap the belt around her tiny waist several times, for it would be dreadful to be thought "a beltless"—a Mongolian woman who never belted her gown. During the last few days she had been practicing walking in the *u-li*, so different from the pedestal shoes she had been accustomed to, and she had pulled her hair high off her neck and braided it into a single queue. Now she tucked her prayer beads into a small bundle of clothes and followed the nun outside. At the edge of town the nun pointed silently at a group of men arguing loudly over chests of tea and after turning, disappeared in the crowded street.

Shu-hsien was on her own.

Taking advantage of the heated argument, she slipped past the men and approached the nearest camel, harnessed to a loaded cart. She had not expected the odiferous stench emanating from the animal to be so powerful, but she had no alternative but to climb the two-wheeled *arba* and slide uncomfortably between two chests. With the soft bundle of clothes propped against her back, she sat quietly, every muscle tense, mind alert to the moment when she would be discovered and questioned about her presence in the caravan. Mother Superior's suggestion of pretending to be mute was a stroke of genius, and all she had to remember was not to use her vocal cords at all.

She prayed that none of the drivers would select her cart to ride on, and when at last the caravan began to move, she could not resist a sigh of enormous relief to see herself sandwiched between two riderless arbas. There were five carts ahead of hers, with a man on horseback urging on the sluggish camels, but she couldn't see behind her. The longer she went undiscovered and unrecognized as a trespasser, the less the danger of her being ordered to return to Urga. Yet she couldn't resist peeking from the side of one of the chests to watch with envy as the first rider ahead spread his bedding atop the chests and, stretching on it, immediately went to sleep. No such comfort for her, for she would have to doze in a sitting position throughout her journey.

The caravan moved for hours at a walking pace over a bumpy, rutted road, through grazing land, bleak and monotonous, dotted occasionally with burial tumuli. Shu-hsien discovered that if she pressed her face close to the rawhide that covered the tea chests, the smell of leather softened the offensive camel odor that was insulting her stomach.

When her limbs became stiff from the cramped position, she moved cautiously, guiding her body through the ancient exercises of *t'ai-chi-Chu'än*, their slow rhythms relaxing her aching muscles and taking her mind off her predicament. Then, at long last, the caravan stopped to rest and eat, and as she climbed down to get some food, she was finally discovered.

"Where did you come from?" one man asked suspiciously.

Bowing in rapid succession so as not to lock glances with any of the men, Shu-hsien repeatedly pointed to her mouth and tongue, shaking her head and hands to convey her inability to speak.

"A dummy!" one rider said. "Who hired this boy?" When no one answered, he shrugged. "Well, why not? Another set of arms to help with the chests in Kyakhta can't hurt!" He handed Shu-hsien a bowl of millet. "Here, eat this, for we'll put you to work when we get there!"

Shu-hsien couldn't believe her luck and silently blessed the mother superior for her suggestion, for frightened as she was, she would have surely betrayed herself with her shaking girlish voice.

The rest of the journey was slow and tedious, for the caravan moved for sixteen hours a day. One of the forward riders took pity on her and shared part of his bedding, so that she no longer had to squeeze her body between the chests and could stretch out at night. Although some men cursed and shoved her when she happened in their way, she took it meekly, aware of the danger involved if she fought back. Punches and foul language directed at her as a boy were infinitely better than the men's reactions would have been to her true identity. The mere thought of such a possibility made her shiver.

Along the way a couple of carts broke down, and the caravan had to stop for repairs. Time dragged interminably, and although surrounded by men and animals, Shu-hsien felt isolated in her silence and wondered how long she could endure her act as a mute without betraying her secret. Then on the fifth day, she almost cried out in excitement when on awakening, she saw the curved green roofs of Maimachin and beyond, for the first time in her life, the five onion-domed cupolas of Kyakhta's Russian Orthodox church.

Safety was near. So very near, and with it, the Buryat Stepan whom she was to contact. All she had to do now was slip quietly from Maimachin to Kyakhta, find Stepan, and ask him to send a message to Yung-lin. She would have to abandon her act as a mute and risk the go-between's suspicions that she was a girl, but once on Russian soil, she would surely be safe under Stepan's protection.

Chapter Twenty-three

The caravan stopped briefly in Maimachin, and Shu-hsien hid between the chests, afraid to be questioned by the Chinese merchants, afraid to see any of her father's men. It might have been only an hour or two, but it seemed like an eternity to her before the cart moved again, leaving Maimachin and crossing the border into Kyakhta.

Shu-hsien looked around her curiously. She had never seen the log cabin izbas before, so different from the curved tile roofs of Urga and Maimachin. She thought them quaint and primitive and wondered how they looked inside. There were no walled-off court-yards, and the last dragon gates she saw were those of Maimachin. The houses in Kyakhta stood directly on the dirt road, with wooden steps leading up to the front door. She was fascinated by the intricate fretwork around the windows of some of the houses, but the majority stood stark and unadorned.

Chinese merchants from Maimachin walked along the road in groups of three and four, gesticulating and talking animatedly, paying no attention to the caravan that labored past them. Strolling along the road were stocky Russian men with bushy beards and hair parted in the middle, dressed in side-buttoned shirts and wide pants tucked into high leather boots. They greeted Chinese merchants with harsh-sounding, loud words that Shu-hsien did not understand. She had never heard Russian spoken before, and the only other language she knew besides her own was Mongolian. Yung-lin had warned her that Russian merchants did not speak Chinese, and she was glad she could communicate with Stepan in Mongolian.

The caravan finally stopped at a large warehouse, in which a crowd of men were sewing rawhide around the tea chests with long awls. The building was packed with thousands of chests and covering the ground was a black, fragrant blanket of tea leaves.

Certain that she wouldn't be able to lift the heavy chests off the carts as she would be expected to do, Shu-hsien took advantage of the general confusion as the men were dismounting, slipped off her cart, and raced to hide behind the warehouse. There she hugged the wall, clutching her small bundle to her chest, sure that the pounding of her heart was as loud as the peal of the Orthodox church bells sounding in the distance. For a moment she forgot the danger of being discovered and listened to them in fascination. It was a rapid, joyous sound of multitoned chimes, and they seemed to beckon to her with a warm and hospitable call. The Russian God, then, was a cheerful one. Would he smile down on her as benevolently as the kind Buddha at the convent in Urga?

Loud, arguing voices interrupted her flight of fantasy. Instead of wondering about the Russian God, she should run while the workmen's attention was diverted elsewhere. Grateful for the soft *u-li* on her feet, she ran noiselessly toward the cluster of houses down the street. She knew that Stepan was well known in Kyahkta and she should have no trouble locating him.

The first three houses she tried were deserted. She was surprised to find the door of the fourth one unlocked and the back room filled with idling Chinese smoking and drinking tea. Mumbling a vague excuse, she backed away and knocked on the door of the next house. Moments later a burly Buryat stood on the threshold, his crafty eyes sizing up Shu-hsien with caution.

"Yes?" he asked, holding the door half open.

"I'm looking for Stepan," Shu-hsien said, trying to bring her voice to a lower pitch.

"I am Stepan. Might you not be Shu-shu, a cousin of Chien Yung-lin?" Stepan asked.

Shu-hsien smiled at the way he used her name and nodded.

Stepan waved her in. "Come in, come in. Don't just stand outside."

Shu-hsien stepped into what she thought was surely the most Spartan and plain interior she had ever seen. A square table in the center of the room looked like one she had seen in her clan's kitchens—deeply scratched, unvarnished, and discolored with dark stains. Four straight chairs stood around the table, and along the walls were long wooden benches. Except for a cupboard and a map of Russia nailed to the wall, the room was stark. Aware that the less of herself she exposed to scrutiny, the longer she would be able to disguise her true identity, Shu-hsien sat down at the table and pulled the chair close to it, so that only the upper portion of her body was visible. She leaned on her elbow and wiped her moist forehead nervously with the palm of her hand.

As she raised her glance to his, she noticed that he was watching her hands. Small they were, with delicate, smooth fingers, and she hid them quickly beneath the tabletop, clasping her fingers together. But it was too late. Stepan took a step forward.

"What the devil? How old are you, boy?"

"Eighteen," Shu-hsien answered, remembering to answer in a lower pitch.

"New to this business, eh? I see the sun and the tea chests haven't roughened your hands yet. But then your cousin Chien Yung-lin may have office work for you in mind."

Relieved at the way the conversation was turning, Shu-hsien shrugged and smiled, careful to say as little as possible.

"Why are you running away from your homeland?"

Shu-hsien thought fast. "My cousin tells me that Irkutsk is a land of opportunity, and—and I want to learn his business," she concluded lamely.

Stepan turned, walked into an adjoining room, then peeked through the door. "Do you want to eat?" he asked, ladling red beet soup into a bowl from an iron pot sitting on top of a stove. "You need to feed that puny frame of yours if you want to survive in this country. Here, kasha is good for you," he went on, spooning into the soup a huge portion of what looked to Shu-hsien like brown millet.

She tried the soup. It was not too hot, but very tasty with cabbage and morsels of meat and thick with the millet he called kasha. When she finished, he poured her a mug of orange liquid and said, "Here, drink this kvass; it will cool you after the hot soup."

Feeling warm all over again, Shu-hsien took the mug gratefully. It tasted like fermented juice, and she drank it all to the last drop.

Stepan winked. "Look out, it sometimes makes you tipsy!"

Shu-hsien placed the empty mug on the table, looked for a hot towel, and, finding none, was about to ask for one, when she thought better of it and wiped her mouth with the back of her hand. She was perspiring. The ventilation in the room was nonexistent, and the air oppressive. Her nervousness wasn't helping either, and the clothes she was wearing had not been changed since she left Urga. All of a sudden she felt her flesh prickle and itch, and she knew that the sweaty odor she smelled was her own. She squirmed in her seat. "Thank you, that was very good. Please excuse me—I am very dirty!"

"You'll have to have a bath then," Stepan said, taking the dishes off the table.

"Thank you, very much. May I have it now, please?" Shu-hsien said, looking in an adjoining room for a bathtub.

Stepan burst out laughing. "Hey, boy, you have lots and lots to learn! I suppose where you came from, you had servants to wait on you, right?" When Shu-hsien neither confirmed nor denied it, he went on. "Over here we have no servants to fill your bath, and as a matter of fact, no bathtub in the house at all! Come, I'll introduce you to a Russian bathhouse."

Suddenly Shu-hsien felt the telltale stinging of tears rising to her lids. She mustn't let them fill her eyes. Boys didn't cry. She lowered her head, pretending to search her pockets.

"I have no money to pay for the bathhouse," she said. "If you have no tub here, maybe I could refresh myself at a washstand?"

"Don't worry about money. Your cousin Chien Yung-lin will pay me later. And as far as the washstand, you need more than that after sitting in a cart all those days. You have to clean up. In the bathhouse the steam is hot, and the birch besoms beat the dirt from your skin real good!" Stepan laughed a little. "Wait and see, we all look like lobsters in there. Besides, it's a good place to collect the latest gossip." He winked at Shu-hsien again and added, "You may learn something, and I promise to show you how to scrub your body our Russian way. Come on, boy, let's go!"

In total panic now, Shu-hsien shook her head. "I—I

can't go with you—I never—I mean—I just can't bathe in a public bathhouse."

Stepan pursed his lips and propped his sides with his fists. "Well, well! Some spoiled brat you are! I told you we don't have any private bathtubs here. You either come with me or stay dirty and smelly, but if you do that, I'll throw you out of my house. I won't have you stinking up my rooms!"

Shu-hsien pressed her lips tight to keep them from trembling. "I've always bathed in private, Stepan, and I'll wash really well over your washstand. I promise you."

"Get up!" Stepan suddenly ordered, his tone menacing now. "Let me see something!"

Shu-hsien rose slowly and pushed the chair back. She stood in front of him with a stoop, as if by straightening she would expose her feminine figure.

"What are you ashamed of?" Stepan said, moving around the table to her side. "Look at you!" he said with a sneer. "Such a small kid, what can you possibly have that all of us don't have?"

He pointed to the lower part of her body and advanced a step toward her. "We all have the same thing down there, or is yours different? Maybe you have two of them?"

Stepan roared with laughter at his own words. "You better come to the bathhouse with me, or I'll take your pants down right here to see if you have anything worth hiding!"

This was too much. Instinctively Shu-hsien began to back away. She couldn't let this big, obnoxious Buryat touch her. How foolish to have agreed to a bath in the first place, but then how was she to know that he had no bathtub in the house? It was the most natural, the most basic, commodity in any Chinese house of consequence. But she had forgotten that this was not a Chinese house

and certainly not of consequence. There was no alternative but to admit the truth—surely Stepan would
treat her with respect if he were to find out who she
was—and then hope that Yung-lin would come to fetch
her before the news spread that Stepan was hiding a
Chinese woman in his house.

With tears streaming down her cheeks, she dropped
to her knees and told him that she was a woman.

Stepan narrowed his eyes and in one leap was beside
her, throwing his arm around her in a firm grip.

His hand landed directly over her left breast, and his
hold was so powerful she could not wiggle out or even
move. For a few infinitesimal moments Stepan froze;
then slowly his fingers started to move over her tightly
bound breast, sliding up and down her shirt; with
lightning speed, his hand slipped inside her shirt as if to
convince himself of what his hand was feeling.

"Well, I'll be damed! *Chort vozmi!* A woman!" He
released his hold and swung her around to face him.
"What the devil! What kind of a game is this? Who are
you? I didn't bargain for a *woman*. No women are
allowed in Maimachin. So what is Chien Yung-lin
thinking of doing when he returns from Irkutsk?"

Shu-hsien lowered her gaze and studied the tips of
her black shoes. "Chien Yung-lin and I are going to be
married and live in Irkutsk."

"So why all the secrecy? Why didn't he go back to
Urga and marry you there?"

She glanced at Stepan's narrowed, suspicious eyes,
then continued to study her shoes.

"I see," he said slowly. "Let me guess. For some
reason, your father is against your marriage, right?
That's why the disguise. Hmm . . ."

Stepan fell silent for a few moments, then slapped his
forehead with the palm of his hand. "*Nu i durak-zhe ya!*
What a fool I am! Chien Yung-lin's clansman Lo Chia-

li's daughter has disappeared, and he's offering a large reward to anyone who will find her. Now I know who you are!"

Tired of pretending, Shu-hsien straightened and nodded. "Yes, I am she. And now that you know, my name is not Shu-shu, but Shu-hsien. Shu-hsien of the House of Lo. I shall stay out of your way the best I can until Chien Yung-lin comes for me, and I promise you that he will pay you handsomely for your trouble."

Stepan beckoned to her with his finger, and she made a tentative step in his direction.

"What do you want?" she asked, dropping the false tone of voice and raising her head high.

The Buryat chuckled, and for the first time Shu-hsien noticed that he had a big girth that stretched his loose side-buttoned shirt taut. The leather belt had slipped low, and his belly protruded like a watermelon. Involuntarily she giggled and quickly covered her mouth with her hand. Stepan looked her over, letting his gaze linger on the areas she was glad were well hidden beneath her shapeless clothes. Nevertheless, his look made her uncomfortable.

"Come closer; I won't bite," Stepan coaxed, his voice suddenly husky and low.

Shu-hsien's skin crawled, her body suddenly tense.

"I said, come *here*, little girl!" Stepan said again.

She did not move. His lips pressed tight, Stepan reached her in two steps and grasped her upper arm so tightly she winced. With lightning speed she wrenched herself free. Although she knew that she could outrun the fat Stepan, she also knew that she had no place else to go so she took a step back and stared at him defiantly.

Stepan's eyes narrowed. "So! You want to play games, do you? Well, well, we'll see about that!"

He reached for her and this time circled her shoulders with one arm, then moved his broad palm over both her bound breasts. A slow leer spread on his face and he tried to slip his hand inside her shirt, and for the first time she noticed that one of his front teeth was blackened and the others were yellow and crooked. Gooseflesh prickled her from his touch, and nausea threatened to overwhelm her. With both hands, she grabbed his wrist and lifted it off her breast to her mouth. With a quick movement she sank her teeth into it and bit as hard as she could.

Stepan yelped and released her, wrenching his hand free.

"Bitch!" he yelled, examining his wrist and rubbing it. "Wildcat!" With one sweep of his other hand, he slapped her across the face and sent her reeling against the wall.

Hiding her fear, Shu-hsien gambled on his greed and stood straight and proud.

"Go ahead and touch me if you want," she said calmly, "but remember, Chien Yung-lin won't pay you a penny if you do."

His eyelids fluttered. "Maybe you're right," he said uncertainly. "Untouched, you might bring a better ransom." He looked her up and down, then sneered. "Besides, you're too skinny for my kind of fun anyway. I'd rather have a milky Russian girl with something to hold on to!"

Still rubbing his wrist, he walked over and paced the floor back and forth in front of her. A slow, crafty smile stretched his lips, and there was something so sinister, so threatening, in that smile that Shu-hsien's heart stood still.

"We shall see who will pay more—Chien Yung-lin or your father, who is so anxious to get you back. We shall see!"

Desperate, Shu-hsien found her voice. "Please contact Chien Yung-lin immediately! He doesn't know that you found out who I am. He'll make it worth your while. Oh, please!"

"Aha! Now you're talking sense! In the meantime, the longer I wait, the more it will cost me to feed you, not to mention the trouble I'll have hiding you here." Stepan averted his gaze and swept some imaginary crumbs off the table. "Let's see . . . it will take several days for the messenger to reach Chien Yung-lin and several days back. I wonder how long your father is going to keep his offer good."

That night Shu-hsien lay on a narrow cot that Stepan showed her in the small alcove off the back room. The area was windowless and stuffy, and although she had refreshed herself at the washbasin, she was nervous and perspiring. Ordinarily she would have fretted and squirmed and tried to dry herself, but all the tension of the last few weeks preceding her flight, the journey itself, and her arrival in Kyakhta, having culminated in that afternoon's encounter with Stepan, now had exhausted her, and she lay quietly, pondering her situation, weighing her alternatives.

Then, as she thought about it with gradual awareness, she knew that she had to yield to fate. Was it something in Stepan's last words or was it his sly look that made her wonder if he would wait for Yung-lin before turning her over to her father? Or was it some other warning instinct preparing her for the future—an instinct born of a lifetime of obedience and custom that was being violated by her daring spirit? That spirit that tried to warp conventions and defy her familiar world to brave a foreign country with its alien customs and rules, that spirit driven by a single force, a force that centered in one human being, her beloved Yung-lin. Was this the reason why a small voice from somewhere deep in her soul reminded her how peaceful and free of fear she had felt inside the convent, surrounded by serenity and a different kind of love—a spiritual love of deity that transcended all tribulation and mundane disturbance?

She had ignored it then only to recognize it now. She loved Yung-lin, would love him always, and if he came to claim her on the morrow, she would follow him gladly and obediently wherever he chose to take her. The happiness she would experience would be the same as that she had tasted once in his arms that lovely moonlit night, the precious memory to cherish for a lifetime. But if not . . . If that kind of happiness was not to be, what would she do? Would she seek contentment among the harmony of Buddha's servants?

The vow of obedience in the convent was for life—an awesome, final step—but obedience to her father's wishes was another matter. In this case it was not a question of obedience, but a question of yielding to a life of hardship and disgrace, for she had shamed her father and knew that the Woo family would not want her now in their clan. Her father would not forgive her and would keep her at home for a while and then send her away to some remote village to be given in marriage to a simple farmer. And that would not be possible for her to accept.

In the dark, small room, alone with the hours of this endless night, Shu-hsien tried gallantly to prepare herself for whatever course her fate would place before her.

Yung-lin . . . the song of tender words, the wine of breath, the silken cushion of his touch . . .

Within her reach or not? Whichever way, she must prepare to yield.

Chapter Twenty-four

Early days of September were beautiful in Irkutsk. Already the cooling air smelled of autumn, with the chimneys threading the fragrant smoke of burning birch and alder. The burnished brown and golden leaves carpeted the ground, and those that still clung to the branches shimmered brilliantly against the background of evergreen pine and cedar. The city savored the lovely time, well aware that it was short-lived and the long months of somber winter were not far off. Everything seemed crystallized in these exquisite days, as though nature, apologizing for the hot summers and the fierce cold that was to come had endowed the air with a balm of sweetness and purity to hold and remember until the following spring.

Today the clouds were few and lacy in the sky, drifting leisurely across the heavens, careful to skirt the sun and float behind the hills and forests. But all this beauty was lost on Alexander as he sat in his office staring at a letter before him. Igor Panfilov had written that he had become supicious when one of the silver idols he received from Stepan seemed heavier than the others. He had had it broken and discovered that it had been cast hollow and then filled with cement.

Stepan is obviously cheating the Chinese, [wrote Igor Panfilov], and this particular idol must have come to my desk by accident. I would ignore this, but since it is here, I must warn you that both our reputations are at stake with Chinese tradesmen as soon as they discover the truth. What do you suggest we do? As I mentioned to you before, I have been reluctant to expose Stepan, but now we must do something to protect ourselves from being implicated in his fraud. Once the credibility is undermined, it is extremely difficult, if not impossible, to reestablish it, and we must act before it is too late. As I said before, we can do it in a couple of ways: One is to confront Stepan with the facts and threaten to report him to the authorities if he continues to cheat. The other alternative would be to report him right away.

Alexander was incensed. He could never compromise his honesty. Back in Russia he could not bring himself to serve his tsar because he could not be morally loyal to him and felt that his oath of allegiance would have become a lie. In his private life he could not lie to Irina about Marya, and he was punished for it by her failure to understand and forgive him. And now he was challenged again. It would be easy—wouldn't it?—in view of the penalty he had to pay for his honesty, to tell Igor Panfilov to ignore this latest development and when the Chinese learned about the fraud, pretend indignation and try to assure their colleagues that they knew nothing about it.

Alexander chuckled and shook his head. The tip of the quill he held in his hand absentmindedly scratched his wrist, and he replaced it in its stand. He could daydream, couldn't he? But even daydreams could be unworthy of an honest man. How foolish even to consider such a possibility. The only course of action was to write Igor Panfilov and tell him that he had to confront Stepan and threaten him with exposure. Illegal deals in silver on the side was bad enough, but to defraud the merchants was intolerable.

With the quill in his hand again, Alexander wrote to Igor Panfilov, and after he had finished, he sat back, pondering the situation. It would take awhile before the whole problem was resolved, and in the meantime, his good friend Chien Yung-lin and his colleagues were being defrauded. Could he, Alexander, knowing what he knew, let this go on without taking some action?

The answer was obvious. He knew what he had to do.

With his desk cleared and papers put away, Alexander left his office, waved the coachman aside, and walked the few blocks to Yung-lin's office.

His Chinese friend rose to greet him and, after inviting him to sit down, poured a cup of tea and handed it to him with both hands. Accustomed to drinking out of a *podstakannik*—silver glass-holder—Alexander struggled to hold the hot Chinese cup that had no handle. Yung-lin leaned back in his chair, folded his arms into the wide sleeves of his gown in his usual manner, and tilted his head, waiting for his friend to speak.

Unexpectedly Alexander found it difficult to begin. Yung-lin was his friend and, as such, deserved to be warned; but he was Chinese, a man who belonged to a far different country, and in some perverted way Alexander felt suddenly that he was betraying his own countrymen by divulging a fraud perpetrated by another Russian citizen. But by withholding the truth, he would be protecting a criminal and allowing his good friend to be cheated.

Embarrassed, unsure of how exactly to phrase his thoughts, Alexander proceeded to tell Yung-lin about Stepan. So concerned was he with his choice of words, so careful to lead up to the facts and make clear why he was doing this that he was not aware for a long time that Yung-lin was unmoved. When at last Alexander became conscious of a slight, bemused smile on Yung-lin's face, he halted in mid-sentence and stared at him in amazement.

"Did I say something to amuse you, Yung-lin?" he asked rather testily, annoyed that such a grave subject should seem humorous to his Chinese friend.

Yung-lin smiled. "I have always believed that you are an honorable gentleman, a man of great integrity, or you would not have found yourself in Siberia in the first place. But I admire you even more now, for I realize that what you are telling me comes from your heart, your desire to warn me. Since you are not directly involved in this fraud, it would be understandable if you remained silent."

Yung-lin paused and looked at Alexander with admiration. "I also know that it is not easy for you to tell me, a Chinese man, that one of your own compatriots is cheating me. I appreciate it."

Alexander's teacup was empty by now, and Yung-lin refilled it unhurriedly, offered him a cookie, then smiled again. "As I have already said, I appreciate your candor and honesty, and I must tell you, my friend, that I have known about Stepan's dishonesty for quite some time now."

"And you did nothing about it?"

"On the contrary. We did something about it and hope the results will be evident soon."

Alexander waited.

"My colleagues and I," Yung-lin continued, "had a conference a while back, trying to find a solution to the problem, and after some discussion we decided to remove some of our high-quality tea from the chests and replace it with the cheaper brick tea."

Alexander was stunned. A slight smile twitched at the corners of Yung-lin's mouth as he studied his reaction. It was an obvious vendetta. Were the Chinese not averse to stooping to Stepan's level of fraud? He would never understand Chinese psychology. He asked, "So that's how you decided to deal with it. A tooth for a tooth. Why not simply expose Stepan?"

"It would be bad business for all concerned."

"I don't understand! Why?"

"For two reasons. If we exposed Stepan, he would be prosecuted by the authorities, and we would lose the services of an experienced man; and for us, we would lose face by admitting that we were initially duped since the hollowed-out idols were not discovered for quite some time. In acting as we did, nothing need be said or done, and everyone saves face. Soon enough Stepan will find that some of our chests contain inferior tea, and he will then know that we are aware of his fraud and are supplying the quality of tea commensurate with the quality of silver received. We are a patient people, and with time the situation should correct itself without overt confrontation."

Yung-lin hesitated, looked uncertainly at Alexander, then inclined his head and cleared his throat. "My honored friend, since you were so honest and candid with me, allow me to return the honor. I have to confess that I have a selfish reason for not wanting Stepan to be prosecuted at this time. As I told you, Shu-hsien is to contact Stepan when she arrives in Kyakhta, and not only do I not wish to attract the authorities' attention to him at this particular time, but I also don't want to antagonize him. Shu-hsien's safety is at stake here. As a matter of fact, in a few days I am leaving for Maimachin. I decided to wait for her there, rather than have her wait for me in Kyakhta."

"What excuse can you give your colleagues for

returning to Maimachin? After all, you don't know whether it will be a few days or weeks before she arrives."

"A few days or even a week would present no problem; there are always business matters to settle. If it is any longer"—Yung-lin shrugged—"then I shall think of a reason when the time comes."

Alexander rose and thanked him for tea. "We shall be waiting for you here, Yung-lin, to welcome your future bride. My wife and I will do everything in our power to make the transition easier for her."

Yung-lin bowed deeply. "You honor me by your concern."

Back home, Alexander found Irina in the parlor. She had just finished the French lesson she was giving to two little girls who came to their house twice a week and was reading some of Pushkin's latest poems that he had sent her. She and Alexander were corresponding with the famous poet who had openly confessed to the tsar that had he been in St. Petersburg that December 14, he would have been one of the Decembrists.

"I can't get over Pushkin's candor," she said to Alexander as he walked into the room. "The tsar must value his genius to have overlooked such an unabashed confession! He says in today's letter that the tsar told him that he would be his personal censor." Irina chuckled and shook her head. "I wonder how our tempestuous Pushkin with his unruly hair that matches his temperament is going to accommodate both the tsar and his muse?"

"He needs a wife to domesticate him. As long as he lives alone in those two rooms in the Hotel Demuth with no one to govern him, St. Petersburg and its pampering society are going to be his ruin."

"Don't be so prophetic, Alexander. Surely the tsar

will keep an eye on him, and now that Pushkin has had a taste of our sovereign's wrath, he should appreciate being allowed to return from exile."

"I hope so. It would be a shame to lose the greatest literary talent we have ever had in Russia!" Alexander paused, then asked, "Where is Olga?"

Irina shrugged. "In her room, sulking. She feels we're keeping her from going back to Russia and forcing her to wait here for Boris. I really have a hard time forgiving her, but I'm doing this for Boris's sake, although I'm not sure that he wouldn't be better off alone. She told me this afternoon that she thinks he would never try to escape and that he said it only to make her stay. Imagine, such disloyalty to her husband. But basically, I feel she is not a bad person, just shallow and spoiled."

"You're a little hard on her, aren't you? She has a right to make her own choices and we can't hold her here much longer," Alexander said, then turned his head and listened. "Where is Sasha? I haven't seen my son all day, remember?"

Irina smiled tolerantly. "You'll see him soon enough before supper. He has to learn discipline early."

"And seeing his father only before supper is part of the discipline?" Alexander said teasingly.

"I mean that he is on a regular schedule, and this is not the time to play with him. Too much frivolity on the floor, and we run the danger of acquiring babytalk ourselves."

"You're going to be a strict disciplinarian, my dear. I'm afraid I am putty in Sasha's presence. You'll have to scold both of us from now on!"

"I have already noticed that. Two children romping on the floor. A slight gap in their ages, but children nevertheless."

Alexander smiled and kissed her hand. "It is the first

glimmer of humor I've heard from you in a long time. It sounds good!"

Irina stiffened. "In the future, as Sasha begins to understand right from wrong, I'm sure there will be times when I shall have to spank him. And what shall I do with you for your leniency with him? Take your favorite *podstakannik* away and serve you tea in a cup?"

"I'd love to elaborate on my future behavior when I'm with Sasha, but there's something else that I want to tell you right now."

Alexander sat down in a chair opposite Irina and told her about his visit to Yung-lin's office. He held nothing back, not even his own doubts about informing Yung-lin, and after he had finished, Irina put down the poems and looked at Alexander searchingly.

"I don't like the whole business with Stepan. He sounds to me like a man whose first interests are in his pocket, and if necessary, he would sell his soul to the highest bidder. It frightens me that he is responsible for Shu-hsien's safety."

"Don't worry. Yung-lin told me he is planning to leave for Maimachin and wait for Shu-hsien there. We shall have to keep a good thought for those two young people who love each other so deeply that they are prepared to sacrifice their heritage and their homeland in order to be together."

Irina lowered her gaze. "We shall certainly do all we can to make them feel welcome in our country. I remember Yung-lin saying that Shu-hsien doesn't speak any Russian. It will be difficult for her here in Irkutsk, and I'll be glad to teach her our language."

"This is what worries me, my dear. Can love alone be this strong? In other words, can it survive through such tremendous upheavals as defying conventions and abandoning family and tradition? Can they still find happiness in a world that is foreign to both of them?"

Slowly, Irina raised her eyes to him. "Much can be accomplished, Alexander, if in addition to love, there is total, unchallenged trust in each other."

Alexander felt a flush rise to his face. They were trespassing again on precarious ground. He rose.

"Saints do not exist among us, Irina. This is where many of us make the mistake of setting our standards too high and then risk destroying the very happiness for which we sacrifice so much."

He kissed her good night and walked out of the room without waiting for her reply. He had exhausted ideas of how to prove his loyalty and love, and although he ached for her, desired her fiercely, he fought his yearning to touch her because her frigid acquiescence to his lovemaking was a greater insult to his pride than the abstinence he had imposed upon himself.

She still loved him, he knew that, and sooner or later she would come to him. But how long must he wait? And what would bring about the change? Time was on his side. But how much time? He poured himself a glass of brandy and downed it in one gulp. Raising the crystal glass against the light, he twirled it in his fingers, enjoying the sparkling, changing hues of the ruby glass, and then he did something he had never done before. With one swift and violent move, he dashed the glass against the wood casing of the fireplace.

Chapter Twenty-five

Soon after Alexander's visit Yung-lin left a retainer in his office and went to Maimachin. His plan was to make a brief stopover in Kyakhta to let Stepan know that he was going to stay in Maimachin until his cousin arrived. This way, he reasoned, Stepan would be aware that Yung-lin was nearby to keep an eye on him and would be glad to pass the responsibility of smuggling a Chinese boy into his hands as soon as he could. Yes. Yung-lin was rather pleased with himself as he reclined in his coach, this time ignoring the rough ride.

He had been touched and not a little surprised by Alexander's confession about the silver idols. How little he still knew of the Russian mind and the depth of emotion in the Russian soul! What had driven the man to confess so openly? Yung-lin had found it difficult to conceal his astonishment at his friend's description of the fraud.

He knew, of course, that the Russians did not consider it as shameful to lose face as they, the Chinese, did. Nonetheless, it surprised him to hear Alexander denounce Stepan so openly. Had the situation been reversed, he would not have divulged a dishonorable business transaction to a foreigner. It would have brought shame on all Chinese merchants as a whole. He would have found ways to handle the situation privately without revealing a double-crosser among his own people.

Yung-lin leaned on the arm of the coach and shaded his eyes. There was much for him to learn yet and teach his beloved along the way. Delicate Shu-hsien with a strong will. She would survive; she would adapt and learn the foreign ways and bring him boundless happiness. Graceful girl with smooth, taut skin, not a blemish on her body, so warm and loving. He would cherish her, protect her. There would be so much to do after their reunion! He had not been able to look for a house or buy anything for her for fear of arousing suspicion among his colleagues and the curious Russian merchants who already had questioned his reasons for wanting to move to Irkutsk permanently.

"But there are already some Chinese residents here," he said to them, trying to evade a direct answer, but they would not be put off.

"Don't give us that!" They guffawed, winking. "We know why you're moving here. You are a virile and healthy man, and you don't like leading a celibate life in Maimachin!"

Yung-lin did not correct them. Let these lusty men think what they would, so long as they were far from the truth. He was more concerned about his Chinese colleagues who would be far more suspicious about his return to Maimachin especially since they would know by now that Lo Chia-li was looking for his daughter and his men would be everywhere, spying and questioning everyone in sight. He would have to be particularly careful to protect Stepan by not visiting him more often than his usual business required. And what if Shu-hsien already there? His delicate Shu-hsien with her soft, shining eyes and her quiet, gentle ways . . .

As his coach approached Kyakhta, his heart—his foolish heart he could not control—began to race. It would take all his self-discipline not to stop in Kyakhta first but to proceed directly to Maimachin, so as not to arouse the slightest suspicion.

A current horse caravan was about to leave from Kyakhta for Irkutsk on its routine run, and if he were lucky, he would join it with Shu-hsien by his side. Stepan occasionally joined the caravan when he wanted to visit his Buryat relatives in the Transbaikal area and, Yung-lin suspected, collect his current contraband of silver. If he were to go with this particular caravan, then Yung-lin would have an ally in case of suspicions or questioning by the authorities as to the identity of his young "cousin".

While he was making these plans and dreaming of how Shu-hsien would greet him, he found himself at the gates to Maimachin and paying his Russian coachman. The town looked the same as when he had left it the previous winter; only the weather was different. This was by far the better time of the year, and Yung-lin walked the narrow center street, greeting acquaintances and reciting a well-rehearsed speech of why he had come back. He was glad for his business ties, for an ongoing transaction that required his knowledge of current prices and official dealings in trade, so that no one could consider his reappearance suspicious.

Right now he had to join other merchants in one of the big houses where they usually collected to discuss the day's affairs, but first, he would have to visit the town *dzarguchay*, for it would be unthinkable to appear among his colleagues before paying his respects to the honorable head official in Maimachin.

After exchanging formalities with the *dzarguchay*, who asked him many veiled questions about Irkutsk, which Yung-lin answered, careful to avoid any reference to his personal life, the older man, resplendent in his brocade purple gown, asked how long he would honor Maimachin with his presence. Yung-lin replied that he expected to leave with the next caravan from Kyakhta, but if the Russian merchants had more orders for him, he would remain a little longer. He was subjected to careful scrutiny by this wise old man with his silvery, slender beard and narrow eyes, and Yung-lin knew that a calm, respectful expression on his face, so carefully cultivated by his countrymen over centuries of training, would be expected of him now. With his eyes closed, his hands joined in front of his face, he bowed deeply and started to back out of the *dzarguchay*'s presence. But the old man stopped him.

"I thought that you were staying over in Maimachin temporarily on your way to Urga. The honored Lo Chia-li may need you back in the clan right now."

So he knows, Yung-lin thought, *and if he knows, then everyone else in Maimachin knows, too.* Outwardly he maintained his calm. "I feel that I would be of more service to the honored patriarch of my clan by being here right now, listening to rumors and possibly learning of his daughter's whereabouts."

For a fleeting moment Yung-lin thought he caught a look of surprise in the *dzarguchay*'s eyes; then the official nodded. "Distances are great between cities, and Maimachin and Irkutsk are no exception. It accounts for your lack of knowledge of what has taken place in Kyakhta and in Maimachin a short while ago."

Yung-lin inclined his head. "I am indeed at a disadvantage. I know nothing of the local news and would be grateful for your information."

The *dzarguchay* began to speak. Something inside Yung-lin's chest squeezed his heart and held it in a vise as he listened to the official sitting before him in the center of the room. Puffing on a long thin pipe between sentences, the *dzarguchay* tore Yung-lin's mind apart with calm, impersonal words.

Shu-hsien had been found in Kyakhta, hiding, disguised as a boy, in the Buryat Stepan's house. It appeared that Stepan had given her shelter before he realized who she was.

"It is not known how Stepan discovered her identity," the *dzarguchay* said, narrowing his eyes against the thin coil of smoke rising from his pipe. "Once he knew who she was, he sent word to her father's er—contacts here that he was willing to hand her over to them."

The *dzarguchay* leaned on the table and busied himself with refilling his pipe. Then he looked at Yung-lin again.

"I am sure that the honorable Lo Chia-li's promise of a high reward helped expedite the matter. Anyway, we all are most pleased that father and daughter are now reunited. This is why I thought you might be going to rejoin your clan during—er—this difficult time."

How had he found his voice to thank the *dzarguchay* for the information? How had he hidden the rage boiling inside him and left the *dzarguchay*'s presence without betraying the truth? He did not remember. All he knew was that he could not face the other merchants in the large house, could not say a word to anyone, for the enormity of the news overwhelmed him.

He had to fight the urge to follow Shu-hsien to Urga, to see her once again, to look for another way for them to be united. But even as he thought these things, he knew how futile they were. Lo Chia-li would never allow him near his daughter, and she would surely be well guarded now until the patriarch decided where to send her away. She had disgraced herself and had caused her father to lose face, and now the Woo family would refuse to take her in their clan. With time, Lo Chia-li would choose a lowly farmer to be her husband. And he, Chien Yung-lin, had condemned her to a dreadful future and brought shame on his adoptive father and his clan.

Yes, he had sinned, but his sin was in wanting Shu-hsien for himself, to have her for his own, not to ruin her life. He hadn't counted on betrayal. Rage blinded him. He had to go to Kyakhta, find Stepan, and vent his fury upon him.

He waited until the gates to Maimachin were ready to be closed at sunset as usual before slipping out with his belongings. It was such a short distance to Kyakhta, only a fraction of a verst, that he decided to walk, rather than hire a coach, lest he look back and find several curious faces watching him leave. It didn't matter now if his colleagues became suspicious about his brief visit or his abrupt and unorthodox departure. Nothing mattered, really, except his all-consuming, single-minded intent to face Stepan. . . .

At the door to the Buryat's house Yung-lin paused and tensed his muscles, coordinating his limbs into deliberate, slow motion by drawing on his knowledge of *t'ai-chi-chu'än* exercises, whereby his mind was in complete control of his body. He would not demean himself before Stepan by showing how anguished he was or dignify the Buryat's betrayal by revealing how deep was his pain.

When he entered Stepan's house, the Buryat closed the door behind him and silently pointed to a chair, but Yung-lin remained standing.

"We made an agreement," Yung-lin said, spacing his words carefully. "Why didn't you notify me?"

Stepan shrugged. "I did! I sent a message as we arranged, but you didn't come in time."

Yung-lin's fists tightened. "You lie! I received no message from you. I came because I expected Shu-hsien to be here by now. You betrayed my trust. We Chinese do not forgive betrayal."

Stepan spread his hands in an apologetic gesture. "You know how it is—business is business! Her father's offer was too good to pass up!"

"How did you learn who she was?"

"That was easy! I wanted to take her to our bath-house. Well . . . the truth came out."

"Did she tell you that she was a woman?" Yung-lin pressed.

Stepan leered. "She did, but I found out for myself!"

The image of Stepan's touching his beloved was terrible. What indignity—or worse—had she suffered at the hands of this uncouth, dreadful man? The thought was intolerable. Flashes of light stabbed his brain, blinded him, destroyed reason and self-control. Seconds later he knew only that his hands were closed so tightly into fists they shook. Slowly he advanced on the Buryat. There must have been something so menacing in Yung-lin's face that Stepan backed away and cried out, "I didn't touch her! I swear, I didn't do anything to her!"

Yung-lin continued to advance on him. "Someday you'll know my revenge!"

Stepan moved to the other side of the table and, from a safe distance, said, "I told you, I didn't touch her. Her father wouldn't pay if I had."

Stepan's last words sobered him. No assurances of honor would have convinced Yung-lin that Stepan was telling the truth, but admission of greed rang true. How unworthy of his proud heritage it would be to sully his hands on a minion like that!

With some of his aplomb regained, Stepan looked insolently at Yung-lin.

"You have no right to threaten me! I could beat your skinny body into scrambled eggs, but you're not worth getting into trouble for. Better get out of here before I call the police. Remember, you're on Russian soil here, not Chinese."

His body and mind back in control, Yung-lin spit on the floor to indicate his contempt. "Our score is not settled yet, and your day of reckoning will come soon enough."

Yung-lin watched with satisfaction a flicker of fear that flashed in Stepan's dark eyes, a fear that did not match his words.

"You don't frighten me. As I said, better get back to your Maimachin, or I'll call the police." With a theatrical gesture Stepan pointed to the door.

Without a word, Yung-lin turned and left the house.

He was weary and suddenly so tired that he halted a horse cart lumbering up the street and asked the driver to take him to the neighboring Troitskovask, where he knew he would find lodging.

All he could do now was return to Irkutsk and hope Shu-hsien would find a way to send him a letter or a message, telling him that she was not harmed, giving him some final words of love.

Tomorrow the caravan was leaving for Irkutsk, and he would go with it.

The horse caravan moved slowly up the road, many of the drivers asleep atop the tea chests. Yung-lin, dressed in his travelling cotton padded blue gown, sat in a cart covered with a curved straw mat, glad not to look outside and face other men. He saw Stepan join the caravan as they were leaving Kyakhta, and he didn't want another confrontation with the man. After traveling for sixteen hours, the caravan camped at night, the men tightening the straps of their cone-shaped caps under their chins and hugging their long sheepskin coats around their legs. The summer heat was over, and the short autumn was heralding the approach of the long winter cold.

Yung-lin slept fitfully, hearing the neighing of horses, the shuffling and stomping of feet, loud voices talking at once in Russian and Mongolian, phrases all mixing together in his ears, taunting him with derisive laughter and imaginary accusations.

He had failed to save his beloved, and he thought he had planned it all so well. He should have known that Stepan would sell his own soul for money, should have gone back to Maimachin earlier, should have—oh, Lord, why chastise oneself; why torture the mind with what he should or could have done? Final is the past, and painful because it *is* so final.

Far worse was the thought that Shu-hsien would one day belong to another man, who could never appreciate or nurture this exquisite flower, as he, Chien Yung-lin, would have done had she belonged to him. This other man, whom her father would select for her—would he appreciate the delicacy of her lovemaking? But then it might be that her husband would never know the joy of her response. He liked to think not. Shu-hsien loved him, only him; she would not give her private love to another—the man who would become her husband.

Why were the horses moving so slowly? Interminable, miserable journey; the monotony of this trodden path! There were moments during the night when his body tensed, aching for Shu-hsien's arms, and he wanted to scream long and loud with an animal ferocity of primeval hunger.

He clenched his teeth. What good would that do? It would bring men running to his cart with questions he could not answer. He would be ashamed and lose face.

Soon they should be reaching the Baikal area; there the scenery would change into wondrous beauty: the mountains with rugged cliffs; the forest; the fast Angara River. Then finally Irkutsk and his Russian warmhearted friends. He needed them now, for he had no one else he could open his burdened heart to and share his misery.

Exhausted, drained of emotion, he fell asleep at last,

and when he awoke the next morning, the magnificence of Baikal thrilled him anew. Although the road to Irkutsk was terribly rutted and twisted, it afforded him a sweeping view of the lush terrain that surrounded the lake. Buryat nomadic tribes scattered their camps mostly in the Transbaikal area, where pastures for their cattle were more readily available, but a few spilled over into this area, hidden between birch groves, pines, and cedars. Sounds were difficult to hide here, for they echoed through the valleys, fading into the distance like an invisible ball bouncing on air.

The echo was deceiving, for often voices seemed near when in fact they were far away, so, when the caravan descended into the valley, and Yung-lin heard the first sounds of galloping horses, he judged them to be far behind. Clear they were, and unmistakably urgent. Pirating the caravans was rare; but isolated incidents did occur, and Yung-lin remembered that only recently he had heard of a new marauding band of Buryats who had attacked and robbed a caravan, taking all the silver it had been carrying. He shifted uncomfortably in his cart. His personal loss and the pain of that loss were so consuming that the intruding thought grazed his mind only briefly and then vanished in the brilliance of an early sun.

But the thudding sound of the horses' hooves did not recede. On the contrary, the rhythmic gallop intensified, grew in volume, and as Yung-lin watched from his cart in astonishment, a large number of Buryats appeared from around the birch grove and were galloping toward them on ponies. Before he could fully comprehend what was happening, the caravan halted, and the Buryats quickly surrounded it. Their loud shouting and the flashing of knives left no doubt as to who they were and why they were there.

With amazing agility the sleepy drivers had jumped

off their carts and without the slightest resistance handed over everything the Buryats demanded. From a nearby cart Yung-lin saw Stepan lumber toward the bandits. A lively argument ensued.

"You're robbing your own people!" he yelled at them. "Shame on you! Why don't you ride south across the border and rob a Chinese caravan?"

"Why should we go that far when this is in our own territory?"

"I told you! I'm a Buryat, too, that's why!" Stepan shouted indignantly, and tugged at the nearest bandit's belt, trying to pull him off the saddle.

Stepan may be crafty and sly, Yung-lin thought, *but he is not very smart.* How foolish to pick an argument with a man on a horse and surrounded by other men all brandishing knives!

The men on their ponies paused indecisively, whispered to one another, and then one of them trotted toward Stepan.

"You must be Stepan from Kyakhta, right?"

Stepan straightened and propped his fists at his sides, pushing his rotund stomach taut against his belted shirt.

"You know me, eh?" he said with a satisfied smirk. "Well, well. I tell you, I have connections, so go away quietly, and I won't report this to anyone."

Three bandits dismounted, each pulling a length of rope out and twisting it around their hands. Briskly they circled Stepan, then grabbed him by the arms.

"What are you doing?" Stepan shouted, trying to wriggle his arms free, but the bandits held him.

"We know you, all right, but not in the way you think," one of the bandits said. "We've been looking for you ever since we got the silver from another caravan."

"I don't know what you're talking about!" Stepan said, shrugging in an attempt to bluff his way out.

An angry glint flashed in one of the men's eyes as he swung wide and slapped Stepan across the face. "Liar! It was hollow! Do you think you can go on casting hollow idols without word spreading around?"

Instinctively Stepan put his hand against his burning cheek. "And what if I had cast a few? They weren't meant for you!"

"But we got them just the same, and you cheated one of your own! You're coming with us!"

The men began to tie Stepan up in spite of his vigorous struggles. Frantically he looked behind him at the caravan drivers, but they all cowered behind the tea chests.

"Chien Yung-lin!" Stepan shouted desperately. "Help me! Tell them—tell them you need me in Kyakhta!"

But Yung-lin sat immobile, his arms hidden inside the wide sleeves of his gown, and watched the scene with half-closed eyes.

"Nobody in Kyakhta knows the business like I do! I have the right contacts! Do you hear me?" Stepan's voice took on a note of hysteria, but no one came to his rescue. It was obvious to everyone except Stepan that the odds were in favor of the armed Buryats, and no one was foolish enough to attempt a confrontation. After the bandits had tied Stepan's hands securely, they hoisted him up on one of the ponies and turned to leave.

In the last frantic effort Stepan cried, "Chien Yung-lin, they'll kill me! For God's sake, talk to them! They'll listen to you!"

The ponies began to trot away and then, gathering speed, broke into a gallop. Yung-lin lowered his gaze and slowly settled back in his cart. The caravan began to move again. He pulled his hands out of his sleeves and, rubbing them gently, studied them. Shu-hsien's skin was the same color as his, but her hands were smoother, silkier. He could never touch them again. She was lost to him forever and would suffer because of one man's greed.

He listened. In the distance the horses' hooves thudded in a gallop. Softer and softer they sounded, then faded into oblivion.

Chapter Twenty-six

In the small cemetery of the little country church Irina had come to love so well, the early-autumn breeze stirred the dry leaves, lifting and rolling them over the graves with a whisper of ancient platitudes for the absent mourners. Irina strolled pensively, reading absentmindedly the carved inscriptions on the crudely erected tombstones—not at all like the elegant, exquisite monuments of white, gray, and black marble of Moscow and St. Petersburg cemeteries. She paused and sat down on a wooden bench to savor the silence and the peace around her.

Inside this quiet, homely palisade she discovered a closer communion with God than among the sculptor's masterpieces in Moscow. The simply constructed tombstones and wooden crosses testified to the love of those who had left their loved ones here. More and more often of late Irina was drawn to this quiet refuge, seeking seclusion to look deep within herself and argue with her soul.

Of late so many demands were placed upon her that she needed to sort them out, choose priorities, and suppress her problems. She smiled, thinking of her little Sasha. He was such a joy to her! A happy toddler now with a language all his own and the wonderful logic of a child. Yesterday, when Anushka brought him to her to say good night, Anisia was pulling the cork out of a bottle of kvass to pour him a drink; but the fermented juice spouted foam, and Sasha stubbornly refused to drink it. Pursing his lips, he pouted. "The bottle is mad at me! I don't want to drink from it!" Then, to distract attention from the hateful bottle, he ran to the window, pointed to the new moon, and asked, "Mama, who bit off a piece of the moon?"

Irina chuckled now, amused by her son's early agility in avoiding unpleasant chores. He was the bright spot in her life. Yet pressures mounted. Olga's presence annoyed her because of her reason for being there. She was also annoyed that Chien Yung-lin was trying to bury his grief over losing Shu-hsien by coming over to their house more often and seeking Olga's company.

She pulled at her scarf uncomfortably. Could it be that she was using all this as an excuse to vent that other, secret frustration that she hated to voice even to herself? Why not be honest and admit that the most difficult inner war she was now waging was against her own stubbornness, or was it just her silly pride? Whatever it was, she was ashamed that she had brought upon herself the punishment of Alexander's withdrawal from the conjugal bed. She never thought she would miss his lovemaking this much, yearn for his arms so much, now that perversely she knew she could not even secretly enjoy his caresses. The cold sheets that encased her down comforter no longer warmed her as she tossed in her bed alone, her body hungry for her husband's hard embrace. How long was it going to take her to resolve this conflict, to *understand* Alexander and start anew? That was the key to the whole problem, she thought bitterly, this inability to understand, to see it from his point of view.

Another gust of the wind, and the rustling leaves gently brought her back to the present. She rose reluctantly and, facing the church, made the sign of the cross, then turned to leave. As she rounded the corner toward the cemetery gate, there, walking slowly toward her, was the tall, patrician figure of the mysterious hermit she had met near Lake Baikal a year earlier. Irina fought an urge to sink into a deep curtsy, so profoundly affected was she by the hermit's serene countenance; she was afraid he might misunderstand her obeisance and judge it to be a reverence to his august birth. Although she was convinced now that Tsar Alexander the Blessed stood before her, she would deem it betrayal of trust to divulge her recognition.

No, her desire to sink to her knees was motiviated by a far more noble, more spiritual awareness of being in the presence of an evolved soul, a saintly man who was standing before her with a kindly smile.

"So we meet again, Princess Dolovina! I praise your decision to return to Siberia of your own free will. It takes a strong and valiant woman to sever the ties of her birthplace and venture so far away from home. I am happy that you now have your family with you and that your husband has been exonerated of all crimes."

"You give me more credit than I deserve, Fedor Kuzmich," Irina said. "I came to love the Siberians during my first stay here and felt we would be happier if we were closer to our less fortunate friends, who are still languishing in prison."

The hermit nodded. "This is what I came to tell you about, Princess. I have a message for you and your husband. I'm afraid I have some distressing news."

Irina's heart skipped a beat. The hermit had access to things that no average monk would know; he had proved it last year when he hinted at Alexander's pardon. What tidings was he about to bring her? She crossed her hands over her chest and waited.

"A small group of fugitives," the hermit began, "are

hiding in a cave near the sourthern tip of Lake Baikal. They are running out of supplies and fear the approaching cold weather. If they are to suceed in evading authorities and making it back to Russia, they need help." The hermit paused, then added quietly, "One of the escaped prisoners is Count Boris Radin."

Although Irina expected this the moment the hermit began to speak, still the sound of her cousin's name made her gasp.

"I am sorry to distress you, Princess," the hermit went on, "but if the fugitives are to survive, they need food and extra clothing, and they need it soon. Frankly I see no future in this adventure even though they are armed with stolen guns. I would urge you to go to the authorities and tell them the approximate area where they are hiding."

"How can you say that?" Irina cried. "How can you advise me to betray my own cousin?"

"Some of the escaped prisoners are simple peasants, hardened to the hardships of Siberian life, and could eventually disappear into the country and be lost to the authorities. But not an aristocrat reared in Moscow. Even if Count Radin succeeded in escaping local police, he would have to live the rest of his life in poverty as a peasant, afraid to divulge his identity to anyone. Is that the kind of life you wish for your cousin? After all, he had only two more years to serve in prison, and then he would have been resettled in Siberia and could have lived comfortably somewhere near you."

"Why have you come to me then instead of my husband?" Irina asked.

"Because no one would question a hermit's presence in the church cemetery, but my presence in your husband's office or home would attract attention. Frankly, although I honor the secrecy of the message I took upon myself to deliver, I am at a loss to understand Count Radin's desire to escape."

Irina bit her lip. How could she tell him that it was Olga who had driven Boris to desperation, that it was his wife who had in effect forced him to commit this foolish act? Yes, foolish it was, but she could not turn him over to the police. No matter how rational the arguments were given to her both by Alexander earlier and now by this strange and mysterious man, she refused to accept it intellectually and reacted emotionally.

"I thank you, Fedor Kuzmich for your kindness and for honoring the secrecy of my cousin's request."

The hermit bowed slightly. "My doubt of the success of Count Radin's escape in no way affects the secrecy of the message entrusted to me."

"I know that what you are saying is true; you wouldn't have any reason to mislead me. Your prophecy about my husband's pardon proves it. But my heart will not allow me to leave my cousin's plea unanswered."

"In that case, I beg you to consult your husband first. Whatever his reaction will be, the message was for both of you, and I hope Prince Dolovin will persuade you not to attempt your dangerous mission. And dangerous it will be, I assure you, for you will become an accomplice to your cousin's escape."

"I *have* to help him, can't you understand that?" Irina cried, wringing her hands and searching the hermit's face for some sign of approval. But the hermit only closed his shining blue eyes and inclined his head slowly.

"I do understand your reluctance to turn your cousin over to the police, Princess. Since you consider it an act of betrayal, I shall leave you with this thought to ponder. In the broader scheme of things, address your vision to the future and ask yourself: given the quality of life that Count Radin will acquire if he escapes recapture, which will be the greater betrayal?"

Unable to speak, Irina pressed her fingers to her lips and stared at Fedor Kuzmich, her eyes filling with unexpected tears. The hermit's features blurred, and shutting her eyes tightly, she covered her face with both hands. She didn't hear him leave, but when she looked up, he was gone.

As Fedor Kuzmich had predicted and as Irina had anticipated, Alexander refused to go into the forest and take supplies to Boris.

"You are out of your mind, Irina," he said angrily. "What has happened to your common sense? You're guided by your emotions and I resent Boris's appealing directly to us. It is not honorable of him to do this, knowing that he is putting us in a difficult position with the police should they find out about this."

"What would you do if you were starving and desperate? How do you know what it is to be pursued and hungry? It's so easy for you to pronounce judgment from the comfort of your home."

Olga rushed into the room, wild-eyed and frantic. "I heard everything you said! Oh, my God, I'll never forgive myself if anything happens to Boris! It is all my fault! He did this to be with me, and I didn't believe him when he told me he would escape! Please help him! We can go to some faraway town where they wouldn't look for us, change our name, and only you would know about us!"

Alexander grabbed her by the shoulders and shook her. "You're talking nonsense! Boris has no chance of succeeding. No chance at all! Do you realize that the longer he evades the authorities, the harsher will be his punishment? He was due to be released in two years, but now his prison term will be extended, I'm sure."

Olga wrung her hands and paced the floor. "I'll go into the forest myself. I'll do what I can to comfort him!"

Alexander caught her by the arm. "Stop it! You'll do no such thing! You don't even know where he is hiding. The police must surely be looking for him by now, and in your distraught state, you'll be the first to be caught."

Irina put her arm around Olga. "Olga, dear, please calm down. Let me talk to Alexander, and we shall see what we can do for Boris. Whatever we decide, you are certainly not the one to take action. You're too upset to be of help."

Olga burst into tears and ran out of the room.

Alexander turned to Irina. "Get any such thoughts out of your mind. As I said, I'm sure the police are on his trail already. Bad news travels fast, and any involvement on our part can only damage Boris, for they will know that he had contacted us in an effort to make good his escape."

Convinced that Alexander would do nothing to help Boris, Irina thought better of continuing the argument. A vague plan was already forming in her mind as she busied herself with household chores.

Tomorrow morning, when Alexander leaves for the office, there will be time enough to talk to Ossip. Ossip would not refuse to help.

Early the next day, after Alexander had left, Irina slipped out of the house before Olga was awake and knocked on Ossip's door. The cobbler let her in and with a deep bow offered a chair. Irina shook her head.

"I need your help Ossip, and I need it in a hurry. Prince Dolovin must know nothing about it."

Without betraying any surprise, Ossip listened until

she had finished, and after she had added softly, "I *have* to find Count Radin and persuade him to give himself up," he thought for a moment, then said, "We shall certainly help the count, Irina Ignatyevna. During my dealings with the Buryats, I've heard them speak often of various hiding places in the forest and mountains around Lake Baikal." He narrowed his eyes and added, "As a matter of fact, I remember their talking about a certain hideaway that one of the fugitives once used in the mountainous region at the southern tip of the lake. They said it was well hidden and quite secret."

"That's it! The message I got was that they were waiting somewhere in the southern area. Do you suppose we can find it?"

"I'll have to remember what I heard, and I'm sure we can find them. Let me start gathering things together. We'll need horses, and I can say that you want to take a ride in the country and are reluctant to go alone, so asked me to accompany you."

Irina felt a surge of gratitude to this wonderful man, who, in spite of the differences in their stations in life, had become her loyal friend. She blinked the gathering tears away and said, "Thank you, Ossip! But please hurry!"

After two hours of riding out of the city, they left the valley floor and started to climb the steep forested hill. Ossip remembered the detailed directions that Marya had once given him when she thought he would travel to the Transbaikal area to buy additional leather. A well-hidden hut, half cabin, half cave, disguised with live cedar branches and set deep in the woods off the footpath, had been a Buryat hideaway for nomadic tribesmen. As Irina listened to his description, she was tempted to ask why he hadn't gone back to the camp and asked for more specific directions. She knew the answer, of course. Besides, the less they asked questions, the better their chances of remaining undiscovered.

No one saw her leave, and she hoped that her absence would not be discovered until Alexander returned late in the afternoon.

But remembering the detailed directions was one thing and applying them in practice was another. They hadn't counted on the depth of the forest or the shrubbery that obstructed their view beyond a few yards, and before long Ossip realized that they had taken the wrong fork in the road. After retracing their steps, Ossip looked up through the tree branches to see where the sun was and then took another path.

After a slow climb they neared the crest of a hill, and at its turn, in the rocky terrian overgrown with moss and cedars, was the opening to a cave. Wooden logs framed the entrance, and it was so cleverly camouflaged that unless one looked for it specifically, it could be passed by, unnoticed. Ossip and Irina dismounted and approached the cave cautiously. Black cinders from a recent campfire were still smoldering at the entrance, and bones and potato peels lay scattered nearby. Irina put her finger to her mouth in a warning to Ossip and then, turning toward the opening of the cave, called, "Boris! Boris Radin, it is I, Irina!"

After a tense silence there was a shuffling and a rustling sound, and four men emerged from the cave. Pitiful they were, and ragged, with overgrown beards, bloodshot eyes, and dusty boots. One of them had bast shoes with strings wrapped around strips of cloth that covered his calves. For a few moments Irina squinted at the men, unable to recognize Boris. Although she knew that the image she had of her cousin as a debonair, handsome dandy entertaining Moscow society with his witticisms was long a thing of the past, still, she was not prepared for these four unrecognizable men. Searching their faces frantically, she panicked, fearing that they had come upon a group of brigands, who would now rob them of their supplies. But as these thoughts lanced her mind, one of the four men, who was behind the other three, moved forward and with shaking hands reached for Irina.

"Irina! Thank God you've come! I prayed that you would. Where is Olga? Is she still in Irkutsk? Tell me, tell me!"

Instinctively Irina pressed her hands against her heart to calm its violent, painful beating and then took a step backward. The man who stood before her was a caricature of the Boris she remembered. He had lost a tremendous amount of weight, and the pallid face with unkempt beard was a dreadful shock to her, no matter how hard she had tried mentally to prepare herself for it.

Irina found her voice. "Olga is still with us."

Boris looked at Ossip. "Who is he?" he asked suspiciously.

"You can trust Ossip implicitly. He's a friend. Here, we brought you food and supplies." Irina motioned to Ossip to hand over the bags. Ossip had thought of everything: potatoes, onions, cucumbers, cooked pirozhki, salt pork, and fruit. There were bandages, alcohol, oil, several pairs of boots he had slipped in from his cobbler's shop, and fresh clothing.

Furtively Boris glanced around him, then pulled Irina aside while the other men greedily checked the bags and started to pull them inside the cave.

"Tell me about Olga!" he asked, searching Irina's face anxiously.

Irina nodded. "She's fine, Boris. I asked her to wait awhile before returning to Moscow. Oh, Boris, what have you done? How in the world do you expect to escape capture? And what of your future?"

"Irina, I don't intend to remain on the run. What kind of a fool do you think I am? These other men are peasants who have been imprisoned for petty crimes. They will easily disappear into the bowels of Siberia, and no one will bother to look for them. It's been done before. But my case is different, and I know it. I joined them to keep Olga from returning to Russia. Don't you see?" His voice rose. "I can't face life in Siberia without her! She told me that if I am resettled in a big town, she may rejoin me. But I know her—once she goes back to Moscow, she will never return. And what guarantee do I have that the place where I am resettled will be a large community?"

Gently Irina touched his cheek. "Oh, Boris, my dear, I didn't know—how could I have guessed?"

"I could not tell my plan to the other men; they would have killed me if they found out that I was planning to be recaptured as soon as possible. I was hoping that Alexander would come and bring the police with him. Then I would be returned to Chita, and Olga would come back." His voice broke, and he looked at Irina with such abject pleading in his eyes that her heart hurt with pity.

"Alexander wanted to go to the police, but foolishly I believed the message and thought you really wanted to remain free. Oh, Boris, I am so sorry! I'll go back and tell Alexander. He'll get the police, and then Ossip can lead them here."

"Thank you, Irina. I'll try to get the men to leave without me. There's no need for them to stay now that the supplies have come." Then he wanted to know all about Olga again, how she looked, what she thought, and Irina found herself covering up the truth, distorting facts to please him. In turn, she asked him about the prison in Chita, and he told her what a relief it had been to have their leg irons removed and how the Decembrists drew moral sustenance from one another. True, they were desperately crowded and had no privacy; but there was comfort in togetherness, and they accepted the personality frictions and tempers that flared as an inevitable part of their confinement.

When the hours stretched into late afternoon, Ossip approached Irina. "We must leave, or we won't be able to reach Irkutsk before dark."

"What about our horses? They can't make the ride back in one day!" Irina said.

Ossip nodded. "I know. We'll leave our horses here and take theirs."

But Boris begged Irina to stay a little longer. "God only knows when I shall see you again! Please, stay until tomorrow. Even if you leave now, it is already too late."

Irina smiled at Ossip apologetically and stayed. When the shadows had lengthened and the air had cooled, Irina shivered. She had not brought an extra coat for herself and now felt chilled.

They slept in the cave with the fugitives, and in the morning Irina was reluctant to leave Boris. Instinctively she knew they would be parted for a long time, if not forever. At last, when Ossip insisted on leaving, she quickly embraced Boris, then moved toward the horse, which Ossip had already prepared with her sidesaddle. As she did so, a hush fell on the small group behind her. In the pristine verdure of the forest, where four desperate men sought shelter in a cave, an echo flew along the sloping shale of the granite cliffs.

Irina listened. She heard the cautious steps of horses' hooves. The sounds intensified and came closer. Her first impulse was to mount their horses and leave the scene before she and Ossip were discovered helping the fugitives.

But there was only one path down and no place to escape.

Chapter Twenty-seven

When Alexander returned home earlier than usual and found both Irina and Ossip missing, he knew at once where they had gone. Careful not to alarm Olga, he told Anisia that he wouldn't be back for supper and hurried directly to Yung-lin's office. There he confided in his friend, rushing through his story and telling him what he was about to do.

The he asked, "Do you know any Buryats who could direct the police to the hideaway?"

Yung-lin nodded. "Your former servant, Marya, told us, when Ossip and I visited them in their camp, that she had gone several times to the forest to leave food for the traveling nomads. Evidently some of her father's relatives had used a cave for a hideaway from robbers, so she could probably lead you there." Yung-lin watched Alexander's reaction to his words and then added quietly, "It would be the quickest way to find them."

But Alexander balked. That was all he needed! Irina and Ossip were there, and then he would show up with Marya, leading the police to the hideaway! That was too much.

"I—I think a woman is more of a responsibility than a help in a dangerous search like this. Why can't her father take us to the hideout?"

"Because he's vague about its location; remember, it

is Marya who has taken food to the hideout, and she knows the exact area," Yung-lin said.

Alexander hesitated. His friend was right. Too much was at stake right now—Irina's safety; Boris's escape; confrontation with the police. His personal reluctance to have the two women meet face-to-face was unimportant just now.

"Well then," he said, pacing the floor and unable to face his friend, "may I impose upon your friendship and ask you to go to the camp? Ask Marya if she would show us the way . . . tell her—tell her that my wife and Ossip are in danger! Meanwhile, I'll go to the police. I'm terribly concerned for Irina. God, how foolish of her to go there! I'll have Ossip's skin for this!"

Alexander started toward the door, then turned. "I'll notify the police and then wait for you at the house!"

Yung-lin nodded. He understood what it must have cost Alexander to agree to Marya's help. It couldn't have been helped. In an emergency the most expedient path ennobled the means. He rose, put his papers away, and after closing the office, took a droshky to the Buryat camp.

It didn't take long to convince Marya to lead the police to the hideout, and when he volunteered to go along, strong, enduring Marya raised her eyes to him, and a river of tears spilled over, rolling rapidly down her smooth olive skin. Surprised, Yung-lin stood waiting. He was reluctant to ask about the cause of her tears, and his pain over his own loss was still too raw for him to offer any comfort to the Buryat girl. As she fought for control, he finally asked, "Is there something I can do to help?"

Marya shook her head and, after wiping her nose with the sleeve of her dress, said, "You don't know? You haven't heard?" and when Yung-lin shook his head, she whispered, "My uncle Stepan—he's—he's dead . . . The bandits . . . They killed . . . He—he was always kind to me when I was a little girl . . . and—and I haven't seen him in such a long time. . . . I wish I had seen him before—Oh, Yung-lin, seeing you made me hurt more because you've dealt with him, you must have seen him recently . . . haven't you?"

There was pathos in her words, an ingenuous plea of a woman who, in the face of grief, had suddenly regressed into childhood. What could he tell her? That he had seen her uncle abducted, listened to his cry for help, and intentionally done nothing about it? Or that her uncle had betrayed him and had paid the highest price for his treachery? No. He couldn't tell her. Let her grieve for the uncle she remembered, the uncle who had been kind—in a child's memory of long ago.

Yung-lin joined his hands before his face and inclined his head. "I regret to hear of your grief. It is most unfortunate, but you must console yourself that your father is here, near you."

Marya did not answer. She turned to get her padded jacket, then mounted her pony. Yung-lin mounted another, and they galloped back to town. When they reached Alexander's house, it was already dark. Alexander thanked Marya for coming, and when he heard that Yung-lin was going to go with them, he grasped his hand and squeezed it silently.

"The chief of police said we'll start early in the morning. I'll see you tomorrow!"

After Yung-lin had left, Alexander turned to Olga, who was sitting in the parlor with her hands clasped tightly in her lap, her eyes red from crying. "Olga, please ask Anisia to share her room with Marya tonight." He then nodded to Marya, said good night to both women, and left the room.

Early the next morning Alexander, Yung-lin, and Marya joined Efrem Orlov, the chief of police, who gave rifles to the two men, before the search party started out of Irkutsk. Orlov rode abreast of Marya, who led the way. As they reached the outskirts of town, he turned to the rest of them.

"All of you! Hold your fire as long as possible!" he called. "I have orders to take them alive, especially Count Boris Radin. Besides, Princess Dolovina is with them, so don't shoot until I give the order! Understood?"

They moved on, and by the time they reached the forested slopes the midday sun was high above them. The breeze that cooled the air in the morning had subsided, and the tall pines stood somber and forbidding, their stately tips seeming to touch the golden sky. Nothing moved. The hollow silence greeted them as they entered the forest, where shadows lengthened, spreading their dark fingers through the birch and cedar branches. The horses moved in single file, stepping carefully over moss-covered logs, cracking an occasional twig that had slipped down across the path.

Darkness deepened, blurring the outlines and confining the vision to a few yards ahead. But Marya seemed unperturbed. Confidently she led the search party on along the narrow path, through a thicket of ferns, past a jutting rock, and onto a small clearing.

It was empty save for a few horses tied to a tree. The smell of smoldering wood and cooked food reached Yung-lin's nostrils, and there, beyond the burned-out campfire, was the entrance to the cave.

The silence was so complete that a frightened squirrel scampering through the birch leaves and rustling the quiet made Yung-lin start.

The search party dismounted, and Efrem Orlov approached the cave cautiously. "This is the chief of police addressing you! We know you are in there. Come out with your hands up!"

When there was no answer, he shouted, "You are outnumbered, so surrender peacefully!"

The reply was a volley of shots, and the policemen scattered for cover.

Efrem Orlov tried again. "Don't be foolish! I'm giving you the last warning—come out or we're coming in!"

After a few moments Irina and Ossip emerged with their hands up. When Irina saw Marya, she stiffened and stopped.

"What's all this?" she asked, looking angrily at Alexander, but before he could answer, Yung-lin stepped forward and bowed.

"We're here this soon only because Marya knew the way to this hideout," he said.

Irina's frozen expression did not change.

"Listen, Irina," Alexander said, moving toward her, but at that moment, Efrem Orlov motioned them to the side, and more shots rang out. With lightning speed Marya moved forward, grabbed Irina by the arm, and pulled her aside, shielding her with her body. Ossip stood frozen to the spot, his glance traveling from Marya to Alexander and back, and as Yung-lin watched the changing nuances on Ossip's face, he could read his emotions clearly.

With a silent gesture Orlov ordered his men to shoot in the air, and moments later the fugitives came out of the cave, brandishing knives and guns. Before Yung-lin could move to protect the women, Alexander was beside Irina, circling her waist and pulling her to the side of the cave and behind a tree. Marya and Ossip were left facing each other, and as Yung-lin stepped toward them, the police moved to take the fugitives. But the escaped prisoners began to fight with knives and then started shooting at random. In an instant Ossip was in front of Marya, pulling her out of the line of fire.

Quickly Yung-lin looked at the fighting fugitives. It

wasn't difficult to identify Boris Radin in spite of his overgrown beard and tattered clothes. His refined features and slight frame were in stark contrast with the robust, weather-beaten faces of the other prisoners. Yung-lin moved swiftly to pull him away from the skirmish, but as he did so, a single shot rang out, and Boris slipped to the ground at Yung-lin's feet. An instant later Alexander was beside him, kneeling by the fallen man. Cradling Boris in his arms, Alexander felt his pulse, raised his half-closed eyelids, then slowly lowered him to the ground.

"He's dead, Yung-lin!" he said softly.

As if mesmerized by the crumpled figure of the fallen man, the fugitives threw their knives and rifles down and reluctantly raised their arms. Suddenly it was all over.

In a few steps Orlov was beside Yung-lin. "You've killed him, you fool!" he shouted. "We didn't want any casualties!"

Yung-lin turned to Orlov. "I did not shoot Count Radin. One of your men did."

The chief of police studied him with open hostility, taking in his dark blue padded gown, his black cap, the thin queue in the back, and sniffed. "Why would one of my men shoot him when I gave orders not to? You were standing right beside him when it happened."

Yung-lin felt a wave of heat rise to his face. He straightened, towering over Orlov by a good head. Without inclining his head, he stared at the police chief. "I had no reason to shoot him. He is my friend's relative, and besides, I haven't fired my rifle."

Efrem Orlov shrugged. "It doesn't matter. You won't be prosecuted. We have witnesses that the fugitives resisted."

But Yung-lin stood his ground. "I cannot ignore a false accusation against me. I wish it to be clearly understood that I did not shoot the count."

The chief of police nodded absentmindedly. "Have it your own way. We have more immediate concerns right now." Appalled by the attitude of the chief of police, Yung-lin thought: *I shall never understand these people. They shall always be an enigma to me. Is Orlov blaming me because he doesn't want to admit that his men disobeyed his order*? He turned toward his friends behind him. Alexander and Ossip were bending over Boris, checking him carefully, reluctant to believe what their eyes were telling them. Marya was holding Irina in her arms, pressing her face against her shoulder to keep her from looking at the slain man.

Ossip was the first to rise. After a slight hesitation he walked over to Marya and touched her on the arm. She looked at him, then released Irina and slowly gave him her hands. He grasped them, and the two looked at each other for a long moment. Neither said a word.

Freed, Irina ran stumbling into Alexander's arms and, hiding her face in his chest, burst into tears.

"You're shivering," Alexander said. "We must get you under cover. There's nothing left for us to do. The police will take—take care of things. Come, darling, let's go!" He turned to Yung-lin. "Come with us, dear friend. The police will feed our horses and bring them back tomorrow. We'll take the prisoner's horses. I'm sorry you became involved in this dreadful tragedy; I beg you to ignore the accusation. We're all distraught and saddened. Forgive us!"

Yung-lin did not answer and watched as Ossip pulled the horses toward them. As they began to mount, Irina looked at Ossip and Marya. The eyes of the two women locked, and Irina's mouth quivered. She left the horse and, after walking over to the Buryat girl, touched her arm.

"You've risked your life to protect me. I want you to

know that I am grateful." Then, having turned quickly, she rejoined her husband.

Olga received the news in shocked silence. For a few minutes she sat staring into space; then, all of a sudden, she let out a rending cry and, wringing her hands, sobbed. "What have I done? What have I done, God? I am guilty of murder—guilty for the rest of my life! How can I live with this?"

Irina stroked her hair gently, sensing that embracing her would be the wrong thing to do, that Olga needed freedom to move about, to express and expend her grief physically.

Irina herself was shaken to the depths of her soul. Boris, her lighthearted, dandified cousin with his clever wit and charm, was dead, killed in a desperate and foolish attempt to hold his wife. It was excruciating to dwell on the circumstances and difficult not to blame Olga for her selfish act, which had boomeranged in such a tragic way. There was nothing left in Siberia that would keep her from returning to Moscow now. Time would heal her wound, shade her past, and Irina hoped, keep selective memories with which she would be able to live.

But what about herself? She had to remain in Siberia, near a constant reminder of Boris's death and, with it, a memory of a courageous act—an act that revealed Marya's largess of character when she had shielded her with her own body. So the other woman did not envy her, did not covet her husband's love. Was this, then, the first glimmer of the understanding that she—the wife—would have to work through in her heart and mind so that in the end she could go to Alexander and love him again?

She would have to think about it, but right now the events of the immediate past were too strong, too fresh to think of anything else but the problems at hand. She was overwhelmed. After Olga had cried herself to exhaustion and been put to bed, and Anushka had brought Sasha in to say good night, Irina lowered herself slowly into a chair in the parlor and began to shake. The fire burned in the fireplace, the heavy draperies were drawn to keep the autumn drafts out of the room, but Irina could not control her tremor. She felt cold.

The day's events returned to shatter her anew, and there was still a lot to endure in the days to come: Boris's funeral; Olga's grief; letters to be written.

Anisia brought in a steaming samovar and placed it on the square table in the center of the room. "May I pour you a cup, Barynia?" she asked, and, without waiting for a reply, poured the tea. Then she put a heaping teaspoonful of raspberry jam into the cup, stirred it, and turned to Alexander. "Barynia is shivering. A little brandy in the tea will help warm her."

Alexander, who was sitting by the fireplace, his eyes shaded with the palm of his hand, rose quickly and went over to the sideboard, where a crystal decanter and several small glasses stood on a tray.

"Here," he said wearily, giving the decanter to Anisia, "do as you think fit."

After the brandy and the jam had been mixed together in the tea, Irina took the cup from Anisia's hands and sipped the hot liquid. It seemed to relax her and control the shivering, but the chill in her hands and feet would not go away. The only thing left to do was to climb into bed and hope that the down comforter would warm her. Working out the details of the funeral and consoling Olga would have to wait until the morning.

Chapter Twenty-eight

The next morning Irina awakened with a chill. Her whole body shook so uncontrollably that she thought her bed was rocking. In spite of an extra down comforter Anisia brought and the hot-water bottle wrapped in a towel that she placed at her feet, Irina's teeth continued to chatter. By the evening she was burning up with fever, and Alexander called the doctor.

While Irina kept the thermometer tightly squeezed in her armpit, struggling to contain her shaking, the doctor took her pulse, listened to her chest, and then checked her temperature. She watched him as he turned to Alexander, who was standing by the window. "Well?" she heard him ask anxiously.

The doctor, a jolly-looking man with red cheeks and a round belly that bounced his watch chain every time he turned, shook the thermometer in the air. "Considering that the high normal is thirty-seven point two, forty point three is high fever indeed. Prince Dolovin, it is a little early to tell for sure, but I am afraid your wife has inflammation of the lungs. I shall stop in tomorrow morning again, but in the meantime, keep her warm, and be sure that when she perspires, her linens are kept dry; otherwise the moisture on her body will chill her. If she has what I suspect, she will start coughing soon. Here's a cough syrup for her."

Toward evening Irina's breathing became labored and caused stabbing chest pains. The cough started late in the night and deprived her of much-needed sleep. By the following morning she was exhausted and hovering on the edge of consciousness, suspended somewhere in another dimension, slipping in and out of a strange, confused dreamworld. Gradually, as the hours ticked away, days and nights blurred into one.

. . . *"Irina! Ce n'est pas comme il faut!" She heard her French governess's reproving voice. In her pink batiste Easter dress she had just climbed out from under the dining room table, where she was hiding from her cousin Boris. She was ten years old. "Oui, mademoiselle," she said contritely, smoothing the flounces of her pretty new dress. Boris grinned and pulled at her cascading curls. It hurt. "I caught you! You are my prisoner!" he said triumphantly. . . .*

The pain increased, spread through her chest and up into her shoulder. The racking cough brought her up in bed. Someone was holding her tenderly. She turned her head and leaned against Alexander's chest. With no strength to support herself, it was good to be in his embrace.

Another violent paroxysm of coughing brought up a rusty-colored sputum, and Alexander held a handkerchief against her mouth. A sluggish thought stirred in the back recesses of her mind. Alexander shouldn't be doing this; so improper to see her like this; embarrassing. . . . Where was Anisia? The words slurred, and she could not string them together.

. . . *"My, my, what an enchanting creature we have become at the important age of sixteen!" Boris's mocking voice sounded behind her as she stood in front of the gilded mirror in her mother's boudoir. . . . She looked in the mirror but saw no one but herself. . . . Abruptly she turned around, and her skirt made a soft, swooshing sound; but Boris wasn't there.* . . . *"Boris? Stop teasing me!" she cried. There was no answer.* . . .

She opened her eyes. Alexander's pained face moved slowly above her, then faded away. A thought floated past. With great effort she grasped at it. What was it? Oh, yes—why was Alexander's face tearstained? Maybe she was dying. Breathing was torture—every breath a dagger in her chest and the cough tearing her apart.

Marya came into focus. Nodding, smiling kindly. What was Marya doing in her bedroom? She turned to look again. . . . *The dark room brightened, and it wasn't Marya at all, but her old, dear* nyanya *in her bonnet and apron, bending over her and shaking her figure. "He's a man and a lusty one, I reckon. Is that reason enough not to marry the man you love? . . . You laugh well together . . .don't forget to laugh together."* . . .

It was bright in the room and warm. Too warm. Then it was hot. Her chest was on fire. Something was burning her chest. The pain was terrible, and she thrashed, pulling at her body and fighting a couple of strong arms that held her prisoner. She opened her eyes.

Marya again. Her chest *was* on fire. The excruciating pain cleared her mind, brought her full consciousness. *Mustard poultice!* The dreadful burning was from the mustard poultice. She tried to tear it away, but Marya wouldn't let her.

"I know how it hurts, Irina Ignatyevna! You've been sick a long time, and we need to do this to help you get well. Hold on a little; I'll take it off soon."

"I can't take it any longer!" Irina cried, and choked on a paroxysm of coughing.

"When there is no alternative, there's a lot we can take," Marya said quietly, and a few minutes later started to unwrap the mustard poultice.

When it was off, she smiled. "There! Doesn't it feel better now? This is the first time you've been truly awake in ten days!"

She slipped the nightgown over Irina's head and helped her back onto the pillows. Her touch was gentle and slow, and the relief was so enormous Irina sighed deeply.

Why was Marya caring for her?

"You need to sleep now. You've been thrashing and coughing all night." Marya's voice was calm, soothing, like a cool brook rippling over her senses.

Had Marya been with her throughout the night? Strange . . . But what was even more surprising was that she did not seem to mind having Marya at her bedside. The thought was confusing, and she could not comprehend it. She felt weak, so terribly weak! Everything, even to think, seemed a great effort.

"Here, take this syrup!" Marya said, and fighting her tremor, Irina raised herself on her elbow. "What are you giving me?"

"It's called loquat syrup. Chien Yung-lin recommended it. He said it's made of eleven different herbs and has cured many of his people of cough and lung trouble."

Irina swallowed the syrup without protest and fell back on the pillows. She was exhausted. Questions whirled in her mind, but to ask them seemed too much trouble. She closed her eyes, sighed again, and, for the first time since she'd fallen ill, drifted into a dreamless sleep.

When she awoke, the heavy draperies were drawn back, and the autumn sun bathed the room with its golden light. Furniture outlines blurred in the hazy sunbeams as Irina's glance wandered slowly over familiar objects. She had purposely furnished her bedroom in Karelian birch; she loved its cheerful golden color and its wavy grain, and she wanted to have a link with her childhood home. As a little girl in her Beryozovka home she had created imaginary castles with their labyrinthine secret passages on her armoire's side, staging pursuits and escapes through the intricate serpentine patterns of the wood.

Her gaze drifted now over her dressing table, covered with crystal perfume bottles, her set of silver hairbrush and combs that she had brought with her from Moscow, the nightstand with its washbasin and medicine bottles, and finally came to rest on her silk-covered chaise longue, where Marya was reclining. The Buryat girl's eyes were closed, her face in repose, and as Irina studied her, she realized that she was able to look at Marya without resentment and that the girl's goodwill had somehow eased her pain. Marya's selfless act in the forest had tempered Irina's bilious anger and perhaps softened even the deep-seated hurt she had felt these many months.

As she thought these things, Marya opened her eyes and saw that Irina was awake. With one quick movement she slipped off the chaise and walked over to stand beside Irina's bed.

Irina squinted at her against the light. "Why are you here, Marya? Who called for you? How long have you been here?" The questions poured, unrehearsed, and Marya waited until Irina had finished.

"You were desperately ill for a long time, and your maid, Anisia, was afraid to touch you. Anushka has to care for Sasha, and Countess Radina said she didn't know what to do. Prince Dolovin stayed by your bedside day and night until he himself collapsed, and finally Ossip came to fetch me. So I came to care for you and brought medicines that Chien Yung-lin has given me. He recommends using camphor oil instead of mustard poultice, but the doctor says that if your cough does not disappear, I am to put the cups on you, for they may draw the inflammation from your lungs better than the poultice." Irina winced, remembering that her mother called the cup treatment a voluntary torture. "I feel so much better already that I may escape the cups," she said unconvincingly.

"You're still very weak, and your cough has not gone away," Marya said. "It'll be a while before you are strong enough to get up. It is important to nurse your energy now."

Irina's lips tightened. It was awkward to be alone with Marya, too soon to have a conversation with her or to pretend that the past no longer mattered. What would the girl's reaction be if she told her that she knew?

She said, "I know, but it won't be easy for me." She hesitated, then asked, "Where is my husband?"

"He's in the parlor with Countess Radina and Chien Yung-lin, who came to inquire after you," Marya answered, carefully tucking in the blankets.

"Please ask Prince Dolovin to come in," Irina said, enormously relieved that her coughing spells were not as frequent now.

Marya nodded and went toward the door. A few minutes later Alexander was beside her and kneeling by the bed.

"Oh, my dearest, our prayers have been answered! Two weeks of not knowing if you would get well. . . . All Dr. Karpov could do was spread his arms and say that he'd done everything he could and the rest was up to you and the Lord. . . ."

Alexander took her hands and kissed them, then pressed them against his cheek and kissed them again.

"I love you!" His voice was choked, and when he raised his head to look at her again, she realized with a shock that there were deep dark circles around his eyes and he looked pale and drawn.

Those days and nights then, when in fleeting moments of lucidity she had seen his face before her with tears and pain in his eyes, had not been hallucinatory images after all. He had kept a vigil by her bedside, agonized for her, feared to lose her.

He truly loved her!

"You look so tired I don't know who is the sick one here!" she said, trying to make light of it, and suddenly her hand, with a will of its own, smoothed his brow and caressed the outline of his face. Alexander grabbed it impulsively and pressed the palm of her hand to his lips. Suddenly there was such an abundance of happiness on his face it spilled over and bathed Irina in its glow.

In an awkward silence that followed, Irina changed the subject.

"How is our Sasha?" she asked, and heard a happy recitation of Sasha's daily pranks and his own special words. Irina listened avidly, suddenly hungry for her family's daily minutiae, hungry for activity, and—and yes, hungry for Alexander's love. But as she raised herself on her elbow, a coughing spell cut off her speech, weakened her again, and brought Alexander to his feet, to rush around the foot of the bed to where the bottle of loquat syrup stood on the bedside table.

"Alex, you look tired yourself," she said after the coughing spell had subsided. "Please go and rest. I'll be all right now."

Alexander hesitated, then said, "Yung-lin came a short time ago to inquire after you. What a concerned and supportive friend he has been! He's so lonely, especially since Shu-hsien has been lost to him."

"Is he still here?" Irina asked.

"Yes, he's in the parlor with Olga."

A vague suspicion disturbed Irina. There was nothing to hold Olga in Siberia anymore. She should

return to Moscow immediately. A widow now, she was
as lonely as Yung-lin. Linked by their tragedies, the
two would surely be attracted to each other. This must
not be allowed to go on. Their background's were so
different, it could only spell disaster.

Irina felt an inner tremor. Every emotional strain
exhausted her. In her weakened state maybe she was
imagining things, exaggerating her suspicions. After
all, she had to admit that they were completely un-
founded, and neither Olga nor Yung-lin had ever
given her cause to suspect that they were anything more
to each other than interested friends.

Contrite, Irina touched Alexander's arm. "Please go
back to them and tell them I am better. Then send
Anisia in with some hot bouillon for me. For the first
time since my illness I feel hungry. Must be a good
sign!"

Alexander smiled and, bending down, kissed her.
Then he straightened, smoothed her covers, pushed her
tousled locks off her forehead, and went out, closing
the door quietly behind him. Then, still holding the
handle, he leaned against the door.

The long days of tension, the sleepless nights, the
anxiety, had taken their toll, and the sudden relief of
knowing that Irina would not die—he could have
strangled the doctor in frustration when he had told
him that she might not survive—was almost too much.
In fact, the events of the last two weeks had exhausted
him, had stretched the limits of his self-control. With
Irina's desperate illness, when any moment he expected
a turn for the worse, and Olga's emotional outbursts
and self-castigation over Boris's death, he found that
Marya's presence had given him a stabilizing equilib-
rium. Embarrassed to admit it, he had drawn on her
equanimity, her quiet support, and her expert ministra-
tions to Irina.

But at the same time he had looked at her in amazement these days, ashamed of himself for having allowed an intimacy between them that had now seemed not only impossible but incongruous. There was no doubt in his mind that Ossip had loved Marya for a long time, and after the tragic incident in the forest when he had forgotten his hurt and in the face of danger rushed to protect her from the fugitives' shots, he must have forgiven her. And ever since, he had been walking with a shy and contented smile on his face and had informed Alexander that he had resumed buying his leather from the Buryat camp.

Weary, Alexander sighed. How wonderful it would be if Irina were to forgive him, too! He had spent hours by her bedside, praying that she would not die, bargaining with God with promises to atone for all the hurts he had caused, and his prayers had been answered. All but one—Irina's feelings toward him. Yet somehow he felt that this illness was perhaps a catharsis of many things in their lives.

Suddenly he was brought up short by Olga's angry voice coming from another room. With a few quick steps he opened the door and entered the parlor.

Olga and Yung-lin were facing each other across the table in the center of the room. Olga whirled toward Alexander, red blotches covering her face and neck, eyes flashing in anger.

"What kinds of friends do you have here in Irkutsk?" she said, her voice shaking with indignation. "I thought Chinese merchants were civilized people, but evidently I've been wrong!"

Alexander glanced at Yung-lin. The Chinese stood erect, his face an enigmatic mask.

"What happened, Olga?" Alexander asked, taking her arm and trying to lead her to a chair, but Olga wrenched herself free.

"This so-called gentleman has just offered me his protection! He had the temerity to tell me"—Olga was choking with anger—"to tell me that he would be willing to have me as his concubine. Can you imagine that? Not only is he offering me something highly insulting, but at a time when my husband hasn't cooled off in his grave yet! That's—that's barbaric!"

Alexander stepped forward. "Yung-lin, I know that you didn't intend to insult Olga. It's a simple matter of misunderstanding."

Yung-lin paled. With eyes half closed, he said, "I do not understand why my offer has been taken as an offense. A concubine may occupy an enviable position in a Chinese household, and since Madame Radina is now a widow, I have offered her my protection. I would have welcomed companionship now, and Madame Radina would have been well taken care of in my house."

"You could have offered her marriage," Alexander said quietly.

Yung-lin looked up sharply. "My grief is deep, and I doubt that I would ever marry again."

Alexander cleared his throat and smiled. "Your offer was well intended, Yung-lin, I'm sure; but you must understand that this is not a Chinese city, and while you may establish a Chinese household here, Olga is not Chinese, and in our culture such an offer is . . . not acceptable."

"Yet you do have courtesans, do you not?" Yung-lin asked.

Alexander flushed. "Courtesans do not live in a household with other members of the family, and they do not hold the same position in our society."

"But our concubines are envied, especially if they bear sons," Yung-lin insisted, still seemingly unable to understand their reaction. "If Madame Radina refuses to accept my offer, I bow to her decision, but to say that I have insulted her is an undeserved accusation."

"In our culture," Alexander said patiently, "there is no such position in a family. Our religion permits only one wife, and a concubine would mean the same thing as a courtesan—in other words—an illicit affair."

Alexander glanced at Olga, who stood breathing heavily, her eyes filling with tears, then quickly looked back at Yung-lin, whose face reddened through his smooth saffron skin. "I can see that there is much for me to learn about the Russian culture," he said. "I can assure you, however, that *my* culture would not permit me to insult a lady in my friend's household. To be accused of such a transgression and be called a barbarian is an insult in itself."

With his arms stiffly at his sides, he bowed formally and walked out, his silk robe rustling in the awkward silence.

Olga's face crumpled, and she began to cry. "How dare he! Just because I'm a widow now!"

"Have you given him any lead to presume that you were looking upon him with favor?" Alexander asked.

"What are you insinuating, Alexander?" she said angrily. "You don't think I've been flirting with him two weeks after Boris died?"

"You'd been seeing him before Boris escaped from prison. He may have thought—"

"He may have thought what?" Olga cried indignantly. "He's been associating with Russians long enough to know better. He had no right to suggest such an unspeakable thing!"

"You may see it only from your point of view, Olga," Alexander said. "You heard what Yung-lin said before he left. He's just as insulted as you are. It's a simple case of mutual misunderstanding and should be treated as such. As a matter of fact, I suspect we've made him lose face—a grave thing to happen to a Chinese. I'll see what I can do tomorrow to make amends."

"Make amends! So! You're siding with him! I should have guessed that you would defend another man. What is it to you if he humiliated me, a lonely widow without a husband to protect her! You men are all alike. Your first instinct is to side with another man, whether he's right or wrong! You men! I hate you all!" Olga started to sob and ran out of the room.

Chapter Twenty-nine

Yung-lin went directly to his rented flat adjacent to his office. He locked the door, drew the curtains, and stood indecisively before an idol of Buddha that sat on a small red lacquered chest he had brought from Maimachin. He needed to think, and he didn't want to be disturbed. Slowly he pulled up a straight-backed wooden chair and sat down. His mind was in a turmoil; there was so much he had to think about. So much!

He had lost face today before his Russian friends, but thankfully they would not understand the deep humiliation that accompanied it. He had behaved honestly in offering his protection to Olga. She had intrigued him with her black hair, her sparkling, mischievous eyes that seemed to signal a willingness to establish a closer relationship. And he was lonely. So lonely! Surely a widow, a woman experienced in pleasing her husband, would have become a good concubine. He was human, wasn't he? It would have worked out, he was sure, and he would have had some consolation during those long, empty nights when nightmares haunted him, those nightmares that had become his only companions. He could not escape the figure of his adoptive father hovering somewhere above his head, shaking his accusing finger at him, or the image of Shu-hsien's dolorous face with tears running down her cheeks.

Was it wrong, then, to want Olga to wipe away those images that pursued him? How was he to know that his offer would be taken as an insult? His people said that a widow brought bad luck. He laughed out loud with a dry, bitter laugh. He already had all the bad luck he could have. Foolish woman. She was condemned, like him, to a lonely life. Would she, a widow, ever find another young and loving husband? He doubted it. So why had she turned him down? Different culture, strange customs. He would never get used to them, never understand them fully; he knew it now. To be accused of being a barbarian before his Russian friend was an indignity, a shameful loss of face.

There was so much he did not know yet, so much to be learned about this strange country. How could he have thought that he and Shu-hsien could adjust to living in this primitive land, among these strange people? They, not he, were the barbarians.

It seemed to him that the Lord Buddha had wrought vengeance on him for having sinned against everyone he loved. And he had sinned indeed. Against the one woman he adored, whose life he had ruined; against his adoptive father, whom he had disgraced and caused to lose face; and against the members of his clan, upon whom he had brought shame.

Yes, he had sinned. The right, the proper thing to do now would be to return to Urga, kowtow to the patriarch, and beg forgiveness for his sins, promise to dedicate his life to his adoptive father and to the service of his clan.

But even as he thought of this possibility, he knew he could not go back. Some' things were beyond a man's endurance. Shu-hsien would be living in the same courtyards, and he would never be able to see her, never touch her, and be always aware that one day Lo Chia-li would send her away. In his folly, blinded by love, he should have remembered the ways of his people and that disgracing one's family was an unpardonable sin. No matter how much Lo Chia-li loved his daughter, he would not, could not, keep her permanently in his clan, and since no respectable family would want a disgraced girl for any of their sons, he would send her away to lead a life of hardships, without happiness or hope.

Involuntarily he looked at the long white cotton sleeves of his undershirt, which were cuffed over his gown to signify that he was from the upper class and would not soil his hands with common labor. Yet his beloved would submit to such an existence.

His sin. The guilt and the pain descended on him, tightened his neck in a noose. As long as Shu-hsien remained in her father's clan, he could not make himself go back. He couldn't even return to Maimachin to live, for once there, among other Chinese merchants, his adoptive father would demand his return to the clan. He was trapped.

But remaining in Irkutsk now was a bleak prospect. He rose, paced the floor. Was it warm in the room? Maybe he should open the ventilation window and let in the fresh air. He pulled open the draperies, reached up to the upper right square of the window frame, and opened the double panes. A blast of cold air poured in, cooling him, soothing him. He stood there for a few moments, breathing in deeply as if the air's purity would wash the shame away.

In spite of it all, he had to stay in this city, which had suddenly become hostile, a city where he now felt more alien than ever; but at least he would stay by his own choice. Somewhere in the back of his mind a memory stirred. In the courtyards of the Lo clan, whenever he suffered physical pain as a child, he had been reminded that he was a brave little boy, and brave little boys must not cry. It was wise perhaps to train the mind to imagine even greater pain, which would then make the real one more tolerable. And now he realized that his loss of face could have been infinitely more shameful if it had occurred in the presence of other Chinese men.

What small consolation! Now that Shu-hsien was not to be his, he yearned to return to his roots, to be a part of old traditions and customs he knew so well. His was the legacy of obedience, of respect to his elders, and he had defied it. What poetic justice! The place where he sought to find supreme happiness had now turned into a prison.

Someday maybe he would find it possible to go back. But right now the image of Shu-hsien in the arms of another man, and a lowly man at that, was raw in his mind and the worst torture of all. Betrayed by a common man, she now had to yield to a comman man; that Stepan had paid the supreme price for his betrayal was no comfort.

No. He could not bring himself to return now. Not yet. So be it. He had no alternative. He would swallow his insult and continue to see the Dolovins and seek their friendship. Olga would be going back to Moscow soon, and in the meantime, he would share Alexander's joy in Irina's survival. The crisis had passed, and her recovery would bring Alexander much happiness.

At the Dolovins' house, rejoicing over Irina's recuperation was tempered by sadness at Olga's imminent departure. As soon as Irina's crisis was over and recovery on the way, Olga announced that she could not tolerate another minute in Irkutsk, where everything reminded her of tragedy and past unhappiness. She wanted to leave for Moscow immediately before the winter months set in and travel became difficult.

Alexander did not insist that she stay, and after a

tearful good-bye to Irina and little Sasha, she left. With her went the last link with Moscow, with Dolovino and their families, but neither Irina nor Alexander voiced any regrets to each other.

Irina was secretly relieved of the burden of handling Olga's difficult personality and keeping suppressed a basic dislike of her cousin's wife. Now especially she had to struggle not to blame Olga for causing—however indirectly—Boris's death, and her presence was a painful reminder of the whole tragic affair. She did not envy Olga's return to Moscow, for emotionally she no longer belonged in Dolovino, and she knew that Alexander felt the same.

Physically she was still very weak, and her cough persisted. The slightest exertion brought on dizzy spells and bathed her in perspiration.

A few days after Olga's departure Marya came in one morning, carrying a tray with cups, an alcohol burner, a glass half filled with alcohol, and a short stick with its end tightly wrapped in a thick wad of cotton. One look at the tray, and Irina groaned.

"Oh, no! I told the doctor I was improving every day. Even my temperature is now normal. I think we should wait another day or two and see how I do."

"Irina Ignatyevna, you know as well as I do that your cough has persisted longer than it should," Marya said sternly, setting the tray down on the nightstand. "Besides, cups are not nearly as bad as the mustard poultice, and you know it!"

Marya's casual irreverence in speaking to her at first had astonished Irina, but in the last few days she came not only to appreciate it but actually to like it. She sighed in resignation. "Well, if it has to be, let's get on with it. It's been such a long time since I had the cups. I think I was only ten or eleven years old, and because I was so thin, it wasn't a pleasant experience, as I remember.'

Marya uncovered Irina's chest. "Well, you're pretty thin now, too. After all, you had little to eat during your illness."

With experienced hands Marya picked up a small tulip-shaped glass cup. She held it in one hand, while with the other, she took the cotton-wadded stick and, after dipping it in the glass of alcohol, lit it from the burner. With a deft movement she swished the flame inside the cup and then quickly pressed it to the center of Irina's chest. Immediately her meagre flesh was sucked into the vacuum of the cup, and before she was able to register its gathering pain, another cup was claiming her flesh above her right breast, and another over her left, and then higher up to her neckbone. Two more went on each side of her chest before Marya was satisfied and extinguished the flame. She was about to cover Irina with the blanket, when the center cup between her breasts slid to the right side, enough to suction a portion of her breast tissue. The pain was suddenly unbearable, and she moaned.

"Oh, please, take it off immediately!" she pleaded, pointing to the offending cup. Marya placed a finger near the rim of the cup, pressed gently on Irina's breast, and with a slight popping sound, the cup released the trapped flesh. Relieved, Irina sighed, but Marya relit the flame and repeated the procedure, making sure this time that the cup stayed in the center of her chest between her breasts. Then, satisfied, she covered her and looked at the clock.

"I'll be back in fifteen minutes, and then we'll do it on the back. As you may remember, the chest is the most painful side."

Irina tried a smile. "Thanks for the consolation!"

As she lay there quietly, the acuteness of the initial pain now dulled, she thought about Marya. It was easier to think about her when she was not in the room, for her presence made Irina feel awkward, and the more at ease Marya seemed to be, the more uncomfortable Irina felt. It was as if Marya had nothing to hide, carried no buried guilt within her, and demonstrated true concern and even affection for her charge. Irina was at a loss to understand it. There was something truly sincere in Marya's smile, her look, her gentle touch, and reluctantly, Irina found herself responding to this simple and caring woman.

Unable to move while the cups were on her, Irina tried unsuccessfully to doze. When the time was up, Marya came back and smiled down at her.

"Well, let's take them off and see where the seat of your cough is!" she said, and after removing the cups, examined Irina's chest. With her head bent down, Irina looked too. The slightly puffed circles differed in color. Some were pink, others purple.

"There!" Marya pointed to a spot below Irina's right collarbone. "This dark one is where the sickness is, see?"

Irina sighed. She had never heard this before, but if Marya believed it, she wasn't going to argue.

"You needed the cups," Marya went on. "Now your cough should loosen and be gone soon. Let me rub you with oil, and then we'll turn you over and put the cups on the back."

She poured some oil into her hand, smeared it between her palms, and then placed both hands on Irina's chest. Gently she spread the cool unguent over her skin, and the soothing, delicate touch was such an exquisite sensation of relief that Irina's eyes filled with tears. Gratefully she turned her head to look at Marya, but instead of the Buryat girl's face, her eye was caught by a dangling ribbon that slipped out from her bodice and was swinging above Irina. And from that ribbon swung a broken piece of coral amulet.

Irina caught her breath. "Why do you wear a broken piece like that?" she asked, trying to keep her voice even.

Marya glanced at her amulet, then looked at Irina. "Because it is an amulet and because I've worn it for as long as I can remember. It's bad luck to have it break, and it did bring me misfortune for a while." Marya wiped her hands on a towel, then sat down on the edge of the bed, took it absentmindedly in her hands, and looked at it. Then she smiled shyly and said, "But my good luck is coming back, and I guess I'll keep wearing it."

"Your good luck?" Irina prompted.

"Yes. Ossip is coming around to the camp again."

A lovely glow illuminated her features, and the happiness that shone through was so genuine, Irina squirmed inwardly from shame. Impulsively, without thinking, she said, "Marya, go over to the wardrobe, and in the drawer you'll find a box. Bring it to me."

Marya looked at Irina with surprise, then got up and did as she was bidden. With shaking hands Irina opened the box and, after taking out the broken coral piece, handed it to Marya.

The girl stared at it for a long moment with wide-open eyes. Then she raised her gaze slowly to Irina. Their eyes locked in silence. If Irina expected to see embarrassment or guilt in Marya's eyes, she was mistaken. Only sadness and genuine concern appeared there. By now tears flowed copiously out of the corners of Irina's eyes as she lay exhausted on her pillows. She tried to swallow them, tried to speak, and could not. Marya took a fresh towel at the foot of the bed and, bending over Irina, carefully wiped her tears. Then she cradled the coral piece reverently in her hand, pressed it against her bosom, and looked at Irina.

"So you know. And so I see many things now. I knew that Prince Alexander was unhappy for a long time; only I did not understand why."

"I could not forgive him!" Irina whispered, avoiding Marya's glance.

"He was lonely. He thought he would never see you again. I understood that. But when you joined him and he was still unhappy, I could not guess the reason."

"I was very hurt when I found out. I couldn't make myself forgive him."

"Forgive him? There was nothing to forgive. He always loved you. Remember, he grieved for you like a widower who has lost his wife to death."

The sparks of old anger threatened to ignite Irina anew. "What about later, after we had returned to Siberia together?" she said testily.

Marya raised her brows. "Who was to blame? Think about it," she said quietly. "He was a guest in my father's yurt, and you know the customs of my people. I didn't go to him myself. My father sent me, and when I came in, he was already asleep and restless. He was moaning, having bad dreams, and talking in his sleep. I listened."

Marya paused and looked at Irina for a moment. There was hidden accusation in that glance as she went on. "I heard him calling a name. Always the same name; only each time he called, it was in a different voice. He called it with love, and with pain, and—and with hunger. Yes, great hunger! It was *your* name, Irina Ignatyevna, that he was calling in his sleep. He was a saddened man, and I consoled him. It was you he touched in his sleep and you he always loved."

"And you did all this without loving him, without—without wanting anything from him in return?" Irina asked.

"I love Ossip," Marya said softly, her voice shaking

for the first time, "and I still don't know if he loves me enough to marry me."

Marya rose and busied herself with turning Irina over onto her stomach, and a few moments later Irina felt the first cup's suction on her back.

"You are a fortunate woman to have a husband who loves you so deeply and so loyally," Marya went on. "Not many of us women are that lucky. I hope your love is strong enough to understand that."

"Your understanding of loyalty is different from mine," Irina persisted stubbornly, her voice muffled by the pillow against her face.

"Prince Alexander's loyalty to you never wavered. Your name was on his mind and on his lips and in his heart. Always."

Suddenly the pain on her back was not as severe as the pain of revelation. That time in the camp Alexander had not sought Marya deliberately. He had hungered for his wife instead, and now, during her illness, he had stayed by her bedside for many sleepless nights, praying for her recovery, until the crisis had passed. And she had driven him away with her stubborn refusal to understand and forgive him, to allow the hurt to heal. What did she expect? She had brought it upon herself.

As soon as she was out of bed and recovered, she would make it up to him. After all, he had told her that he would not touch her anymore and that it was up to her to come to him first. Well, she would do just that. The thought sent her pulse racing.

A wave of such happiness flooded her now that even the cups on her back no longer hurt, and when it was time to remove them, Irina lay quietly until Marya smoothed the oil on her back and helped her turn over. She took Marya's hand and looked at her with a smile.

"I hope Ossip will realize soon what we all can see,"

she said, and watched Marya's face flush. "He loves you, I'm sure. The way he rushed to protect you in the forest—I'm afraid it's obvious to all of us except him. Well, it's that age-old tradition that he must have a virgin bride. A man's pride is a force to be reckoned with, Marya. Be patient. He'll come around."

"Ever since the shooting in the forest, he has come back to buy leather from my father," Marya said. "And as for what you've said about his pride, well—I am what I am, and I hide nothing."

I hide nothing—the words lingered with Irina long after Marya had left the room. She believed her.

Life was ever so, wasn't it? *We create our own rules,* she thought, *adhere to them tenaciously, and when they are broken, and our preconceived ideas are challenged, we place the blame on someone else without looking deeper within ourselves.* It had taken her a long time to see the light, and now Ossip must do the same. Somehow she felt that he had already done so.

As for herself . . . she smiled dreamily. A few more days of recuperation, and then she would undertake the loving task of convincing Alexander that the love of their early days together was about to begin again. Only this time, maturity through suffering would give it poignancy, depth, and a special awareness of themselves to cherish.

She stretched languorously under the covers. Yes, she would convince him. . . . And it would be a delicious task. . . .

Chapter Thirty

During the past week, snow flurries had powdered the roofs of neighboring houses and, today, as Irina sat by the window, she marveled at the dazzling sight before her. This October of 1828 the winter heralded its approach with several days of heavy snowfall. When the storm abated, the sun burned its way through the clouds and sprayed the snowflakes with twinkling sparkles. Now the snow reflected the turquoise sky with a clarity and brilliance that blinded the eye, and a morning hush pervaded the streets, as though man and beast were awed anew by the majesty of nature's beauty.

Bundled in padded coats and thick wool scarves, children waddled along the road and fought with snowballs. Vapor curled above their mouths as they laughed and tumbled into snowbanks. Little *mishki*—bears— Irina thought indulgently, envying the boisterous energy of the very young. In a few years Sasha would be out there, playing with other children, enjoying the winter fun.

The crisp, pure air that Irina inhaled through the briefly opened ventilation window smelled of burning wood and freshly moistened pine and cedar. She rose from her chair and stood on tiptoe, enjoying the morning freshness.

But she was allowed only a brief contact with this

outside world, for Anushka, who had brought little Sasha to see her, shook her head and quickly closed the window. Although her cough had long disappeared, it had taken quite a while before she felt herself truly strong and recovered. She smiled at the two-year-old Sasha, who was climbing laboriously onto her lap.

"He's been asking me something all morning," Anushka said.

"What was it?" Irina asked, ruffling Sasha's locks.

Anushka chuckled. "Why don't you ask him yourself?"

Irina looked into her child's large eyes. "What is it you want, Sashenka?"

"I want a little sister to play with, Mama. Anushka says you can buy me one at the marketplace."

Irina's mouth twitched, and she glanced at Anushka quickly.

Anushka shrugged. "What else could I tell him?"

Sasha tugged at his mother's skirt. "Mama. Mama, buy me a sister!"

"Why do you want a sister? How about a brother?"

Sasha shook his head vigorously. "No! A brother will fight. Choose me a small sister, please, with long curls to pull."

Without waiting for his mother's reply, Sasha climbed down from her lap and ran to the window. "Why is snow on the roofs? Anushka can't pull me on a sled up there!"

Then, realizing that his mother had not answered him, he came back, and, leaning on her lap, looked up at her. "Mama, you are still sick. Can Anushka go buy me a sister?"

Irina laughed. "I'll talk to your papa about it, Sasha. I promise!"

After Anushka and Sasha had left, Irina rose and looked at herself in the mirror. She had lost weight; but the pallor was gone, and with all the rest she had been getting, her skin was glowing and a healthy pink blush tinted her cheeks.

"I shall not touch you anymore until you come to me yourself! Alexander had said to her that last time they had an argument. *Oh, my dear* she thought, *twice now I have almost lost you, and I won't let it happen again!*

Indeed. The first separation through exile had been dreadful, but she had endured it through trials and suffering and her determination to join him; the winter journey across Siberia, the attack by the wolves . . . she had survived them all; and the second time, more insidious, more pervading, had been the separation of souls through her anger and hurt, and it was this second time that she had nearly destroyed her happiness.

She thought these things with sadness and regret, aware that tragedy and pain had matured her. She mustn't think all this, for now a renewed happiness was within her reach. Her heart overflowing with a more meaningful love, she was more convinced than ever that it was time to make the first move.

She would take time this morning to groom herself with special care. Alexander had promised to come home early today, for Yung-lin had sent a message that he would like to call on them that afternoon. She frowned. Why had Yung-lin sent a message? Strange. He usually came unannounced. Suddenly an uncomfortable feeling took hold of her. He had been withdrawn and uncommunicative of late, as if he had built a wall around himself to guard his privacy. Well, she would try to break through that wall to impress upon him that he should not shut out his friends.

Yung-lin had indeed built a wall around himself to imprison the tragic failure of his life. His Russian friends were kind and thoughtful. Would he come for a sleigh ride with them on a sunny afternoon? Take tea with krendel and stay for supper afterward? They tried. . . . They truly tried! But he declined.

A door had shut to be forever sealed inside his heart, a door to kindness or love. Suppress desire, and yield to fate with equanimity that was instilled in him through training of a lifetime. A pain without hope of healing was his heritage to bear. And guilty thoughts, those torture implements of his exhausted soul, must be controlled and sublimated by daily duties of his life.

His business was good; he was rich, respected. His agent in Kyakhta, a stocky fellow with a rusty beard and cheerful smile, came often to Irkutsk, reporting profits, proposing deals with Maimachin merchants. He listened. Nodded. Disagreed at times; approved at others.

And then, one day, his agent brought a Chinese merchant with him to Irkutsk. Between discussing shipments of chests of tea and the busy winter trade, the Chinese, a young and slender man, mentioned, without looking at Yung-lin, that Lo Chia-li's daughter had dedicated herself to the life of service to Buddha and had entered the convent in Urga.

That night Yung-lin did not go to bed but sat by the window, watching the light of an invisible moon float above the clouds.

So Shu-hsien had chosen a noble path. She was free of human fetters and now belonged to Buddha. But she would never know the happiness or the honor of motherhood, never again enjoy the touch of the man she loved. And he was the cause of her misfortune. He rose, slipped his hands inside his sleeves, and looked down on the street.

The moonlight was diffused, endowing nature with a pallid hue. The house across the street, its shutters closed, stood somber, unadorned. Yung-lin remembered blues and greens and reds in Urga and Maimachin. His courtyards, dragon gates, his home . . .

Shu-hsien was gone. In spite of his guilt, he was relieved that she would not be chained to another man. The clan was empty of her presence, and he could now return. He would not even try to see her in the convent. She was a memory of sweetness, of tasted, fragrant fruit that he had stolen and had lost. He had violated his country's traditions and for that had paid a woeful price. And now his goal in life would be to serve his wronged adoptive father. He would see him, kowtow, and pledge his lift to him and to the service of the clan. For that is where he belonged.

Yung-lin straightened, drew the draperies together, and went to bed. That night he slept without nightmares for the first time in many months.

Saddened by the news that Shu-hsien had entered the convent, Irina and Alexander were nonetheless astonished by Yung-lin's decision to return to his clan in Urga. They made no effort, however, to dissuade their Chinese friend from leaving Irkutsk, for the aura of formality and aloofness that emanated from Yung-lin as he announced that he was leaving Siberia precluded any further discussion of the subject. His choice of words seemed flowery and rehearsed, not at all like the warm and considerate friend they had come to know.

His hands stiffly at his sides, Yung-lin bowed ceremoniously and refused to stay for tea.

"I must depart immediately. I want to express my gratitude to you for your kindness in the past and say that I shall remember you always. I deeply regret that it has become impossible for me to remain in Irkutsk, but my duty to my adoptive father requires that I return to my clan."

Impulsively Irina touched his arm. "I hope you find happiness among your own people, Yung-lin. Perhaps even a good wife."

Yung-lin lowered his gaze. "My life now belongs to my adoptive father," he said, avoiding a direct answer.

Irina felt an imperceptible distance growing between them.

"We wish you well, Yung-lin!" she said sadly, offering him her hand, but Yung-lin either did not see it or pretended not to. He bowed stiffly and left the room.

Alexander shook his head. "I guess we shall never bridge the differences in our cultures. The gulf is far too wide!"

"Perhaps not now," Irina said, "but I can't believe that the day won't come when we shall learn at least to understand each other."

"I'm so sorry that his hopes did not materialize," Alexander said pensively. "Anyway, let's hope at least that he finds contentment in his life in Urga." He looked at Irina and smiled. "I have to return to my office for a while, my dear, but will be home for supper."

As Irina settled down to read alone in the parlor, there was a knock on the door, and Ossip and Marya walked in. Shuffling their feet, moving hesitantly forward, they stopped in the center of the room and waited.

What a sight they presented! Marya was beaming with happiness, a broad smile illuminating her face, but Ossip was frowning. His hands worked overtime, kneading his lamb's wool cap, and he pretended to be so intent upon it that Marya giggled, covered her mouth briefly with one hand, and then tugged at Ossip's shirt. But he elbowed her away, and continued with his task.

Oh, poor man! Irina thought, trying not to show her amusement.

Finally, Marya said: "We have prepared a speech together, but I guess I'll be the one to say it." She cleared her throat, then went on: "We're going to be married soon, and since my mother is dead, we would like you, Irina Ignatyevna, to be my sponsor at our wedding."

Marya glanced at Irina anxiously, then bowed deeply and touched the floor with her fingertips.

Irina smiled at the gesture. A memory stirred. She had done the same to Alexander's mother when she arrived at Dolovino on the day of her wedding. An old Russian custom of obeisance.

"I shall be delighted, Marya," she said. "I'm so happy for both of you!" Then she frowned, perplexed. "But you're a Buddhist, Marya! Our priest won't marry a non-Christian. The Church forbids it!"

Ossip raised his head. "Marya has agreed to become a Christian. She will be baptized in our church before the wedding."

Without a word, Marya took something out of her pocket and placed it on the table. It was the coral amulet.

"I won't need this anymore," she said solemnly.

Irina nodded. "I'm so glad, Marya!" was all she could say. She knew what a devout Buddhist Marya had been, and now to become a Christian—why, her love for Ossip must be strong indeed!

Ossip was a lucky man.

That night, after the stars and the moon had vanished above the gathering clouds, and the snowflakes drifted slowly upon Irkutsk, Irina and Alexander sat warming themselves by the fireplace in their bedroom. Dressed in her mauve peignoir, her golden brown hair combed loosely down her back, Irina watched her husband sip brandy in the love seat opposite her. There were fine lines of stress newly etched at the corners of his dark eyes, which now reflected the restless flames as he looked pensively at the fire. She moved from her chair and sat next to him, not knowing how to begin.

"Alex," she said lightly touching his hand, "I want to make a fresh start, a new page in our lives, a—a new chapter."

Alexander moved his hand away, put his brandy glass down, and turned to her. His face was somber and unresponsive. "You sound so academic, like a school-teacher assigning a lesson to her class. When I stayed by your bedside and prayed for your recovery, I did it because I love you, not because it was some sort of obligation on my part for which now you have to be grateful. Spare me your charity."

His last words sounded bitter, and impulsively Irina took his hand and held it.

"No charity, Alex," she said softly, and then, after hesitating for a moment, looked deeply into his eyes and added, "In many ways, this illness was a blessing, darling. A revelation even. So many pieces have fallen into place. I feel as though a blindfold had been removed from my eyes. I see a wonderful world around me now, a world where the sky has been suddenly cleared of a persistent fog."

Embarrassed by her long speech, Irina rose nervously and after walking over to the window, pulled the draperies apart. Then she chuckled. "Well, the sky is not exactly clear tonight, but the sight is beautiful just the same. Come look!"

Alexander walked over, and together they looked out. The clouds had thinned, and although the moon was still obscured, its blue light shone upon the snow-covered ground with an ethereal cast, illuminating the large snowflakes drifting leisurely past their window. Below them a downy carpet had covered the street, the pure, unblemished snow hiding the packed snowdrifts. Her life could be the same from now on—a fresh approach to love built on a solid foundation. She leaned on Alexander.

"I love you, darling. Do you understand? I love you!"

Alexander paled. "Say that again!"

Slowly Irina reached for the sash of his smoking jacket, untied it, then tugged at the jabot of his shirt. Suddenly Alexander caught her hands in his; kissed her palms with lingering kisses. Then he took her face between his hands.

"Irina!" His voice shook. "Irina, my own, my dearest love. . . . How I've hungered for you these dreadful months!"

In the fireplace the wood crackled, and the flames leaped, danced, and ignited a brighter fire. The human fire ignited, too, spread, and enveloped the two lovers as they reached for each other.

Through the half-drawn draperies the moon had found its way into the room to embrace them in its pale aquamarine light.

Gently, slowly, he gathered her into his arms, pressed her against his firm body, and held her a willing prisoner.

He felt her in his arms, yet he did not feel her, so light was she, so supple and so fragile. But she was there, wasn't she? He held her, enjoying her scent, that fragrant scent of roses on her hair and on her neck and shoulders. He closed his eyes and tightened his arms around her, to savor and to touch each tiny spot, afraid to miss some silken part, some hidden place, that now lay open to his loving.

To love this much, was it a sin or heaven? To gain her back in body and in soul was an awaited gift, so long denied, so desperately yearned for. This was a dream—a dream of past remembrances, of future longings, a dream come true. Past images recede; sharp memories become diffused, then blur. He had forgotten how it was to have his love returned with intensity that matched his own. A huge wave swelled inside him, like a surge in the ocean, then lifted him to float weightless, his senses acute, reaching a peak of such glory, such ecstasy, that surely, he thought, no earthly man deserved.

Her face was cushioned between his tender hands. His eyes looked deeply into hers; his warm and tender lips brushed over her exposed and trembling shoulder. She slipped into his arms, fitting herself gently against his chest, hiding her face in the hollow of his neck. Soft it was, warm and intimately hers. With her arm around him, she threaded her fingers through his dark hair, pulling his face slowly toward her until their mouths met in a lingering kiss.

How had she existed all this time without his touching her? How had she managed not to seek his closeness, that intangible closeness that is without reservation, without conscious thought—a private secret of two human beings? To know that he was on her side, completely, always on *her* side, no matter what, was a renewed and welcome joy. And because of that, the sharing of their thoughts and souls was more than bodily love.

The shadows in the room softened; the moonlight reached their arms above the covers and kissed them with a cool and silky touch. Contained within their walls, the air was soft, warmed by the embers in the fireplace and by the vibrant love that spilled to fill the room. His eagerness of loving and her passionate response were now united in a poignant expression of themselves.

She kept her arms around him in the afterglow of lovemaking, afraid that sated dreams would overtake her to convince her that this was not reality but an illusion and that the fleeting images of sleep were truly life.

Time flowed. Seconds, minutes, hours—the night was theirs to hold forever. This was their season for glory. The fire had died down in the fireplace, and the burned logs glowed, throwing a faint crimson light over the carpet. Irina moved under the down comforter, the warmth of love reaching to the tips of her toes to tingle and excite anew. Beside her Alexander stirred, raised himself on his elbow, and bent over her, tracing the contours of her face with a feathery touch. It tickled.

Suddenly Irina giggled. "Oh, Alex, I forgot to tell you that our Sasha came to me this morning with a special request."

"And what does that little rascal want now?"

"He wanted me to go to the marketplace and buy him a little sister, with long curls, mind you, so he could pull on them!"

Alexander laughed. "Smart little man we are bringing up! Well, what did you tell him?"

Irina cuddled against Alexander. Hiding her face somewhere between a pillow and his warm chest, she said, "I told him I'd speak to you about it!"

"Marketplace, no less! What happened to the stork idea?"

"Anushka told him that we'd have to buy him a sister at the marketplace, so now he's asking that she go to the market instead of me, while I'm still not well, he says."

"Enterprising young man. I like his tenacity. Well"—Alexander smiled at Irina—"we don't need to go to the marketplace to please him, do we?"

Irina smiled and put her arms around him. "No, darling, we don't!"

The hurt that had chained her to herself and had deprived her of objective thinking— she had lived with it so long, so blinded by anger! She grasped him fiercely, to shake away intruding, taunting thoughts.

The past was there—a stern reminder of her doubts, suspicions, hurts, that had nearly ruined their lives.

No. Chase away those thoughts, the cruel thoughts that hung somewhere in space. Think of tonight. Of love and the union of that love. Its sweetness, softness, languor. The giddy days of happiness ahead. Think of the nestling snow in the trees, the sleigh rides, Christmas, Sasha, children. Her love. Her winter song.

Outside, the streets of Irkutsk were hushed in the frosty night, and no man nor beast dared brave the cold; but inside, the warmth of love had spread its glow to touch two hearts and bind them forever.

Historical Postscript

After the exiles had completed their various terms of hard labor, some were resettled in and around Irkutsk. Princes Trubetskoy and Volkonsky lived in a nearby village and eventually moved into the city.

Upon the death of Tsar Nicholas I in 1855, his son and successor, Alexander II, amnestied the Decembrists in 1856, restoring their rights, privileges, and titles, but of the one hundred sixteen men exiled, only fifty-five were still alive. Thirty-four lived in Siberia, and the rest were resettled in other parts of Russia.

Not all the Decembrists elected to return to Russia. After thirty years of exile some felt their roots were in Siberia and chose to remain. Of those who returned, a few realized that their true home was in Siberia and went back.

The amnesty, however, imposed certain limitations on their freedom: They were forbidden to live in Moscow or St. Petersburg and to the end of their lives were under police surveillance.

Princess Katasha Trubetskaya died two years before the amnesty and was buried in Irkutsk. Princess Marie Volkonskaya returned to Russia with her husband and died in 1863.